MIZ CATFISH

by Portia Gray-Goffigan

Poems by Tara Morgan

Cover Art by Alexa Gustafson

Miz Catfish

Miz Catfish © February, 2013 Portia Gray-Goffigan

Published by Nature Woman Wisdom Press

First Edition. Printed and bound in the United States of America. All rights reserved. No part of this book may be reproduced in any form or by any electronic or mechanical means, including information storage and retrieval systems, recording, or photocopying, without permission in writing from the publisher, except by a reviewer, who may quote brief passages in review or where permitted by law.

Copyright © 2013 Portia Gray-Goffigan

Published by Nature Woman Wisdom Press

ISBN-13: 978-0615768045
ISBN-10: 0615768040
Printed in The United States of America

FEBRUARY 2013

10 9 8 7 6 5 4 3 2

Library of Congress Cataloging in Publication Data

Gray-Goffigan, Portia

    Miz Catfish
Fiction

    Miz Catfish
    by Portia Gray-Goffigan
Romance

    Miz Catfish
    by Portia Gray-Goffigan
Women's Issues

    Miz Catfish
    by Portia Gray-Goffigan
Abuse

    Miz Catfish
    by Portia Gray-Goffigan

This book is dedicated to Michele (Woodland) Hinds. We are sisters of different blood lines, and skin color, but the same soul.

I give many thanks to the former Mayor of Attleboro Judy Robbins, Allana Schaefer, Gene Moore, The Writer's Group at the Attleboro Public Library, Milagros Ramos and Mariangeli Vargas.

To my sister Alecia who is my all time, anytime cheerleader. Thank you Auntie Melverine for your support in the beginning of my book process. To my supportive buddy, who thought the character in this book wearing muu muu dresses, is based on her. Your supportive words made all the difference, and helped me push through the last mile to completion. My characters are so realistic due to the interviews with people in my life like my sister, Pamela, and one of my favorite neighbors Brenda. Thank you ladies.

To Debra, my thanks for your encouraging words.

Thank you cousin Tara for allowing me to showcase your gift of poetry in my work. I hope everyone else enjoys them as much as I do.

Major shout out to my Gemini niece Joy Chaunte'! ☺

Miz Catfish

To Rone'tia, Ronae', DanielleChina, Rae'ven and Delores, don't be a catfish. To Armani, Sherel and Travis, don't look for a catfish; you can stand on your own. ☺

Table of Contents

Chapter 1 .... page 7
Chapter 2 .... page 21
Chapter 3 .... page 31
Chapter 4 .... page 39
Chapter 5 .... page 57
Chapter 6 .... page 61
Chapter 7 .... page 75
Chapter 8 .... page 81
Chapter 9 .... page 87
Chapter 10 .... page 95
Chapter 11 .... page 105
Chapter 12 .... page 109
Chapter 13 .... page 129
Chapter 14 .... page 135
Chapter 15 .... page 147
Chapter 16 .... page 165
Chapter 17 .... page 181
Chapter 18 .... page 195
Chapter 19 .... page 219
Chapter 20 .... page 241
Chapter 21 .... page 251
Chapter 22 .... page 265
Chapter 23 .... page 309
Chapter 24 .... page 329
Chapter 25 .... page 381
Chapter 26 .... page 389
About Portia .... page 395

Miz Catfish

Miz Catfish

Chapter 1

As she felt the heel of her right shoe give way, Macy made a mental note not to buy anymore "value priced designer quality" shoes from the small, back alley store called VALUE SALES. Some of the girls at the club raved about the selection of colors and styles that were available there at lower prices than the large department stores. She had been a nude dancer for the past two years, and used her learned skills to quickly maneuver her way out of the clumsy situation by kicking the broken shoe to the back of the stage, then lightly flicking the perfect one off her foot into the crowd.

The shoe was grabbed out of the air by an excited customer as the men cheered and whistled. Macy got down on all four and crawled teasingly across the stage. The last two minutes of her set went by smoothly ending with an accumulation of dollar bills in her hands and garter belt. She quickly picked up the money from the stage and ignored the catcalls for "More." She picked up the broken shoe on her way through the heavy velvet curtains that separated the front of the club from the dressing area and hallway in the back.

It was a shame to lose the teal four inch pump from her vast collection of shoes at home. She had to admit, before finding out about the cheap quality of the merchandise she had been excited about the find of such a unique color. While walking towards the dressing area she came to a large garbage can and allowed the shoe to slip from her hand and land inside with a loud thud. After peeling the pastel teal and yellow pasties held on by body tape from her nipples, and the matching garter belt, she got back into her jeans, a t-shirt, and sneakers. She took a taxi home, where she showered, and popped the tab of a cold beer. After flipping channels on the television and realizing that there wasn't much on of interest at three o'clock in the morning she turned off the set to get some rest before going to her full time job at 4 o'clock that afternoon. At eleven o'clock, Macy's co-worker came in to relieve her.

Instead of waiting for the bus, she walked the five blocks home. For the moment "home" meant one of ten rooms in a shabby, run-down rooming house. She lived there for the cheap rent and the lack of a yearly lease, allowing her to move on at any time as she was used to doing. The room was just that, a room. All of the tenants in the house shared the bathroom and kitchen. She had a bed, television, small refrigerator, sofa, and bureau, but her prize possession was a small fish tank containing a guppy with a fan shaped tail in beautiful hues of golden yellow, azure blue, and burnt orange. Between the male and female guppy, only the female's tail had such brilliant color. The guppy's companion was a silver catfish with black spots, described as an upside down catfish because of its ability to swim back up as well as belly up.

She entered her room, put her pocketbook and shoulder bag down, and then went over to the fish tank. She smiled as she peered into the water searching for its inhabitants, picking up the small can of fish food, she pinched off a few of the pale yellow, green, and pink flakes into the water.

The guppy spread her fins and glided upwards to snatch at the flakes, she was able to get to a few of them so quickly that they were still dry on the surface. All that she couldn't suck in fell silently, landing on and amongst the toast colored pebbles on the bottom of the tank.

Catfish slowly made an appearance from behind the safety of an artificial green plastic bush. It ventured into the middle of the tank, using its Hoover type mouth to suck up food; catching a pebble or two and spitting it back out with lazy force.

Guppy caught a flake as it made its way towards the middle of the tank, and then in a graceful loop returned to the surface where she lingered with her fins in full expansion, and waving as if to give oneself relief from the heat of summer. The catfish rolled over belly to back, appearing dead to the unknowing viewer, and then returned to a belly down position. Not very graceful, but for an upside-down catfish, nature allowed nothing more. Although there were no distinguishing signs, the catfish was a female, her black spots and silver metallic body drew attention, but not in the same commanding manner as her roommate. Catfish returned to the safety of the green plastic.

Macy's telephone began to ring, "Hello."

"Hey babe. What's up?" Michael's voice crooned.

"I just walked in." Macy hoped he'd hear the weariness in her voice.

"Can I come over tonight?" he pressed.

"I don't think so. I'm kind of tired."

"Oh, come on babe. I haven't seen you in a week. You kickln' me to the curb?" Michael pleaded his case.

"No. I just don't want any company."

"Sounds like you're in one of your moods. Why don't I come rub your back?"

Miz Catfish

"If I talk to you nicely you don't hear me! I said 'NO!' so get off my damn phone!" Macy screamed into the phone before she slammed it down onto its cradle.

Usually a phone call from Michael would send her grabbing for candles and soft music. He was good company and a great lover. She'd known him for the year that she'd worked at the store. One night he came in as a customer. They entered into friendly conversation, and a companionship grew.

Once their relationship became an obvious mutual attraction she invited him to her tiny dwelling. He didn't shudder at the shabbiness of the conditions. He in turn invited her to his home where they were able to enjoy a broader range of privacy and hours of great conversation. They cut up vegetables together in his kitchen and made homemade meals, went to the movies, and jazz concerts together. They took turns massaging each other's backs. Her moods swings didn't scare him off, he simply moved aside and let her have space. If he didn't hear from her after more than two weeks of silence he'd call her. Not knowing if she'd be friendly or aggressive, but leaving behind the assurance that he had no intentions of being pushed away. He allowed her to be herself, to feel whatever was going on inside at the moment. His ability to do this gave her a feeling of comfort and stability. Unlike the other people in her life, he would not leave or be run off. He actually had gotten past her hard core shell and was working towards her heart strings. It all scared her, but felt good at the same time. He was getting as close as anyone else had to winning her heart and her trust.

Tonight Michael's call held no magic, he was correct in his statement that she was in one of her moods. On her walk home from work tonight she had allowed her mind to open doors that she preferred kept shut. She had begun to think about the life she'd lived in foster care.

She'd been placed in foster care at birth, and couldn't even remember the number of homes she'd passed through. She knew nothing about her birth family or ancestry. Taking a guess never brought her to definite conclusions. Her skin was honey brown, and her chestnut brown hair was heavy with thickness and curls that hung to her shoulders. Her eyes though light brown were not distinctive to any particular race. Was she African-American, Spanish, or Caucasian and African-American? Spanish and Caucasian? Spanish and African-American? Would she ever find out the truth? She tried to keep the puzzle shut away in the back of her mind with all the other years of baggage that she didn't want to deal with. Years in foster homes had taught her to control and use her emotions like an actress. Some of the homes actually had people that cared about the foster children they took in, but the majority of them did not. She got slapped around, kicked around, hugged and kissed, went hungry, ate well, fought with girls of all ages and dodged the hands of men and boys of many ages. She'd learned very few morals, values, or proper use of emotions from others.

On her eighteenth birthday she was considered an adult, and was released from the custody of the state. Since being out on her own she'd lived many places throughout Massachusetts. She would become bored with the neighborhood or start to feel closed in by the same old walls of her apartment, and then she'd move on.

Her resume was full of retail stores, restaurants, convenience stores, and nursing homes. She missed some of the people that she'd met, but had become accustomed to people coming and going through her life. She wanted to understand the emotions of a relationship within a family of a mother, a father, sisters, and brothers, even the feelings toward a mate. She couldn't let her guard down. "Why get close to anyone, when they all leave, or lose interest in me, or send me away?" She thought they said "I love you." but it always meant, "I love me, or my own."

"I'm in charge of protecting myself," she reminded herself. Yet she was human, and the thought of having someone to care for her, and someone to share the struggles and pleasures of life, remained in her heart.

The cozy town of East Boston in Massachusetts was bordered by the Boston Harbor, and water had a calming effect on her. One of the positive things about working at the store was the fact that it was across the street from the harbor. Sometimes she would take her break sitting at the water's edge, listening to the waves. Once, as she enjoyed her favorite spot, an elderly gentleman sat down beside her and offered the history of that area of waterfront. "It had once harbored Donald McKay's Clipper Ships, and was part of the great Boston Harbor." He spoke with pride in his voice as if he quoted his very own past.

Macy felt a calmness within that she hadn't enjoyed in a while. She listened to a message from that little voice in the back of her mind telling her that this could be a good spot to stay a while and it was close to her job at the store. There was a building down the street from the store that had an "APARTMENTS FOR RENT" sign in the window. She decided to pay a visit to the place in the morning to ask about an apartment. She slid the dusty window open for some air. After pouring herself a glass of water and getting into her favorite night shirt, she climbed into bed. Feeling a bit agitated, she decided to read a little until she fell asleep. She was scheduled to work the five to eleven shifts at THE CORNER STOP, a neighborhood convenience store, where she'd worked for almost a year.

The sun's bright rays shone bright through the cracks of the sheer curtains at the small window beside Macy's bed. She woke with a burst of energy, and the excitement of moving out of her cramped quarters. She didn't even know if she'd get an apartment today, but she was going with the positive attitude that she would be successful. Think positive, think positive. She got out of bed, did a long stretch resembling a large cat then collected her toiletries and headed down the hall to the bathroom. Back in her room, after her shower, and wrapped in a big, fluffy towel, she stepped before the mirror on the bureau, and picked up her hair comb. As she pulled the comb through her hair it became tangled in a mass of curls. The comb tugging at her hair and the mirror being used to guide her through the tug-of-war seemed to team up against her as their actions caused her to remember a day long ago when a comb tugged through her hair.

At the age of seven, Macy had only the memories of multiple foster homes, and foster families. Her greatest wish was to have a permanent home where no social worker would show up at the door to tell her that it was time to go. She had been with the Kleins for six and a half months, the longest time that she'd spent in any placement. With each day that turned to night Macy's crossed fingers twisted tighter with the hope that maybe the small family would keep her, maybe even come to love her.

The Klein family consisted of a mother, father and daughter her own age, Macy couldn't ask for more. She tried to be on her best behavior at all times, and out shined her foster sister Muriel in completing daily chores. Macy waited anxiously for a sign that her diligence was paying off, but no sign came forth, and as she stood against the floral print, wall-papered wall she wondered what she was doing wrong. What was so wrong with her that kept her from being loved? Macy's heart ached as she watched her foster mother Suze comb Muriel's long blonde hair with ease, and patience, into a ponytail that strongly resembled fine corn silk being bound by a red satin ribbon. The bond between mother and daughter caused the room to appear three times brighter with sun light. The gleam stung Macy's eyes with loneliness, and longing. She pressed her small body closer to the wall, preferring to feel one with the wall paper than to feel ignored.

Suze completed the red bow, and patted Muriel's head in a dismissive gesture. "Go play honey, you're all done, and pretty as ever. Come on Macy. Why are you over there? What are you trying to do, blend in with that wall?" Macy pushed her body off the wall and moved herself across the floor to stand in front of Suze. Maybe today would be the day; maybe Suze would speak to her in a soothing tone, and touch her lovingly.

Macy felt the pressure of Suze's hand in her hair, and then the tugging and pulling as her tangled hair struggled to move through the aisles of the blue plastic comb. There was no patience shared with her today, no tender mother's touch.

"What am I supposed to do with this mess?" Suze's tone was irritated. Macy's heart sank; this wouldn't be the special day. There was no gentle touch for her. The comb tugged, and the words cut.

"My Lord, I wonder where they get some of these children. I've never seen hair the likes of this!"

"Ouch!" Macy yelped, raising her hands to her head in a defensive motion.

"Put your hands down! This will take long enough without you slowing me down."

Tears moistened Macy's cheeks as she withstood the rest of the racking, only to end up with a thick, unruly braid on the back of her head. From the tone of Suze's voice when she dismissed Macy, the girl did not need a mirror to know that a red ribbon was not wrapped around her braid.

The sharp pain of hair being stretched pulled Macy back into the present, and the realization that it was her own image in the mirror pulling at the hair on her own head. Tears had begun to make a slow drip from her eyes, and she swiped at them with the back of her free hand. "Suck it up, you big baby! You've made it this far without falling apart, so don't start now." she spoke quietly to herself.

Macy untangled the hair and pulled herself back into the positive task for the day of finding a new place to live. She dressed in black stretch biker shorts, a mid-way white tee shirt and black open-toed mules for her dainty little feet. Of course the toe nails matched the finger nails, she wouldn't have it any other way. She quickly picked up her black purse and was out the door. She felt full of energy and again she decided to skip the bus and walk. Her hair was pulled into a pony tail and it flopped up and down as she did a light, jolly strut down the blocks to what she hoped would be her new home.

It felt strange to be on the same street as the convenience store and not go to work. As she walked down the street she noticed the once empty store front next door to THE CORNER STOP was sporting a Pet Shop Grand Opening sign. She could see a crew inside the store setting up fish tanks and other items on the walls and shelves.

She continued up the street to the apartment building. After entering the hallway she checked for names on the mailboxes. Apartment seven read Mae-Belle Smoot/landlord.

Macy walked further into the hallway and started up the stairs, stopping on each floor to take a peek at the set up of the building. She reached the top floor and putting one hand, fingers crossed, behind her back, she knocked on the door with the other. A woman opened the door holding a steaming cup of liquid, wearing a purple head scarf tied on the side, and a solid purple muumuu.

"Good morning, my name is Macy Jenkins. I saw the FOR RENT sign downstairs, and I'm looking for an apartment in the neighborhood."

"Oh sure, come on in." The woman said moving aside to allow Macy into her apartment. "I'm Mae-Belle Smoot, the landlord and owner."

Macy walked into the apartment and sat down. She took in the colorful neatness of the home. The leather of the chair was the softest that she'd ever felt. It was a rich hunter green with toss pillows. Her coffee table was in the shape of a baby elephant, made from white marble. The little elephant was standing on all fours. Its trunk and back held a piece of oval shaped smoked glass which matched the glass on the dining room table. An area rug the color of soft butter lay under the little elephant's feet and a tall hunter green ceramic vase stood in the center of the table holding a mixture of daisies and baby's breath. Five foot tall ceramic floor lamps in the shape of Victorian columns stood on each side of the sofa. Facing the sofa on the other side of the elephant table was a love seat. Hanging on the wall behind the sofa was a painting of six multi-colored hummingbirds sucking from flowers on a bush, against a pastel background of sherbet orange and yellow. A Victorian style brass sconce, holding a tulip edged votive cup with a small white votive candle, hung on each side of the painting. The brass of the sconce matched the frame of the painting.

All five of Mae-Belle's large living room windows displayed a hanging plant and a hunter green balloon valance window treatment. Nothing else blocked the view of the windows, so that all the bright morning and afternoon sunlight could be enjoyed. The kitchen and living room stretched one into another. There were three rooms lined up side by side on the wall farthest back in the apartment; a bathroom, and two bedrooms, one used as an office.

"Do you have any children?" Mae-Belle asked.

"No, it's just little ole' me."

"Well, I guess you'll only need a studio or one bedroom?"

"I think the studio will do just fine. How much is the rent?"

"Its four hundred and fifty dollars a month, utilities included. I don't allow dogs, cats, you know, animals of that sort. There are washers and dryers in the basement, so I ask that the tenants don't put them in their apartments. There is a finished roof top for sitting out in the fresh air. Would you like me to show you round?"

"I'd love it."

They went downstairs to the second floor. Mae-Belle opened the apartment on the left side of the hallway.

"This is one of the two identical studios that I have available."

Macy immediately noticed the beautiful shine on the hardwood floor.

"All of the floors are hardwood, but you can put in carpet if you like."

They entered a small kitchen area, which was separated from the living space by a three foot tall, five foot long counter with tan and black marbled butcher block top. Cabinets on either side of the sink were the same oak stain as the floor. On the same wall as the sink, in the right corner was one large cabinet panel with a handle half way down. Mae-Belle walked over to the cabinet and pulled the handle. Macy's mouth fell open with excitement when the panel swung out and became the door of a hidden refrigerator. It contained all of the same compartments as an average sized refrigerator. Macy stepped forward and stuck her hand inside to feel the coldness as if to assure her senses that this wonderful appliance was real. She looked at Mae-Belle and asked "Where did you find such great ideas and pardon me, not have to charge enormous rent for a place with a set up like this?"

"Well," Mae-Belle laughed, "my father owned a storage company for the public and businesses on this very spot. After he died I decided to renovate the building into apartments, so I went back to his old phone book of business customers and made a few calls. Most of the old customers have known me since I was a kid so I got "good stuff cheap", you know what I mean. As far as the rent goes, sometimes you have to think about giving other people a break and not simply lining your pocket. Blessings put out, means blessings will come back." Mae-Belle smiled at Macy and walked into what was to be the living room/sleeping area. Macy closed the refrigerator door and went to stand with Mae-Belle who was waiting in the middle of the room.

"This is the living room, dining room, and bedroom all rolled into one."

Four windows, two at each end of the room let in breath taking amounts of light. There appeared to be more than ample space available to make the room into a comfortable living space. They walked across the room to see the bathroom. The tile covering the bottom half of the wall was golden tan, the same tile was around the top of the wall where it met the ceiling. Next to the bathroom was an enormous walk-in closet, perfect for storage and hanging clothes.

"This place is beautiful."

"Well I tried to make the studio as comfortable as an apartment."

"I would love to take this place today if possible. I can write you a check for the first month and the deposit if there is one."

"That'll be fine sweetie. Come on back upstairs, and we can take care of the keys and lease."

After Mae-Belle and Macy finished their paperwork, Macy left Mae-Belle's apartment and decided to sit at the water. She had expected this move to be like all the others, the simple physical actions of packing boxes, and changing her route to work. But something was different this time. Macy found herself feeling melancholy. Time was moving on and she was getting older. She knew that she would one day have to make a firm decision to settle down permanently and stop looking for "FOR RENT" signs. A glance at her watch reminded her that she had to go to work.

Chapter 2

Amber got her name from her tufts of curly brown hair with its flecks of golden highlights. Along with her fair hair came her fair skin. Throw in a few freckles and hazel brown eyes with golden flecks and it became easy to be moved by her angelic glow.

Her parents had died in an automobile accident when she was sixteen. After her parent's death she lived with her mother's sister. When she turned twenty-one, she felt the urge to spread her wings, and see past the parking lot of the town's mall. She left a note on her aunt's table explaining how she felt closing out with a simple "I'm going to be alright. Thanks for the support. I love you."

She boarded a bus leaving Chicago heading to Boston, Massachusetts. Once she arrived at her destination she inquired about a place to stay temporarily and was directed to the YWCA. She rode the public transportation system all over the city in search of available apartments. After the first week of searching she noticed a "FOR RENT" sign in the first floor window of an apartment building. A woman in a fuchsia muumuu, and matching head wrap was sweeping the stairs.

Amber pushed the "STOP" request bell on the bus, got off at the next stop, and walked back to where she'd seen the sign. The brown-skinned lady wearing the bright dress was still sweeping the stairs.

"Do you know if there is still an apartment available here?" Amber asked.

"Sure is, sweetie. As a matter of fact there are five available. I've just began to rent. You can have your pick of the lot depending on how many bedrooms you need," the colorful lady sang. "Are you the one needing a place?"

"Yes, and I only need one bedroom or a studio will do just as nicely."

"Alright then, I'll show you what I have."

They walked up the few stairs into the newly renovated building.

"Excuse the paint splatters, the painters just finished this morning. The mail boxes are here in the entrance." Mae-Belle pointed out the shiny new metal boxes on the wall just inside the hallway. "By the way, my name is Mae-Belle Smoot, what's yours?"

"Amber Munroe."

"How old are you sweetie? You look a little wet behind the ears as the old folk would say. You're not a run away are you?"

"No ma'am. I'm all of twenty-one, but this will be my first apartment. I've been here for two weeks, staying at the YWCA. I'm from Chicago.

There were two apartments towards the rear of the building. Mae-Belle directed her towards the door on the right, a one bedroom. It was early June and eighty three degrees outside, but inside the apartment was cool and crisp with newness.

"I put in basic white appliances, so any furniture colors that you choose will match. I left all of the floors throughout the building in hardwood as they originally were. You can carpet if you'd like." They stepped out of the kitchen and around a wall into the bedroom.

As Mae-Belle opened folding doors to a large walk-in closet, Amber stood in the middle of the waxed shiny hardwood floor wondering if she could afford the rent on a place as gorgeous as this one. She only had seven hundred and fifty dollars left in her back pack. Her aunt had given her an allowance and she had worked to save as much as she could, thinking one day she would buy a car, instead it had become her travel and living funds.

Mae-Belle closed the closet door and moved on to the living room space. Her slippers slapped across the hardwood floor as she headed towards another door. The muumuu flowed around her like the bottom of a bell.

"Behind this door is also a coat and storage closet" Mae-Belle said while pointing.

"Ah, Miss Smoot." Amber mustered.

"Call me Miss Mae-Belle, honey."

"Okay, Miss Mae-Belle, this place is gorgeous but before I get my hopes up please tell me how much the rent will be?

"It's four hundred and fifty dollars a month. The utilities are included. Can you swing that?"

"Well I only have seven hundred and fifty dollars. Can I pay you my first month rent and owe you for anything else?"

"Sure sweetie, I'll allow you that break. Everyone needs one from time to time. You can pay me the four hundred and fifty dollars for rent and owe me the same for the security.

"I'll take this one. I'm going to look for, no; I mean get a job as soon as possible. Thank you, Miss Mae-Belle! Thank you so much!" Amber chirped as she spun her body around in the middle of the floor, with her arms spread wide like a bird's wings in flight.

"You'd better keep the rest of that two hundred and fifty dollars to get yourself some groceries and essentials." Mae-Belle cackled at the young girl's openness. "After you get yourself settled in come on up to the top floor, I made the attic into my apartment. I'll give you your keys and you can sign your lease. While you're there maybe you'd like a cool drink and something to eat." Mae-Belle turned on her heels and slapped across the floor to the door.

Amber stood at one of the large sunny windows with her head spinning. This was really her first apartment. All hers! She placed her backpack on the countertop in the kitchen, and went into the bathroom. The floor tiles were done in black and white. The walls were painted white with black tiles around the top of the walls where they met the ceiling. Amber leaned over the sink and splashed water on her face, and caught a glimpse of herself in the mirror. Her eyes looked tired. The golden flecks, usually bright, were dull. Her hair was held back by a rubber band and needed a good shampooing.

She needed to find a store to buy shampoo, soap, toothpaste, and a few groceries later on, but right now she'd take Mae-Belle up on her offer of a cool drink and something to eat. With all of the excitement of bus riding and finding the new apartment she'd forgotten that she hadn't eaten all day. She went back into the living room and stood in the middle of the floor. She made a slow circular turn, looking around from one room to the other trying to take in the reality of her new residence. She left her apartment and headed up the stairs to Mae-Belle's apartment. On her way up she quickly took in the two apartment doors and a large artificial potted plant on each floor. Once on the fourth floor, what Miss Mae-Belle called the attic, there were another two doors. The first door looked like the other apartment doors throughout the building, but the second door had a small window in the center. She looked into the window and saw another stairway leading to a space above the attic floor. She knocked on the door that looked like the apartment doors. She knocked twice and heard Mae-Belle's slippers slap across the floor.

"Come on in sweetie."

"This building is so big, and your place is beautiful!" Amber said, while looking around. "I hope that I can do justice to my place."

"It takes time." Mae-Belle said as she led Amber into her kitchen.

"Don't rush."

Amber followed Mae-Belle into the kitchen. The kitchen had bold yellow appliances. Cactus plants of various varieties sat on the window sill of the large window. Floral curtains with yellow as the primary color completed the window treatment. Her smoked glass kitchen table held a bowl of fresh fruit in its center.

"Sit down Amber. I'll get us some drinks. Would you like soda, water, or lemonade?"

"I'll have lemonade, thanks."

"I hope you like southern food, because I just fixed some potato salad, fried chicken, and corn bread, with a sweet potato pie for dessert. I'll have some fried okra ready in about five minutes."

"Sounds great, and I'm starving!"

Mae-Belle brought plates and bowls of southern delicacies to the table, put a large serving spoon into each one, and a tab of butter on top of each slice of cornbread.

"Amber, why don't you get us a couple of plates out of the cabinet above the sink, and forks from the drawer next to the stove, and dig in."

Amber opened the cabinet to dishes with the same pattern as the curtains. With two plates and forks, she returned to the table. She helped herself to a portion from each dish and accepted the large cold glass of lemonade that Mae-Belle handed to her. As they ate they discussed the weather, the grocery stores in the neighborhood, and furniture stores. When Amber could eat no more she asked Mae-Belle about the door beside hers in the hallway.

"That door leads to the roof. I had it black topped and fenced in. I hope that the furniture I put up there is comfortable and sturdy. I'm hoping that it'll be a nice place to sit out during hot summer days like this one has turned out to be. If you'd like we could take our drinks and go on up there."

"Sure, I'd love to. Could I help clean up here first?"

Miz Catfish

"Oh no, don't worry about this, I'll get it."

Amber got up from the table and sat in the living room waiting for Mae-Belle to clear the kitchen table. Mae-Belle excused herself to go into her office to get a lease for Amber to sign and explained to her the no pets or washer/dryer in apartment clause. Amber signed her lease, and received a copy of it along with a set of keys.

"Grab your glass and we'll get going."

They left Mae-Belle's and went through the door with the window in the center, up the stairs to a heavy, insulated door which also had a window in the center. Mae-Belle pushed the door open and the warm June air flowed into the stairway brushing their faces like a floating feather. The air carried with it a sweet smell of blossoms and crispness mixing together. As they stepped out of the hallway onto the roof, Amber was caught by a feeling of comfort. If she didn't think about the fact that she was five floors up, she would think she was in the backyard. Sitting on the turf were a pair of cement benches, and in the turf covered corners were matching oriental ceramic pots, each containing gardenia bushes displaying large white blooms. A cement barbecue grill sat in each corner of the part of the roof not covered by turf.

Three lounge chairs, two matching chairs, and a round picnic table with umbrella completed the scene. A chain linked fence bolted into cement surrounded the entire roof. A mixture of bug lights and lanterns hung alternatively around the fence. A large black metallic storage chest sat next to the doorway to store out-of-season roof items. The women sat on the roof for half an hour enjoying the quietness surrounding them until Amber realized she'd better go shopping before it got too late. She didn't know the neighborhood and did not want to take any chances being out by herself at night. Although Mae-Belle assured her that the neighborhood was friendly, she'd feel better after she found out for herself.

She said "Goodnight." to Mae-Belle and went downstairs to get her wallet. She left her apartment, and came to a stop in the entrance of the building, taking time to take in her new surroundings. To the right was a hardware store, and in front of which was an empty building for rent. Next to that, a new pet shop, then a small twenty-four hour neighborhood convenience store whose sign blazed "THE CORNER STOP".

Amber sat her items on the counter, and waited for the cashier to turn around.

"Is that all you'll be needing tonight?" Macy asked the customer waiting at the cash register.

"Well yeah, except, after I get these things from you could you tell me where I can find a place that's still open this time in the evening, and close by, to buy some blankets and a pillow?"

"Sure. Just continue down another block, and around the corner. They're open 'till nine o'clock. It's only seven now. You've got plenty of time to shop. The prices are decent and there's a lot to choose from. I don't recognize your face, are you new in the neighborhood?" Macy added.

"Yeah, I just moved into the building down the street at 105."

"105 Shawnee Road?"

"Ah-huh, I moved in today."

"I live there too! On the second floor. How's your place? Mine is gorgeous!" Macy rattled off.

Amber jumped in when she could. "Well, the whole building seems to be pretty good. My apartment is beautiful, rent is not bad, and Miss Mae-Belle is a nice lady."

"By the way, my name's Macy, Macy Jenkins. What's yours?"

"Amber Munroe."

"Well Amber, your groceries come to fifty-two dollars and ninety seven cents."

Macy took fifty five dollars from Amber's out-reached hand, and for the first time since speaking with her Amber noticed her fingernails.

"Wow! Those nails are great. Can I see them? Are they yours?"

"Sure are." Macy held out her hands to show the orange and black tiger striped, inch-long nails.

"Do you get them done around here?"

"Nope. I do them myself. Years of practice, you know."

"Maybe you could do mine one day. They sure could use the help." Amber laughed, holding out her hands to display bitten nails.

Chapter 3

"Amber." Mae-Belle knocked on Amber's door. "Amber?"

Amber came to the door. "Good morning Miss Mae-Belle."

"Did you make it to the stores alright yesterday?"

"Yes I did. Come on in. Maybe you can tell me where I could go to find an inexpensive bed."

"I know of an excellent place. They have a large variety of styles, and prices. I could go with you, if you'd like."

"Oh boy, would I? Can we go today? Oh-h I guess I'm running ahead of myself huh?" Amber stopped to catch her breath.

Mae-Belle laughed softly, "Sure, I'd be glad to. We'll take my car. How about around twelve o'clock? That way we can take our time getting dressed."

"Thanks, you're a great help! Amber said, giving Mae-Belle a big hug.

Truth be told, Mae-Belle would enjoy the company. Without her father she was lonely. Daddy had required so much of her time as an assistant with the business and had been so protective as a father, that she had not made friends with anyone at school or in the neighborhood.

"Were you comfortable at all last night?"

"Yes, I went to the five and dime store down the street. I brought two pillows and a blanket. They worked great as a temporary bed. I also found some great dishes, silverware, and a decent thirteen-inch television. I'd say I was as comfortable as possible for a beginner. By the way I brought some groceries at the twenty-four hour store last night and the cashier lives upstairs.

"That's right. I forgot to tell you that the other tenant would be working at the store I directed you to. I'm happy that you two met each other. I guess I should stop yakking and get dressed, huh."

On the way upstairs Mae-Belle stopped and knocked on Macy's door. Macy answered on the third knock.

"Hi Miss Mae-Belle."

"Hello Macy. Amber and I are going out to look for a few things for her place. Would you like to come?"

"I don't have to be at work until five, I'd love to tag along. Thanks."

"Good, we'll be leaving at twelve o'clock, and taking my car. See you then."

Macy dressed and headed down to Amber's apartment.

"Open up new neighbor!" Macy sang.

Amber opened the door. It seemed as though the building was coming to life with the presence of Macy's energy. "Come on in new neighbor", Amber repeated. The women giggled.

"This place is great." Macy said, looking around. "That lady really put some time and interest into this building. You'll have to come upstairs to see my apartment when you get a chance. Oh yeah, I hope you don't mind, but Mae-Belle invited me along to go shopping."

"No problem. I was thinking that maybe I could go down to the store before we leave, and fill out a job application. What do you think?"

"Yeah, now's probably a good time. Hank's on now. He's the day manager, and an okay guy. I'll come with you."

Amber slipped into her sandals and the two women left the building together. They were quite a stunning pair, Amber with her soft brown curls and Macy with hers dark and pulled back. Both were a statement of youth and beauty. They shared the ability to adjust quickly to new environments. This ability made it easy for a friendship to begin between the two.

Amber filled out a job application, while Macy cleared the path for an immediate interview. She got a job as cashier, working the hours of eight o'clock in the morning until four o'clock in the afternoon, Mondays through Fridays and other times when they needed her to fill in.

The pay would be enough for her to handle her rent and live on until she decided to do something else. She'd start work the next morning. As she and Macy started back towards their building, Amber linked her arm through Macy's and they walked with a skip in their step. Each enjoyed the feeling of excitement of new jobs, new living quarters, new friends, and feeling good about the future. When they got in front of the new pet shop they both stopped to look in the window. The crew was still busy setting up the store, but a sign on the door advertised the opening date to be a week away.

"Maybe I'll get a pet." Macy said trying to see further into the back of the store.

"We're pretty limited by our lease," Amber reminded her.

As they stood in front of the window conversing, a man started in their direction and stopped when he was about two feet from Amber's side. He pretended to also look into the window. After standing there for half a minute he turned to Amber and said "It's been a long time since there's been anything in this store front. A pet shop should be interesting. I noticed you through the window of my hardware store; you must be new in the neighborhood."

"Yes I am." Amber replied. "Do you work in the hardware store?"

"Yeah, well, actually I own it. So did you move in somewhere in the area?"

"Uh-huh. The three story at 105. Do you live in the neighborhood too?"

"No, I don't.

"I haven't seen much of town yet. The water across the street is very peaceful to watch through my windows, and the bus line is convenient." She suddenly realized that Macy was softly nudging her in her side.

"What?" she whispered out of the corner of her mouth in an attempt to be discrete.

"Stranger." Macy whispered.

"Oh yeah." Amber whispered back. "Oh, I guess I'm talking too much." she said in a normal tone.

"No you're not. I wanted to meet you. My name is Jason Michaels. What's yours?"

"Amber."

"Well Amber, I better get back to the shop. Someone's got to watch the store as they say. Hope to see you again."

"Okay, see ya. Jason, right?"

"Exactly. Bye Amber. Oh, where are my manners? I'm sorry, good day, um-m-m."

"Macy." Macy stated in a guarded tone.

"Good-bye Macy. It was nice to meet you."

After he had gone a distance, Macy turned to Amber. "Girl be careful who you talk to, there are some crazy people around these days."

"I know, but he doesn't look dangerous. He's too cute."

Macy thought of Amber's response, "He's cute." She wondered how many wolves the girl had allowed into her life just because they were cute.

"How old are you, if you don't mind my asking?" she asked Amber.

"No, I don't mind. I'm twenty-one."

Over the years Macy had developed the ability to sense when a person was vulnerable, and naïve, or might not be able to protect themselves against the worlds' many twists and turns. Intuition told her this girl had been and would be prey to many. She herself had been preyed upon by many and over the years she had found herself becoming an advocate to others that seemed unable to protect themselves in any number of situations.

At this moment she felt something for Amber, something was tugging at her heart for this younger than herself. It was always possible that she would be wrong with her assumptions, she had been from time to time in the past, but until she saw an indication of anything different she felt led to look out for her.

The women headed back to the building, where they met Mae-Belle to go on their furniture shopping spree.

Mae-Belle bought a new desk lamp for her office. Macy loaned Amber money to buy a bedroom set, and a brass table lamp. Macy had decided to leave all of her furniture in her old room and buy all new things for the apartment. She bought two bar stool chairs to put at the kitchen counter. The trio took the escalator up a floor to an area of living room sets. They walked around admiring and sitting on different chairs. They entered an area of funky, contemporary furniture and Macy fell in love with a vivid purple sleep sofa. The other two women thought she was joking. The sofa was so-o-o purple. Macy assured them that she was serious. It was definitely the sofa for her. She next picked out a pair of floor lamps in black, and a desk and chair for the office space she was going to create in the large closet. After Macy and Mae-Belle paid for the items and set up a delivery time, the women went back down two floors, to the house wares area. Amber had chosen to do her kitchen in light blue so she chose a set of white dinnerware trimmed in small blue flowers. She picked up cutlery and cornflower blue cookware. Macy was feeling bold and spicy. She chose solid black for both her dinnerware and cookware.

Miz Catfish

With bags in hand the trio moved down another floor to electronics. Macy picked out a thirty two inch color television, and a stereo system, a wall unit to hold them both and a boom box for Amber as a gift of friendship.

The women left the store to find lunch. By the time they got home it was time for Macy to go to work. She left her extra key with Amber to let her deliveries in, and then she ran off to work.

When she got home later that night her furniture had been delivered and set in the center of her living room floor. As she arranged the new furniture she didn't like the plainness of the large wall behind the sofa. After standing back from different angles and looking at the wall for about ten minutes she pulled the chair away from the wall. She rummaged in her pocketbook until she found an eyebrow pencil, and began to doodle on the walls as she would a clean slate.

She began with a bouquet of flowers but after three roses she decided that the idea was too common. She sat on the floor in front of the wall with her hands cupping her chin, trying to visualize something bright and detailed. After fifteen minutes and a bag of Spanish peanuts that she found in the bottom of her pocketbook, she jumped up and ran to the wall with a brain storm. She started with grass and palm trees, went on to a parrot, flamingo, a small monkey which was her favorite, stopping a few times to sharpen the expensive pencil, she continued until she had a huge outline of a jungle complete with animals. Now she'd have to contain her excitement of seeing it complete until tomorrow when she could buy paints at the hardware store next door. Filling in the color would be really fun. She also realized that her stomach was rumbling. It had been a while since she'd used her hidden talent for drawing, and she had gotten carried away with the fun of it all and the thrill of the new apartment. Another rumble of her stomach bought her back to reality.

It was four o'clock in the morning; her only choices of food would be cold and lacking in nutrition. She ran down to the store, chose a pre-made cold cut sandwich, bag of plain potato chips, and large soda. A package of vanilla cream cookies for desert and she had a meal. She fell asleep on the sofa using a coat as a throw. She woke five hours later and walked back to her old place to turn in her keys and begin to move her personal possessions. Macy stopped in front of the fish tank. Sometimes the occupants appeared to come to the glass as if to greet her. Did they know she was there watching them? Macy took the tank to the bathroom and poured some water out in preparation for transport. She peered into the bowl. The catfish was hidden completely behind the artificial bush.

"Come on out girl. Don't hide, we'll be alright. You'll like the new place. Who knows maybe we'll stay awhile."

She called for a station wagon taxi and with the fish tank safely in the crack of her arm, hauled her few boxes and bags back to her new place. She wouldn't miss the shabby dwelling or furniture that she'd left behind - just another chapter in the steadily growing book of changes in her life. Another move: new characters to learn. So she thought. Little did she know this move would become an amusement park of emotional rides.

Chapter 4

Aisha could feel herself losing consciousness as Shawn tried to choke the stubbornness and defiance from her body, darkness mixed with pinpoint dots of blue and red filled her head as she felt for something within her reach to use to get Shawn's strong hands from the grip on her neck. She felt the telephone within her grasp, and with one quick movement she snatched up the receiver. The fight started after Aisha found a crack pipe in the pocket of his jacket while doing laundry. She confronted him with the evidence that he hadn't stopped smoking crack cocaine as he'd promised and therefore he had to leave their home for good.

To which he responded "Bitch, I'm not going nowhere!"

"Yes you are!"

"You're my wife, we have two kids! I'm not going nowhere!"

"Either you leave, or we will."

"You better not try to take my kids from me!"

"I am and you can't stop me, you raggedy ass crack head! What happened to the baby's diapers? I'm sick of living this way, my babies deserve more. You'd probably sell the drawers off your mama's ass if she turned her back long enough!"

Those were the last words she spoke before feeling Shawn's hands around her neck.

She felt a surge of energy flow through her body as she brought the phone receiver down on top of his head. The feeling of survival took over her emotions. Self preservation, the scientists call it. The first hit shocked Shawn, a second sent him falling sideways holding his head.

"You bitch!" he yelped as the second blow made contact.

Shawn sat on the floor holding his head. He wasn't sure if he should stay still, or leave and save his own life. Maybe he'd pushed her as far as he could. They'd been together for five years and married for three, long enough for them to learn each other inside and out.

Through the five years, Shawn had become used to Aisha being an easy person to have his way with. They had two children together, a daughter named Teri, and a son Shawn Junior. Teri was now four years old and Shawn Jr. was two years old.

Shawn knew that as long as Aisha had their children he'd always be in her life. In his own demented way he loved Aisha. He knew his drug addiction was getting the best of him and ruining his entire life, but the proverbial monkey had a tight hold on his neck. He couldn't seem to shake it. He sat on the floor and fell into a drug assisted dazed sleep.

After seeing that Shawn was sleeping, Aisha replaced the phone on its cradle, then picked it back up and called the police.

"Please send the police to 549 South Ave", she said as calmly as she could.

"What's the problem ma'am?" the dispatcher asked.

Miz Catfish

"I need my husband removed from the house."

"Where is he now?" the concerned dispatcher asked.

"He's sleeping in the bedroom." Aisha responded calmly, but she felt shakiness beginning in her hands and a warm stinging sensation in her eyes. She knew that she wouldn't be able to keep up the deceptive attitude of control much longer. She had almost lost her life. What type of existence was she living? What in the hell?

"Ma'am. Ma'am?" the dispatcher called loudly, breaking through Aisha's private thoughts.

"Huh! Oh, yes." Aisha snapped back to the attention of the conversation.

"Does he know you're calling?"

"No. We just had a fight. He choked me. I've had enough of him hitting me, he almost killed me today." Aisha began to cry.

"Calm down ma'am. Stay calm, you're doing fine. I'll get a patrol car over there immediately!"

Aisha hung up the phone and tried to gather her senses. This wasn't the first time that she had really been afraid for her life. Shawn's drug use was getting worse. The money for the baby's diapers was not the only issue, but the latest. The bills were all behind. The VCR was supposedly at his friend's house. His gold chain necklace and bracelet had "gotten lost" some weeks ago. On his payday she rarely saw him before midnight and by then his pockets were empty. He was looking skinny and pasty in the face. Teri rarely ran to him anymore when she got the opportunity to see him home before she went to bed. Instead she and her brother clung to their mother, afraid of their father's next outburst.

He didn't like any of her friends, and didn't want her to go anywhere without his knowledge. If it was a place that he didn't want her to go he'd say "I don't want my kids there!" If she found a sitter he'd say "I don't want that person keeping my kids." Anything to keep her home!

At the age of twenty five she felt trapped. When she met Shawn five years ago he was so suave, and charming in a "bad boy" way. She fell for him immediately. His tall, slim frame, and large white smile against his caramel-brown skin, made him stand out in a crowd. He was always dressed in slacks, dress shoes, and masculine jewelry. He still looked sharp to the people outside of the house, while on the inside Aisha watched his debonair appearance unravel. She knew that he would sell his sharpest outfit for ten dollars or a piece of crack.

Many women had been introduced to drugs by their partners as a form of quality time spent between the two. Shawn had tried to get her to indulge in the poisonous candy. If she wasn't so involved in the needs of their children, and the fact that she couldn't imagine anyone else, like her mother or Social Services raising them under any circumstances other than her death; she might have given in to the curse as others in love had done. The thought brought a cold shiver through her body. "There but for the grace of God go I." she knew to be the truth of that situation.

She had gone to the kitchen waiting for the police to arrive. She heard Shawn begin to move around in the bedroom. A

Miz Catfish

siren could be heard outside of the house. Shawn came into the kitchen looking rumpled and dazed.

"That better not be the police coming here Aisha!"

She didn't respond. Bolts of heat from fear shot from her toes to her knees. Aisha couldn't back down now; things were out of control, she wanted out before someone got fatally hurt. What if the police didn't offer her any help? What type of help did she want from them? Did she want Shawn in jail? Did she want Teri to hear this commotion, wake up and see the police taking her father away?

The nervous heat continued to flow through her legs and feet. There was a forceful knock at the door. "Police."

Shawn looked at Aisha with venom in his eyes.

"Isha, you'll pay for this, you bitch. After they leave I'm going to beat the shit out of you! You're gonna learn who wears the pants around here! Open the door and tell them that everything is okay. You're my wife and those are my kids in that room, I'm not going nowhere. I've already told you." He reached into a cabinet drawer and pulled a butcher's knife handle half of the way from the drawer, just enough for Aisha to see it. "I'm not playing with you girl, open that door and tell them to go away!"

Aisha heard Teri's small voice calling from the children's bedroom. "Mommy. Mommy?"

Aisha made sure that she went towards the front door in the direction that gave her the most distance from Shawn. As much as it tugged at her maternal instincts, Teri would have to wait. She got to the door, flung it open and yelled. "I want him out! He tried to kill me!"

Shawn quickly let go of the knife and closed the drawer.

"I don't know what she's talking about! She's crazy!" Shawn said.

"I'm not the one who's out of control, you are!" Aisha yelled.

The two policemen stepped into the apartment as Teri came out of her bedroom and into the kitchen. Shawn picked her up into his arms.

"Come to daddy, baby girl."

Teri wiggled out of his arms and ran to her mother when she saw the policemen.

"We received a call for assistance at this address", said one of the policemen. The one with the angry face.

"Uh-huh I called. I want him", Aisha said, pointing towards Shawn, "out of my house."

"Your house!" Shawn yelled. "This is my house too, and I'm not going nowhere!"

"Oh yes you are!" Aisha shouted.

Shawn moved towards Aisha. The second policeman moved forward to block his path.

"Hey guy, don't even think about it!" cautioned the policeman.

"I was only going to get my daughter from her." Shawn said in a snide tone.

"You're not getting her, so stay over there." Aisha heard Teri whimper and picked her up.

"She's my daughter too; don't tell me I can't hold her!"

"I take care of both of these babies, so just because you gave sperm don't make you a daddy. If you wasn't so busy chasing your pipe maybe you could earn some Father's Day points!"

"Yeah, you talk your shit now, wait 'till I get your neck again bitch!"

"That's enough, calm down you two, there's a child here. Ma'am, there was a mention of a fight. Was there any physical contact?" Officer One asked.

"Yes, look at my neck." Aisha stepped towards the policeman. He recorded the red bruises and welts on Aisha's tawny colored neck.

Officer One spoke to Shawn. "What's your name buddy?"

"Shawn Brown. I'm her husband, and there's no problem here."

"From the looks of your wife's neck I'd say there is a problem. Mr. Brown, here in Pittsburgh we frown on beating women. I think we better take you in just to give you a little time to come to your senses and to find some respect for the opposite sex." , the policeman standing between Shawn and Aisha reached for his handcuffs. "Hands behind your back please."

"Aisha! I know you not gonna do this to me!" Shawn yelled as he felt the policeman tightening the handcuffs around his wrists. "When I get out I'm gonna fix your ass. Just watch and see."

"It takes a pretty stupid guy to threaten someone in front of the police", snarled the second policeman. "I'm going to put him in the car Mike."

As the policeman walked Shawn toward the door. Shawn looked toward Aisha and spit at her. Aisha flinched from the pool of spit and her husband's venomous words. She knew he meant what he said.

"How long will he be locked up?" she asked the policeman that remained.

"Well, since it's after five o'clock, the courts are done for the day, so he'll at least be held until he goes in front of a judge tomorrow. It'll be up to that judge what happens from there. He'll be charged with Assault and Battery with intent to do serious harm. He could be further held or let out on bail. I'm going to go out to the patrol car to get my camera. I need to get a shot of your neck with the bruises. The picture may even help the judge hit him with a stronger charge. If he gets out on bail do you think you'll be safe? You can get a restraining order in the morning. That should stop him from coming back here if he gets out. If he does come here, all you have to do is call the police and they'll take him back to jail for breaking the order. Do you have family here to help you out?"

"Yes, I have family here; my mother lives a few buildings away. I have more family living near by, but he's not afraid of most of them. He once pulled a gun on one of my cousins."

"I'll be sure to put that in my report. It may help us hold on to him a little longer. Let me go get my camera. I'll be right back."

Miz Catfish

The policeman came back with the camera and a concerned look on his face. "Ah Mrs. Brown, while I was out at the car, your husband was making it clear that he's not exactly intending to reform himself when he gets released. I advise you to seriously think about not being here when he gets out. Here's a card with the 800-number of a group that provides assistance to women in your situation. From what I hear they're resourceful and act very quickly. I can't force you into anything but I do strongly advise that you consider calling them. This guy looks to be a loser and they have little fear or remorse from their choices. Did I hear you mention earlier that he uses drugs?"

"Yes sir, he does."

"Well from my experience in these situations that only makes the person more likely to be uncontrollable, or unpredictable."

Baby Shawn started crying from his crib, and Teri was holding onto Aisha's neck as if for dear life. Aisha felt the urge to scream "The baby is crying. The other baby is hanging on my neck. Shawn is in the police car just outside that window. Teri watched her father get arrested by Officer Friendly and the other one is standing here taking pictures of my neck and telling me to get help because he fears for my safety from my own husband. Lord! Help me! Lord I can't fall down now, my baby boy is crying."

All of these thoughts jumped around in her mind, fighting to be the most important. While she fought to make sense of them all, the only one that she could grab from the lot was that Shawn Jr. was crying louder, and that Teri was squeezing her bruised neck tighter. She took the card from the policeman's hand and convinced Teri to get off of her hip long enough for more pictures to be taken of her neck. The policeman told Aisha that she could get a copy of the report that he would be filling out on today's incident by tomorrow morning at the police station.

"Goodnight Mrs. Brown, and please think seriously about what I told you."

"Thank you officer, what's your name?"

"Officer Jameson."

"Thank you Officer Jameson, good evening." She left him to let himself out as she checked the refrigerator to see if there was enough milk to make a full bottle for the baby, there wasn't. She'd have to make more. Junior would have to settle for apple juice for the moment. She grabbed a clean bottle, filled it with the juice, then filled a cup of the same for Teri.

"Mommy's coming, honey." she called in the direction of Baby Shawn's room. "Teri get up to the table and drink your juice."

The following morning, it took Shawn one phone call to a friend to come up with his bail amount of two hundred dollars, and he was back on the streets. While Shawn was in the holding area, Aisha had already gone to the court house to get a restraining order as the policeman had suggested she do. It had been very embarrassing to stand in front of a court room full of strangers, and explain to the judge the things that Shawn had done to her to make her fear for her safety. Explaining the events so vividly bought flashbacks as if she were reliving them and tears threatened to spill from her eyes, a court officer discretely offered her a tissue. She had to keep the goal at hand in the fore-front of her mind in order to follow through on the disturbing procedure. By the time the judge felt that he had heard enough sufficient evidence to make his judgment of her request, she felt completely naked. Standing there in the middle of the floor, in front of strangers who now knew some of the worst private haunts in her personal life like a soap opera actress on day time television. The judge granted her the restraining order, he explained the usage of the order and gave her a copy, she couldn't think of anything else other than getting home, behind closed doors, away from the prying eyes now upon her.

During the late hours of the night Aisha heard a key in the door. She knew of only one person who had a key, and she braced herself for the drama about to erupt. She thought about her copy of the restraining order in the shoe box of her red open-toe sandal. Shawn was to be served with his copy earlier while he was still locked up in the jail. She knew that she had to hide her copy in order to keep him from doing something as crazy as trying to make her eat it. Was putting him in jail worth it? It had only made him angrier and more likely to strike out violently.

"Isha I'm baack-k-!" he teased.

She jumped up from the bed and ran to the closet, reaching into the shoe box; she snatched the order out and shoved it under the mattress jumping back into bed as quickly as she'd jumped out. She intended to ask him to leave and use the court order if he wouldn't. It crossed her mind that if he came into the bedroom to start a fight she'd have to grab what ever she could get her hands on, something she could use to defend herself. The telephone would have to serve as a weapon again, as it had before. Time seemed to crawl by, second by second.

She wondered when the other shoe would fall, when would the mad man on the other side of the door decide to lash out? What felt like a grip around her chest, moved further and further up towards her throat. Maybe it was a scream but it felt like a strong grip.

At some point she fell into a much needed but not planned slumber. When she woke the next morning Shawn was not in bed. Pieces of paper had been thrown all over her and the bed while she slept. She picked up enough pieces to get an idea of what they had once been. It was a copy of her restraining order. She could make out parts of her and Shawn's names, as well as their address. Quickly she moved off the bed and reached under the mattress to check for her copy, it was there. Her copy was a different color from the shreds of paper on the bed. The confetti had to be the copy served to Shawn. She crept over to the bedroom door. Opening it slowly she stepped from the room into the hallway which divided all of the small rooms in the apartment. She saw the two small mounds of brown skin and juvenile print fabric of the sleeping children in their beds in the bedroom that they shared.

As she entered the living room she saw Shawn sprawled out on the sofa. She crept closer to where he lay to get past the sofa and into the kitchen and caught a glimpse of the man that she had fallen in love with. In his slumber, his handsome features were allowed to fall freely without disfigurement from anger or mischief. She felt the wall of rationale getting shaky as the emotion called LOVE trying to surface. It had been tucked away for so long now that the thought of having someone to love almost felt good. They had made two beautiful children together, although the pregnancies were spent mostly with family and her girlfriend as opposed to him.

The children were neat, well fed, and slept in warm comfortable beds. The sex was so powerful, so emotional. The positive list, it was very short. The negative list of memories was much longer and the thought of each entry brought her wall of protection back up to full strength, once the addition of this latest incident was added to her memory, she was again able to focus on the reality of today. Quietly she made her way to the kitchen, got a bottle ready for Junior, made a bowl of cereal for herself, and cautiously took it back to the bedroom. She didn't want to wake Shawn; she wasn't up for another physical fight. He would surely be more than ready to torture her physically as well as emotionally when he woke. She had come to realize that sometimes you challenge and fight back to the best of your ability, other times you keep yourself out of harms way and are very careful not to push your luck. She hoped that by already having a bottle ready for Junior, when he woke she wouldn't have to walk so close to the rabid dog in the living room again, she'd just have to go directly into the children's room which was close to her own.

The cereal that she brought into the bedroom had turned to mush. Her stomach felt empty, yet she couldn't get herself calm enough to imagine chewing and swallowing. She turned on the television and lowered the volume as low as she could to not disturb Shawn, but without losing the sound all together.

Another half hour went by before she heard the shower water running in the bathroom. "Hey Isha." Shawn pushed the bedroom door open with so much force that it slammed into the wall behind it. She jumped unable to control her nervousness. He walked over to the closet, brushing closely past her legs as he went. "So you got yourself a restraining order huh? Those things are only worth the paper they're written on." He searched through the hanging clothes humming a little ditty as he chose an outfit and got dressed. She sat still, looking in the mirror from as many angles as she could. Walking back towards the bedroom door, he stopped in front of her and used his hand to shove her forehead, forcing her head to arch back at an uncomfortable angle. She fought the urge to jump up and dig her nails into his face, to bite his arm, kick him in the groin, anything to get back some of the pride from which he was stripping her by taunting her. Instinct told her to stay still and stay as safe as possible in this situation that she really couldn't control. She'd only be throwing gasoline on a smoldering fire. He'd been locked up and held over night, which meant that he hadn't been able to get drugs. She was sure that would be his top priority this morning, but she did not expect him to let her get away with hitting him in the head with the telephone or calling the police. He'd blame her for getting arrested, and not take any ownership for his own actions. There would be some sort of revenge against her. He was too vindictive to be this calm; surely there was a storm to follow.

"See ya Isha!" he sang walking away.

She heard him shut and lock the front door on his way out. The children were still sleeping, and with tears of frustration, and fear running down her cheeks she sat on her bed wondering what he was up to. She didn't bother to wipe them away, just let them run down, some ran over her top lip and rolled between her lips, giving her the slightest taste of warm salt. She felt so lonely and alone. There is a difference.

She could use the restraining order to keep him from returning, but she'd have to wait for him to be there, or at the door, before she could call the police. What if it took them too long to respond to the call? She didn't know if she wanted to take that chance. It sounded too easy, and he had proven when the police were in their home that he wasn't afraid of them. They'd take him out and he'd come back angrier than he'd left. She went to her underwear drawer and reaching deep under the colorful mixture of fabric, pulled out her poetry notebook. She kept it hidden so that Shawn wouldn't get a hold of it and read her inner most thoughts. Something had to remain untouched by his poisonous hands.

Flipping through the pages Aisha realized how much time she spent reflecting her emotions into words, and then onto paper. She stopped turning pages at a poem for which she strived to one day be her anthem.

I AIN'T YO SLAVE

Get in the kitchen and fix me a cut
I'n fixin you nothing, jus look at you gut
Clean up this room 'cus it is a mess
Keep runnin yo mouth and you'll be starin at my fist
Get back to work and make me some money
I ain't yo slave, I ain't doin nothing for you honey

Bring me a beer from outta the fridge
No, how bout you getting outside and clippin that hedge
Do sum'In wit yo hair, do sum'in wit yo clothes
You talking bout me wit yo notty afro's?
Get back to work and make me some money
I ain't yo slave, I ain't doin nothing for you honey

Bring me my slippers so I can relax

Miz Catfish

Keep talking that mess, you gone need some ice packs
Who are you talkin to, I know you ain't talking to me
I think you are the only one around here I see
Get me my paper, let me check out the score
I said, I ain't yo slave and I ain't doin it no more!

- Tara Morgan

Then with a shaky hand, and unsure grip on the pen, she wrote a new work:

Crack Man

The witches are out on the prowl tonight
Looking for zombies to torture and fright

Dressed in all black, hoodies and sweats
Gold rings, and gold necklaces, and gold teeth,
How about that

The zombies look up to them and idolize them for sure
And NO matter what, they keep going back for more

They can't pay their bills
They can't love their wives

They can't love their kids
They don't value their lives

All in all they just look a damned mess
But the root of it all is hiding from stress

Miz Catfish

The witches are out on the prowl today
With little white pills, OH,
How they make the zombies pay

The zombies are running around eyes open wide
They've lost all their luster, they don't have any pride

They can't clean their houses
They can't make their beds

Their husbands are furious,
Going upside of their heads

And all in all, they just look a damned sight
But that doesn't stop them from roaming the night

The witches are stunning and prosperous for sure
But to all of these witches I say Stop it! No More!

Down, Down, Downward they'll come
NOW….Who will the zombies get their little pills from?

- Tara Morgan

Miz Catfish

Chapter 5

Amber's heart skipped a beat when the cute guy that she and Macy met in front of what is now the Pet Shop entered the store. She quickly turned her body to the left and pretended to straighten the assorted brands of cigarettes stacked in a metal rack on the wall. As long as she stayed tucked away behind the counter he wouldn't notice the way her legs were shaking with nervousness, and excitement.

Jason started down the aisle. He stalled in front of the case, giving the impression that he was choosing from the vast selection before him.

Actually Jason was taking the time to plan what he hoped would become conversation with Amber. He remembered her name from the day he'd met her and her friend in front of the new store on the block. He'd been watching her walk back and forth past the window of his hardware store. Twice while on his way to open the store in the morning, he saw her going into the "THE CORNER STOP". He began to wonder if she worked in the store. He decided to take a chance on finding out if his assumption was correct. Jason was attracted to the girl, he liked what he saw and wanted to get into her life, and maybe a little more. He'd have to find out if she was in a relationship. Pulling an apple juice from the cooler, he made his way back to the register.

"Hi."

"Oh, hello." Amber returned shakily, still trying to appear busy with the cigarettes.

"Can I have this juice free? You look busy, and maybe you're too busy to ring me." he joked.

"Yeah, right! Imagine the store surviving on that theory." she laughed.

"Maybe you could run a tab for me, that is unless your significant other would have a problem with that."

"No tabs allowed, and no significant other on board."

"Too bad on one, so good on the other."

"Fork over that dollar fifty buddy." Amber flashed a big smile. If she wasn't mistaking, that had been a flirt.

"Since you said that you don't have a significant other, would you be willing to get together for a drink one night after work? Maybe a glass of wine?" he asked.

"That would be fine." Amber hoped her voice was coming across smoothly; she didn't want to appear anxious.

"How about around eight o'clock Saturday, your place?"

"Great. You know where I live, I'm in apartment one on the first floor."

"Well, I guess it's a date." he winked as he placed two dollars on the counter.

He left the store and took up the bottle of juice, enjoying the progress made with Amber; he absentmindedly twisted the white cap in preparation to take a drink of the cold liquid. The clear glass bottle let out a loud suction noise caused by the breaking of its safety seal, Jason tilted his head back and took a gulp of the amber liquid. An involuntary gag reaction caused Jason to spit the liquid onto the sidewalk. "Damn, I forgot I don't like apple juice!" he cursed to himself. He looked around hoping no one had seen him.

Chapter 6

Shawn walked back into the house at eight o'clock in the evening, two days later. Aisha was in the kitchen cleaning away the mess from the children's supper. She had cooked a large pot of spaghetti figuring she'd put some away for herself to eat later when she had more of an appetite. What ever was left after she separated hers would go into the garbage to keep Shawn from eating since he had become so stingy with what he gave her towards the food bill. This time he came back before she could throw the extra food away. He came into the kitchen.

"Hey Isha, what did you cook? Smells good." He said as he strolled towards the stove. He spoke as if the past seven days had not happened. He still wore the denim outfit that he'd left the house in. His face looked worn and he faintly smelled of sweet, musty smoke.

As he reached for the lid of the pot, she came to stand next to the stove, fully prepared to stand her ground. "You're not getting anything to eat in here, so don't go into my pot."

"Why not?" Shawn managed through a laugh. Surely she must be joking, thinking she could stop him from doing what ever he wanted to do in his own home.

"Because, where ever you've been you must have been eating, so go back there and tell HER that you're hungry."

"Why does it have to be a HER?" he asked innocently.

"I'm sure that you haven't been with the guys these past two nights. To be honest with you, I really don't give a shit where you've been, but you won't come back in here acting like nothing has happened."

"Don't start, Aisha. You always have to find something to bitch about. That's your problem, your damn mouth is too big."

"What ever. Just don't touch the food."

"Shut up girl." he said as he reached for a plate and fork.

Aisha went to the sink, reached under and pulled out a jug of bleach. Before he could dig his fork into the opened pot she quickly emptied some of the pungent, clear liquid into the well seasoned spaghetti.

"What the hell did you do that for you crazy bitch!"

"Because I told you that you're not going to eat anything in here. Now if you want to ignore me and you think I'm joking, let me see you eat that! Help yourself."

"If I wasn't so tired I'd punch your stupid ass face in." Shawn hissed.

He threw the plate and fork down on top of the stove and headed out of the kitchen. She followed behind him.

"Where are you going?"

"Mind your business Isha", he said as he walked into their bedroom, sat on the edge of the bed and began taking his shoes off.

"Don't get in my bed", she said feeling a lack of control over her emotions. She knew that she was treading on dangerous ground, yet she could no longer stand the disrespect, and abuse. There was a screaming sound growing inside her head.

"Isha get the hell out of my face will you!" He got off the bed, grabbed her by the arm and half walked and shoved her out of the bedroom door, slamming it behind her.

Her bantering had no effect on him; he'd been hearing it for years. She couldn't control him so who cared what she felt. He took his clothes off and climbed under the covers.

Aisha's nerves were in such poor condition that the slamming of the door seemed to send an arrow of hot anger from her head to her toes as if a sharp knife had been dragged down her body. Her mind began to feel scrambled. Confusion, anger, fear and pride were trying to find perspective in her emotionally clouded mind. One thing she was sure of was that he was not going to continue to walk in and out of their home as if he were a room-mate instead of a husband and father.

Even though their relationship was in a shambles she still hurt to think of the slap in the face of knowing that Shawn was with other women. For him to come back and slide his body between their marital sheets as if he had not played a part in any such behavior was the last straw for her on this evening.

She dressed the children in their coats, leaving them in their pajamas, and took them to her mother's house a few buildings away. She sat them on their grandmother's sofa simply stating that she had something to do and would return shortly. Actually she didn't know if she'd return or not, because what she planned to do might either land her in the jail house or dead.

As she walked back to her building she thought of the pain and anguish that she had felt while going through the years of chaos with Shawn. The telephone calls from other women, and late at night texts, Shawn answering messages, leaving soon after, and returning home the following evening. The black and blue marks under her eyes, and the red marks on her tawny colored skin, around her wrists, on her thighs, and one on her back from being shoved backwards into the bureau. The broken dishes, pulled down curtains, and ugly black metal monkey statues. Yeah, those statues were on her list too. Two of them that Shawn had gotten from God knows where, and had put one on each end of the coffee table. They never got broken during a fight. They just sat there, *ugly*. Other than the large red lamps, they were his only contributions to the living room.

She marched back towards her building in body, but not in thought. She felt mechanical. All she knew was that she had to get rid of him. Couldn't take anymore! COULDN'T! WOULDN'T! He must go! Marching like an angry momma going to the playground to defend her hurt child, she reached the building. Climbing the stairs on shaky legs, she got to her front door and as silently as possible, entered the apartment. She looked for Shawn. Their bedroom door was still closed. She imagined him lying in bed, resembling a king in all his glory. Quietly she went to the kitchen. After rummaging through the cabinets she found some newspapers and matches. Then rolling the paper into a cone she put match to paper and began a race through the house to the bedroom where Shawn lay. Quickly grabbing the door knob and shoving the door open, she threw what was now a torch onto the bed, hoping that it would land directly on his lap. She pulled the door knob and closed the door completely.

Her toes couldn't keep a grip in her slippers in her hurry to get back to her mother's house, and they slipped off as she broke into a run. She didn't even notice their absence.

A sudden flash of intense heat seared Shawn's thigh causing his eyes to rush open and he bolted into an upright position. He looked down to find a ball of flames made from newspaper. Fear surged through his body, forever scarring his memory, and gripping his heart in a grid iron brace. Through a fog he realized what had happened.

"Uh-h-h! You crazy bitch! What the hell are you doing? I'm gonna kill you! You stupid bitch!" he beat at the flames with a pillow, imitating a large, angry bird flapping it's wings while jumping up and down.

Once the flames were out, he snatched up his pants and almost tripped himself trying to quickly get both legs in at the same time. He grabbed the first shirt that he saw lying near, not worrying about matching his outfit as he normally would have done. Had he taken the time he would have noticed that the white t-shirt he picked up was one of Aisha's that read "IN CASE OF PMS ATTACK, FEED ME CHOCOLATE" He slipped into his brown loafers usually not worn without socks, but socks were the last thing on his mind at that moment. He wanted to get to Aisha's crazy ass. She would be sorry for being so bold and thinking that she could get in his face and punk him. No female would ever punk him, not even his wife! He ran into the living room, noticing that Aisha was not in sight and the children were gone as well. The living room door was ajar. He headed to his mother-in-law's house thinking she'd go there first.

Aisha's mother tried to call Shawn on the telephone. She wanted to ask him what was going on with her daughter. It was hard to keep out of her daughter and son-in-law's marital problems, but when she saw her daughter hurting physically or emotionally, she went directly to Shawn's face for an explanation. Through the years she had learned to let Aisha handle problems her own way, in her own time. She realized that she couldn't tell her daughter who to love. To try and force Aisha to leave Shawn could have a negative result. What if Aisha chose Shawn over her and she had to be without her daughter completely? Love sometimes worked that way. If Norma could have her way with things Shawn would have been found in an alley a long time ago.

She disliked him to that extent. She was sure a few of her nephews would be more than happy to teach him a few lessons about hitting women, but she knew if Aisha found out the names of anyone involved she would probably turn them in to the police.

Aisha had come running back through her front door with nothing on her feet. Her hair was in complete disarray, and she was out of breath. Her daughter had made no clear sense as she slammed and locked the door behind herself, rattling some words about being fed up, tired, and burning. At the time of Shawn's knock on the door, Aisha was on the sofa rocking slowly back and forth. The children were in their grandmother's bedroom watching television, away from the excitement.

The first few knocks did not register in Aisha's clouded mind. She sluggishly returned to her surroundings. The banging noise invaded her haze in time to realize that her mother was on her way to the door. She yelled "Ma don't open the door!" Her mother came to an abrupt halt, spinning on her heels to face her daughter. "What in God's name is going on?" Shawn yelled into the door "Aisha! Isha! I know you're in there! You'll come out sooner or later, and when you do I'm gonna kill yo ass! You hear me!"

Aisha's mother could no longer stand to see her child in such a state, and from the tone of the threats and disrespect coming from the other side of her door, she decided to call the police and told Shawn as much. When the squad car arrived and the officers knocked on the door Shawn was no where in sight.

The officers reporting to the call were the same two that had responded to Aisha's call days earlier, and they recognized her. They got as much from her as they could in her agitated state before they again suggested she consider the use of the domestic violence network. This time she realized that she needed the protection and that something had to change, things had gone too far today, way too far. Before she could talk herself out of going she said "Yes I'll go." If Shawn had been present during this conversation he may have succeeded in getting Aisha arrested for attempted murder, but because these policemen knew this to be a volatile situation, they quickly surmised that the victim they had previously assisted again had been attacked. They chose to try to change the situation themselves by giving Aisha an out to safety.

Officer Jameson went with Aisha to her apartment to get a small amount of personal items for the children and herself.

The officer entered first; there was no sign of Shawn. With shaky hands, Aisha focused on her task of selecting needed items only, instead of packing like a cautious mother. What's the difference? Emergency packing: diapers, formula, two clean outfits for each child, etc, the minimum. What did it mean to pack cautiously? Pampers, is this enough? Clean outfits. Four for each child because someone might get dirty or wet themselves. Snack foods, medicines in case of pain, toys, etc., but the maximum that could be folded into tiny cubes until there is no room for left behind possibly needed items. Aisha spent less time and thought when grabbing her own things, making sure to snatch up her poetry notebook along with some underwear. Then the two walked quickly back to her mother's house.

The police officers called for a plain clothes female officer from the Domestic Violence Unit, who arrived at Aisha's mother's house within ten minutes. The small family was allowed a moment longer for well-wishing, stay-in-touch hugs and kisses between mother, daughter, and grandchildren. Then the female officer ushered the small family out the door to a plain black car and off to a hidden shelter. Aisha would be unreachable but would be able to call after a few days.

After being in her own apartment for four years, it was not easy for Aisha to be under someone else's roof, with their possessions, and their rules. The realization of being thirty years old and having to start over again as well as removing her children from their own toys, and bedroom, made her long to return to her own home. Maybe Shawn would smarten up after seeing how she wasn't going to allow him to continue with his abuse and disrespect, maybe he missed them already and would change his ways to keep them. She wondered if it

Miz Catfish

would have been easier to stay with the familiar and its negativity rather than sharing a six bedroom house with four other women and children.

Frayed nerves surrounded the entire house like barbed wire. Blackened eyes, bruised arms, necks, faces, hearts, souls and spirits, children whose innocence would never return, who would misunderstand the word LOVE, and associate it with hitting, screaming, tears, pain, and police.

Every concerned mother and staff member within those walls wondered which child in the house would be an abuser or victim when older. Which child would get hit, which one of them would break the cycle as opposed to continuing it? On this day they all looked the same, like innocent children. Now that Aisha was away from Shawn, she began to realize that restructuring her own attitude was not going to be easy. She had always been the type of person that openly voiced her opinions, fighting with Shawn verbally as well as physically, had made her very defensive. Here she had to swallow those instincts. There were too many different personalities, and the need to blow off steam could give any of the other women the slightest reason to let the fists fly. They all had to learn to be patient and try to stay out of each other's way. Even though all of her bouts with Shawn had made her unafraid of a battle with anyone, she realized that she was sort of boxed out at the moment. All of the latest events had drained her energy, not only emotionally, but physically. She made sure to stay out of the way of any confrontations.

If she needed to relieve her stress with a bitching and moaning session, she'd call her mother. Children ran amuck, mothers squabbled like farmyard hens, and counselors offered comfort and counsel to those allowing their protective walls to be penetrated.

The purpose of staying in the shelter was not only for the instances of emergency housing, but with the goal of finding permanent housing as well. On a daily basis each adult client had to attentively search for housing. Aisha waited her turn each day to get a glance at the classified section of newspaper for the town and surrounding areas.

The last telephone conversation with her mother lingered heavily on her mind. Norma reported to her that Shawn had been hanging around her house, and calling her constantly telling her to remind her daughter that he was still her husband, and the father of the children.

"Tell her that I'll find her and my kids. She can't hide forever and I won't give up my family. Let her know that I owe her for this burn mark on my hand."

She and her mother cried together over the sadness of the entire situation, her mother pleaded with her to be careful. She missed her daughter, but knew that the situation had gotten further out of control than they could handle on their own, and Aisha was doing what needed to be done for her and the children's safety.

Aisha reported the conversation to the director of the shelter. Shawn was correct in the fact that the children were his as well as Aisha's. The staff made arrangements with their legal services to help Aisha get full physical and legal custody of the children. This would take away Shawn's rights to have say in where they lived with their mother, as well as removing his ability to take them at any time without Aisha's permission.

Although the temporary restraining order had given her temporary custody, she still needed to make the move legal.

Copies of the police reports, and the abuse photos were faxed from the police station in her home town, along with the copy of the restraining order from her court, were used in the request to the court for full custody of the children as well as an extension of the restraining order for one year, at that time she could go back to any court to request another extension. Shawn would not receive a copy of this restraining order, so that he would not receive information to indicate Aisha's location. The other task of hiding from Shawn was changing her name as well as the children's. They were no longer Aisha, Teri, and Shawn Junior Brown. They would now be known as Janice, Jamie and Johnny Trenton.

All of the court actions, the name changes, and living changes had her head spinning. Things were moving at a cannon ball rate of speed, leaving no time to absorb the horror of her old life, or the mystery of her new life. She felt enormous amounts of anger at Shawn. Why had he forced things to go this far? Why didn't he care enough about her and the children to care about their feelings, their necessities? How was it that her life was up-side down and not his? She had lost all control over her own life. The shelter had a curfew that all clients had to abide by. She couldn't even stay out as long as she wanted. She couldn't even remember the last time her own mother had set the time for her to come in the house.

She knew that she would only feel safer if she moved far away from Shawn, although he'd continue to ask questions of his mother-in-law with the knowledge that she wouldn't give him any answers, anyone that knew him knew that he wouldn't give up his quest. His family was a part of his legal possessions. In his mind he owned "them". He'd make the decision on when the relationship would end, not her.

She agreed to allow the shelter network, made up of other shelters from state to state, to link together on finding her what would hopefully become a safe and permanent home. In the back of everyone's mind they knew that she would always have to be aware of her surroundings in case Shawn found his way around her new protective shield.

Since moving into the house Aisha had only gotten one chance to sit down to do some work in her poetry notebook.

I'm Always Guilty

No matter what the case may be
I am always guilty
No matter what my eyes may see
I am always guilty
Why is it that it's always my fault?
Even when I try to talk
You never want to take the blame
You know that is a sorry shame
But yet and still
No matter what the case may be
I am always guilty

Why can't you be responsible?
For the pain you cause?
Instead of pointing your finger at me

Miz Catfish

Why can't you just apologize?
Instead of glaring your eyes at me
Why can't you see that it's your fault?
Instead of all that rough and tough talk

I know why!
Because no matter what the case may be
I am always guilty

You see a tear drop from my eyes
Instead of calming down my cries
You point your finger and place the blame
And sometimes make me so ashamed
But the reasoning is so clear to me
Because no matter what the case may be
I am always guilty

You tell me I'm not smart enough
But I am always guilty
You tell me I need to toughen up
Still, I am always guilty
It's always that I did it wrong
And I am always guilty
It's my fault when we don't get along
Because I am always guilty

Because you choose to raise your hand
Tell me to sit, when I choose to stand
Because we forgot to make the bed
Because of all that stuff we said
Because we could not afford to pay
That bill that was due on yesterday
Because when we choose to sit down and talk

Miz Catfish

The words I speak don't touch your heart
Does not induce the case to be
That I am always guilty!

- Tara Morgan

Chapter 7

"Callate! Callate nino! (Shut up! Shut up boy!) Shut your mouth." CeCe yelled from her native Spanish to English at her six year old son Manuel, who sat on the sofa crying. He wanted to go outside to play. CeCe had told him "No" because she had to go get ready for work and didn't have time to go outside with him. CeCe whose entire name was Cecilia Ana Maria Ortiz had been nicknamed CeCe by her co-workers on the job that she started after coming to Massachusetts from the Dominican Republic. As long as she could remember, there had been talk of a life of riches in America, and along with other islanders, like CeCe decided they would try to make a better life for themselves and their children by making the trip to the land of opportunity. She was twenty three years old, and had the full responsibility of single parenting a child.

Now that she had been in America for a month she began to completely understand the greater possibilities to better her life. In her old home, no one had explained to her how uncomfortable and scary it was going to be living as an illegal alien in the new country. She knew it would entail some use of trickery on her part to even get a job here, but she had not been prepared for the pressure of doing so. She had no adult companion to share her worries.

Manuel's father Luiz had been one of the pickers on CeCe's grandfather's farm. He was six years older than CeCe, and had talked her into giving up her virginity behind the smoke house.

After six months of hiding their relationship CeCe realized that she was pregnant and had to tell her family. Her father and uncle chased Luiz off their land and threatened to kill him if he ever returned. She carried the pregnancy to term, gave birth to her son, and the events of which included his conception and paternity were never spoken again.

Even though it would not be easy, at least here she had a chance to earn money and possibly save enough to send her son Manuel, to a modern school. She wanted the best for him. If she had stayed home in the Dominican Republic she would still be living with her large family who were not middle class people, but not poor either. Through the day her thoughts often went back to when she had helped her family pick her grandfather's tobacco crops, getting them ready for sale at the market. People from the area were also hired to help work the crop. Some of the workers were American and she learned English from them as well as from the people at the market.

Her grandmother and mother stayed home cooking plantanos and rice and beans. They sang songs passed down by their mothers as they cleaned the house and tended to cows, goats, horses, and a donkey.

CeCe thought of these things as she, Manuel and ten others waited for midnight to sneak to the shore. Once there they would board a boat owned by a fisherman who had become wealthy selling seafood during the day, and illegally transporting people wanting to leave the island at night. Everyone crowded onto the boat except the owner who, collected five thousand dollars, in American value, from each person, and stayed behind. He kept his hands clean.

Each of the passengers was given motion sickness pills and told to stay below deck in the dark and be very quiet. The crew was afraid that any light or noise might attract the Coast Guard, constantly on surveillance for illegal ocean travelers. The trip was long, and frightening, never to be forgotten. Manuel was the only child on this trip, and he clung to his mother closely.

"Tengo miedo." (I'm scared.), he moaned. "Donde estas abuela y abuelo?" (Where are grandma and grandpa?)

"No llores. (Don't cry.) I know that you are afraid, but everything will be alright. "Abuela y abuelo estan en la casa." (Grandma and grandpa are at home.) She pulled her son's small body close. Cecilia understood his fear, and she felt the same. Unfamiliar faces surrounded them and the boat was filled with a mixture of fish odors, aromas of cooked food, musk, sweat and pungent cigar smoke. Three of the men passed cigars and matches among themselves and heartily indulged in comical conversation. The women, including CeCe, held onto sacks of homemade foods, sandwiches, chicken, plantanos, and plenty of water.

She was lucky to make the trip after her time of the month and not before. CeCe did not want to draw too much attention to herself. She had been warned that all women would be watched very carefully, any sign of a female on her monthly and she would have to go over board. It was believed by male travelers that sharks would smell the warm odorous blood and come after the vessel for a meal. By throwing the female overboard the attraction would be eliminated. CeCe hoped that all of the women on board had been as careful. She couldn't imagine seeing such a thing happen to anyone. The men with thick smoke clouds above their heads laughed loudly and slapped each other on the back as women tried to move around them without getting pinched on the behind. The men passed around a bottle of homemade liquor and had to be reminded by the captain to quiet down. He then took a few swallows of liquor from them as payment for their rowdiness. While he was taking his share of drink a young man climbed past him to get above deck to the railing. The motion sickness pill wasn't working for him and he hung over the side vomiting violently.

The lack of windows and the darkness inside the boat prevented anyone from noticing the changes from day to night back to day, but it was very apparent when the small boat entered the rough area of ocean waters called the Canal de la Mona. The water there was feared because of its powerful waves. Immediately the group heard the knocking of the water's forceful waves against the outside of the boat. A vessel as small as theirs was no match for the large swells surrounding them. The boat tilted from left to right so violently that it nearly capsized. The motion threw everyone, men and women, and child, against the walls, the floor and each other. CeCe clung to Manuel whose crying could barely be heard amid the cries of the other passengers praying to the Virgen de la Altagracia, the Mother of God.

It was hours before the small boat reached calm waters. A cigar was lit in the corner, and it's orange-red embers glowed softly against the grey darkness of the cabin. The fusing of colors and the return to passive water helped to soothe one's nerves after the hair raising experience.

The smell of food filled the cabin. The contents of knapsacks were being spread out and shared. Food and water had to be eaten and drunk with caution because the duration of

Miz Catfish

the trip was unpredictable. The lack of water would be most unbearable.

Five days later they landed on the shore of Miami. The group was instructed to quickly grab their bags and move into brush and the boat was prepared to be sunk, to prevent the border patrol from seeing the vessel and starting a search, for they would immediately assume the boat belonged to illegals because of the deserted area in which it had landed.

They had arrived in total darkness and had to wait until the following evening to be picked up and moved to a "safe house". During that time most of the women amongst the group were raped. The sounds of the women pleading, the heinous laughter of the men, and the fear of being found by police was unbearable for CeCe.

She felt her bladder fill, and left Manuel and their bags in one spot while she crept off farther into the wooded area to find a hidden spot to urinate. After urinating and wiping at herself with extra food napkins, she saw what is usually thought to be a curse. Her period was coming. She knew that only this would stop her from being attacked like the other women. When she reentered the group a grungy, musky smelling old man grabbed her crotch, but after feeling an extra bulge caused by folded napkins, he backed off and yelled her good fortune to the rest of the men. They laughed loudly, then moved on to other women who were not as lucky.

The next day, everyone stayed hidden until the evening when they were loaded into a large white van. Manuel clung to his mother, afraid of all the new faces and asking about his grandmother and grandfather. Whenever he was tired or afraid he knew his "abuelo" his grandfather, would make everything alright. He'd sing to him songs sung by their ancestors, and would walk through the fields with him on his shoulders, making him giggle to be so high above the others.

"Ma Ma, donde' esta abuelo?"

"Sh-h-h, Manuel, no ahora, te quiero, dame un abrazo. (Not now, give me a hug)" CeCe tried to soothe her son.

CeCe was trying to teach him English and although she still spoke to him mostly in Spanish, she slipped the English translation in as much as possible so her son would soon understand the language of his new surroundings, and not feel so completely alienated.

The van stopped at a ranch style house in a town called Rincon. About five of the crowd left and went their own way. This was as far as they'd paid for transportation. They only wanted to make it to the United States, and had no wish to go further. The other seven people, including CeCe and Manuel, traveled on. CeCe had received the money from her grandfather for boat passage, and shelter at a hideout in Miami until two seats were available on a plane to another state. The person who was in charge of the hideaway or safe house had a friend at the airport who called when seats were available on a flight. Many waited until the plane's destination was one where relatives had already settled, but not CeCe, she would take whatever she could get and make the best of things.

Chapter 8

Amber completed her shift, and exited THE CORNER STOP with the thought of catching a glimpse of Jason on her way home. She hadn't seen him since his visit to the store one week ago, and she found herself thinking of him constantly.

As she got closer to the hardware store her mind scrambled to devise a scheme for needing to either buy something in the store, or speak to Jason.

Amber straightened her shirt, and ran her fingers through her hair. She waited until she was directly in front of the large hardware store window and allowed her pocketbook to fall to the ground. Her plan worked, Jason looked up from the stack of order forms on his counter in time to see Amber's golden curls go down, and her perky behind come up. He walked over to the door to find out what had her attention, and to get a closer look at that perky bottom.

"Hey, what's so interesting down there?" Jason asked Amber as he allowed his eyes to scan the shapely formed body in front of him. A loose curl of hair fell across Amber's forehead and a sudden urge to reach out and smooth it back into place came over him. He pushed his hands into his pockets in an attempt to control himself.

"I'm so clumsy! I dropped my pocketbook." Amber said.

"Well, I guess I better help you pick this stuff up before someone kicks your" He picked up a tube of lipstick and turned it upside down to read its label. "Fluffy Pink lipstick down the street." he joked.

"Why thank you my savior." She smiled.

They bent together picking the small quantity of items off the ground. Jason straightened up first, then Amber, holding a pack of gum in her hand.

"Would you like a piece of gum?" she offered.

"No thank you, but I'll counter offer that by offering you a cold drink."

"That offer I will accept." Amber said with a wide smile. She had succeeded in not only getting to see Jason, but was going to get to spend some time with him as well. The day couldn't be better.

"Come on in." Jason said holding the door for Amber to enter the store.

" Head straight to the back, past that ladder hanging on the wall," he instructed her as he turned the square plastic sign that hung on the door from OPEN to CLOSED.

"This place is a lot larger on the inside than it looks from the outside." Amber said while looking around at the variety of supplies. She had no idea that so many cartons of boxes and cans could be stacked so high without falling.

Jason walked over to a small refrigerator in the corner of the room "Would you like a bottle of water, or a can of ginger ale? Apparently that's all I have today."

"I'll take water. Thanks."

Jason passed Amber the cold, plastic bottle making sure their fingers touched during the exchange. They both felt a tingle run through their stomach.

"So how was your day? Jason asked Amber. "I assume that you're leaving the store."

"It was okay, but you wouldn't believe some of the kooky people that walk through the door of that place." Amber laughed.

"Yeah, tell me about it. I think you guys send them to me after they finish driving you crazy, because I get some whackos too."

"Uh, excuse me; it's more likely that you send them to us." she snickered, pouring a little water in her hand and flicking it at him.

He dodged the liquid drops, moving close enough to reach out to her and tickle her in the rib area.

"Hey that's not fair! I used one hand, and you're using two." She sat the bottle and her pocketbook down on the floor. They tickled each other into a mini wrestling match, backing themselves against a stack of paint cans in a corner. Without giving her notice he pulled her into an embrace and began to kiss her, she did not resist. The kissing became passionate and the movements of the participants became sexual demands needing to be fed.

Jason's fingers fumbled in his haste to unbutton the top of Amber's jeans, and then his own. He stopped kissing her long enough to look her in the eyes, looking for a sign of consent. Amber returned the look, acknowledging the tension felt within the room. She unzipped her jeans and along with her panties pushed them down, allowing them to drop to the floor. Ignoring the coldness of a paint can that now touched her bare skin, she leaned back to pull a foot out of the mixture of denim and cotton at her feet.

Jason pushed his jeans and plaid boxers down, also freeing a leg from fabric. Amber wrapped her arms around his neck as a means of keeping her balance as he lifted her leg. The thought of the appropriate conditions under which they were about to have sex for the first time made Amber feel like a teenager behind the bleachers, "But then again," she thought as she drew in a deep breath at the most pleasurable feel of Jason's invasion.

While holding her upwards, he moved in and out of her wetness with the precision of a football player holding onto the ball in concentration of the goal zone. His reaching the goal was what caused Jason's head to loosely fall back with his mouth agape, and to loose his footing only long enough to step back one step with his right foot. In his sudden stillness, his penetration caused Amber to experience an orgasmic explosion. His immediate cessation of her bouncing motion with his arms brought her to a sense of dizziness. Slowly he lowered his arms placing both her feet on the floor. Still in her orgasmic dizziness she slightly stepped back.

"Whoa, don't fall! Imagine me calling the ambulance to come into the back room of my store to pick up a pretty girl, naked from the waist down, and covered in one of my most expensive brands of paint." Jason joked as he helped Amber steady herself on her feet.

Miz Catfish

"Yeah, but just think, if the ambulance attendants like what they see I'll be able to get special taxi rides from now on to any place I want to go throughout the city." Amber laughed.

They both bent to pull up their clothes and began to make themselves appropriate once again for the public.

"Ouch!" Amber yelped mid pull, twisting at the waist in an attempt to see her left buttock." I'll have the print of a Benjamin Moore Red Cherry paint can handle on my ass cheek until tomorrow thanks to you." she laughed.

"Well you're welcome madam." Jason responded bowing at the waist.

"Maybe you'd like to paint your bedroom that color as a memory." he offered.

"I'll think about it smart aleck." Amber buttoned the top button on her jeans, picked up the plastic water bottle, her pocketbook off the floor, and followed Jason to the front door.

He turned the plastic sign back to OPEN, and opened the door for her.

"I'll see you later?" Jason asked.

"I hope so." Amber hoped that she didn't sound too anxious.

Jason gave her a quick whack on her behind as she exited the doorway. She giggled like a happy school girl.

He closed the door and took the ladder off the wall, then went back into the stock room and set the ladder up under a window over the refrigerator. Pushing up on the wooden frame, he opened the window two inches to allow air to circulate throughout the room. Then he went into the bathroom to do a quick bird bath wash up of his private area.

Even though he would hear the drag of the heavy front door if a customer entered the store, he hurried with his task so that he could get back to the cash register, and his order forms.

Jason knew he would have to be careful about getting used to sneaking the girl into the backroom for a treat as sweet as he'd just been allowed. But a little every now and then...well who would that hurt?

Amber walked home practically in a skip. She hadn't done anything as naughty with a guy before. The shame from her conscious fought with the pleasure felt in her body.

Chapter 9

After two days, a call came offering three seats to Boston, Massachusetts. CeCe and Manuel took two of those seats. The white van showed up again and took them to the airport. She was given a small piece of paper with flight information and an address for possible living arrangements. When she arrived at Logan International Airport in Boston she found a taxi and gave the small piece of paper to the taxi driver as she had been instructed. She paid the taxi fee out of money that she'd saved separately from what her family had given her for the trip. Her money had been changed into American dollars by a person in the safe house back in Miami.

The taxi stopped in front of a large three-family house. Stan, the owner of the house, was an old friend of the person in charge of the safe house in Miami. There was an arrangement for Stan to take in illegals for a portion of the shelter fee from Miami. CeCe took Manuel by his hand and with her few bags of their possessions walked up the worn, cracked wooden steps, one of which was missing, to the front door. She knocked three times before a tall, thin-framed man came to the door. Immediately after the door opened the smell of cigar smoke, dirty diapers, and the tall man's cologne invaded CeCe's nostrils. Manuel moved behind his mother's legs clinging tightly to a piece of her shirt. The man looked CeCe up and down from head to toe. A cigar releasing thick smoke hung from the corner of his mouth. He stared at CeCe and she looked at him. Finally she got up the nerve to speak first.

"Habla inglés?" she asked.

"Yeah. What cha want?" Stan growled from behind the soggy cigar.

"I need a place to stay for myself and my boy."

"How you gonna pay?"

"I'll find a job. Could I work around here to earn my rent?" CeCe asked with genuine fear and pleading in her voice.

"I'm not sure if I want any more help around here. What else you got?"

"Nothing." she replied as she reached behind her back to loosen Manuel's grip on her shirt.

"Yeah, well we'll think of something." He said with a wink of an eye, as he moved aside to allow their entrance.

CeCe knew what the wink meant and the thought of a strange man touching her body made her nauseous, yet she knew that she had to do what it would take to make it in her new surroundings.

"Everyone takes care of themselves. Put a lock on your door if you want to protect your stuff. I'm not responsible for anything stolen. I need fifty dollars a week; you buy your own food and everything else. There's an empty bedroom on the second floor in the back. I'll expect your money every Monday and you can cook and clean up around here until you can come up with the money."

CeCe reached into herself and pushed past her strong sense of pride, she mumbled, "Thank you" to the slimy man standing in front of her. He stepped aside to allow her and Manuel to pass through the doorway.

"Up those stairs." he said pointing to a stairwell leading to the second floor.

This was CeCe's first time in a house of this type, three floors, separate dwellings, inside bathrooms, and kitchens. Back in the Dominican Republic her family's home consisted of a four room flat, living room, dining room, and two bedrooms. A small cubicle on the side of the house was used as a bathroom, it was called an outhouse, and water for the house came from a spring within a mile away.

Here everything was so loud, and busy. She could hear car horns, and sirens coming from the street below. She heard Manuel whimper and stroked his head tenderly. CeCe couldn't concentrate on her son's emotions at this moment; she needed to focus on what had to be done. Looking down at the top of her son's small head, covered with shiny marble black hair, she realized that he didn't understand any of the recent strange happenings. The fear she felt must have been one hundred times stronger in her son.

She kept telling herself that she was doing this to get the best for him.

("We're going to live here now, don't be afraid.) Vamos a vivir aqui ahora, no tengas miedo." She leaned to kiss him on the head.

She went over to the dingy, stained mattress against the wall and reaching into one of her two bags, pulled out the blanket that had covered her and Manuel during their boat trip. She used it to cover the mattress and she and her son laid down and fell into a deep slumber for the first time in four days.

They were awakened by loud knocking on their door. It was the owner banging and yelling about her holding up her end of their deal, that she would cook and clean for him.

"I'm hungry," he barked. He was also anxious to check out his newest prey. Taking advantage of the confused women in need of his aide was something he looked at as being a positive benefit to his position. He waited downstairs in the kitchen for CeCe. All of her questions about where she could find things or put them away were answered gruffly. She felt his eyes on her skin and wondered how long she could keep away from him. She took some of the leftovers from the meal up to her room for herself and Manuel.

Her curiosity was answered on the night of her second day in the house. Late in the night after the house was quiet she heard the turn of her squeaky bedroom door knob. She had not had time to get her own lock. She froze with fear and anger at the invasion. Immediately her thoughts turned to her innocent son, she didn't want him to see the ultimate violation, that of his mother. She had not been able to shield him from the violence that had already occurred to other women during the trip but nothing had happened to his mother. Now the violence was focused on her, and Manuel was lying right next to her. She pulled the blanket up around his small shoulders and slid off the mattress so that he would not be disturbed by what was about to occur.

She walked towards the tall male figure that now stood in the shafts of moonlight shining in through the torn areas of the window shade. He reached for her as if he were a lover sneaking in a late night visit. She knew the situation in this new environment left no room for her to give resistance. It was obvious why he had come. This stranger would be the second man that CeCe would be involved with sexually. Manuel's father had been the first. Both experiences would forever scar her mind with sadness and anger, first to be tricked into a sexual relationship by an older man, now to be violated by this foul predator. He positioned himself behind her, and leaned her forward over the back of a rickety, worn wooden chair that had been left in the room by many a boarder before her.

As one of Stan's heavy hands held onto her shoulder, the other roughly reached under her tattered nightgown in search for her underwear, the fabric went down. CeCe cringed at the pain of the scraping of her flesh as the elastic tried to hold its position. She didn't dare whimper out loud from the fear of waking Manuel, or to allow Stan to hear her and lose what little of her pride she was determined to hold onto. There was nothing to do but focus on her reason for being there. This sacrifice was what this mother would endure to ensure a better future for her child.

CeCe's body was dry and not prepared for intrusion, Stan was not patient and his thrusting invasions were harsh. Each thrust went deeper with the purpose of wanting to hear the moan of conquest from a prisoner. The moan never came and finally CeCe's prayer of the horror coming to an end was answered as she felt her predator's body stiffen against her behind and the backs of her legs, then the quick withdrawal of the penetrating object. The heavy hand released her shoulder, and with a slap to her behind, Stan slipped back out of the room as quietly as he'd come.

An involuntary chill shook CeCe's body as warmth oozed down her inner thigh. The reality of Stan's fertilizing seed swimming quickly throughout her body made her want to scratch at herself, to gauche at her own body with repulsion. If it is fact that every time a woman has sex with a man, he leaves his seed and takes a piece of her soul; then Stan the devil had just made off with a piece of CeCe's and she felt the loss in her humiliation. Manuel slept peacefully while she pulled her clothes back in place. He never heard the click of the door closing or his mother softly crying. CeCe waited a few minutes, then crept to the door, and down the hallway to wash up in the bathroom, and then went back to the bedroom. She crawled back into bed with her son, unaware that she would endure the landlord's visits for the next two nights.

On the fifth morning in the house she prepared to go about the task of finding a job. As an illegal she could not simply go anywhere to look for work, she needed to go where her situation and alien status would be ignored. Who could she ask for the whereabouts of such places? Unfortunately the landlord was her only source for the moment.

Asking him for help took all the emotional strength that she could muster. This man was a predator on the vulnerable and she felt she gave his actions approval by speaking to him, and needing his assistance in this strange environment. While speaking to him, she focused her eyes on the floor as often as she could, but could not see his directional gestures using this technique. When she finally looked up at him for eye-to-eye contact she was unnerved by the darkness of his eyes, the twinkle of devilish, mischief that surrounded the pupils. Her grandmother said the eyes are the window to the soul. These eyes show a dark picture. After giving her a name and place to

Miz Catfish

go and directions, he smiled at Manuel and ruffled the hair on top of the child's head in a friendly manner. Manuel cringed against his mother's side. It is said that children and animals are able to sense wickedness even before it is revealed. CeCe grabbed her son's hand and left the house on her journey. The pet shop that he sent her to was not far and they were able to walk. She had no time to stop along the way to enjoy the views new to her and her child but she made a mental note to walk slower on the way back so that she could write her first letter back to her family. She missed them dearly, and felt almost physically ill with the sadness of being away from them. CeCe got the job of stock person keeping the shelves of pet products neat and fully stocked. She started work two days later, and she would get paid in cash every week.

New people came and went from the house. A young woman had arrived earlier in the week, she made friends with CeCe. CeCe was happy to have someone near her age to converse with about the roller coaster of emotions she felt. She was also happy to have someone to help watch Manuel while she worked.

Miz Catfish

Chapter 10

Four weeks after moving into her apartment Macy started out to the convenience store for milk and noticed that the new pet shop had opened. She walked in and rubbed noses with a kitten, then yipped with some puppies. After playing with the animals, she realized that she had grown quite fond of the pet fish she already owned. She decided to purchase a twenty gallon fish tank, with all of the necessary equipment, as well as a few additional fish. Macy called a clerk over to where she stood in front of a display of a variety of fish tank decorations, plants, gravel, rocks, and under water housing. The clerk scooped out her selection of two female guppies, and three neon tetras. As she reached out to pick up a bag of purple gravel for the floor of the tank, the clerk noticed Macy's long fingernails. They were peacock blue with three rhinestones circled in white on each nail. In her heavily laden Spanish accented English, she asked to see the nails. The two women conversed.

   The clerk was nervous about speaking to strangers, but it was the only way to learn about the town. They exchanged names and Macy answered all of the clerk's questions about fingernails, and neighborhood resources. After the girl named CeCe, short for Cecilia, mentioned that she walked to and from work everyday, Macy mentioned to her the fact that the building she lived in had empty apartments, and was only buildings away, which would put CeCe closer to her job.

Hearing about the empty apartments had given CeCe a ray of hope through the dark cloud mess of her personal life. Just the thought of moving out of the dreary run-down house she was currently living in as a housekeeper and sexual servant made the rest of her day enjoyable. After work she walked down to the apartment building and inquired about a vacancy. She hoped she'd run into the friendly woman that she'd met earlier and lived in the building. She thought seeing Macy again would help her to feel less nervous about approaching another stranger. Maybe Macy could tell this person that she had sent CeCe over and that would save CeCe from having to come up with answers to a lot of questions the perspective landlord might ask.

After making her purchase Macy hurried home and released her new fish into the old tank with her other fish, while she set up the new tank with all of its accessories and goodies. She forgot about needing milk or eating. She added the fish to their new home and watched them explore the territory. The guppies spread their fins allowing yellow hues to be illuminated by the sun's rays streaming in through her windows.

She pecked on the glass trying to draw at least one of the fish close enough to get a close up glance. She sprinkled brown flakes of fish food from a can that advertised the ability to be helpful in giving your fish a disease free coat of protection, as well as nutritious vitamins. In her regular brand of fish food the flake mixture was made up of pale pink, yellow, and green colorful flakes, but she had run out of that food and the new pet shop did not sell the brand. The guppies quickly swam to the surface, doing a graceful water dance as they plucked the food from the surface. The catfish quickly appeared from behind the plastic treasure chest, suctioned food from between pebbles on the floor with its Hoover vacuum type mouth, and wasted no time returning to the safety of the chest. It settled for the food that fell to the bottom, not even bothering to rise to the top to join the dance.

Macy's mind drifted from the color of the thin flakes to Mark Lewis, a six-foot, blue-eyed loser, with the broad shoulders of a football player, and bow-legs of a bronco rider. When they made love he'd pick her up and she'd wrap her legs around his waist. He opened doors for her, and fed her food from his fork. When they slept he spooned his body around hers.

She in turn helped him with his car note when he lost his job for being late too often. The electricity in his apartment stayed on three months at a time by a game he played of leaving the shut off note where she could see it, and pay it, with the promise that he'd repay the money.

On his twenty-fifth birthday, Macy threw a birthday party for him, and invited his buddies. They marveled at the burgundy, leather living room set. She listened to him accept compliments on the chairs, and then brag about the quality of the fabric, and the variety of colors they were available in, little did they know that she was making the monthly payments on his credit card. He didn't mention that she had a hand in the deal at all. Macy poured herself a glass of wine and sat in the up-right back, wooden chair in the dining area. Mark was in the living room laughing in his loudest voice and never noticed that she had left the room.

The presence of the cardboard can enclosed in her fingers returned her mind to the present. The memory of Mark faded, but the thought took its toll, and left her anxious. She gave the tank one final glance, looking past the décor in search for the catfish. At times she felt that the fish mirrored her image of herself.

She decided to dance a few sets at the club after work at the store to get rid of her haunts, and tension. She called Kenneth and asked him to put her on the schedule for the night. Macy's eyes caught a glimpse of the clock. She was surprised at how fast the time had gone by and left the tank to put the finishing touches on her wall art until it was time to go off to work at the store.

There was a knock at Macy's door, she opened it to find Amber, smiling and holding two cans of soda. She bounced past Macy and into the living room, holding out one of the sodas to her friend on her way in. She stopped in front of the colorful wall and voiced her admiration for the imaginative work. Macy invited her to grab a small brush and help with the trimming of the detail lines with black paint. Amber accepted the invitation and the two pulled the sofa away from the wall.

"Hey Macy, guess who stopped me on the street today on my way to work?" Amber said in a girlish tone.

"Who?" Macy asked.

"That cute guy who owns the hardware store next door. He asked if he could come by tonight with some wine. I told him yes. Do you think that was alright?" Amber asked sheepishly.

"Well, if you think he's cute I say go for it."

"He's a bit older than I am, and I haven't had that many boyfriends. I'm kind of excited and nervous all at the same time. I do want the company. I've been bored, and lonely."

Miz Catfish

As the new friends talked and painted they each felt a comfortable closeness forming between them. They were both in need of another person to share their thoughts, the trials, and joys, their fears, giggles and secrets.

The wall was finally completed, and the two sat on the floor admiring the image. Macy got up and went to the refrigerator. She returned with two sodas, and handed one to Amber.

"Let's celebrate this jungle and your date. What time is he coming?"

"Eight o'clock. He's got to close the store and get to the liquor store. I love your fish tank. Those guppies are so colorful." Amber said as she watched the fish dart around the tank. "What are the other ones?"

"They're called neon tetras. I like the red dot over their eyes."

They sat enjoying their cold drinks. Silently bonding as they watched the fish travel the distance of the tank. Amber caught a glimpse of the clock and selfishly left Macy rearranging the sofa.

*****

She met the colorful Mae-Belle, who didn't ask as many questions as CeCe thought she might. Mae-Belle promised CeCe a two bedroom apartment on the third floor. It would take CeCe two weeks to accumulate the money to move in, but the two weeks would be a breeze to wait through knowing she had something to look forward to.

Amber returned to her apartment with plenty of time to prepare for her date. She tidied up the kitchen, showered, and dressed in a clean pair of jeans and t-shirt before there was a knock at her door.

She opened the door to find Jason standing on the other side with a boyish grin on his face. His curly black hair enhanced the twinkles in his blue eyes. She moved out of the doorway allowing him to enter. They discussed her feelings about her new living arrangements, her family, and his store in the hardware business. After sharing a bottle of wine and a quick goodnight kiss Jason was on his way, saying that he had to get home early so that he could open the store the next morning without feeling tired. He asked Amber if he could return the following evening and she said "Yes." After letting him out and locking her door, she turned on the radio and danced around the living room, felt light headed from the wine, the kiss, and the remaining fragrance of Jason's cologne in the air. She turned off the lights in the living room and kitchen, dancing her way to her bedroom. Climbing into bed she enjoyed the snug feeling between the sheets, and within fifteen minutes she fell into a comfortable slumber with a content smirk on her face. She was strongly attracted to Jason, and the fact that he was an older man did not hurt her ego either.

As Amber slid between her sheets, the taxi Macy requested pulled up to the curb in front of the apartment building. The driver honked the horn repeatedly allowing his cigarette to dangle carelessly from the left corner of his mouth.

Macy exited the building and snatched open the back seat passenger door.

"Hey! What's your damn problem! You in a hurry or is your ass on fire?" she yelled over the back seat at the back of the driver's head.

"Yeah, yeah," the driver responded in a nonchalant tone. "Where to?" a thumbnail of ash fell onto his leg.

She gave him the address of the club and sat back into the contour of the seat, trying to redirect her attention from the driver's rudeness to being in a calm state of mind before her dance set.

As Macy's eyes adjusted to the dim light of the entertainment section of the club, she noticed that the crowd was sparse and scattered. Even under these conditions a dancer had to give an impressive show as if the room were full to its capacity. Acknowledging this rule of the trade, and keeping it forefront in her mind, still she chose not to throw one hundred percent of her physical energy into her performance. She decided on a soulful strut across the stage, and a few slow seductive twirls around the pole in the middle of the stage.

One of the few male customers seemed to enjoy the show a little more than the others. He hooted and cat-called from a table directly in front of the stage, and stood to his feet in anticipation of seeing her up close, with the stage light gleaming on her body. He felt the tension growing tighter in his stomach, and groin area with anticipation. He simply had to touch and smell her. Making his way to the front of his table he waited patiently between the table and stage like a cat stalking its prey.

Macy glided to the front of the stage with ease. She noticed a customer standing at the front of the stage waving money.

They locked eyes, as she had done with so many other customers but for a quick moment the face looked familiar. She smiled and returned her attention to the rest of the crowd. Setting her right foot forward to reach the final area of the walkway, she felt a tug on her foot.

"Come here baby! Let me lick those beautiful toes!" he yelled above the music being played by the DJ.

A twenty dollar bill fell from his hand as Macy pulled her foot from his grip. She could feel drool across her big toe and the toe next to it. Goose bumps rose on her arms. Two husky bouncers rushed to the stage and grabbed the excited man by the shirt and arm. They roughly dragged him to the front door entrance and flung him out into the street. One of the bouncers went back to check on Macy who was collecting her small amount of tips from the stage floor.

"Macy are you okay?" he asked in a concerned voice.

"Yeah Joe, I'm alright. You guys didn't hurt him did you?"

"No. He only got a few scrapes if anything," he laughed "Is your set over?"

"Oh yeah, I'm done. That's enough drama for one night. Thanks."

"Come on now, you're a professional, let me go get him. You can do a few more sets and make some more money. You never know who has a fat wad in their wallet." Joe joked.

"You let him anywhere near me and I'll kick his ass, and yours!" Macy joked back as she turned with her gains and headed towards the back of the stage and the dressing area.

After getting fully dressed in her street clothes she found Kenneth for a ride.

"Kenneth my boy, could you give a lady a ride home."

"No problem. Just let me shut these lights off and lock up. It's my turn tonight."

"Did I tell you that I moved?" she asked.

"No. Where'd you get off to now?" he laughed.

"Near the water on Shawnee Road, my job and my home on the same street, that worked out to my advantage."

"Moving on up huh?" I suppose almost anything is better than that room." He said with a grin as he flipped the room's light switch into the off position.

"Yes to both of your smart ass comments." she responded as she poked him in the side.

"Hey do you think you can work tomorrow night? It's the colorful Fourth of July, and you know that's usually a standing room only night around here. I'm giving you first dibs at the pole."

"Sure, why not. I didn't plan to do anything special. I'll be here."

*****

Aisha usually enjoyed a loud, and colorful, Fourth of July, with a hot barbecue grill. She and her mother would pre-cook chicken wings, and pat out fresh hamburger patties. Hot dogs were also a necessity for the children. As the darkness of night settled in they'd join other town residents in the center of town for a fire works display. Teri was at an age that she could enjoy the colors and ignore the loud explosive sounds that used to make her jump with fear. This Fourth of July, Aisha didn't have the spirit to celebrate. She didn't want to cook fresh burgers for the shelter residents, or stand around with them oou-uing, and ah-hing at fireworks. She let the day go by like any other.

Chapter 11

Jason came out of the stockroom in time to catch a glimpse of Amber passing the window. She was headed in the direction of her home. The time on his wristwatch indicated that she'd probably just finished her shift at the store.

He hadn't gotten a chance to spend time with her since he went to her home the previous week, and he yearned to feel her again. Acting on a knee-jerk thought, he picked his keys up from the counter, locked up the store, and walked down the street to Amber's house.

Jason climbed the stairs of the building, hoping that he wasn't making a mistake by dropping by the girl's home without an invite, but he felt driven.

Amber was in the kitchen making a sandwich when she heard a knock on her door. Thinking that the person on the other side was most likely to be Macy she swung the door open wide.

"Surprise!" Jason said with mock excitement in his voice.

Amber's face registered just that, a surprised expression came over her face as her eyebrows moved in an upwards motion, causing her eyes to open widely. "Um-m-m, hi. This is a surprise indeed, but at least it's a good one." Amber's face caught up with the change of her emotions and her facial expression changed to smile.

"Come on in." Amber offered, moving aside.

"Thanks. I apologize for dropping by unannounced, but I saw you go by and I got a vision of you in a Benjamin Moore Red Cherry teddy."

"Oh my, you are a bad boy."

Jason moved close to Amber and pulling her close to him he began to kiss her. Amber took hold of Jason's knit, short sleeve Henley shirt by the hem, and stepped away to pull it over his head. Both his chest and abdominal muscles were well defined, as if done by a chisel. Amber found the image almost intoxicating. She couldn't allow the Adonis like statue to stand before her without taking in a bit of its beauty. By slightly bending her head, she was able to flick his right nipple with her tongue, then catch hold of it with her lips and indulge in a sucking action.

"Don't do things to a person that you don't want done to you." he managed between the jolts of pleasurable sensations that traveled through his body.

Amber straightened up "I'm a good sport."

Jason pulled Amber's t-shirt over her head and reached one arm around her to unsnap her bra, while his other arm held her around the waist.

"What a talented man!"

"I'm glad that you're impressed. Now let me impress you with another sample of my talents."

He bent his head and returned the favor of manipulating both of her nipples with his tongue and teeth. Using both hands Amber gently grabbed Jason's hair and pulled his head back into an upright position.

"Are we going to continue to stand here in the middle of the floor?"

"Do you have a better idea?" Jason said while kissing her neck.

"How about you help me pick out a wall in my bedroom to paint red?"

They walked hand in hand into the bedroom, stopping at the side of the bed.

"I can't stand beside you like this a minute longer, come here." he pulled her to him, and they fell onto the bed.

Early July heat engulfed the bedroom, causing the slight breeze off the water that drifted through the open window to appear absent. The kissing, groping, and stripping of their last pieces of clothing caused a light sheen of sweat to cover Jason's forehead. Amber climbed on top of Jason into a straddling position, using her hand she guided his erect sweetness into her body.

She lowered herself completely with a force that caused him to penetrate her deeper than she had imagined, and they both moaned. She pulled his arms above his head, and held them there while moving her body in a quick, continuous horseback riding motion, holding onto his arms as if they were the reigns that controlled the horse beneath her. They climaxed simultaneously, with Amber getting an immediate headache from the quick rush of blood flow through her veins, while Jason's toes curled into tight folded positions.

"Oh man, I just got the head rush of a life time." Amber said rolling off Jason's body, and onto the bed.

"Well my toes will need chiropractic attention to get the knots out! So touché!" Jason laughed as he sat up and swung his legs over the side of the bed. "I'd better get along. I have a shipment coming in." he said as he got dressed.

"Do I have to walk you to the door? I don't think I can stand, I'm drained."

"That'll teach you to take off other people's clothes," he laughed, "and no I don't mind letting myself out." He leaned onto the bed and gave her a quick kiss disrupting her as she began to fluff her pillow in preparation for a nap.

Chapter 12

On Tuesday morning, three weeks after entering the shelter, Aisha was asked if she would accept an apartment in East Boston, Massachusetts. It was a two bedroom apartment in a newly renovated building. She would have two days to pack. She felt apprehensive about the responsibility of making the decision to take the apartment. This decision would force her to concede to the fact that she would be permanently leaving her mother. Once everyone's chores were complete, the house was dark and quiet, and her children were asleep, she allowed herself to consume as much as she could of the entire mess of a situation. She purged through her tears. What other way could there have been? It seemed that she had little control over anything else in her life.

She felt Shawn Junior snuggle closer under her side as he pushed the nipple of his bottle into his mouth. She cut off her tears, in fear of her trembling body motions waking the baby. She had to accept the offer in the morning, she didn't have a choice.

Thursday morning, Darlene, a young college student with an air of arrogance and a pencil thin waist called Aisha into the front office. Darlene was the housing coordinator, she was the staff member with the responsibility of helping clients find housing, whether it be permanent or something in a step towards permanent housing. After wishing Aisha and the children the best of luck, she gave Aisha three pre-paid bus tickets along with a sheet of paper explaining to her what to do when she got off the bus in Boston at the South Station bus terminal. The paper also had a pink receipt stapled to the back with the proof of transfer of funds to pay the first two months of her rent. She was to keep hold of this receipt in case her new landlord lost her copy.

Darlene gave the family a ride to the bus terminal and barely gave Aisha one minute of her time as she waited for the mother to get her bags and children from the back seat of her car. As soon as she heard the thud of the door closing she checked her rear view mirror to confirm that the client had completely exited her vehicle and drove away. Although she was doing her internship in Sociology at the shelter for the past seven months, it still bewildered her at the number of women that allowed themselves to not only get into an abusive relationship, but to stay long enough to come to the point of needing assistance to this degree. She shook her head from left to right in a gesture of confusion as she reached down with her right hand to turn on her car radio.

There would be another shelter worker to meet her at the bus terminal in Boston. Aisha had the instructions from Darlene on who to look for when she got off the bus. She held onto three tickets with the strange, new names on them now belonging to her and her children. Teri was told about the name game, a trick that they would get to play on everyone around them, Teri, now Jamie, was excited about the new game.

The long bus ride took its toll on Aisha's nerves. It would have been so easy to turn back to the life that now seemed like it would be easier withstood than beginning this journey into the unknown. Entertaining the children for so many hours was not easy. They both wanted to move around but couldn't until the bus stopped at rest and transfer points. When they reached their destination, a large plainly dressed woman stood in the exit door of the bus terminal with Aisha's new name on a card. The adults collected the few bags belonging to the family, and were off to a small station wagon in the parking area of the large bus terminal.

*****

Macy manipulated the strings of the two shopping bags that hung from the fingers of her right hand. Her left fingers were just as busy poking through the large hole of a large plastic bag. She used her foot to force open the steel framed door with the scratched plexy glass window and the neon red "EXIT" letters above it.

She made her way to the sidewalk curb, and without putting her bags down, used her head to indicate to a taxi that she needed service. Two strong nods and the dingy white car with the peeling black words that once proudly spelled TAXI, pulled up in front of her. The driver got out of the car to assist her with her bags. This was done more with the hope of getting a tip than being a gentleman.

"Wait a minute, pretty lady. I will help choo with those bags." The driver offered as he rushed quickly towards her without waiting for her response. Macy immediately recognized the driver's face. She realized that she knew him. He had been a steady customer at one of the clubs she'd previously danced in. He was an odd character, with his thick

Spanish accent, and white tape used to hold on the right arm of his black plastic framed glasses.

  Character was the first descriptive word that came to her mind the first time he approached her at the bar after a set. He offered to buy her a drink and introduced himself as Jorge Tomas Ortega, preferring to be called Ortega, he said. To the dancers a paid for drink was a drink, only on rare occasions were drinks from the customers turned down. But as Macy sat on the bar stool, taking in the likes of Mr. Ortega, she couldn't help but feel like she should pass up his offer. Something about him gave her a creepy feeling when he looked at her, a feeling like that of a cat sitting at the gate watching the bird on the porch. Although he jibber-jabbered on about how her ass twirled the pole the best, she paid less attention to his words and more to his hands that were busy working at lottery scratch cards. He worked one card at a time, using a penny to scratch all of the grey areas first, and then pulling the card closer to his face, he would check it for a winner, put it on the counter and begin to scratch another card, all the while continuing to talk to Macy. Macy never gave him so much as a "Huh-huh." in response; she just kept watching those thick weathered hands. She couldn't shake the feeling that Ortega would try to touch her at any moment. The thought of him stroking her thigh was making her stomach tight. After deciding that the risk wasn't worth the drink and the possible tip that might come her way from him, she gave up on watching him scratch his cards, and excused herself. He may have had potential to become an admirer who paid good tips for conversation and lap dances, but she had made up her mind to pass on the chance.

Miz Catfish

She hadn't danced at that club in eight months. It was located in one of the many areas that Macy had written off and moved on from. These areas were dangerous, and she'd had to begin carrying a box cutter in her coat pocket when ever she came or left the entranceway for the dancers, and employees.

Here were the thick weathered hands, grabbing her shopping bags from her. He looked at her, "Where choo want to go-o-o? Hey, it's choo, my pretty lady! Where have choo been?" Ortega smiled like he was indeed greeting a long lost friend.

"Hello to you too, its Ortega right?" Macy couldn't help but to stare at the white tape on his glasses. It was like a headlight in the dark. She smiled, and so did he. She laughed to herself and thought "What a character!" He put her bags in the trunk, and then strutted to the front passenger door preparing to open it for her, all the while, wondering if she still swings a pole."

"For choo, my ladee." He reached for the car door handle.

"Oh, no thank you, I'll be just fine back here." She chuckled, shaking her head from side to side as she opened the door to the back seat and slid her body in, quickly closing the door behind herself as if she still worried about him touching her leg.

"Are choo sure? I like pretty ladies up front with me."

"I bet you do, but no thank you."

He gave up quickly, thinking he'd go at her another way, another time, now that he'd get to see where she lived. "Okay, I will ride choo like a princess today. Where is the address?"

"If you mean where I'm going, it's to 105 Shawnee Road. Do you know where that is? It's over near-r-r."

113

"I know the place very well." He jumped in cutting off her response. "A lady should let the man drive."

"What's that supposed to mean?"

"It means a woman can not tell a man how to drive." he proudly proclaimed.

"She should if THE MAN might get her LOST!" Macy responded with a huff, thinking "This guy is a nut."

As Macy's taxi pulled up to the building, she noticed Mae-Belle standing on the front steps speaking with two women. One of the women held a sleeping child while an older child ran up and down the stairs. Macy got out of her taxi and helped the driver put her few bags from various department stores on the sidewalk. As she paid the driver she saw out of the corner of her right eye the older child, a little girl with golden brown skin and long shiny black ponytails slowly walking over to check the colorful bags. The little person walking towards Macy was an exact image of the way she remembered herself at about the same age. It was uncanny. It had been a long time since Macy had even allowed herself to think of those days from so long ago. Quickly she pushed the image out of her mind and focused on the task at hand. The taxi drove off and Macy turned to speak to the small detective.

"Hi there."

"Hi." the small voice responded.

"What's your name? My name is Macy."

"Teri."

The younger of the two strange females yelled "Come over here Jamie."

The little girl ran over to hide behind the legs belonging to the owner of the commanding voice. Macy noticed that the name the little girl told her was different from the one the woman had just called her, but she didn't give it a second thought as she continued to gather her things.

Mae-Belle called to Macy "Hi Macy, you have a new neighbor. She's moving in below you." She made introductions as Macy headed toward the group with her hand outstretched. Macy and Aisha shook hands, and Macy continued up the stairs with her bags. Mae-Belle, Aisha and the shelter worker headed towards the empty apartment on the first floor.

"This is my largest apartment," Mae-Belle said to Janice, now being called Janice, as they entered the living room. Janice sat the now awake little Shawn, now being called Johnny on the floor. Jamie was already viewing the apartment on her own while the two women stood in the middle of the room.

"You have two and a half bedrooms here" She directed Janice to the largest bedroom. It had a large walk-in closet and two windows on one wall. The next bedroom was smaller than the first but still a decent size. The half size bedroom was large enough for Johnny's crib, a bureau, and a toy box.

"All of the rooms are painted white but you can paint them other colors if you'd like. I know white walls are probably a little drab for children, and will be hard to keep clean. There's a hardware store next door."

"How many people live in the building?" Janice asked.

The shelter worker walked around the empty apartment with the children, keeping them busy so that their mother could focus on the business at hand.

"There are six apartments, two on each floor, and I still have three empty now that you are here. I would give you a choice of the others but none of them would be large enough for you. Also I figured with the children running and playing you wouldn't be over anyone's head. The woman you met out front, Macy, lives above you, and a young lady Amber Munroe lives across the hall.

"Are there any other children in the building?" the shelter worker asked from across the room.

"No. Not yet, so far these little guys here are the only children." Mae-Belle smiled in the direction of Jamie and Johnny.

Mae-Belle directed Janice towards the bathroom, then all the closet spaces and a spacious walk-in kitchen with all of its cabinets and drawers along the walls. The refrigerator was hidden in an alcove on the left wall farthest back from the entrance way. All of the cabinets were honey colored sharply contrasting with the frost white of the refrigerator and counter tops. The large sixteen pane window over the sink allowed the morning sunlight to spill all over the high ceilings in the room. The warmth of the sun's rays felt soothing to Janice's frayed nerves. She missed her mother and the comfort of her familiar apartment now a part of her past. Trying to stay focused on the future she accepted the beauty and potential in her new home, as well as the friendliness flowing from her new landlord.

She was grateful to the shelter staff for having been so supportive. The help they had given her would be enough to

Miz Catfish

get her furniture for the apartment. They also helped her get cash and food benefits from the welfare department. The domestic violence network had been a blessing that she would never forget.

"Come upstairs to my apartment. You can sign your lease and get your keys." Mae-Belle said.

On the way up the stairs they passed Macy running back up to her place with the last of her things. After finishing the paperwork and a bit of small talk Mae-Belle gave her the telephone number for the taxi company. She called for one to take Janice and her children grocery shopping. Janice's telephone wouldn't be turned on until the following day. The shelter had to share the basics of Janice's situation with Mae-Belle and she hoped that she was helping the woman feel as comfortable as possible under her circumstances.

Macy saw Janice standing on the stairs and asked if she needed help. The women discussed Janice's plans and Macy decided to take the ride with the family to the supermarket. Macy also had a brand new mostly empty refrigerator in her apartment.

When they got back to the building the taxi driver helped the women unload their groceries into the first floor hallway. They said their "good-byes" and went their separate ways on promises of getting together at a later time. Macy hurried to put her groceries away in order to make it to the hardware store to pick up the paints and brushes to paint the mini-mural on her wall. She spent any extra time she had on completing the jungle scene. While allowing the paint on the wall time to dry she rearranged the furniture in the room. The brand new purple sofa looked powerful, yet confusing against the colorful wall. The scene reminded her of herself, colorful and confused.

A floor below, Janice tried not to succumb to the feeling of being overwhelmed by what seemed to be a never ending list of tasks. The groceries were put away, the children were tucked in their beds, and she sat on the new sofa wiggling her tired feet. The furniture voucher from the shelter had allowed her to purchase decent bedroom, living room, and kitchen sets, as well as a small television set. She used her cash to buy curtains, kitchen items, towels and other essentials. Even a few toys for the children made their way to the register.

The quietness seemed to envelop her. She needed to get into her new bed and get some rest. Yet as tired as she was she could not get over the feeling of being lonely. Even though Shawn had been a disastrous choice for a mate, she was accustomed to having another adult's presence in her home. No, he had not been home every night, but he had been a major part of her everyday existence. She wasn't missing him so much as she was missing having someone. It had been a long time since she had slept alone as she would now. She thought fleetingly of all the events that had occurred in the past month and could no longer ignore the fatigue that fogged her mind. She got up from the sofa, turned off the lights and went down the short hallway to her bedroom. She undressed, got into the gown that she'd brought from home, and felt the stiffness of the new sheets surround her body. Sleep did not follow. She lay in the new bed in her new home listening and learning the sounds of the building and the neighborhood.

A poem formed in her mind. She slid out of bed, dug her notebook out of her top bureau drawer and climbed back into bed. After unclipping the always ready pen from the cover, words began to pour freely from her mind onto the paper.

All This Sorrow

> More than ever I'd like to know
> Why all this sorrow envelope me so
> Why the happiness left my heart
> And tore my lil ole world apart
>
> Is it not my destiny?
> To live my life happy and free
> To know that when I wake tomorrow
> My heart will be free of all this sorrow
>
> But yet and still my soul is sad
> Just thinking about the life I've lead
> And all this sorrow so full in my heart
> Has torn my lil ole world apart

- Tara Morgan

The creative moment passed as quickly as it had come. She allowed the pen to lazily drop from her hand and fall onto the blanket. Her mind took in the sounds around her.

A cat fight went on somewhere in an alley and a startled dog began to bark. The cats moved on, the dog settled down, and silence returned. Still the comfort of sleep evaded her.

Across the street from the building, the sun rose above the harbor. Baby birds began to chirp, Johnny began to whine, and still Janice lay wide eyed between her sheets. She swung her legs off the side of the bed, and sat still allowing herself to adjust to her surroundings. Jamie ran past her bedroom door with one of her new toys in her hand.

"Good morning mommy." she sang in a giddy tone.

"Hey baby girl."

"I'm not a baby anymore! Johnny is!" Jamie yelled back as she ran into the living room. Janice smiled as she listened to her daughter's response filled with innocence and playfulness. She envied her, it had been a long time since she'd felt either. She went to check on Johnny and heard a knock at the door.

"Hello?"

"It's Macy-y-y."

With a look of bewilderment on her face, she headed towards the door and opened it to find her neighbor standing in the hallway with a large brown bag.

"Good morning Janice, I hope I didn't wake you guys."

"No you didn't. We were already up." She replied as she felt Jamie's small body pushing between her and the door.

"Hi." Jamie managed to mouth past her mother's body.

"Good morning cutie," Macy returned.

"Come on in," Janice said moving aside dragging Jamie with her.

Macy entered the apartment. She walked over and put the bag down on the table.

"I went to the store this morning, and spotted these heavenly looking blueberry muffins. I hope you guys will eat some with me. How about it?"

Miz Catfish

"Sure the kids love them. How about something to drink with them? Milk, tea, juice?"

"I'll have some tea."

"Alright, just let me get Johnny a bottle and a dry bottom, and then I'll put the kettle on."

She went off to see about the baby and left Jamie trying to sneak a peek into Macy's bag. They were soon joined by Janice and Johnny. After their muffins were eaten and the remnants scattered on chairs and floor, the children went off to play and the women nursed their tea.

"So how do you like your apartment?" Macy asked.

"I like it just fine, and as soon as I'm able to sleep at night I'll like it even more."

"Well it's a great building and neighborhood. I'm sure you'll begin to feel more at ease soon."

"I hope so, because I'm feeling really tired from lack of sleep." Janice groaned.

"If you want me to watch the kids for a while I'd be glad to."

"I'll keep that in mind. I could use a relief pitcher sometimes."

"Just remember the offer stands. I guess I better get upstairs. I've got some company coming." Macy said as she stood to excuse herself.

"Thanks for stopping by. See you later."

Macy barely made it back upstairs before she heard a knock at the door. She yelled "Come in." Kenneth entered the apartment, closed the door behind him and stood in one spot looking around. Macy stood at the kitchen counter watching him.

"What are you looking at?" She asked with a cool smirk.

"This joint is pretty cool." Kenneth said with an authoritative tone.

"Thanks. I'm so glad to have your approval. Maybe you wouldn't mind paying my next month's rent."

"We'll see. Maybe you'll find it within your heart to be a good girl today."

"Now it's my turn to say we'll see. I haven't heard from you in about three weeks." Macy sassed back.

"I didn't think you needed me." He said in a pouty manner, as he crossed the floor to where she stood, and began to nibble on her neck. She moved away from him and sat on a stool on the other side of the counter.

He went over to the refrigerator and pulled out a beer, then walked around the counter pinching her thigh on his way past her, and stopped at the fish tank.

"I like this tank setup. Where'd you get it?"

"At the pet shop down the street."

"Nice choices of fish. How'd you pick them? By color, or did you have help," he joked, "but that catfish is ugly. They let you down there."

"I chose them all by myself, thank you very much, and I have a special relationship with that catfish, so back off. Besides I had three of them at the old place, you just didn't notice. Maybe your interests were focused elsewhere?" she huffed.

"You and your pretty but smart ass mouth!"

"Whatever!"

"Who did the painting on the wall?"

"Guess." she said smiling.

"Not you! No way!" he said, genuinely surprised.

"Yes way, and of course!"

"Boy, you have more talents than I realized."

"Never put all of your cards on the table at one time." She said winking her right eye.

"That purple sofa looks just like something you'd buy!"

"That's right. If it's different it's for me. I'm going to take a shower. Make yourself comfortable." She headed off towards the bathroom.

She and Kenneth were old lovers so she didn't bother to close the door. He waited for the sound of the shower's spray and then began to take his own clothes off. When he could tell that her body was in the water he stepped into the shower with her. Just as she had known he would. She felt his hand on her shoulder, the other on her thigh. Traveling from her shoulder to her belly, his hand felt smooth and sent tingles into her legs. As she turned to face him, she raised her arms around his neck and her legs around his waist. He was tall and every muscle flexed into position as he held her and made love to her. As he felt himself begin to release he moaned and bit her softly on the neck. His blonde hair was matted to his head from sweat and steam. Their cream and tawny body parts were intertwined together, resembling coffee with cream on the first stir. They stepped out of the shower, dried off together and returned to the living room. She pulled a towel around her naked body and jumped into the black chair, folding her legs beneath herself. He sprawled out on the sofa.

"I've got a gig lined up for tonight. You wanna work?" he asked.

"Yeah. I could use the money. My till is not where I like it to be. You know how I like my security. What time can you pick me up?"

"Be ready about nine o'clock. Wear your sassy stuff."

She said "You got it boss" and made a salute motion with her hand to her forehead.

He got dressed and reached into his pocket for his wallet.

"How much is that rent?" he asked.

"Just donate six dead prez, and I'll take it from there."

He handed her the money and left. Macy continued to sit in the chair relaxing and day dreaming.

After finding a sweatshirt to throw on, she found her cosmetics case and pulled out her temporary hair dye. She chose Fierce Red as her hair color for the evening. She packed her favorite duffel bag with everything she'd need, and then went to work on her hair color. While waiting for the color to take she dropped food into the fish tank. The guppies ate from the surface while the group of tetra swam as one after what fell into the center. Macy almost lost track of her task at hand as she got caught up in watching the graceful movement of the fish.

She washed, rinsed; blow dried, and brushed her hair back into a neat ponytail. Then for the first time since she'd purchased it, she pulled out her sleep sofa, put sheets on it and took a nap.

Macy woke to the sound of Jamie and Johnny playing outside the building, and Janice scolding Jamie not to go too far. Deciding to rise on that cheerful note, she made herself a grilled cheese sandwich and chose a soda. It felt good to sit at the counter. The stool was comfortable. In her old room she always ate sitting on her bed. She hadn't seen Amber all day, and decided to pay her a visit after lunch.

Amber wasn't home so Macy decided to ask Janice if she wanted to come up to the roof top with her. Janice accepted the invitation and Jamie led the way running with her seemingly never ending source of energy. They noticed a little boy sitting on the stairs of the second floor. He hadn't been there when Macy came out of her apartment.

Jamie was the first to speak to him, "Hi." No response came from the little boy. His head hung sadly, and his face reflected his body language.

"Do you want to play?" Still no response came.

CeCe entered the hall from the stairway. She yelled to the little boy, "Veneca! ("Come here!")" The boy got up from the stairs and went to his mother.

"No puedes ir para afuera. ("You cannot go outside")."

"Por que?" ("Why?") the boy's small voice responded

"No me hagas preguntas. (Do not question me)." voiced the maternal response.

Macy spotted CeCe. "Hi." I see you took my advice on checking this place out. That's good. I think you'll like it here. We're on our way up to the sitting area on the roof. Do you want to come?"

"No thank you. I'm cleaning."

"Well can the little guy come up with us? He'll probably enjoy playing with the kids and you can get some cleaning out of the way." Macy offered.

"Okay, that would be nice for both of us. This is my son, Manuel. He's six. He doesn't speak any English, but I'm trying to teach him. I'm sure he'll enjoy the company of the children and the fresh air." CeCe had almost said "No." out of fear and the need to stay hidden, but Manuel deserved to begin to feel like a child again, and she had to begin to ease them both into this new life.

"Come on Manuel." Macy held out her hand.

Manuel looked at CeCe for approval. CeCe nodded and he took Macy's hand.

"Oh yeah, CeCe this is Janice, the children's mother. Janice, this is Cecelia."

"Hello, Cecelia." Janice said with a welcoming smile.

"Please call me CeCe. They do on my job."

"All right gang, let's go." Macy led the group.

Macy hung out on the roof top until it was time for her to get dressed. Mae-Belle had joined the group and brought along some lemonade and cookies. Manuel enjoyed the playtime. He couldn't understand a lot of what Jamie said to him, but they got along just the same. It had been quite some time since he'd gotten the chance to enjoy being a carefree child. When CeCe came to get her son she was brought to tears by the sight of his happy, innocent smile. The other two women were confused by the tears, and rushed to her side. She explained away the emotions as being a side effect of the move, the new job, and needing a good night's sleep. The answers she gave were true; she had simply left out the story of her trip, and the getting away from the lecherous ex-landlord.

As the evening sky drifted lazily across the water, the building at 105 Shawnee Road settled down with everyone in their own apartments. Amber had returned home after a day's work at the store. CeCe and Manuel slept comfortably on blankets Mae-Belle had given them. CeCe slept with ease for the first time since being in America. She finally had the comfort of knowing there would not be a dirty predator waiting to prey on her. The quietness of the building felt like the comfort of a warm bath. She drifted peacefully, holding back any fears of being an illegal until daylight came again.

After Janice had given the children their baths and tucked them in for the night, she fought the tired heaviness that tightened her shoulders, and settled on the sofa in front of the television with a letter pad and pen in her lap. She was going to write her mother before she fell asleep. She knew that Norma would be happy to hear that her daughter and grandchildren were comfortable in their new home.

She stood at the bathroom sink rinsing the last remnants of toothpaste from her mouth. As she turned the knobs marked hot and cold, she heard a loud click. She straightened into an upright position and stood still waiting to hear if the noise would come again. Her senses were heightened by her constant fear of Shawn following through with his threat to find her and the children. Shaking her head, as if to clear her thoughts, she opened the mirrored medicine cabinet door, and reached in to retrieve the over-the-counter remedy for the tension in her shoulders and the headache she felt coming on. She returned the door to its closed position and jumped with shock, and surprise at the sight of Shawn standing behind her. His mouth contorted into a sinister sneer. "Hi Isha." he whispered, and then let out a guttural chuckle as he raised his arm.

Five inches of shiny, silver steel glistened above her head and disappeared as his arm dropped from sight. She felt a sharp piercing pain between her shoulder blades. Her mouth fell open in an attempt to cry out for help, but only a faint groan escaped.

Janice woke to her own groaning noises, the letter pad and pen, lay on the floor at her feet. She forced herself to walk through the apartment first checking on the children, making sure that they were as safe as they had been before her nightmare. She went back into the living room, and picked up the pad, ripping the letter from the rest of the pad, she decided not to add the ordeal of the nightmare into the letter and further worry Norma, her hands shook as she prepared it for a send off. She lay back on the sofa, preparing to sleep there instead of down the hall in her bedroom. To be in her bedroom would take her too far away from the entrance of their den of protection. Tonight she would sit watch as sentry at the gate.

Mae-Belle was also settled in for the night, and was sitting in her chair next to her living room window that faced the front of the building. It was from this window that she kept a watch over the comings and goings of the building. She saw Macy get into a waiting vehicle.

Miz Catfish

Chapter 13

Kenneth pulled to the club's back door in the alley to let Macy out. Once at her table in the dressing area she released her red ponytail and shook loose her shoulder length hair. Four other women spoke loudly, discussing their problems at home and daily aggravations. Macy wasn't ready to talk; she was concentrating on getting into character. Someone behind her lit a joint. Macy didn't want to take a hit herself but didn't mind the contact high that would most likely be coming her way.

"Hey! Come on, pass that joint this way!" Sheila demanded as she fluffed her big hair.

"Damn I just got it. Hold your horses!" the possessor yelled back. "You know this ain't gonna hold me over through the entire night."

The smoke swirled around Sheila's head as she said, "Just say the word girl; you know I got the real stuff. Hell it looks like I'll never get but a whiff of the joint anyway."

"Who'd you get it from Johnnie?" asked possessor still holding the joint.

"Yeah, he came by last night." Sheila said in a bragging tone.

"Pull it out now! Shit I'm feigning like a bitch!" Shelly joined in.

"Shelly you are a bitch!" Pam instigated.

"Ha, ha! Shut up Pam. I can't take your shit tonight. Sheila you gonna cook or not?"

"Yeah, but you're not first! Hey Macy, you want some?"

"Nah, I don't do that stuff. Anybody bring a bottle?" Macy asked.

"Yep! Now you're talking up my alley." responded Pam, who went over to her oversized bag and dug out a bottle of vodka, and passed it to Macy. Macy took a few long swigs from the bottle then passed it back. She stepped into her red four inch heels, straightened her metallic red G-string undies, and glued on the tasseled nipple cups. She heard the whistles and claps indicating the end of the previous act. She was next.

"Alright Macy, let's go!" Kenneth bellowed down the hall.

"I'm coming! Hold your horses!" she snapped in return, as she rubbed baby oil down her legs.

Macy made her way out to the stage feeling the alcohol begin to cloud her head. She couldn't stand the men around the stage like drooling dogs, just a big girl instead of a young one, but still with a male waiting to touch without permission as her body went into shimmy-shake dance moves she let her mind drift into another place. She thought about things she wanted in her apartment.

When she left the stage, she made her way to the bar, smiling and brushing off touches all the way. It didn't take long for a customer to slide up to the counter beside her and offer her a drink, she accepted and he began to question her about her plans after the club closed. She quickly swallowed the amber liquid, allowing the empty glass to thump the countertop loud enough to have gotten the pleading companion's attention, and understanding. Her method worked, and he immediately ordered her another drink. She was losing her high from the back room, and had to get enough alcohol into her system to continue through the night. It was only twelve o'clock, two hours left until the club closed. Kenneth came over to her, and pinched her ass, while he spoke into her ear.

"Guess what cookie? You get to enter lap city for the next round. Aren't you lucky!" he snickered.

"Yeah. Just so-o-o lucky." she replied in a snippy tone.

"Five more minutes, then hit the seats."

"Yeah, yeah."

Lap dancing was still hard for Macy. When a dancer was on stage the men were at a safe distance. When working the crowds the bouncers protected you, lap dances left you vulnerable, some customers lost control, touched the girls, and got dragged out of the club by a bouncer. Those customers weren't allowed back into the club. Lap dances usually brought a dancer a fairly decent tip on the other hand. Since the dancers got a minimal base pay they depended on their tips to make a night worth while.

Macy went through the crowds winking, and making small talk with the customers. She offered a lap dance to the ones that weren't too grungy and looked like big spenders. Her first two dances went without incident; the third caused her to end her night early.

While mid-hump she felt a warm wetness on the inside of her thigh, and looked down to find that the dim lighting of the room had prevented her from noticing that her customer had gotten his member out, was fondling it and had ejaculated on his leg. She jumped away from him as if she'd sat on a hot toilet seat.

"You sick bastard!" she shoved his shoulders as she moved.

"Sorry honey, but you made me so excited." he replied with a sheepish grin.

"Where's my damn money!" She didn't let up.

He reached into his pocket and pulled out a fifty dollar bill. Macy snatched it and went to tell Kenneth that she'd had enough for the night. He agreed, knowing that Macy's hot temper wouldn't hold out much longer and she'd probably hit the next customer that irritated her. Calling it a night was a good idea, he made sure that she got a taxi, kissed her on the cheek, and bid her a good night.

When Macy got home she put away her travel items and took a shower. The hot water felt cleansing against her skin, yet no matter how hard, or long she rubbed she didn't feel clean. The thigh violated by the customer was beginning to feel raw with every stroke of her wash cloth, and still she scrubbed. The violation brought back old memories of the little girl Macy in the foster home. The money may have been good for spending, but it was not good for the soul. All the scrubbing in the world could not cleanse her soul. Wrapped in a large towel, she went to the living room and counted her earnings for the night. Five hundred and twenty dollars was not a bad take. Maybe she'd dance a few more nights. If all her nights were like this she'd rebuild her stash quickly. She decided to call Kenneth in the morning. Without pulling out the sleeper, she threw a blanket on the sofa and fell asleep.

Amber did not hear Macy come into the building. She was in the arms of her new lover. Jason was not Amber's first, but he was her most experienced. He satisfied her over and over again. She felt safe from the outside world as she lay wrapped in his soothing arms. Their toes rubbed together lazily under the sheets that were moist with the dampness of their bodies.

He leaned up on one arm, nibbling on her ear lobe to keep the bodily contact.

"I'm sorry babe, but I've gotta run, I have some things to take care of early tomorrow."

"Oh-h-h, do you have to? I'll miss you." she groaned.

"Hey don't pout. You're going to distract me from my commitments, don't make me feel like a jerk. You know I wish I could stay." He swung his feet off the side of the bed and began to collect his clothes. He'd brought her a large screen television for the bedroom. She remained in bed with the remote control and began flipping channels.

"Why do you have to leave?" she whined.

"Honey, I have a lot of responsibilities. I can't ignore them. I promise I'll stay a whole night with you when I can clear my schedule."

"You promise?" she pouted.

"You promise?" he imitated her. "Stop pouting. I'll see you soon."

They kissed and then he was gone. Amber lay in the mangled sheets holding a pillow close to her chest. She felt tears of disappointment trying to rise to the surface. She wanted him to stay, she enjoyed his company. Jason paid attention to every part of her body from her head to her toes. He touched, he rubbed, and he nibbled. He made her feel special, beautiful, and sexy. He gave her money to turn her telephone on so they could stay in touch when they were apart. The telephone company promised to have someone at her house first thing in the morning. She would be able to call him at the store when he opened. She fell asleep with the anticipation of hearing his voice.

Chapter 14

CeCe awakened to find Manuel looking out of the window. She lay watching his small frame surrounded by morning sunlight. His small ears stood out slightly, like his father's. There were times, such as this, that the memory of her son's father slipped invasively into her thoughts. It was not often that she allowed herself to think of the man that had a hand in changing her life so drastically. She dismissed this thought as quickly as it had come.

"Buenos dias, mi hijo. (Good morning, my son.)" she called.

"Buenos dias, mama." Manuel returned.

She rose from her blankets on the floor, and after washing up, went into the kitchen to prepare breakfast before going to work. She stood in the middle of the floor taking a moment to absorb the beauty of her surroundings. The only smells that invaded her senses were the eggs in the skillet mingling with the fading scent of fresh paint. She wouldn't have to deal with the offensive odor of a smelly cigar, or invasive hands touching her without permission during the night. No one would cause her son to tremble behind her legs with fear.

Everyone that she'd met in the building seemed to be friendly. CeCe's biggest problems were hiding her personal situation, and having to leave Manuel unattended while she went to work. She couldn't allow him outside she worried about him wandering away and getting lost, or making friends with someone outside who might ask questions and involve officials in their life. It never left her mind that he was young and had a right to be afraid to be left alone, but she'd made the trip to the United States with the intention of giving her son the best start in life. She was determined to pursue her dream.

Pulling her mind back to her chore, she put plates of waffles and eggs on the counter top.

"Ven a comer tu comida. (Come eat your food.)" she called.

Manuel left the window. His face did not show hunger, it showed sorrow.

"Porque' estas triste? (Why are you sad?")" she asked.

"Porque' me hace falta abuelo e abuela." he responded quietly.

"Yo se que te hacen falta, pero vamos vivir aqui ahora. (I know that you miss your grandparents, but we are going to live here now.) Tu comida. (Eat your food.)" Her response was stern, but inside her heart ached with her son's pain.

CeCe got dressed and gave Manuel instructions to follow while she was gone. She left him a prepared lunch in the refrigerator.

"Voy a trabajar. (I'm going to work.) Recorda, no puedes ir para afuera! (Remember you can not go outside!) No le habras la puerta a nadie. (Do not open the door to anyone.)" She pulled him to her. "Te quiero dame un a brazo. (I love you, give me a hug)."

Once outside of the building, she looked up at her windows to wave at her son, whom she knew was in one of them watching her.

Miz Catfish

Manuel waited until he could no longer see his mother then put on his shoes and left the apartment. He knocked on Janice's door hoping to play with Jamie and Johnny.

Janice opened the door to the weak knock, and was surprised to see the little person alone on the other side. "Hi Manuel, did you come to play with Jamie and Johnny? Does your mother know that you're here?"

Manuel stared up at Janice, unable to respond to her due to the language barrier.

"Oh yeah," Janice said to herself, "you don't speak English yet. Come on in little man. Your mother must have let you come down to play." She moved aside and touched his shoulder as a gesture for him to enter. He played with Jamie and Johnny, and ate lunch with them.

Ortega bounced up the front steps like a young man in his prime. He was taking a chance by dropping in on Macy unannounced, and expecting her to have time to entertain him, but that was Ortega's way with women. Men made the decisions for them, and they followed. Softly whistling to himself, he knocked at the door three times before deciding that she probably wasn't home.

When it was time for the children to go down for nap, Janice spoke, and motioned to Manuel that he would have to go home. He left, but instead of going into his apartment he went to the front stairs and sat looking in the direction his mother had disappeared. He wondered if he could go the same way and find her, he missed her. Mae-Belle returned from the store. She rubbed the little boy's head on her way past him as she entered the building, and made a mental note to speak to CeCe about the dangers of the child being outside by himself.

Ortega left Macy's apartment with thoughts of a return visit already being formed in his mind. As he reached the front entrance of the building, he noticed a child sitting on the steps. The small, thin, shoulders moved up and down ever so slightly. Ortega walked down the steps until he could look into the small face. He stood with his hand stretched towards the small hand that drew circles in the sand on the step. Manuel looked up into the face with a mixture of fear and confusion. He had not seen any men around the building since he had come to live there with his mother. His mother warned him to stay in the apartment and that strangers could mean trouble. Yet this stranger looked safe, and almost welcoming. He reminded Manuel of some of the many uncles and workers that he missed so much on his abuelo's farm.

"What's wrong little hombre?" Ortega smiled at Manuel.

Manuel hunched his shoulders and continued to make swirls in the sand.

"Where do choo live? I don't think choo can be here alone. Are choo rund away?" Ortega tried to befriend the child.

Manuel looked up and didn't bother to wipe at the tears that had began to run down his face. Ortega reached out and swiped at them with a handkerchief that he'd pulled from his pocket.

"No, no hombre. Why choo get so upset?"

"Mi madre. Yo quiero a mi mama." the little boy sniffled.

Ortega was relieved to hear the little boy speak Spanish which was also his primary language.

Miz Catfish

"Do choo live here? Porque tu estas tan enojade?" he remembered to switch to Spanish.

"Si." The weaker voice returned.

"Who is watchin' choo?"

"No-o." At that point Manuel remembered what is mother had told him about the problems that talking to strangers could cause them. He would be in trouble with his mother.

Janice looked out of her window, and noticed Manuel in conversation. She immediately went out to get him. By telling him to go home, she had in no way meant to put him in harms way.

"Manuel, why are you outside alone?" she questioned.

"He say he very sad." Ortega answered hunching his shoulders to show confusion at the boy's quietness.

Janice stuck her hand out and curled her fingers in a "come here" motion.

"Come on Manuel," she said with authority. "I don't think you should be out here alone. Come with me until your mother gets home."

"He does not speak englees." Ortega interrupted.

"No kiddin." Janice hissed at the stranger.

"Ladee, choo are like a bee in a shut up car." he said as he stuffed his handkerchief back into his pocket.

Janice watched from the window until CeCe returned home, and explained to her what had happened with Manuel, and the fact that he'd been speaking with the stranger. CeCe thanked her neighbor and pulled her son home.

"No me obedeces. (You do not obey me.) Vete adrento.(Go inside.)" she snapped.

Manuel obeyed his mother, and once they were inside, again she explained to him why he needed to stay inside while she was at work.

Mae-Belle came down later and invited them to the roof top for drinks and snacks. CeCe accepted the offer. She felt a warmth from the woman that allowed her to also trust her. While they were there she discussed with CeCe the importance of Manuel's safety. CeCe longed to share her situation with the motherly woman. Maybe she could help watch Manuel while she was at work, but she couldn't take the chance. She felt utterly alone in the world, at least in this part of the world.

After returning to her apartment Mae-Belle put away the snacks and returned the remainder of the lemonade to the refrigerator. She settled herself in a chair in front of her living room window. The moon was at a perfect half crescent, and its brightness lit the evening sky.

A car pulled up in front of the building. Jason Michaels the owner of the hardware store down the street got out. She had known him for years; his father had owned the store before him. When her father was alive, from time to time she'd go with him into the store for things he needed.

It was past business hours, and she noticed that Jason didn't carry a bag from the store as if he were doing a delivery. As he climbed the stairs to the building Mae-Belle wondered who he was coming to see. All the residents in the building were single, but Jason was married. Mae-Belle had seen his wife and children in the store many times. It suddenly occurred to her that her building was no longer going to be empty and quiet. It was now taking on a life of its own, and as she quietly watched, she was beginning to get an uncomfortable maternal feeling of oncoming unrest. She sat in the window a while longer thinking about the events of the day, wondering to what extent she would get involved in the lives of these young women. Mae-Belle decided to turn in for the night, and as she left the window to get undressed, a couple elsewhere in the building indulged in the newness of desire. Mae-Belle never knew that the car parked below did not leave its parking space until the following morning.

The beauty of the crescent moon was lost to Amber as she lay comfortably in Jason's arms. She twirled the hairs on his chest, as she nuzzled her nose into his neck. She felt free of any responsibilities and worries, unconfined as she reveled in these few precious hours. He slept silently, looking angelic and peaceful. A ringlet of hair fell over his forehead glistening with sweat. She gently swept it away. He stirred, and moaned a small purr. He opened his eyes and smiled at her. Pulling her to him, he drew her small body on top of his. He felt quivers in his groin, as well as his thighs as her petite hands roamed over his upper body. Her innocence made her love making seem wilder and full of charged energy. Her body responded to his needs. She yearned for more and he gave it to her. They answered each other's desire for satisfaction. He felt guilty about sneaking away to spend time with another woman. If he had to explain the reason for cheating on his wife he would not be able to, there was no good explanation. Yet he found himself drawn to this person, to the freshness of her body, her voice, her face, her hair. Everything about her pulled him towards her. They made love tenderly, touching every part of each other's body, enjoying the adventure of newness. In the end they lay spent in each other's arms, content and full of emotions. Each thinking their thoughts, with Jason's on the easiest way to remind Amber that he had to leave.

He knew that he should be going home. Debra would be expecting him. He had to be careful with this new activity, and very creative with his excuses for being late. He couldn't afford to become attached to the sweet, young beauty that he held in his arms. He loved his wife, and children. Nothing would get in the way of that part of his life. "Alright babe, I have to get going. I've got some things to take care of." he said as he slowly pulled himself away from her, not wanting to seem too eager in his exit.

"Oh-h-h, I was hoping that we could go out shopping today. Then have some lunch" she whined.

"Come on; don't give me a hard time. I'll be back. It's not like I'm going away for good." he said using a stern voice for her good as well as his own. As he reached for his underwear and jeans, he caught a glimpse of the disappointment on her beautiful face and felt a tug at his heart. He needed to install discipline within himself to continue with what he knew his responsibilities were. "We'll try to do those things another day." he hoped to sound convincing as he zipped and snapped his jeans.

"Why another day?" she persisted with a frown twisting her face.

"Why an-not-ther da-ay?" he mimicked in a high pitched tone trying to lighten her mood. "Give me a hug and take that scary frown off of your face. Come on, get over here!"

Acting as if she were a defiant child, instead of reaching across the bed to him, she got off the bed on the side where she lay, stopping to put on her bra and panties.

"Do me a favor and bring my socks from over there on your way will you?" he requested.

She didn't verbally respond to his request, although she'd heard him loud and clear. Instead she reminded him of her irritation at their situation by bending at the waist to pick up the socks, and while in a curved position straightening the string of her pastel pink thong between her smooth buttock cheeks, allowing the fabric to snap into position. There was nothing seductive about the snap action, and the message sent was clear. Jason had been watching and had enjoyed the view. He couldn't help but laugh out loud, but when Amber straightened up and turned toward him, he noticed that her face did not show a smile. She continued around the bed carrying the socks, and allowed them to drop on top of his foot when she reached his side she then continued on to find her own clothes and got dressed. The hug was purposefully forgotten.

"Why don't you get yourself something at the store and surprise me. Take a few dollars and smile will you!" he ordered.

She took what turned out to be one hundred dollars from his out stretched hand, and then gave him a hug. Her heart ached to see him leaving. He was beginning to occupy a place in her heart that had never been touched. Her previous lovers had been boys that were inexperienced, fumbling, and stumbling, as if dancing with someone stepping on her toes. This man gave her a waltz. She was falling head-over-heels for what would turn out to be a wolf in sheep's clothing. He finished getting dressed then left the apartment, passing Macy on her way to Amber's. They nodded as a way of acknowledging each other, and continued on their way.

"Hey girl! What's up? I haven't seen you in a few days. I just passed Mr. Hardware in the hallway." Macy spoke in a sing-song manner.

"Hi Macy, it's been a while since we've crossed paths, and don't mention Mr. Hardware. I'm kind of angry at him. Wanna come shopping with me? I've got some spare time before I have to go in to work," Amber asked.

"You don't have to say the word shop to me twice. Where are we off to?"

"Somewhere that I can buy something catching to the male eye, something with no fabric here, a little fabric there, and frills around here." She moved her hands from one area of her body to another to demonstrate what she meant.

"I know the perfect place. Let's go!"

Macy waited for Amber to shower, get into fresh clothes, and put on make-up, then they started on their way out of the building. Janice was sitting on the stairs. She held a jar of pickled pig's feet in one hand and a fork in the other.

"What are you eating?" Macy asked curiously, as she squinted her eyes and wrinkled her nose.

"Pickled pig's feet. One of my favorite snacks, want some? Janice offered, as she held up the jar of floating baby pink, mixed with the softest beige, mounds of over marinated trotters, one with a protruding nail.

Both women recoiled in disgust. All three women laughed loudly, until slapping knees and holding stomachs. Janice had begun to make peace with her new life and enjoy the friends around her. Although nothing could replace what she'd left behind, the friends that now stood laughing with her were an accepted blessing. They didn't pry into her life, or invade her space when she felt like being alone in her apartment with the children. They had all begun to enjoy the roof top in accommodating weather. Little by little bonds were being formed.

Janice continued to eat her treat, as her friends continued on their way to the store. Amber and Macy ran past their job site feeling naughty about not looking in to see if things were running smoothly. Giggling was an allowance given to women no matter what age. On this day they enjoyed their freedom and their allowance.

CeCe looked out of the window of the pet store. She checked the sidewalk from time to time, making sure that Manuel was not out roaming the street. She couldn't see very far up the sidewalk towards the apartment building, yet her maternal instincts kept her from being able to concentrate on her work. Mae-Belle and Janice had both warned her about an agency called the Department of Social Services. Janice had explained to her that this agency's job was to make sure that children were properly taken care of if not the children would possibly be removed from the home. They told her that because Manuel sat in front of the building alone, someone that passed by and saw him was bound to call this agency out of concern. Manuel spent a lot of time with Jamie and Johnny, but he longed for his mother in her absence and preferred to sit outside waiting for her. He knew he would be chastised when she arrived, but he disobeyed her anyway.

Manuel sat crying on the stairs. His heart ached; there had been too much change and not enough explanation. The large building, noisy sirens, and strange faces were overwhelming. There was no grandfather to hoist him up on his shoulders. No grandmother to hand him warm platanos. No chickens to chase or tall fields of crops to run through. CeCe saw these emotions in her son, but couldn't help him, her hands were tied, and she was trying to make things better for him.

A black Buick passed by the building. The female driver noticed the small boy, sitting alone on the stairs, with his chin cupped in his hands. The next day when the same black Buick drove past the building, again the boy was sitting on the stairs. The car parked in front of the pet shop, and as the driver got out she couldn't help but look back at the small person. Their eyes momentarily locked as he stared at her with returned curiosity. A mental note was made by the driver to find out who the child was.

CeCe assisted a customer that came into the store to purchase a bag of bird food. She admired the look of quality of the woman's skirt and blouse and longed for the day when she would be able to buy such clothing for herself. The customer left the store, and through the window CeCe watched her get into a black car.

Mary Rivers pushed her briefcase into the passenger seat of her car, putting the bag of bird seed next to it. She started up the quiet machine, pulled away from the curb and headed towards her office located within the mammoth sized cement building downtown that housed the government offices. Her office was one which caused great fear, known as the Department of Social Services.

Miz Catfish

Chapter 15

Amber opened the door for Jason wearing a new outfit she'd purchased with the money he'd given her. She turned away from the doorway, leaving him to close the door. She turned on the radio and began to dance in the middle of the room. Until she repaid Macy for the furniture that she'd bought for her, she would not worry herself about a living room set, so Jason allowed himself to sink into the large pillow on the floor and enjoy the treat.

He reached out to her, she took his hand, pulled him to his feet, and they danced their way into the bedroom, where they made love through another three songs before Jason broke the mood. It was eleven o'clock and he was planning the excuses to make his exit.

"Hey." he whispered "I've got to get going."

"Why do you have to leave?"

"Don't give me a hard time Amber. I just can't stay alright!" he snapped.

"Where are you going? Can I come to your house?"

"I told you that I live with my sister. She's a bitch about strangers in her home. Can't you just leave things alone? I'll be back to see you as soon as I can." He walked into the living room tucking his shirt into his pants. He held his ground, knowing that if he could he'd gladly stay.

Amber, still naked, followed behind Jason, she was not giving up in her quest to spend more time with her lover.

"At least give me your telephone number so I can call you at home. I'm getting tired of only being able to speak to you during store hours." She forgot about her nakedness as she leaned against the wall with her arms folded.

"I can't give out my sister's phone number. She'll kick my ass! Stop asking questions will ya?" Jason snapped as he turned his back to her in an attempt to not be drawn back into her naked arms. "The answers aren't going to change."

"Can you come early tomorrow morning so we can have breakfast?" She tried to settle with an agreement as he tied the laces of his shoes.

"We'll see." He kissed her on the forehead and left.

The door closed firmly, releasing a soft click to confirm its finality of position. The click as soft as it filled the room, reached Amber's ears as loudly as if a bell had been rung, and as if responding to the bell, tears began to roll down her face. She cried out of anger, loneliness, and fear. She wanted to tell him that her period was late. Her cycle was always regular, without fail, and she was afraid to think of the reason why now it was not.

She looked at the clock, it was late. She wanted to speak to Macy, and her head ached from the disagreement with Jason. Goosebumps stood up on her arms drawing her attention to the fact that cool air enveloped her body. Giving into the pain in her temple, and the need to cover up her nudeness, she went into her bedroom and climbed back into her bed, gripping the sheet between her fingers she pulled it over her head. Talking with Macy would have to wait until a later time.

Mae-Belle was at her window watching the moonlight beam off the surface of the water. She noticed the car belonging to Jason Michaels parked in front of the building again tonight. It was too late in the night for any other explanation. One of her tenants was heading down a bumpy road.

Macy would not have been home to receive Amber's visit, she spent the evening with Janice watching television and having a few beers. While the children slept, the women shared some "girl time". Macy explained to Janice about her childhood in the foster homes of Pennsylvania. They discovered that they were born in the same area of Philadelphia, and shared some similar childhood memories. Some people that Janice knew Macy knew as well, and one of Macy's foster mothers lived in the same neighborhood as Janice's grandmother.

The picture of a baby wearing a two-tooth smile sitting on the end table caught Macy's eye.

"Who's this pretty little button?" Macy asked as she picked up the wooden frame.

"That's Jamie when she was one, just about the time she learned to walk and destroy. Don't let the innocent grin fool you."

"Spoken as only a mother would, I'm sure." Macy laughed. "But you can't deny the fact that she's a beauty."

"Okay, I concede. Thank you."

Macy continued to hold onto the picture; lost in the small innocent face staring back at her that looked so like her own had at that age. She remembered the day she met Jamie in front of the building. The similarities between herself and the little girl had struck her that day as well.

"If I told you how much this picture looks like I did at this age, you wouldn't believe me." Macy said loud enough that Janice could hear, but mostly to herself.

She quietly sat beside Janice, holding the picture as if in a trance. Tears began to roll down her face. The tears tasted of sorrow, curiosity, and longing. She thought how funny it is that tears were only described as tasting salty. She trusted Janice enough to try to explain her mixed emotions.

"When I look at this picture and see Jamie's face, it makes me think of my foster mother at that time. She was so loving, her name was Betty Jenkins. I remember the picture of myself that looked like this one; it hung on the wall above a large floor model television. She kept my ponytails so neat and pretty. I lived with her until I was five years old. When she became ill and couldn't take care of me anymore, they put me in a new home. I never saw her again."

"How old are you?"

"I'm twenty three." Macy replied.

"I'm twenty five. Only two years older than you. I wonder if I ever saw you at Miss Jenkins's house when I visited my grandmother. I'm going to ask my grandmother if she remembers you. I'll call her tomorrow." Janice hoped that she sounded comforting, and supportive of her new friend's feelings.

Macy continued to sit quietly staring at the picture. Emotions that had been silent for years had been awakened. Loneliness engulfed her like a glove. She gently replaced the picture to the table, and wiped away the last of the tears.

"Do you mind if I have another beer?" Macy's voice was tight with emotion.

Janice noticed the change in her friend's mood, she now seemed sullen, and in private thought. She allowed Macy to quietly sip her beer, and waited for her to introduce conversation. Macy finished her beer, and gave Janice a hug goodnight, then went home. No further conversation had followed.

Janice felt heavy at heart when she thought about Macy's story. She hoped that she could be helpful in getting some closure for these questions. She took the empty beer cans to the kitchen, and returned to the sofa to watch a little mindless television.

Macy struggled to regain control of her thoughts as she entered her apartment. The colorful mural on her living room wall may just as well have been black and white. She couldn't focus on anything in the room. Her mind raced with the possibilities of what Janice's grandmother could help her find out about her past. Maybe she could get a lead on finding her parents after all.

She pulled out the sleep sofa and slowly crawled onto the mattress, allowing the slight haze from the beers that she had drank while sitting with Janice to slip her into an alcohol induced slumber. Macy woke the next morning trying to force all of the previous night's events back into their dark place in her mind. She called Kenneth.

He answered, "Hello."

"It's me." she responded matter-of-factly without giving her name.

"Me who?" he joked.

"Ha, ha! You got any work for me?"

"Sure, when can you be ready?"

"I want something tonight. I need to keep busy. I have to work at the store today so pick me up after eleven."

"You got it babe. Your voice sounds edgy. Are you in that devilish mood of yours?" he asked.

"Yeah, I guess you could say that."

"I suppose asking you what's wrong won't do any good."

"No it wouldn't, because I don't want to talk about it."

"Okay."

Amber woke to waves of nausea. She sat on the side of her bed for a moment before getting up and going to the bathroom. No red stain spotted her underwear. Reality was sinking in, but she held on to a string of hope that maybe her period was just mixed up this month. Maybe she could explain the nausea away as an on coming cold, and maybe the pressure in her chest and her shortness of breath was not an anxiety attack. Maybe her underwear was slightly tinged and she'd missed the faint color. Maybe, maybe, maybe!

She threw on a tattered robe from her high school days and went through the hallway and up the stairs to Macy's. It was time to share the fear with someone. Macy opened her door on the third knock.

"Good morning Amber. What's got you up here so early?" Macy asked.

Amber walked in and flopped on the sleep sofa that was still pulled out. She crawled to the top of the bed and pulled the sheet up to her neck, holding onto it with both hands.

"Girl, what's wrong?"

"I didn't get my period last month, and now I'm late for this month." Amber whispered.

"Have you ever been late before?" Macy asked.

"No, never!" She replied, pulling the sheet totally over her head.

"I won't ask if there's a possibility of you being pregnant, because if there wasn't you wouldn't be hiding in my bed. Let's start from scratch. First you need to find out if you've got something to worry about." Macy took charge.

Macy got out of the black chair and went into the smaller room. She came out within seconds wearing a t-shirt and blue jeans, pulled her hair into a ponytail and slipped on her flip flops that she used as slippers. Amber realized that she didn't hear anymore conversation from her friend and pulled the sheet back to her lips to see where she was.

"What are you doing dressed?" Amber asked.

"I'm going to the store to buy you a pregnancy test."

Amber continued to hold on to the sheet. She tried to imagine how silly she must look to Macy, but she felt safe here. She knew that her friend would help her through this. Everyone needs a place to go where they can be taken care of like a child. Macy's colorful three room apartment was such a place.

Macy returned with the test, and laughed to find Amber still tucked under the sheet.

"Come on out of there. It's time." she commanded.

"I don't think I want to do this." Amber whined.

Macy grabbed the sheet and yanked it from Amber's grasp. "You don't have a choice." she said. "Take this package and go into the bathroom. I would give you my pee, but I'm afraid it won't be of much help to you here." she joked hoping that she could take some of the worry off Amber's mind long enough to bring a smile to her face. "The test is for anyone more than five days late. That's definitely you."

Amber took the box and went into the bathroom. She followed the directions on the instruction sheet, and then went back into the living room to sit with Macy.

"Now what?" Macy asked.

"Well in three minutes we should see a positive or a negative sign." She handed Macy the test stick. "You look, I can't do it."

They both stared at the stick in disbelief as a dark blue plus sign appeared in the small viewing window of the plastic stick. It had not taken three minutes. One minute was the test needed for its chemicals to mix with Amber's urine and reveal the results.

"Oh shit!" Amber tried to sound strong.

"Well, now you have to make the next decision. Are you going to keep the pregnancy or not?"

"I don't know."

"I'm going to make a guess that the father of the baby is the hardware store guy right?" Macy asked.

"Yeah."

"Well you've got to discuss it with him."

"This should thrill him to death. We just argued about him not giving me a telephone number to reach him outside of the store. I've never been to his home. He says that he lives with a sister. I don't think this information is going to make him feel very excited." Amber explained in a nervous tone.

"Don't you think that it's a little bit strange for a man who owns his own business to be living with his sister?"

"Yeah, I guess so."

"Well, I guess that's not the most important thing at the moment. Now you've got to look at your options."

"I know. My head is spinning. I can't believe this."

"What did you think was going to happen if you continued to have unprotected sex? The purpose of sex is to procreate. Why the surprise?"

"You're right. I guess I didn't really worry about the consequence. I always wanted my own little prince or princess. Have you ever wanted children?" Amber asked.

"I never gave it much thought. After being in foster homes I didn't think that I could give a child the stability that it would need, emotionally, or morally. You see a lot of things in foster care. Most of it isn't something that you want to pass on to someone else." Macy responded, to herself as much as to Amber.

Amber touched one hand to her stomach. "There's a little person growing in there. Wow! Now I feel really weird."

"If you're keeping it, time won't matter. But if you're going to get an abortion, you're on a count down. They won't do one after a certain number of weeks."

"I don't believe in abortion, at least not for myself, but to each his own for everyone else. I guess I better go call Jason."

"Since you're going to work soon, and I'll be going in later, I won't see you until tomorrow. I'll check in on you in the morning. Don't panic, you'll be alright."

Macy gave Amber a hug. While holding her she felt the younger girl's shoulders start to shake.

"Oh Amber don't cry! If you cry, I'm going to cry."

"I can't help it. This is weird, and I can't believe it." Amber sniffed.

"I guess you better let it out instead of trying to be brave and keep it in. Let it flow. Prego women are supposed to be emotional any way."

"Name calling already!" Amber laughed a nervous giggle. She swiped at the tears coming from her eyes and looked around the room for something to wipe her nose.

"Here." Macy said as she handed Amber some tissues. "Don't wipe your snotty nose on my sheets!"

"Stop making me laugh, you clown! Can't a person have a good wet cry in peace?"

"Not when you bring it to my door! Now get out so I can get ready for my exercise work out, or keep sitting there and I'll fold you and that kid up in the sofa." Macy giggled.

Amber got up to leave. She grabbed her friend again and gave her another hug. When she got downstairs to her apartment, she saw Mae-Belle was coming from the mailboxes.

"Hi sweetie, how are you?" Mae-Belle asked in a sing-song voice.

"Hi Miss Mae-Belle, I'm hanging in there." Amber returned with forced happiness in her voice.

"When are you going to come back upstairs for some lemonade?"

"Soon, real soon."

"I'll be waiting for you." Mae-Belle hoped that the words sounded warm and inviting, because she had a feeling that the young girl might be in need of a comforting ear in the near future.

Amber tried to keep the conversation short so that she would not have to look Mae-Belle in the eyes. She knew that the older woman would be able to tell that she'd been crying. She was nowhere near being ready to share the reason for the tears with anyone other than Macy and Jason. She got into her apartment and closed the door quickly behind her as if an intruder was on her heels.

Mae-Belle had noticed the red eyes. She wanted to reach out to the young lady, but decided to wait until Amber came to her.

Amber called the hardware store. The answering machine came on. She hung up the telephone, then picked it back up and tried again. Again the answering machine came on. This time she left a message.

"Jason this is Amber. Please come see me tonight. We need to talk." she pleaded.

She hung up the telephone and crawled back into her bed. She had no energy and the nausea had returned. Again her hand went to her stomach.

"Hi, little one, it's mommy. I just found out today that you're snuggled away in there. I don't mind telling you that I'm still in shock. I haven't told your daddy yet. I bet he'll be as shocked as I am. Now that I know about you for sure, I think I can get used to you. You'll have me, your daddy, and Auntie Macy to watch over you."

Amber fell to sleep with one hand on her stomach, and the other still holding the tear stained tissues. Jason did not call back. She got dressed and went to work. On her way past the hardware store, she noticed a sign in the window. It read "GONE ON VACATION. BACK IN FIVE DAYS." Amber's heart felt as if it enlarged in her chest. Her mouth watered with nausea and a feeling of faintness came over her. She leaned against the wall of the store to regain her composure. Her thoughts were erratic. She remembered that she was on her way to work, but she was pregnant and the store was closed. On vacation, why didn't he tell me? On vacation with who? His sister? I need to tell him about the baby, our baby.

She pushed herself off the wall and continued down the sidewalk to the convenience store. Her hours at work seemed to stretch out interminably. She tried to do little things to keep herself busy, like dusting the shelves, and straightening anything out of line. She needed to tell Jason her news. She needed to see the surprise on his face, and to hear him say that every thing was going to be alright.

A lady came into the store pushing a baby carriage. Amber peeked inside and caught a glimpse at the sleeping baby. A light weight, pastel pink blanket covered her body, leaving only the top of a tiny white cap visible.

"How old is your baby?" she asked.

"She's two months." the woman replied.

"What's her name?"

"Rachel Marie." the customer answered with pride.

"That's a beautiful name."

"Thank you."

She noticed that the young lady was not wearing a wedding ring. Although Amber had been raised by her parents to not so much as dream of having children before she was married, she saw women every day such as this one, who were doing just that. She thought to herself, "I suppose I could do it too."

She finished her shift and began her walk home. Before she began her relationship with Jason, the hardware store was just another store front. Now it stood out like a neon sign, it would not only stick out today, but felt like a razor cut as she went past the "GONE ON VACATION" sign again. She dreaded the emotional trip.

She made it past the hardware store and was drawn to the first window of the pet shop by puppies covered in brown fluff that were jumping all over each other, nipping each others ears and using their paws to slap one another around. She moved on to the next window and was immediately drawn into the serene view of a twenty-gallon fish tank. She thought of the tank in Macy's apartment that she had enjoyed many times. After watching a small red-tail shark chase a clown loach, twice its size, around the tank, Amber decided to buy a tank for herself. She entered the shop and made her way down the aisle, passing spiders in tanks, and hamster cages along the way. She tried to ignore the different odors mixing in her nostrils, but knew that she would not be able to stay long before nausea would overcome her. She spotted her neighbor holding a puppy, lightly stroking its fur.

"Hi CeCe."

Cecilia looked up startled and clutched the puppy to her chest. "Hi um-m-m." CeCe recognized her neighbor's face, but raced to remember her name.

"I'm Amber, your neighbor from the first floor. I didn't mean to scare you." Amber noticed how the woman was holding the dog, and tried to soothe her neighbor.

"I'm just a little jumpy. It wasn't your fault." CeCe said as she held on to the puppy protectively. "Is everything okay at home? Is Manuel in trouble?" CeCe's words stumbled over themselves in her nervousness.

"No, no. I just wa-a." Amber tried to say as CeCe interrupted her.

"Arth choo?" CeCe's voice was panicky causing her Spanish accent to become stronger in her speech.

"Yes! Calm down CeCe. Really, I was walking by on the way home from work at the store, and the fish tank in the window caught my eye. I decided to come on in and buy one. I don't want anything big, just something to hold two or three fish."

CeCe's eyes searched Amber's face as if looking for a sign of whether her neighbor was telling the truth about her visit. She replaced the puppy to its holding cage. "Do you know which tank you want?"

"Not really. Could you show me what you have?"

CeCe showed Amber around the pet fish items, and caught the red-tail shark, and dark grey catfish that she selected. Amber paid for her purchases and prepared to leave the store.

"I'll see you at home." CeCe said in a dismissive tone.

Amber realized that communication was over. Maybe her neighbor wasn't ready to make friends, and she shouldn't take it personally. She certainly hadn't meant to make CeCe uncomfortable. Why had her presence caused such upset? There was no way that CeCe could have concerns greater than her own.

After Amber left, CeCe continued to question the girl's sincerity in coming in solely with the intention to buy a fish tank.

Amber took her new pets home, and after Macy got home from work called her to come downstairs and help set up the tank. Once everything was in place, they watched the fish feel out their new home.

"It's really weird how both of us chose a catfish. They're not the most attractive fish in the window." Macy said in a thoughtful tone.

"Yeah well, I don't know what yours means to you, but I brought mine because when I saw it gliding around the bottom of the tank, it reminded me of the way that I feel about myself today."

"What way is that?"

"Really low. Barely making it from one point to another. Have you been outside yet? There's a sign on the hardware store saying that Jason is on vacation. He didn't even tell me that he was going. Now I'm here nauseous with his kid, and purchasing a shark fish I've named Jason to blow off steam."

"Ugh. Those fish sure pack a whollop of emotions. My little guy mirrors the way I feel about myself at times. My childhood in foster homes was an ugly period in my life, and has left me struggling to see myself as anything but ugly. I heard that I was ugly over and over again. Sometimes I feel like I'm as average to pretty as any other woman, but other times I can't help but hear the voices in my head from the past. When I bought my catfish, I guess the voices of the past were shopping with me." Macy's voice seemed to get more emotional as she spoke.

"Wait a minute; let's not get too bogged down in this mental garbage." Amber nudged Macy in the side. "If we both go under, there'll be no one left to pull me up."

"I'll ignore your selfishness today, and go back to Jason being on vacation. Have you discussed with him any thing about where this relationship was going?"

"No, not yet."

"Well, I think you better get to it my dear."

Chapter 16

Mary Rivers walked into the building at 8:30 a.m., stopping at the mail boxes that displayed the names and apartment numbers of each tenant. Box number four was the only one that had a Spanish name matching the Spanish features of the little boy she'd seen on the stairs to the building. The knocking woke Manuel from a sound sleep. When CeCe opened the door a neatly dressed woman stood before her on the other side. As she and the woman stood in the doorway Manuel poked his head in between the two women.

"Well, hello there little fellow. How are you?" the lady said smiling at Manuel. She recognized him as the child from the stairs. CeCe pushed Manuel back into the apartment.

"Is that your son?" the stranger asked CeCe.

"Si." In her nervousness CeCe slipped into her native language, realizing this she quickly corrected herself, "I mean yes."

"I'm from the Department of Social Services. My name is Mary Rivers. I'm a case worker. I've noticed your little boy sitting outside alone quite frequently. He's much too young to be left alone, and I've filed a report that requires our agency to make sure that he's in a safe environment. Would you mind if I come in?"

Cecilia moved aside and allowed the woman to enter. CeCe thought for sure the stranger could see her heart beating through her shirt, because she thought it was going to jump out from her throat with the vomit that threatened to spring forth from fear. She didn't know what to do. She had to let the woman in, but could only imagine what the woman must be thinking about the emptiness of her apartment. She recognized the woman as a customer that had come into the store recently. Now here the woman was again, but this time standing in her home. Mae-Belle and Janice had warned her about the agency. She wondered if the woman had truly seen Manuel outside, or if someone in the building had called them.

"May I ask your name, and your son's?" the woman asked.

"Cecilia Ana Maria Ortiz and Manuel Ortiz."

"How long have you lived here?" the woman continued.

"About two months now." Cecilia tried her best to speak with out any hint of an accent.

"Does you son go to school yet?"

"Yes, but he had been out sick lately with a cold."

"Have you taken him to a doctor?"

"No, children get many colds, I'm sure that he'll be fine."

"Well, that's true, but you should check with his doctor if the cold lasts too long. I know that you haven't lived here very long, but you must make sure that he has a doctor. In the mean time you've got to keep the little guy inside, and supervised. I'm sure you realize that allowing him outside alone is very dangerous. I have an appointment that I must get to." the woman said looking at her watch. She reached into her briefcase and pulled out a business card, and handed it to CeCe. You can reach me at this telephone number. If you need help with anything."

Miz Catfish

Cecilia could see the woman's eyes searching the apartment as she spoke. Manuel watched the conversation from his blanket on the floor. His face showed confusion, and fear.

"I'll get in touch with you. Do you have a telephone?"

"No."

"Okay, well, I'll drop by again soon. Please take the time to think of any services that you could use help with, such as getting some furniture, food, or finding a doctor. Good bye Manuel. I'll see you again soon." Mary Rivers gave Manuel a smile

It wasn't until Cecilia closed the door that she realized that she was shaking. What could she do? She would be found out. She had to think fast.

She dreaded the thought she would have to go back to the house where she had begun. The thought of being back under the same roof as the perverted landlord made her skin crawl, but she had no choice. If she could hold out two more days, she'd get her pay for the week. Then she'd wait until the dark and leave with her few possessions and her son. She'd miss her new friends, but she didn't know which of them she could trust anymore. Her only choice was to sneak away quietly.

She needed someone to talk with. It would have been nice to have another adult to share her burden with. Yet she was too afraid to take the chance with anyone else in the building. As she stood with her back to her living room door, Manuel went to the window in time to see the black Buick, that he'd seen drive past the building so often, pull away from the curb.

Macy finished her hours at the store then went home to pack her travel bag before Kenneth picked her up. She had only been in the house ten minutes before she heard a knock at her door. She yelled "Who is it?" thinking that maybe it was Amber, or Kenneth.

"It is me. Jorge Tomas Ortega." sang back a proud masculine voice thick with Spanish flavor.

"What! How did you find me?" she feigned surprise as she threw open the door and reluctantly stepped aside to allow her guest to enter her living room. He stood in the middle of the room looking around and walked over to the fish tank.

"They are beautiful. Muy bonita!" he exclaimed.

"Thank you, they're good company."

"They look hungry." he added.

"How in the hell can you tell when a fish is hungry?"

"Wheen they are all een a corner chasing the other's tail. Dass is how." Ortega responded proudly. He liked to feel that he had knowledge on all subjects.

She sprinkled some fish food flakes into the tank. All of the fish scattered around chasing and eating the food.

"How come that little fish down dare is not eating with the others?" Ortega asked.

"Oh, that's my buddy, Miz Catfish. She eats what falls to the bottom." Macy laughed.

"Maybe she knows of more important thinks than the others." Ortega suggested.

"I doubt it. I think it's more like she's just used to being down there."

Miz Catfish

"Can I seat down?"

"Sure, but don't get too comfortable, because I'm going out soon." Macy warned.

"Okay, I guess I come back another time." Ortega didn't argue.

"That'll be fine. Sorry I can't sit and talk longer."

She walked him to the door and hugged him goodbye. The next knock on her door would be Kenneth and he'd be impatient. Macy chose a nude body suit with thigh-high black suede boots, put everything in her duffel bag, zippered it up and used the rest of her time sitting in the black chair getting herself mentally ready for the night ahead.

Janice was on the phone talking to her grandmother. She had a close relationship with her mother's mother. She had spent a lot of time playing in the large backyard that was full of flowers and plants but had a section fenced off for the grandchildren to play and run free. Teri and Shawn had been in the yard twice in their lives, and Janice looked forward to taking the children again. It was heart warming to watch her own children play in the same house that she had as a girl. After greetings had been worked through, Janice grabbed the chance to ask some questions.

"Grandma do you remember Miss Betty who used to live next door?" she asked.

"Yeah, baby, I sure do. I still see some of her children now and then. As a matter of fact I just saw her oldest grandbaby on Tuesday. No, maybe it was Wednesday. No, no, I think it was Tuesday because I was going to the supermar..," her grandmother dragged on with her thoughts.

Janice jumped back into the conversation before her grandmother got carried away with the other five days of the week. "Grandma do you remember all of those foster children that she used to have in her house?" she asked.

"I sure do. Sometimes I swore she had more children in that house than a coop had chickens! Ha, ha." she cackled.

"Well I think one of them is one of my neighbors. Her name is Macy Jenkins. Do you remember her?"

There was silence on the other end of the telephone.

"Grandma? Ma did tell you that I had to move didn't she? Grandma?"

"I'm here baby, I'm here. Yeah, your mom told me that you and the babies moved." her grandmother responded.

"What's wrong?" Janice asked.

"Oh, oh, I'm alright. What did you say her name was again?"

"It's Macy Jenkins."

"What does she look like?" Grandma asked softly.

"Well she looks mixed, because she is very light-skinned and has medium brown eyes. Once we started talking she mentioned having been in foster care. That's when she told me that she was from Pennsylvania, and that her first foster mother's name was Betty Jenkins. Grandma you wouldn't believe how much Teri looks like her, only with darker skin. The more I see her the more I remember playing with her when I was little."

Miz Catfish

"You know what, baby? I hear someone at my back door. I'm going to go now and take care of them. I'll call you back as soon as I remember about the chile you're talking about okay?" Grandma tried to sound sincere but her voice sounded unsure, "Love you."

"Alright grandma, goodnight. Love you too." Janice thought her grandmother's silence and abrupt exit from the conversation was strange, but she pushed it aside.

Later that night Janice fell into her bed tired from a day's work with the children, and happy about hearing her grandmother's voice. On the other hand her grandmother did not feel such peace. She sat rubbing the cover of the family Bible. There was a newer one in the drawer of the end table that had been a gift her last birthday, but this one with its tattered page corners, and fold lines on its covers held the records of birth of each child, and grandchild. She had carried it to family weddings, funerals, births, and deaths. Tonight she held it and prayed for inner strength.

As the last light was turning off at 105 Shawnee Road, Macy was snaking her way across the stage on her baby oil slicked belly towards a customer holding up a five dollar tip. In her mind she viewed him as a pig sitting on its hind legs in a chair. She smiled as she took the money from his hand in her teeth. The crowd around her roared and whistled. The excitement in the room kept her mind off the conversation that she'd had with Janice. She finished her set on stage and entered the crowd. Before she could make it to the bar three customers asked her to do a private dance for them on her next set. She promised them that she would, then continued on to the bar to work the customers there. As long as the customers were buying the girls drinks that meant that they were spending money in the club, which made the owner happy. After two drinks with the same person, Macy moved from the bar to get back into action. She spotted Kenneth in the crowd and told him that she was going to do a private dance for some guys for the next set, then went back stage to change into a thong and neon body paint.

"Hey Sheila, do me a favor and come over here. I need someone to put some of this paint on my back." Macy yelled.

"Alright, but you owe me one for having to touch another bitch's body for free!" Sheila responded.

"Oh shut up! It's not like you haven't done it before. Bring me one of those valiums out of your bag too, will ya?" Macy quipped back playfully.

"Damn you want everything don't you bitch!"

"Yeah. Gimme, gimme!" Macy laughed.

She handed Sheila the neon green paint, and Sheila handed her the pill that would help her glaze through the rest of the night.

"You going back on stage?" Sheila asked.

"No, I'm getting ready for a private run."

"Ah man, I hate those damn things! Why don't we girls just make up another way to give those type of customers what they want without havin' to watch the drool run down their chins?" Sheila snorted.

"Yeah!" chided Marilyn. "How about if we pick an empty room and cut a hole into the door and a money slot. Then each guy can just walk up to it while we sit on the other side, out of sight. Then the guys can get in line, and one by one walk up to the hole. Which ever one of us that has "hole duty" will slap "it" around and yank "it "a bit. We'll make our money, they'll get off and the drool will stay out of sight."

Carol joined the conversation "You forgot one thing, you nut case! What about the drool that's going to come out on your end? Also I didn't hear you mention rubber gloves or a safety door to slam shut on any dirty, or smelly pee pee that comes through the hole. Those types don't get their money back either. We get to keep it for subjecting us to the cruel punishment."

All of the women laughed loudly, each visualizing their own image of "The door" After Macy took her pill she entered the private dance room. She was still laughing about the crazy conversation that she'd just heard as she switched on the black light so that the paint on her body would glow as she danced. She opened the curtain that separated the private room from the staged area of the club, and nodded to the three customers that had requested the private dance. The three men were probably business partners who had come to the club together for a little excitement. This was a secret life that many business men in suits led behind their wives and partners backs.

They entered the room, but Macy continued to stand at the curtain until one of the club's bouncers noticed her. She had forgotten to do this the last time she did the room and it had been a big mistake. After they caught each other's attention he came over to stand inside of the room. The bouncers protected the women from touchy or harassing customers. They were paid bodyguards. Macy started her shimmy top, shake bottom around the room from customer to customer. She recognized the face of one of the men as a customer from a few of the clubs that she'd previously danced in her mind she replayed how she had originally begun to dance.

Two years ago, Kenneth had bumped into her in the supermarket. The impact of the two shopping carts caused the eggs in her cart to jump.

"What's your problem mister?" she snapped.

"I guess I was blinded by your beauty." Kenneth replied.

"Bull shit! Watch where you're going next time!"

"Do you eat with that mouth too? Who pissed in your Cheerios so early in the morning?" he teased.

Macy couldn't help but to laugh at his frankness and they became friends on that day. After knowing her for three months he repeatedly mentioned to her how beautiful her body was. He told her that she could make fast and easy money dancing at a club that he managed.

Macy resisted for three months until she gave in to the temptation of the money. It was money that brought her back to the stage. She would have to prepare herself for the demeaning feeling of being naked in front of a room of strangers, both physically and emotionally.

She had showed up in the dressing room area, duffel bag in hand.

"I'm Sheila. Did your man send you here?" the colorful Sheila blew a large blue bubble from between her full shiny pink lips.

"No. I don't play that game." Macy responded sternly. " If I work, my money is all mine."

"Good for you, I wish I could say the same."

Sheila reached into a Gucci shoulder bag and pulled out a prescription bottle. "The little beauties called valiums. They'll help you coast right through almost anything. You want to try one?" Sheila offered.

"Yeah, thanks. I'll take you up on your offer."

Macy went through the night of nude dancing dazed from the drug and realizing that her naked body had a room full of men yelling and throwing money. It always gave her a feeling of euphoria. For almost eighteen years of her life she had heard how ugly, different, and unworthy she was. She was in a room where her presence was being called for as she left the stage. But she knew from the past that the feeling of euphoria would be followed by the feelings of being looked at as a piece of meat, a cheap whore, and a person with no respect for herself. Sure some of the customers looked at her as a piece of fine art, but others yelled horrible words at her. Tell tale signs of what they felt about a woman who took her clothes off in front of strangers. Becoming a dancer had put her in the confusing position of being praised for her outer beauty, and punished for it at the same time.

It was times like this, shut in a dark room, showing her body to strangers when she would ask herself "What in the hell am I doing here?"

When the dance was over, two of the three men handed her forty dollars each. The third customer waited for the other two to leave. He approached Macy with his hand outstretched. She thought it held money but instead he handed her a jewelry box. The bouncer moved closer to be aware of the customer's intentions.

Macy was not intimidated by this customer. He had been a regular in the club as long as she could remember. He seemed harmless, never aggressive, and had often given her gifts. She'd received outfits, jewelry, fruit baskets, and vacation offers. Most of the gifts came from this customer. He seemed to take a liking to her for some reason, more so than any of the other girls. She had named him "Santa"

"Hi Santa. What's this?" she cooed.

"Just a little something for you." He shyly replied.

Macy looked down at the burgundy velvet ring box. She opened it to find a pear shaped topaz with six diamond baguettes on each side. She gasped at the beauty of the stones. They glistened even under the black light in the room.

"Oh Santa is this for me?" she shrieked.

"Yes it's for you."

She kissed him on the cheek, and he took the chance to hug her with one arm, knowing that with the bouncer standing so close he'd never get a chance to put both arms around her. She probably wouldn't let him fully hug her any way.

"You deserve it, you're so beautiful. Will you have a drink with me?"

"Sure just let me cover up a little, okay. I'll meet you at the bar."

Santa left the room beaming from the simple kiss that the beauty had planted on his cheek. He was crazy for the dancer. He gave her gifts because he wanted to. He had more money than he could ever spend and he chose to spend some of it on the toffee colored nymph. Her shaking body lulled him into peacefulness. Even if he never got anything from her in return, he enjoyed giving her gifts and watching her smile. He walked over to the bar and waited for her to join him.

Macy and Santa finished their first round of drinks, and ordered seconds while they continued to discuss the weather, current news, and the stock exchange. She had slipped on her new ring and each time Macy lifted her glass to her lips the lights of the club collided with the cuts in the stones of her new ring. It gave off an evening light show. She purposefully held her glass with her ringed hand so that the gift giver would enjoy the sight of his well spent money being worn with majestic beauty. After the second rounds of drinks were empty she made her thank yous, and explained that she'd had a long day and was ready to go home. He was content with the quality time that she had just spent with him and did not pout. He would love to have her to himself all of the time, to keep her off the dance stage showing everyone her naked body. But with his type of upscale lifestyle, he was expected to have a mate of the same qualities. His family and friends expected him to find a mate in a woman from a well-to-do family, not a nude dancer. Macy informed Kenneth that she needed a taxi.

When Macy entered the building Amber pounced out of her apartment causing them both to jump with excitement.

"I'm sorry!" Amber exclaimed. "I've been waiting for you to get home. I can't sleep, too much on my mind." She pulled her door shut and joined Macy in her walk towards the hallway stairs.

"Did you speak with the future dad?" Macy asked as they entered the apartment.

"No, I didn't get a chance to." She began to pull pillows off Macy's sofa, knowing that her friend would be pulling out the sleep sofa. "He's not back yet remember?" She flopped down on the now pulled out sofa bed.

Macy had been listening from the back room as she unpacked her bag and undressed. She slipped an oversized t-shirt over her head and pulled her hair into a ponytail. With a fluffy bed pillow under each arm, she left the small back room and joined her friend. She hit Amber with one of the pillows and then tossed it onto the bed.

"What a mess you've gotten yourself into girl! I told you to leave that cute stranger alone on the first day that he approached you. Who in the hell is he supposed to be on vacation with? His sister? Yeah right! Honey, let me be the first to say that your Mr. Hardware, that scum sucking bastard is married!"

"No way! Macy don't be so negative. Just because he didn't tell me that he was going on vacation, doesn't mean that he has a wife. We haven't actually declared this "thing" Amber made the gesture of quotation marks with her fingers, "between us a relationship. Maybe he just doesn't feel that he has to check in with me."

"I guess that's the reason you think he won't give you a home telephone number too, huh?"

No response came from Amber as she began to cry. She tucked herself under the sheet along with the pillow that Macy had tossed at her, and allowed the confusion and fear that she felt to take over her body. Macy realized that she had been too frank with her friend before the girl was ready. She felt horrible about Amber's situation but was certain that she was correct in her assessment of Jason. She too climbed under the sheet.

"Amber?"

"Yeah."

"I'm sorry if I was too hard, but I don't like seeing you stressing out. It makes me feel bad, and I don't want to see any jerk ass man take advantage of you. Big sisters protect you know," she elbowed Amber in the side, "and don't get your snots on my sheets."

They both giggled and then fell into much needed slumber, Amber with a hand over her stomach.

The morning sun streamed through the apartment through cracks in the blinds in the windows. Amber was the first to wake up. Nausea kept her from staying in a lying position. She sat up hoping to keep from throwing up. Macy stirred, and turned over to look at the clock on the kitchen wall. It was nine thirty in the morning. She sat up and swung her feet over the side of the bed. The sun's rays caused a glare to bounce from her new ring. She had forgotten to put the gift away. The ring was so beautiful but it represented ugliness. Adult games were confusing. If she enjoyed the ring, did that mean she enjoyed the way that she'd gotten it? The velvet box that the ring had come in was in her bag. She raced to the closet to put the ring away as if closing the lid over the ring would stop the thought flooding her mind. First the conversation with Janice, now the after effects of strip dancing. She came out of the closet feeling light-headed from swelling emotions.

Heading towards the kitchen, she stopped to sprinkle fish food into the fish tank. Miz Catfish poked her head out from behind one of the plastic plants. It rushed out from its cover to eat the flakes hitting the bottom. The guppies at the top of the tank performed water aerobics as if there was an award to be won. Macy reached into the cupboard over the counter and pulled down a package of Oreo cookies. This morning she did not want her body to feel sexy. Sexy made men look at her, drool for her, buy her jewelry. "Oreo cookies" she thought "would help change that." She poured herself a glass of milk. Six cookies, the seventh held between her teeth. "I'll keep eating until they stop looking."

Amber focused sleepy eyes on Macy. "What are you doing eating cookies first thing in the morning?"

"I don't have time to eat anything else. I grabbed the first thing I could that didn't have to be cooked." Macy had not shared with her friend her means of making extra money. She was not sure if she would. "I'm going jogging. You wanna come?" She realized that a conflict existed within her. The urge to eat until she was unattractive but on the other hand, the need to stay fit and in shape. She did not understand the conflicting desires; maybe someday she'd ask a psychiatrist.

"No thanks. I think I'll go shower, and then go upstairs to visit with Mae-Belle before I go to work. I promised her that I would and maybe the sun will feel good on my tired body if I sit long enough."

"Well I'm out of here. Pull the door closed behind yourself, and I'll catch up to you later."

Chapter 17

CeCe tossed the blue rubber ball to her son. The ball was sold in the pet shop as a dog toy, but she had purchased one for Manuel to play with. The sun's rays felt warm and soothing. Today was CeCe's day off and Manuel was happy to have her home.

"Cacha! (Catch) Manuel!" CeCe yelled excitedly. She threw the ball towards him, and it flew over his shoulder, landing on the ground, where it began a steady roll down the sidewalk.

The blue ball stopped against the sole of a well worn black, dusty, laced up Army boot. Manuel stopped to retrieve the ball as Ortega reached down and scooped it up.

"Hola, mi amigo!" Ortega bellowed joyously. "Como esta? Choo ar-r-e smiling today. Hah!"

Manuel felt a sense of ease when this man spoke to him. It was a feeling that he hadn't enjoyed since he and his mother had left their family. The man was taking an interest in him like the men at home. He could speak to this man in Spanish like the people he'd grown up with. Everyone in this strange place spoke words that Manuel couldn't understand. He couldn't ask anyone where his grandpa was, or his mother when she leaves him home by himself. This man was speaking to him in what sounded like a melody to his small ears.

"Ven aca pequeno, tu' tienes que estrechar la manode sus manos. (Come, little man. You must shake Ortega's hand. All men shake hands.) Come." Ortega stretched out his right hand to Manuel, and held onto the ball in the other.

Manuel stepped forward to shake the hand in front of him, taking notice of the long black hairs curling out from the back of it. They matched the thick mustache that formed a hairdo under his nose. He quickly glanced at the back of his own miniature hand for the signs of manhood. "Not yet" he thought.

"Manuel! Manuel! Ven aca aqui! (Come now. Quickly!") CeCe snapped as she rushed toward her son. ("I told you not to speak to anyone.) Yo te dije que no le hablaras a nadie. Tu' me tienes que obedecer. (You must obey me.")

Ortega released the boy's hand, and passed the ball back to Manuel. As the blue sphere landed in the middle of the small palm, CeCe's heart skipped a beat. She was now close enough to hear the voice of the stranger speaking to her son. The sound of his heavy Spanish accent, along with his dark Spanish facial features knocked her off balance and reminded her how home sick she was for her native land and family.

"He is safe weeth mee. Wee are being friends." Ortega said as he ruffled the top of Manuel's hair. "If choo were not so lovely, I thought that choo could be a bull coming!" he joked. "I am Jorge Tomas Ortega. Tu' hablas inglés? (Do choo speak English?") he asked CeCe, switching from English to Spanish to comfort the protective mother.

"Si. I mean, (yes,) I speak English. My name is Cecilia Ana Maria Ortiz. You've met Manuel my son?" She felt her imaginary woven basket of strength begin to unwind, and tears began to stream down her cheeks. Ortega pulled a handkerchief from his pocket, and wiped a tear from CeCe's face who was still uneasily tossing the ball from one hand to the other.

Manuel watched the adults.

"I have not heard anyone speak Spanish since I've been living here, I am very home sick for my family back in the Dominican Republic. I guess your conversation with my son caught me off guard. I'm sorry. You must think that I am silly to stand here crying like this." She used the back of her hand to wipe at the rest of the tears that remained on her face.

"I am in quite a mess here in this country; I have had no one to talk to that I feel would understand. My son does not understand the problems that we could face." She stopped short of finishing her sentence and looked Ortega in the eyes to see if he was on to what she was about to say. She didn't know this stranger. Yet she couldn't hold back any longer her need to share her visit from the woman at the Department of Social Services, and her illegal status in the country. She needed a confidant.

"My time here has been very stressful. A lady came to my door from an office that threatens to take my son from me. I have no papers to show them, I do not want to go back. I can't handle all of this sneaking around any longer."

Ortega put a finger under her chin and forced her to look directly at him. He gave her a confident, macho grin, and said "Sh-h-h. Choo will bee okay. We weel figure things out. Choo are too beautiful to have such worries. Some matters are for the man of the house. Tell me about this woman that has scared choo so, and the rest of your woes and I will take care of them." he said confidently.

They sat on the stairs of the building and CeCe told Ortega her story from beginning to end. She felt lighter knowing that she had someone to share her problems, but she would have to wait to find out if this person could truly be trusted. Ortega stood and gently rubbed the back of her shaking hand.

"Choo and the little man get some rest now. I will come back another day to further discuss this situation, and I will know what to do to help. My friend Machie lives here; and I was coming to see her. I will walk choo inside." he ended with his usual confidence.

"Manuel. Vena ca! Nosotros vamos a la casa ahora. (We are going in the house now.)" CeCe called.

She took Manuel's hand and headed into the building. Ortega followed close behind the pair, watching CeCe's behind sway in her blue jeans. He went on to Macy's apartment door but not without remembering to be alert to the possibility of running into Janice and her sharp tongue. He got no response at Macy's door. He left the building without disappointment over the missed visit because now he'd stumbled upon a Spanish damsel to woo.

CeCe listened to the sounds of the night, and the ticking of her alarm clock on the kitchen counter. She'd been lying restlessly for hours, waiting for sleep and certainly of her decision to come. Who was Jorge Tomas Ortega? She turned onto her side, trying to calm herself by changing position on her blanket. CeCe's thoughts sounded so loud in her mind that she worried the commotion would cause her to cover her own ears.

CeCe was entering into her second relationship with a strange man since the landlord at the rooming house. Dealing with that stranger had helped her progress towards her goal, and this man would have to be handled in the same manner, a step further towards her goal. Manuel stirred in his sleep, letting out a slight snore.

Amber sat across from Mae-Belle on the roof top. The younger woman stared off into space. While the older woman watched birds fly past and blend with the clouds in the sky, both women nursed glasses of iced tea that had once been cold, but now had lost its frost in the sweat that run down the sides of their glasses.

Amber's voice broke the silence. "Mae-Belle."

"Yes sweetie."

"I'm pregnant." Amber tried to keep her voice from revealing her nervousness. What would the older woman think of her?

Mae-Belle turned in her seat to face Amber. "Are you sure?"

"Yes. I took a home pregnancy test, and I haven't gotten my period."

"How do you feel about this?"

"I'm not sure. I'm somewhere between amazement and complete fear." Amber's voice shook, threatening to reveal her true emotions.

"Have you told the father yet?"

"No. Not yet."

"If you don't mind me asking, who is he?" Mae-Belle asked hoping that she was not being too forceful.

"Jason Michaels. He owns the hardware store down the street." Amber tried to loose eye contact with Mae-Belle. She was wondering what Mae-Belle was thinking.

Mae-Belle was quiet for a few seconds while she pondered on a way to comfortably find out if Amber knew of Jason's marital status. She looked at the innocence on the girl's face and concluded that she probably didn't.

"So you're who he's been coming here to see. I've seen his car in front a few times, and I wondered who he was visiting in the building. I've known him and his family for years." Mae-Belle paused, regretting the task of what she was about to say. "He's married sweetie."

Amber's eyes fluttered as if she would faint. Mae-Belle noticed the girl's body physically slump backwards as if she'd been punched in the stomach. Her rosy pink lips were noticeably agape until they were covered by her hand to muffle the groan that was about to flee her throat.

Mae-Belle lightly touched Amber's knee "Amber? I'm sorry. I had to tell you."

Amber slowly removed her hand from her mouth, "Are you sure?" she asked in between gasps for air.

"Oh, I'm sure. I know his car, and like I said I've known his family for years. My father used to buy supplies from the hardware store. I know all of Jason's brothers and sisters. I've become friends with his wife and children." Mae-Belle calmly explained.

Amber doubled over onto Mae-Belle's lap sobbing loudly. Her words were muffled by the butter yellow cloth of the dress beneath her face.

"What have I done?"

"I can't hear you sweetie." Mae-Belle said lifting the girl's head from her lap.

Amber swiped at her eyes. "What have I done? I've gotten myself in a terrible mess. Why would he do this? Why'd he lie?"

Janice sat on the front stairs of the building with her favorite snack of pickled pigs feet and a can of soda. Ortega walked up to the building. He stopped in front of Janice, looking at her as if she was to pass him a message that he was expecting. She looked at him from his small pea green colored hat, to his dark, shiny "I can see you, but you can't see me" sunglasses. Her gaze skimmed past his pants and stopped again on his square toed black boots. He looked like a wannabe, or used-to-be Don Juan.

"Hallo. Do choo know if Machie and Cecilia are home?" Ortega asked with caution.

"Why are you asking? Janice asked with a mother's protective glare.

"Why choo lookin' at me like I should go back to the dirk?" Ortega quipped.

"The what!"

"The dirk. The dirk! Choo know on the ground."

Mister, I don't care where you come from. You stopped to speak to me. I didn't say anything to you." Janice snapped.

"Why are choo so evil? Choo lookin' for a husband?" he tried to soothe in his manner.

"You better get away from me! I saw you here once before speaking to little Manuel, but you don't know me. Who the hell are you anyway?" Janice's tone became threatening.

"I am Jorge Tomas Ortega. Never forget that name; it belongs to a very special person. Choo believe me?"

"I don't have to believe you or give a care. You're a nut!"

"Choo need me to be your man. Choo won't be cranky any more." Ortega offered with the wink of an eye.

"You better go see Macy, or CeCe before you say anything else. You're getting too comfortable with your lips and your tongue." Janice warned.

"I'll come for you later. Goodbye, beautiful lady."

He tipped his hat as he passed on the way into the building. She shook her head and went back to eating her snack.

Macy answered the door sweaty from her jog. "Hi Ortega."

"Hello Machie."

"Come on in but I warn you I'm not in a good mood." Macy snapped.

"Your friend downstairs is cranky because she needs a husband. Choo got the same problems?"

"What friend downstairs? Are you bothering my neighbors?"

"I don't know lady. Sometime choo lookin' funny to me. Choo lookin' to me like someone in love!" he teased.

"Ortega I'm not in the mood for your foolishness. So shut up or leave. Don't get used to dropping by anytime you damn well please either!"

"Okay, okay. I can give choo a massage. It'll make choo feel better." he offered.

He moved over to where Macy stood and put out his hand towards her back. "Ortega don't even try it!"

He continued on with his thought and as soon as Macy felt his hand on her back she yelled "OUT! GET OUT! You're aggravating me. You cuckoo nut!"

She stomped to the door and swung it open, allowing her right foot to loudly tap the floor while she waited for him to exit the apartment. She slammed the door loudly on his heels.

Ortega's hat swayed as his head moved from side to side. His hands flailed in mid-air as he mumbled to himself in Spanish about the temperament of American women, as he made his way to CeCe's apartment.

Ortega took hat in hand, and put on his most gentlemanly, sincere face, as he knocked on CeCe's door.

"Hello." CeCe's voice nervously responded from the other side.

"It is me, Jorge Tomas Ortega."

CeCe opened the door a small crack, peeped out allowing only one chestnut brown eye to show, and then opened the door entirely to allow her visitor inside.

Ortega entered and immediately began walking around the apartment. Manuel's eyes widened with excitement as he stepped out of the bathroom and once again got to be in the company of his new friend.

"Hey, my little man!" shouted Ortega at the sight of Manuel.

"Hola!" Manuel responded.

Manuel turned back in the direction of his mother, searching her face for approval of his friend. Ortega also turned to face CeCe. She was still standing by the door as if she had entered as a visitor.

"Why does your face look so sad? Come over here with the men, we are happy over here. I come to fix your problem. Come on now, smile." he encouraged.

CeCe dragged across the room to hear Ortega out. What ever he had to say it couldn't hurt to listen. The woman from the Department of Social Services would be back soon and she had to be ready for the visit.

"Come on Cecilia. Let's see your beautiful smile." Ortega urged.

"Call me CeCe, everyone does." CeCe offered giving herself more time to collect her thoughts.

"Well the way I see things ladee, if we go to another state not far from here called New Hampshire, for a marriage, the process could be done right away, and a person that I know there will make sure that all of your information will be fine for a cost."

At the mention of the word marriage Ortega noticed CeCe's eyes go wide and tear up. He pushed forward with his proposal.

"I am Puerto Rican, so I can make choo a citizen. I will move in here with choo and little man, but of course this will all take some changing around of my very busy life. Would choo be able to get some money?"

Ortega was a genuine con artist and felt no shame in his offer, or in taking advantage of the girl's situation. He wore a comforting smile on his face.

CeCe tried to catch her breath, and couldn't find words to respond to Ortega's proposal. Yes, it was an answer to her problem, but did she want to marry herself to this Puerto Rican stranger who had just strutted into her home like a rooster from her farm yard at home? Did he say that he was going to move in today? She was not even sure that she could trust him or that he wasn't a murderer even.

"CeCe? Are choo going to let me help you?"

"Si…Y-yes-s. Okay." She answered unsteadily. The blue ball hopped into the air and landed on her lap. She passed the ball back to Manuel. The small hand belonging to her son reminded her once again of her reason for making these distasteful choices. She steeled herself in preparation to deal with Ortega and the situation at hand.

"How much money? I'll have to get in touch with my parents. Do you know a quick, reliable way to do such a thing? I will ask." CeCe tried to sound in control.

"I will need at least five thousand American dollars. This is very important, they will understand." he pushed. "I will take good care of choo and we can make a good family." Ortega smiled. "We can send your message to your family by wire service today."

"Alright, we'll go today. How will I ever thank you enough Mr-r." What was she to call her future husband?

"Jorge." Ortega corrected. "We will be husband and wife soon. I don't think Mr. Ortega will work for choo any longer."

"Choo work?" Ortega asked trying not to sound as excited as he felt. "A woman who works is not lazy to take care of her family, and help her husband climb to his dreams. Where do choo work?"

"At the Pet Shop down the street from the building. I have one day off, and six days I work."

"That's good, that's very good. Choo are a good woman. I will come back in two days for your answer."

CeCe's head dropped into her hands. Manuel moved to his mother's side protectively, not understanding the sudden changes in his mother's emotions - and now she was crying. Ortega wrapped his arms around the nervous woman. She felt warm and supple against his body. He reminded himself that this was a new situation for the young woman and not a good time to move his hands down to her round butt cheeks.

CeCe felt the arms enclose her, and the smell of masculine musk and sweat invaded her nostrils. She realized that becoming a wife meant that these odors would become a presence in her life. The arms that enclosed her were also about to become a part of her life as well. CeCe's sobs reached from her lungs to the pit of her stomach as she entered another passage of her journey. Ortega stroked her long, dark black hair.

"Choo must never cut this beautiful hair. I like it this way." He was making a statement not a request.

CeCe wired her parents for the money with a complete explanation of her situation. She expressed the urgency of their response, and asked for a blessing over the marriage. Even though it was for business purposes she'd treat her vows and husband as if they were sent to her de Dios.

Carlos and Mariana Ortiz promptly responded to their daughter's wire. They sent the money, their blessing, and shared their worry about CeCe and their grandson's situation.

CeCe cried, holding onto the Western Union envelope from home. She held the cardholder beneath her nose, as if to smell her mother's perfume, tobacco leaf, anything to bring a native touch of the Dominican Republic to her lonely spirit.

Miz Catfish

Chapter 18

Janice got up from the stairs and went into the house to check on her napping children.

As she entered her living room, the telephone rang. She answered it quickly before it could wake the sleeping children.

"Hello."

"Hi Aisha."

"HeyGrandma!"

"How are my babies?"

"They're fine. Right now they're sleeping." she said smiling.

"I forgot to ask you the last time we spoke, are they asking about their father a lot?"

"Well, Teri was for a while, but I notice that lately she hasn't."

"Your mother tells me that he shows up from time to time still asking about you."

"The thought of him finding me scares me to death. I feel bad that he's bothering my mother." Janice allowed her fears to reflect outward.

"Don't worry about her honey. She can handle him. You know how tough your mama is." her grandma reassured.

"Grandma, did you talk to my mother about Mrs. Jenkins?"

"Yes, I did. She wants you to call her."

Janice felt giddy with excitement. "Does she remember Macy?"

"Call your mother okay? And give those babies a hug for me. I can't talk long, these calls cost money you know." Grandma chastised.

"Okay then, I'll call my mother later. I love you. Bye."

Janice sat down on her sofa with a look of confusion on her face. Why did her mother want her to call instead of simply giving her grandmother any information that she could remember? She decided to wait until later in the evening to call her mother. She checked on the children again before going back outside.

Once back on the stairs, Janice had more time to think about the confusing conversation with her grandmother. Why hadn't she heard from her mother? She was beginning to wonder if she had opened a can of worms by asking about Macy and Mrs. Betty Jenkins.

A tall, slender, dark-skinned black man got out of a forest green Jaguar in front of the building. He walked over to the stairs and realized that he couldn't get past Janice who sat in the middle of the doorway. She didn't look like the friendliest person to strike up a conversation with. Not that he wanted to, but he did want to get into the building.

"How are you? Do you know what apartment Macy Jenkins lives in?"

"Yeah, are you a friend of hers?" Janice questioned.

"Well, I guess you could say that. Are you the landlord?" he inquired.

"No, and if you're her friend then how come you don't know which apartment she lives in? Is she expecting you?" Janice was making a habit of protecting Macy. He had spotted the mailboxes in the hallway behind Janice. "Not really I'm surprising her. Can I get by now since it doesn't seem like you're going to help me with an apartment number?" Realizing that he didn't need her any more he cut the conversation off. "Excuse me." He entered the building and stopped at the mailboxes. Skimming across the names in the name slots he came to Macy Jenkins's apartment number three.

Macy was sitting on the floor in front of the fish tank mesmerized by the occupants aquatic performance when a knock at the door broke the spell.

"Hello?" Macy yelled from behind the door.

"Michael."

"Michael?" She opened the door quickly and threw her arms around his neck.

"Well, hello to you too. Does this mean that you're happy to see me?" he asked with hope in his voice.

"Of course I am!"

"I wouldn't have guessed it by the mood of your security guard downstairs. You're going to have to give me your telephone number so I can call before I come. Then maybe you can let her know, so she'll back off. I think she was going to frisk me!" he laughed. "Waiting for you to call me was hell."

"What kind of hostess am I? Come on in." She let go of his neck so that he could move in from the hallway. "Let me show you around the place. It's a thousand times different from my last place." She moved to the window to see the person on the stairs that both Ortega and Michael had spoken of. The only person that she could see on the stairs below was Janice. She smiled to think that the new friend, and maybe old childhood acquaintance was taking a personal interest in her. It felt nice to have someone looking over her. She hadn't had much of that in her life, and she would definitely not say anything to Janice about her self-appointed position of security guard.

Macy returned her attention to her guest. "Were my directions easy to follow?"

"Yes, perfect."

Macy had not seen Michael since his last visit to her old home. She had to admit that seeing him again felt good, and she'd missed him.

Michael sat on the sofa and stretched out across its length. He called her over and pulled her down next to him. She snuggled into the crook of his arm, and wrapped her arm around his chest, enjoying the masculine broadness. Sex was not necessary. Macy was grateful that the visit had not turned sexual. She didn't want to be looked at sexually today. Every time she danced at the club, she was nothing but a sexual exhibit. Just being treated like any other woman who needed her emotions stroked was what she needed today.

Outside daylight turned to sunset causing the room to become gray and shadowed. The two friends continued holding each other comfortable in the silence that had fallen between them, until Michael's stomach began to rumble. He laughed, "Do you want to go out for dinner?"

"No thanks. I don't feel like going out tonight. How about if I cook up something?" she offered.

"Okay with me. I won't be picky, as long as I eat." he rubbed his hands together.

They ate French fries and cheeseburgers, chased down with cold beers. Michael gave Macy a check as a housewarming gift, then fter a long, sensual kiss, he left.

The knock at the door was one that CeCe both needed and dreaded to hear. While Ortega's return meant that she would not be an illegal any longer, it also meant that she would soon become the bride of a total stranger. She took a deep breath, a glance at the Western Union envelope on the counter and opened the door.

"Hola!" Ortega tipped his pea green hat at CeCe. "Hello beeutiful ladie." He had a way of making his voice and vocabulary seem to be a non-stop serenade. "Choo arre lookin' muy bueno today. Am I too soon?" Ortega was in the room and closing the door behind him before CeCe realized that she'd moved out of the doorway.

"No, you are in good time. I have an answer from my family." CeCe moved on shaky legs to pick up the colorful envelope, and handed the money to Ortega without looking him in the eyes.

"Don't worry, Ortega will take very good care of choo." Sticking the money in his wallet, Ortega tried not to reveal the eagerness that he felt to get to the bank to change the money into American dollars.

He would be able to pay back the money he borrowed from his boss at the taxi company. There were retired taxis in back of the office and now he'd be able to buy one of them. The family would need a car, and appropriate furniture for the house. The rest of the money would become his savings.

"I have some things to take care of. I must call my friend in New Hampshire to prepare for the marriage I promised choo." He reached out with both hands and turned her around to get a clear look from all angles. What size do choo weer? Choo will need a nice dress to become a wife. Your feet are a cup full, what size do choo need?"

CeCe answered Ortega's questions, feeling helpless to do anything else but follow his lead into the next stage of his plan.

"Don't worry any longer. Promise me that choo will get a good night sleep," he touched a finger to her chin. I'll be here at ten o'clock tomorrow morning to pick choo and Manuelito, that is little Manuel, up for our trip."

Ortega left, sucking his air of confidence out of the room with him, and leaving CeCe standing in the middle of the floor unable to reconnect to her thoughts after listening to Ortega think for her. When finally able to gather her thoughts, she realized that Manuel would need an explanation of the next day's event.

CeCe gave Manuel a short, child's version of the changes that were about to occur in their life. She explained to him that Ortega was going to marry her and come to live with them, and keep them safe.

The reality of the adult version was much more complicated. The man that promised to make her problems go away was a total stranger. What if he didn't come back? Who else could she go to for a solution to her problems? If he did come back how could she trust his intentions? Maybe he'd run off with the money, and not follow through with the agreement?

After Manuel was asleep, CeCe went into the bathroom and knelt on her knees in prayer. There was no need to continue to grieve over the choice that she'd made, she could only pray that she'd have the strength to perform her duties as a wife, and become at peace with the newest changes in her life.

Ortega arrived promptly at ten o'clock, with a dress bag and shopping bag in tow. He didn't have a free hand so he lightly kicked the door.

CeCe opened the door, surprised by the sight of the department store bags. Ortega wore a black suit, the pants were slightly wrinkled, and barely touched the top of his black boots, and the sleeves of the jacket rose a bit too much above his hairy wrists.

"Hola! Buenos dias.(Good morning.)" he kissed CeCe on the forehead as he rushed past her. "Hola Manuelito."

"Please speak to him in English Orteg, I mean Jorge. Spanish is alright because I want him to keep his native language, but he needs to learn English."

"Si Manuelito your mother is correct. A good woman in the home is very importan,." Ortega conceded. "My friend is waiting for us to arrive, but first choo must get dressed proper for my wife," he passed her the bags.

"These are for choo."

"Gracias (thank you.)" CeCe spoke softly. She took the gifts into the bathroom and was surprised to find a bright pink dress, a pair of strappy white sandals, and an artificial pearl necklace, with matching earrings. The items were thoughtful, but it had been a long time since her clothes were picked out by someone else, and the pink dress was dreams away from the white hand sewn wedding dress, with a long veil and train trimmed in lace, made by CeCe's grandmother, and worn by CeCe's mother and waited for her in the back of her mother's closet. Everything about today was dreams away from yesterday. She dressed in the bathroom and returned to the living room feeling like a mannequin.

"Choo will be like a princess complete after choo pull your beautiful hair up in a bun. Even in America all Spanish women need to be Spanish, even Dominican. Okay?"

CeCe mumbled "Yes." as she lifted her arms and began to pull her hair into a bun. She dug into her bag and pulled out a rhinestone hair pin that she'd bought at the convenience store down the street. She felt mechanical.

"Manuelito, my little man, let's go. We are the men; we have business to take care of."

They climbed into the car that read taxi on the doors. Manuel hadn't been away from the building since they'd moved there, and he was excited at the idea of leaving the

Miz Catfish

front steps. He slid his bottom across the spongy back seat until he could close the door, then found the window handle and cranked the glass up and down until his mother chastised him in their native language to behave himself. He left the window slightly lowered and slid back in the seat. He wondered why his mother wasn't excited about the ride. Instead she seemed irritated.

Ortega spoke to Manuel during the entire drive to New Hampshire. He made plans with him to take him to an amusement park, a lake to swim and fish, and pointed out large rocky areas along the highway as the white striped, black topped road stretched out in front of them. CeCe added to the conversation only when spoken to. All of the scenic beauty that passed along the road may have well been falling on blind eyes as far as her mind was concerned. The only thoughts running through the girl's mind was the marriage that she was about to enter into, with the owner of the hairy hands that gripped the steering wheel.

They pulled into the small parking lot of a square building that looked to be no larger than the Pet Shop where she worked. Even with the red, white, and blue American flag draping from the tall black pole, and the engraved words CITY HALL over its doors, it still gave off no suggestion of importance. Ortega turned off the ignition and opened his door; Manuel took signal from him and swung his open as well. They both slammed their doors shut and headed for the doors of the building, as if they had been there many times before. CeCe fumbled with her door handle, trying to will her fingers to close around the warm piece of steel that would open the door to another drastic change in her life. Ortega looked back, and CeCe quickly shoved the door open and swung her legs out of the car, in order to not appear indecisive as whether or not she was going to go through with the ceremony. She didn't want the man to think she was ungrateful for what he was doing for her and her son, and maybe get angry and take her back to Boston without having gone through with the ceremony.

She left the car, smoothed her clothes, and steadied her legs to follow her men into the building. Besides she couldn't back out now, he knew her secret and might tell someone.

They stood before the Justice of the Peace, a tall man with a face red from too much sun, and were married. This was the first of five scheduled marriages of this type for Michael Kearn who had been a Justice of the Peace for twenty two years. He didn't consider it his business if illegals came into the country, so he made a little side money when his neighbor sent people to him for assistance with legal paperwork. Michael made sure that the names, birth information, and dates were filed in properly, and he personally walked the paperwork to the clerk's office to have it stamped and approved. Ortega handed him the envelope with the money for the marriage, and the additional money for the social security cards that would make his new family officially legal. Ortega drove through a McDonald's drive-through and bought Manuel his first cheeseburger Happy Meal. CeCe accepted a cup of ice water, not feeling the urge to eat anything. She wasn't even sure of the proper spelling of her new last name.

Once back home Ortega dropped his family off and went back to his place to pack. He moved out of the shabby rooming house without looking back. Taking on a wife and kid would not cause any disruption in his life. It would be nice to have hot cooked meals, washed clothes, and a warm body to

Miz Catfish

snuggle up to. He would prefer to stay with a Puerto Rican woman, but this last year of being without a "good woman" couldn't come to an end soon enough for him. He needed a woman in his life to do "woman things" and a young Dominican girl would have to do. Watching her fill out the marriage license he saw her age to be twenty three. He was a strong fifty two years of age, and would have to get CeCe used to seeing him keep his hair black with hair dye, maybe even doing the task for him.

   Ortega moved his few pieces of furniture into the apartment allowing Manuel to carry his large caballero style hat and poncho. Manuel wanted to carry the shiny brown guitar that lay on the back seat of the car, but Ortega explained to him that he was not ready for that responsibility. Ortega knew that his old bed would not make the best impression on CeCe, but with a new mattress they would at least enjoy the comfort of being off the floor. He promised Manuel that he'd only have to sleep on his old sofa for a short time, then the two of them would go to the store to buy Manuel a bed shaped like a race car, and a few toys. CeCe wasn't aware of this conversation pertaining to future purchases. Ortega didn't feel she had to be. He'd continue driving taxis, and she would continue her job at the Pet Shop.

   CeCe came home from work to find the two sitting on red milk crates watching a television that Ortega had sat on the counter. Manuel greeted her with a hug and a smile that she hadn't seen in a long time. She wasted no time getting dinner started, filling the apartment with the mingled odors of plantains, refried beans, and beef cubes pre-seasoned with Sofrito.

Miz Catfish

   The vision of the bed sitting in the middle of her bedroom floor caught CeCe off guard, causing her stomach to tighten along with the feeling of heat running through her veins. It had slipped her mind that she'd have to, be expected to, sleep with Ortega and have sex with Ortega. This man was her husband, but in her mind he was the third man with whom she'd share her body. She dreaded the nights to come with Ortega just as she had spent her nights waiting for her previous landlord. This time her predator would be legally lying beside her every night. Rubbing his hairy hands on her back and his yet to be seen feet would touch her legs. Moving quickly to the bathroom she barely made it to the toilet before she vomited. She simultaneously used her left hand to turn on the faucet in an attempt to use the water to over shadow the sound of her wretching. She knew her nerves were on the edge to say the least, but there was nothing available to her to fix her situation except to wash her face and go back into the living room that was now filled with the sounds of guitar strings being pulled and sizzling plantains.

   Ortega answered the door on Mary Rivers's third knock. He stood in the doorway admiring her appearance by openly allowing his head to move vertically from her head to the tips of her shoes.

   "Is Cecilia at home?" she said, breaking the silence.

   "No. She is not here now. Would you like me to help choo?" he offered while still eyeing her.

   "No. Not unless you live here. Do you?" she asked.

   "Yes I do live here. How did choo know, or are choo as smart as choo are beautiful?" he flirted.

"Would you mind if I came in to ask a few questions? Ms. Ortiz knew that I would be coming, she just didn't know exactly at what time," she explained.

"Welcome Madame." he moved aside allowing her to enter the apartment.

Immediately after entering the doorway she noticed the fullness of the rooms that had not been bare before. There was living room furniture, curtains, pictures on the wall reflecting Spanish culture, and a picture of the man that had opened the door.

"Is her son Manuel here?" Mary asked as she settled herself on the sofa.

"Si, but he's taking a naps right now. Why are choo asking for my family by name, but I don't know your name?" Ortega asked.

"My name is Mary Rivers. I'm from the Department of Social Services. I was here before and I don't remember any mention of you. Are you related to Ms. Ortiz?"

"I am her husband. We are a private people, so if choo didn't ask CeCe for her business why would she tell choo? Do choo work for the police?" Ortega shot at the woman invading his home.

"I work for the Department of Social Services as I previously stated. I have already had a talk with Ms. Ortiz concerning the situation of her son being left unattended to, and I told her that I would have to return. Is she at work?"

"Si. My wife is at work. Actually her name is Mrs. Ortega, but because here a woman can think that she is a man, she had decided to use her family's name. Also Manuel is not my own son but she must show family unity for him. Soon we will have other babies and they will be Puerto Rican strong like myself with my name only. I am sure that your husband would understand." Ortega smiled while allowing his right hand to stroke his mustache.

"Well just tell Ms. Ortiz that I came by as I said I would. But I won't need to come by again. Our main concern was that the little boy was not being neglected. Obviously that is not the case here. If she had mentioned to me that she was married, for how long did you say?" she decided to throw the trick question into the conversation. If he was lying, maybe she could catch him off guard and get the truth about the young lady's and boy's legal status.

"For two years, and three months. We have our paper in the frame on the wall over there." pointing to the silver scrolled picture frame next to his portrait on the wall. He proudly retrieved the frame from the wall and handed it to Mary.

"You got married in New Hampshire. How did you come to be in East Boston?" she asked.

"My cousin here needed some help with his business. My job there in New Hampshire was not doing so good I brought my family here, and went to work for Jose."

"Do you find Massachusetts likable compared to New Hampshire? The winters are different. New Hampshire has a lot more snow, but then again the view of the harbor from the windows here in this building are lovely. Well it's good to know that your wife has someone to help watch Manuel. Are you able to work your job schedule so that he is not left alone in the apartment?"

"I was not aware of the problem but that is over I assure choo. But now that is no problem. As choo can see, I am home now while she works. I am gone most nights. Sometimes I fill in for workers that are not coming to work. I drive a taxi."

Mary handed him the frame, and he returned it to its place on the wall. She rose from the sofa and ran her hand down the front of her skirt to smooth out the wrinkles made from sitting. She moved back into an upright position and noticed Ortega seductively watching her.

"Well Mister…what did you say your name is?" Mary asked while taking her pen and notebook back out of her large black shoulder bag.

"I am Jorge Tomas Ortega." he repeated with a toothy smile. "Feel free to call me Ortega. If you ever need a taxi give me a call. I will come immediately for a beautiful ladie like choo." He removed his wallet from his back pocket and pulled a business card from it. He handed it to her, making sure not to take his eyes from hers.

"Thank you, Mr. Ortega. I rarely take taxis, but if I ever need one, I'll think of you and your offer." She tucked the card, her pen, and the notebook into her bag. "I'll be leaving now." She felt Ortega's eyes watching her backside as she walked to the door. The hair stood up on the back of her neck. She opened the door enough to squeeze her body out pulling it shut behind her. She made a mental note to herself to never call for a taxi from the company name on the business card that he had given her. A taxi that pulled up to her door with him behind the wheel would leave with out a passenger.

When CeCe returned home from work later that evening, Ortega told her about the visit from the woman of the

Department of Social Services. Assuring her that the woman would not return, he reminded her that all she'd needed was a husband in her life. He pulled her into his arms and kissed her long and aggressively, using his hands to grip her behind and rub in a circular motion. The thought of these moves of affection leading to the act of sex almost made CeCe want to push him away. Wouldn't that be ungrateful after all that he had just done for her and her son? Wouldn't she be shirking her wifely duties? He wasn't letting her go, his grip on her behind had tightened, and she could now feel his body beginning to slowly move her towards the bedroom. Manuel was watching the new television that Ortega had bought home last night after work. His little face was cupped in his hands, as he lay on his stomach on the floor. The bright variety of colors and movement in the cartoon that he watched prevented him from noticing the adults leaving the room.

Hopefully Ortega would not want to cuddle, or have his back scratched. She had to learn to endure his touch and the act of sex, but the extra acts of spending quality time alone was more than she could get used to at the moment. After all this wasn't someone that she had fallen in love with, or was even attracted to. While Ortega wasn't hard on the eye, had a nice healthy head of hair, still had tight muscles throughout his body, and walked with a rooster strut like the rooster on the farm at home, sometimes the clothes that he put on for the day matched and other times they were mis-matched and wrinkled when he put them on. He always wore a hat when going outside. The hats varied from the kind worn on a golf course to ones worn with trench coats on a brisk fall morning. He had a black scarf that he wrapped around his head Rambo style when he wore his Army fatigue pants tucked into his worn black Army boots. He reminded her of some of the older men at home on the farm that shopped in town and mixed their American imported clothes with their home made ethnic clothes. He was very proud of himself and no matter what he wore, he wore it with confidence. He was beginning to take notice of CeCe's limited wardrobe, and told her that he'd take her shopping soon for some clothes that his wife should wear. He was attentive to her in that way. Always coming home with treats he thought she and Manuel would like. He helped brush her hair in the morning before she went to work, and told her to put her feet up after she'd finished cooking supper, and doing the dishes. Sometimes he would come home from work late at night with a cup of coffee and donut for her as a late night snack. He assured her that it was okay to enjoy some things without her son. Maybe she hadn't gotten the worst of the deal. But still after all those thoughts, the end was still the same she hadn't fallen in love with this man and chosen him as a husband or a lover. The sexual situation was again forced on her, and she was learning quickly that prostitution came in many forms.

Amber spent the time waiting for Jason's return drinking ginger ale, cups of tea and eating toast. She assumed that he'd been back from his trip for days, although he hadn't opened the store, or returned her calls when she called him. The days seemed like weeks. What would she say to him now that she knew that he was married?

She struggled to sort through her feelings since her visit with Mae-Belle. It would be wrong to continue seeing him now that she knew about his family. But how would she be able to stop seeing him now that she was in love with him, and carrying his child. There was a rage burning in her gut that caused her to clinch her jaw muscles at the thought of Jason being away with a family that she didn't even know he had. A feeling of betrayal easily turned to embarrassment with the thought of Jason laughing at how naïve she was. "I can't give out my sister's telephone number." He had told her one lie after another, tangling her life in his web of deceit.

Jason had been back from his trip for days. When he finally decided to visit her, the knock on the door startled her. Amber had returned home from work early barely controlling the nausea that threatened to take over her daily existence. The pregnancy demanded to be acknowledged. It caused her breasts to ache, and all of her spare time to be spent sleeping. A knock at the door broke that sleep.

Jason stood on the other side of the door preparing to explain to Amber about his vacation with his sister and her children. He'd explain how he had to go along to help keep the children under control. Then he and Amber would have wild sex. Considering the time of night he expected her to answer the door in her night shirt with her hair tussled and smelling of soap and shampoo.

To his surprise the door was opened by an unkempt person, pale in appearance with a scowl on her face.

"What's wrong babe?" he asked.

"You bastard!" she shouted. She attempted to slap his face, but her swing was weak and slow, giving him time to move out of the way. "What in the hell is wrong with you?" he asked as he held onto her wrist long enough to get both of their bodies into the apartment and close the door.

"Jeez, I thought I'd get a better greeting than this." he said innocently.

"Why are you here at all? Did your sister let you out? Or did you get permission from your wife!" she snapped.

Jason tried to be prepared for this moment. He knew that the building belonged to Mae-Belle Smoot. He'd known her for years, and she knew that he was married with a family. He wasn't sure if she lived in the building with her tenants or not, still he took the chance of visiting Amber and allowing lust and deception to send him into what might be the end of life as he knew it if he ever ran into Mae-Belle and she told his wife. Instead Mae-Belle must have seen him and had told Amber about his family.

"How did you find out?" he asked trying to appear unshaken by her accusation.

"What difference does that make?" she snapped. "Will that change your lie?"

"No. I just want to make sure that you got the truth," he said in as stable a voice that he could manage.

"What more truth is needed to know other than the fact that you're married? What kind of game are you playing? Where's your wedding ring?" she was on a steady roll now, emptying her mind of all that had accumulated over the past few days.

"I don't wear a wedding ring anymore and I'm not playing a game. I didn't tell you because my wife and I don't have a marriage in the way that you think. We stopped communicating a long time ago, and we don't have sex any more. I'm there for the children. She knows that as soon as they're older I'll be gone.

"So you're telling me that you two sleep together every night, even go on vacations together and don't touch each other?" she yelled as she picked up one of the pillows and tossed it at him.

"I'm telling you the truth, Amber. Why do you think I'm here instead of there?"

"Well you don't stay here long. You're running home to something."

"Yeah, to my kids."

They stood in silence. Amber quietly felt out what Jason had just told her, and Jason waited to see if Amber would accept the story he'd just spun. He wanted to feel her firm young body in his arms. To his surprise he'd missed her while he was on vacation.

He stepped forward and pulled her into an embrace causing her anger to fade to relief. She allowed him to direct her into the bedroom where he undressed her and then himself. They lay back onto the bed together and she allowed his body's sexual language to draw her further into his tale of marital woe. She dropped her guard and went along for the sinful ride.

Amber and Jason lay side by side entwined in the cherry red sheet that had become unfolded from beneath the mattress, revealing the padded top of the light blue mattress.

A startled Jason sat up with a jolt of confusion as Amber struggled to untangle herself from the sheet. Almost tripping over the sheet that now dragged the floor, she almost regained her balance long enough to place a clammy hand over her mouth, and lunge herself out the bedroom door and into the bathroom. Jason followed behind her wrapped in the sheet reminiscent of a Greek god.

"Amber what's wrong?" he entered the room in time to find Amber hanging over the toilet vomiting. "Are you okay?" he asked, hoping that the red alert bells going off in his head were wrong and she'd say, "Yes." After three pregnancies with his wife he'd watched the bathroom rush before, and knew fully well what it meant this time.

"No. I'm not." Her voice bounced around the inside of the white porcelain bowl.

Jason couldn't find words; there was no wind in his lungs. Fear had cut off his normal breathing pattern and replaced it with erratic, choppy, short breaths, and his palms were sweaty. He went back to the bedroom, allowing the red wrap to sag in the front. After putting on his boxers, he returned to the bathroom. Amber was at the sink splashing cold water on her face.

"Amber what's going on?"

"One guess, two if you really need it." she tried to sound carefree, as she spoke from behind the blue fluff of a hand towel.

"Don't tell me that you're pregnant!" he said incredulously.

"You guessed."

"Are you sure? How do you know?"

"I took a home pregnancy test last week and I haven't had my period for two months."

"But you haven't gone to the doctor yet?"

"No, not yet."

"Damn, when are you going to?" he snapped.

"Don't snap at me! I guess I haven't thought that far yet! I've been busy trying to deal with the news of you being married."

Jason stumbled back to the bedroom to sit down. His face was pale. What was he going to do? If his wife found out he'd be screwed. He didn't want to lose or leave his family. No one, not even Amber was worth that.

Jason felt cornered with fear and panic, but tried to keep his composure as he pulled a last effort of survival out of the bag.

"You have to go to the doctor to find out for sure, and then you can deal with your options. Have you told the father yet?"

Amber noticed that Jason looked like a deer caught in the headlights of a car. His words forced through the painful realization that the man had children and was married. He was not lifting her off the floor and spinning her around, or touching her stomach. He was using words like, "Why didn't you...options and tell the father." Tell the father? What options. She was pregnant; wouldn't her only option be that she was going to have a baby? What other option was there? She had heard stories of abortions from girls in high school. It had never, ever, occurred to her that she would have to entertain such an event in her own life. Could this man who was the father of her unborn child be suggesting such a thing, as well as the possibility that it was not his child?

"Jason, what the hell are you trying to say? Are you trying to suggest that I was seeing someone else as well as you? You no good bastard!" Amber could barely get her words out before the tears of disappointment, and anger consumed her and there was no point in attempting to say anything else because the words would only be lost in the tears.

Effort down in flames, Jason couldn't do anything more at the moment than to admit to himself that there was a hell of a mess to clean up, and as quickly as possible. "I didn't mean anything by it Amber. I'm just thinking out loud, okay. Make an appointment first thing tomorrow." He hoped to sound concerned with the situation at hand, and not the outsider he'd made himself to be. He'd never get her to do right by him, if need be, by making her angry. The sooner this situation was taken care of the better. There was no way Debra could find out.

"I'll make the appointment. Are you going to come with me?"

"No, I can't. The store had been closed for more than a week. I need to get it open again as soon as possible. Call me tomorrow and let me know the details." He dressed and was out the door like Amber had a plague. To him she did.

Miz Catfish

Chapter 19

"I can put my coat on by myself, I'm not a baby!" Jamie demanded as she tugged her jacket out of her mother's hand.

"That's fine, but mind your manners little girl. Put your coat on before the taxi comes."

"Can I have a bag of Skittles?"

"We'll see. Let's get to the grocery store first."

Jamie heard the taxi's horn and was the first out the door and down the stairs to its yellow door. Janice didn't share her daughter's excitement about their new life that revolved around the three story building that had become their home. Day and night she listened to the other occupants of the building coming and going she longed to re-enter the adult world with adult activities. Macy came to visit her, but she'd never gone up to Macy's. Her life had become a whisper of an existence. If she could stay quiet and therefore non-existent, she would not draw Shawn's attention and lead him to her. But to stay non-existent her home had become a prison. Her children, the contents of her apartment, the building, Shawnee Road, and the water across the street, as beautiful as it was, served to make up the environment of the fish bowl life style that Janice occupied on a daily basis. She was a catfish, hiding from sight, from Shawn, focusing on making sure that the children's needs were met, while trying to block Shawn's threats of retaliation from her mind. His voice taunted her. "You bitch! Isha your mouth is too big, shut up! I didn't come home last night because you don't know how to treat a man. Go get my dinner."

Jamie's voice penetrated Janice's thoughts. "Mommy! Can I get my Skittles now?"

"Jamie, wait until I tell you to get them okay, don't ask again." Janice warned the little girl, whose face was now long with disappointment.

After placing Johnny in the shopping cart, Janice started down aisle one picking up a box of cereal, and two bottles of apple juice. Jamie ran ahead to aisle three and ran back with a bag of Oreo cookies, which she threw into the carriage with a thud. Aisle five stocked canned vegetables, and as Janice handed Jamie the cans of peas, then corn, a can of beets escaped the shelf, rolling to a stop just outside the entrance of the aisle. Janice chased the dented can and picked it up, looking left to right to see if anyone was watching her chase the aluminum, and there he stood at the dairy case.

His brown hand reached for the opaque, white container of milk with the surety of a bowler grabbing a familiar number twelve ball. A black cap sat slightly at an angle over his neatly trimmed haircut. His denim shirt was a perfect match to the sharply creased jeans that hung neatly above the brown leather loafer.

An old familiar tune "You'll Always Be My Baby" by Mariah Carey floated through his puckered lips, and floated on air to Aisha's ears. The song was a favorite of Shawn's. As the man pulled back into a standing position he began to turn in Janice's direction. His profile, the nose, that chin, confirmed her fear, it was Shawn! Here in the supermarket, in

Massachusetts. How long had he been following her and the children around the store?

The children! She allowed the aluminum can to drop back to the floor as she turned and rushed back to the children. She quickly pulled Johnny from the shopping cart, yanking him upwards too soon, causing his small shins to smash against the handle of the cart. He yelped, but his sounds went unheard by his mother. She yanked again successfully pulling her son from the plastic seat. Grabbing a fist full of the red, and blue, plaid fabric of Jamie's sweater, Janice pulled the girl down the aisle, balancing the little boy on her hip. Johnny bobbed up and down as his mother's feet picked up speed. Jamie had trouble keeping her small, mini footsteps in unison with the large ones of her mother. She tried to look up into her mother's face to get a sign of what was causing her to act so angry. Had she done something bad? She hadn't asked for the Skittles again.

Janice hit the electronic door with her shoulder assisting it in its slow swing. She needed it to move at a faster pace, it blocked her way to safety. Yellow taxis lined the sidewalk waiting to be of assistance for transportation. Janice yanked the door open so violently that the handle slipped from her grasp as it swung outward to its fullest degree, and then bounced on its springs flinging it back into an attempt to close once again. The driver, reading a newspaper was startled, then annoyed at the abuse of his property.

"Hey lady, watch the merchandise!"

"105 Shawnee Road." Janice huffed between short breathes, not acknowledging the driver.

"Mommy, I didn't get my Skittles." Jamie groaned. Janice didn't hear Jamie; her focus was out the rear window of the taxi as it pulled away from the curb. She watched the supermarket "exit only" door as if it were about to release the bulls into the streets. Imagining the damage that Shawn would do to her if he got his hands on her, she could easily compare him to an angry bull.

"That'll be five dollars and ninety cents." the driver requested.

From shaky fingers, Janice paid the driver six dollars, and pulled the children from the seat of the taxi, and up the stairs into the apartment. She twisted the locks, each one twice, making sure that she'd placed a barrier between herself and Shawn. The taxi had left the curb before he came out of the store, not giving him time to follow them home, but did he already know where she lived?

Calvin placed his gallon of milk, grape jelly, and cream cheese on the counter. He pulled off his black cap to scratch his neatly brushed hairline, and then replaced the cap cocked at a sexy angle. His brown loafer barely missed a small puddle of pickle juice in front of the snack rack. Quickly he noticed that the cashier was a cute young number and not being able to pass up a chance to add another telephone number to his rolodex, he made sure to allow his caramel brown hand to linger as he paid for his groceries. She was too young to be impressed by the song he sang, "You Will Always Be My Baby".

The following morning, Macy helped Amber find a neighborhood clinic where pregnancy tests were done for free. She went with her to take the test, and held her hand while the nurse reported the results that were known, but needed to be confirmed.

"Ms. Munroe." the nurse called out into the waiting room.

"Yes, right here."

"Please follow me." the nurse requested.

Amber and Macy followed the woman into an office. "Please have a seat. Your test came back positive. It will take an internal examination to be sure of exactly how far along you are in gestational weeks. If you can wait we can get you in today with our visiting doctor. Then if you are ready, someone will discuss your options with you. According to the information that you gave on your intake sheet you figure to be around eight weeks. Are you sure of those dates?"

"Options. What options?" Again someone speaks of options to her.

"Yeah." Amber quietly mumbled.

"Are we moving too fast for you, or do you think that you want to proceed as I have offered?" the nurse pressed on.

Amber looked at Macy for support on a decision. Macy nodded her head in an affirmative motion.

"Yes. I'll stay to see the doctor, and to speak to someone." Amber mumbled again.

Amber and Macy walked back into the waiting room. Macy saw Amber's eyes fill with a pool of tears that waited to spill over. This sight tore at her heart.

Amber was uncomfortable with the heavy silence in the waiting room.

"What a mess this is, huh?" she broke the silence.

"You said it girl! On top of that I just realized that I'm in a room full of pregos. Jeez, what if this shit's contagious? I think I'd better stand up. If I sit in any of these chairs I might get pregnant too." Macy teased.

"Ha, ha! You're so funny, I forgot to laugh. Is that like getting VD from the toilet seats?"

Both women laughed. "Ms. Munroe?" the nurse called. The laughing stopped. Amber began to walk towards the voice. She stopped in her tracks when she realized that Macy was not beside her. She reached back and grabbed for Macy's arm, but Macy pulled away.

"I'm not going in there with you! I don't wanna to see your ass! I'll wait right here until you come back out. Thank you very much."

"Come with me plea-z-z-ze." Amber pleaded.

"No." Macy stood firm.

"Ms. Munroe." the nurse called again.

Amber responded to the nurse's second call. "I'm coming."

Macy shook her head. "No." Amber gave up and followed the nurse down the hallway to an examination room. She was given a sheet to wrap around her waist and was told to undress from the waist down, and then the nurse was gone, leaving her alone in the room to wait for the doctor. The coolness of the room, the entrance of the doctor, and all other actions that occurred in the room whizzed by in a blur. She saw the doctor taking off his gloves, and knew that she could leave. Mechanically, she allowed her body to slide off the steel padded table, with the white noisy paper that covered it making its crinkle, and threatening to rip noise. She dressed and picked up the pamphlets of material on adoption, abortion, and beginning pre-natal care early. What was she supposed to do with them? Throw them on the floor like dice and see which one landed face up.

Macy could tell from the vacant look in Amber's eyes that a period of quietness was needed. She couldn't even imagine what her friend was going through. They left the building in silence, and continued that way until they got off the bus and began to walk towards their home.

"When are you going to discuss your choices with Mr. Hardware?" Macy asked.

"Today I guess, and will you stop calling him that. He has a name."

"Yeah, I could think of a few of them. Like jerk face, or ass-s." Macy began.

Amber stopped walking to confront her friend, "STOP IT MACY!" she felt an allegiance to the love of her life, the father of her unborn child. "You don't even know him."

"I might not know him personally, but I know his type. I've made many of them drool while I shake my ass in their face and take their money. A dancer meets all types at one time or another in their career. The ones that don't try to touch, and the ones that do, the ones that drool, and the ones that don't. The ones that are going home to someone they still love, and the ones that don't want to go home at all. Where did your man tell you that he fits in?" Macy snapped.

"I believe that I just heard you say that you're a dancer, who shakes her ass for money." Amber snorted. "So who in the hell are you to point your finger at anyone else? He told me all that I need to know about the situation between him and his wife. Their marriage has been over for a long time. He's only staying for the children. When they're old enough he's going to leave. So lay off, will you? Mind your own business!"

"You don't have to tell me twice. When you come down off of your fantasy cloud to walk amongst the humans you know where I'll be!" Macy snapped.

Amber didn't reply, she turned from Macy and continued down the street. She stopped in front of the hardware store and went in. Macy's heart stung from the whip of her friend's betrayal. She went on alone to the apartment building. She saw Amber enter the hardware store and wanted to go in to protect her from further pain, but realized that she had to step back and give Amber the space that she needed to grow from her situation. She was undeniably angry from the argument, but deep down inside she also knew that when Amber needed her again that she'd be there for her.

Amber entered the store's doorway and a little boy about the age of six ran past her chasing a puppy. A young woman behind the counter yelled "J.J. stop running inside. Take that dog outside if you want to run around!"

She turned to Amber, who had made her way to the counter. "Children are so busy. They never sit still. What may I help you with today?" she said smiling. Amber was stunned. Could this woman be Jason's wife? Could J.J. be Jason junior? Was the puppy the family dog? A curly haired little girl resembling Jason, about four years of age, chased the puppy from the other end of the store. "Katie, you and your brother go outside with that dog, now! Your father would skin us alive if he knew that dog was running around in here. Come now, come, come." She stepped from behind the counter and headed towards the door to let the children and the dog go outside. "Don't forget to put on his leash J.J."

What felt like a bolt of pain hit Amber in the chest and caused her to lean heavily against the counter, when she realized that the woman that had come out from behind the counter to open the door for the children was largely pregnant. Her maternity smock ballooned around her swollen belly. She waddled back to the counter after closing the door behind the trio. Amber caught a glimpse of the ring on her wedding finger that sparkled against the lights in the ceiling.

"Are you okay? You look pale. Would you like to sit down? Maybe a glass of water? My husband has a small stool back here somewhere." The woman offered. She turned around to check for the stool, but when she turned back to speak to the customer no one was there. "Well, I sure hope she's alright, where ever she ran off to." she murmured to herself as she refolded the foot stool.

The pain in her chest gripped tighter around her lungs, as Amber ran blindly to the apartment. Her tears clouded her vision. She dodged Jamie and Johnny playing on the sidewalk and ran past Janice sitting on the stairs.

Being inside her home brought no solace. The picture of the pregnant woman who had to be Jason's wife still played in her mind. Macy had been right in her assumptions. Jason was a creep. He had deceived her. She had angered her friend by protecting Jason's honor. Her protection was misplaced, and now she had possibly lost her closest friend.

Another image of the woman's swollen belly flashed into her mind and Amber remembered her own condition. She thought back to the information the doctor had given her. He told her that she would have to make a decision soon if she was thinking of terminating her pregnancy. He also told her to consider the option of giving the child up for adoption to a waiting, childless couple. There was also the choice of becoming a single mother, and raising the child herself.

Amber wanted to discuss these choices with Jason. She wanted him to say supportive things, like "Everything is going to be alright, we'll raise this baby together." or "Let's get married and have a family, me, you, and our baby." Now she had to realize that she would not be able to have those dreams come true. She needed to speak with Jason immediately, to hear his voice, to be reassured that she was not alone at this time of need. She decided to try the store, maybe Jason had returned.

"Hello. Michaels Hardware. May I help you?" a female voice responded.

"Yes. Is the manager there?" Amber asked trying to keep her voice steady.

"No, he's not."

"Please have him call Ms. Munroe at 555-1212. Tell him that the supplies I ordered were incorrect in the measurements, and I need to give him some corrections." Amber fibbed.

"I'll be sure to give him the message, Ms. Munroe," the voice.

"Thank you."

Both women returned their telephones to their cradles. One woman went on about her activities. The other cried from mixed emotion of deceit, both received and now practiced.

Macy knocked at Janice's door, but got no response. She looked outside to where she knew her neighbor's favorite spot was and found Janice and the children in front of the building. Jamie spotted Macy on the stairs and ran over to give her a hug, even little Johnny felt comfortable enough to run over and pull on her pant leg.

"Hey you guys, this is a nice greeting. I could get used to these types of hellos." she said to the children.

"Alright, don't hang on her you two. Go back and play." Janice ordered the children. Jamie obeyed her mother and pulled her little brother along with her.

"Have you heard anything from your grandmother about Mrs. Jenkins?" Mary asked.

"Yeah. My grandmother called me back the other day. She wanted me to call my mother about our question. But when I called my mother she didn't answer anything she just told me that she's coming here to visit and that she's looking forward to meeting you. She's arranging her flight and will call me when she's got all of the information on her arrival time. Would you like some pig's feet, or a soda?" Janice answered.

"Girl you eat so much of those pig's feet that you're damn lucky that yours haven't started looking like them. But since you did offer, I think I will have one and a soda." Macy giggled.

Jason pulled up to the curb and parked. "Hi there ladies," he said, side stepping the children.

"Hello." Janice replied.

Macy did not respond to the greeting. Instead she gave him a glare. He assumed that she knew Amber's situation. The two women had gone past his store window together many times. He could still feel Macy's stares as he went into the building.

Amber opened the door and walked back into the bedroom. When Jason caught up to her she was laying in the bed under a sheet.

"I got your message." he said in a dry tone.

"You mean the message that I left with your WIFE, the pregnant woman in your store!" Amber whipped at him.

"We'll discuss that later. Right now I need to know if you went to the doctor yet." he said, ignoring her thorns.

"Yeah I went to the doctor alright."

"What did they say?" he asked in an agitated tone.

"They told me what I already know. That I'm pregnant."

"How far gone are you?"

"I'm eight weeks gone as you call it."

"What are you going to do?" he said in a "let's speed things up" tone.

"What do you mean "YOU?" I think this problem is more than just mine.

They suggested that I should discuss my choices with the baby's father, and that's you!" she felt an urge to punch him.

"How do I know that you weren't seeing anybody else?" he gave the dodge of responsibility another try.

"Are you going to try that shit again?

Janice and Macy ended their conversation and both turned their heads towards the hallway at the same time.

"I was just asking." Jason backed down, changing his tone to one of innocence.

"My ass you were! That's the second time that you've hinted at this not being your child, and it's insulting. I'm not a whore! I don't sleep with everybody."

"Yeah, yeah, alright, I'm sorry, calm down will you, and stop yelling. I don't need everyone in the building knowing my business. I can't give you the cash until next week."

Amber was confused. "The cash for what?"

"For the abortion. What else?" he said matter-of-factly.

"Who said that I was getting an abortion? I don't even believe in them." Whoa! What's going on here? Amber felt like she was doing a doggy paddle in a large body of water, and she was about to go under.

"I can't deal with this situation," he said, dropping his head into his hands. "If my bitch of a wife finds out, she'll divorce me first and take me for everything."

"Well you should have thought of that before you decided to start getting in my bed."

Completely ignoring Amber's comment, Jason rose from where he'd been sitting on the bed and began to pace the floor. "I can't take care of two families at one time." He spoke more into space than at Amber. Without realizing he had repeatedly run his fingers through his hair. It was becoming unruly, and giving a visual to his mental state of mind.

"What do you expect from me right now?" he gave Amber a bewildering look. She felt his anguish, temporarily forgetting her own plight. "I have to get out of here!" Jason continued, seemingly gasping for air, and walked out the bedroom door. Amber stood in the middle of her bedroom floor encased in a fog. She didn't know whether to walk behind him, or to stay put and allow him space to continue to rant. He re-entered the room with a quickness that caused her to jump, she was expecting to hear her front door close from his exit.

"Amber! You can't do this to me! I can't lose my kids, and my store. Help me out here. Now he was pleading.

Tears came to Amber's eyes. Was this the way things were supposed to be? Her first experience with carrying a child, and her first love, turning out to be a married man who wanted her to terminate her pregnancy. Where was her prince charming, with the offer of a house with a picket fence?

"What are you saying to me?" Amber asked through a throat tight with sorrow.

"I'm asking you to work with me. You know my situation!" he continued to lay it on thick.

"Did you say these things to your wife when she found out that she was pregnant?"

"No, I didn't because she's my wife, and any way Amber, that's not what we're discussing now, and that's none of your business. Let's just focus about this."

Miz Catfish

"Yeah, but supposedly she's a wife that you don't sleep with anymore." she reminded him of what he'd told her of the situation in his home.

"Grow up Amber, shit happens! Just go get the damned abortion." he snapped. We can have kids later. I can't deal with this right now. If she finds out about this I told you what she'll do to me. My life would be hell. How could I do anything for you and this kid if I have nothing? Use your head will you? Do you want to raise this kid on welfare, because I'll have nothing for you? I inherited that business from my father. I won't let anything destroy it."

What if I want my baby?" she challenged.

"Then you're on your own." His eyes were cold as he stared into hers.

He pointed his finger into her face, "Then you're on your own. I'll deny everything you claim and your life will be hell." he threatened.

The sound of Jamie and Johnny playing outside broke the silence that now filled the apartment. Amber was aware that Janice must be sitting on the stairs. She felt embarrassed at the thought of her neighbor hearing the conversation between herself and Jason. How could she face Janice again? The most frightening event in her life other than losing her parents had just been shared with a stranger. She did not know that Macy was also sitting on the stairs.

Janice tried to ignore what she had heard. It made her uncomfortable to hear a man yelling personal information loudly. Shawn had done such a thing to her so many times that she could not count. It was an embarrassment that she never wanted to hear, or feel again.

As Macy was about to knock on Amber's door, Jason opened it, and continued out, passing Macy so quickly and aimlessly that his arm brushed her breast. He left the building and couldn't seem to be able to get into his car quick enough. After sitting a few seconds he pulled away from the curb and drove away. Macy walked into the apartment and closed the door behind her?

"Amber? Where are you?" Macy called.

"I'm in here." a weak voice responded.

"What are you hiding for?" Macy ad libbed. She didn't know what to say to her friend. How could she help her feel better at a time like this?

Amber entered the living room, "I thought that you'd never speak to me again for being so dumb." She stopped in front of the window preferring not to look Macy in the face, bracing herself for words of smugness, not the touch of a hand on her shoulder. Amber allowed herself to be pulled into the embrace of her girlfriend's arms. Tears flowed from both women, but for different reasons. One for the reality of the real world's coldness, and the other because of the pain one feels when a loved one is in distress.

Amber broke the seriousness of the moment, "Are you going to hit me?"

"Hit you for what silly?" Macy asked.

"Because I'm so stupid, and you were right."

"Well, I was right, but this isn't the time to rub it in so I'll reserve that right until this mess is under control."

"I didn't think you'd speak to me ever again after I told you to butt out of my business." Amber admitted.

"I was going to let you wallow alone for a while in this pig shit of a mess that you've gotten yourself into, but I couldn't ignore Jason's yelling."

"You heard him? I thought only Janice was out there on the stairs."

"No. I was out there too. He's a real insensitive jerk. I'd like to rip his jewels off and flush them. That way he wouldn't pull this crap on anyone else!"

"You're so violent!" Amber laughed.

"Uh-huh, and you're so in love!" Macy quipped.

"Ouch! You didn't have to hit below the belt!" Amber said as she folded her arms across her waist and bent over.

"So do you want to talk now, or later?"

"Since you've already heard most of the conversation let's save the rest for tomorrow. I'm tired." Amber begged off.

"How about coming outside for a while? Janice and the kids are sitting out there." Macy offered.

"Yeah, don't remind me. How am I going to face her again? She heard the soap opera too."

"Don't worry about Janice, she's cool. She's probably been through her own drama I don't think she's the judgmental type. Come on, I'm sure you could use some air, and you'll sleep better."

Amber joined the two women on the porch. She sat down on the step next to Macy and greeted Janice with a sheepish "Hi." Janice looked at her and replied "I know how you feel. It's not easy to face the neighbors after a personal shouting match. At least you're amongst friends. My business got blabbed to floors of strangers. It's not easy, but you'll survive. Would you guys like to cook a few things on the grill on the roof?"

"Sure, I could go for a grilled hot dog." Macy responded.

"I guess I could nibble on a hot dog too." Amber joined in."

Amber spent the rest of the evening with her friends who made sure to try to distract her from her problems. When the evening turned into late night, Janice had to leave the group to go put the children to bed, leaving Amber and Macy alone.

"Macy." Amber began in a weak voice. "His wife is pregnant too. I saw her with my own eyes. They also have two other children, a little boy, and a girl. The boy is a junior. There's even a cute little dog. She thought I was a customer when I went into the store. She was so nice to me. I don't want to hurt innocent people. He says that if she finds out about me, she'll take him for everything, leaving him nothing to give me or our baby. He says that if I give him this time to clear things up at home that we'll have lots of time together in the future and a lot more babies too." she ended with a loud exhale, allowing her shoulders to slump.

"What was that last part?" Macy asked.

"He says that we could have lots of babies later." Amber repeated.

"So what is supposed to happen to this one?" Macy raised an eyebrow.

"He says that he'll give me the money for an abortion. Why are you asking me what he wants? You heard him yelling."

"Yeah, I heard him, but I want to hear you say these things out of your own mouth. Now tell me what you want to do."

"I don't know if I can deal with this Macy. I didn't know that he was married. I can't hurt those people that I saw in that store. I think I'm going to have the abortion."

"The decision is yours. I won't judge you no matter what your decision is, but make it one that you can live with when you sleep at night. Have you thought about adoption? Or keeping it?"

"I didn't get a chance to discuss those things with Jason. He stormed out before calming down enough to talk instead of yell." She looked off into the dimly lit sky. "He promised me a future." Turning back to look her friend in the eyes she admitted, "I love him Macy."

"I'm not going to touch that subject again, but I must say that men like him rarely leave their wives. If he does, do you think you could ever trust him to be true to you?"

"Macy you're probably right, I can't go on like this. I don't know how I'm going to live with myself after today. I messed up big time didn't I?" Her voice was almost at a whisper.

Macy didn't answer what probably wasn't really meant to be a question, just a thought spoken out loud. It seemed to her that Amber had already made up her mind. There was no reason for her to get into another argument with her by throwing in her two cents more of advice. Maybe Amber would be sorry later, maybe not. Macy had learned earlier in the day to be supportive from the side line.

"Macy? Why aren't you answering me?"

"I think you have the answer to that question already. You don't need me to help you beat yourself to death. The horse is already out of the barn, no use trying to close the door now as the elders would say."

"Don't go wise old lady on me now." Amber jokingly pushed Macy's shoulder. "I guess I'll be having the abortion." Amber repeated trying to get a reality on things by continuing to hear the word out loud.

"I thought you said that you didn't believe in abortions." Macy challenged.

"I don't, but if I give the baby up for adoption I'm afraid I'll pine away for it through the years."

"You know there are many avenues for adopted children and birth parents to find each other. Maybe you wouldn't pine away forever. The kid might find you."

"You and your parents have never found each other."

"Well I haven't tried. So don't make your judgment by my situation."

"I'm exhausted. I think I'd better get some rest." Amber said.

Macy agreed. "I'll see you tomorrow. Go get some rest." Once in solitude they both turned to their own thoughts. Macy thinking about her own missing parents, and the possibility of Janice's family giving her some information.

Amber's thoughts would not allow her to dismiss the fact that she did not want to have an abortion. She'd be doing it for Jason, and not herself. What if she couldn't deal with the decision later? At least with adoption she could find the child later or vice versa. If she kept the baby she would not have to deal with either of the other problems.

Another picture of the pregnant woman talking to the happy children in the hardware store flashed in her mind. Then she heard Jason promising her a hard time if she went against his wishes. She turned off the movie in her mind and focused on sleep before she had time to change her decision.

Miz Catfish

Chapter 20

Samantha Kelly, preferably called Sam, was third among six children born to Ralph and Cheryl Ann Kelly. Ralph had done his best to support the large family, but trying times prevailed. Clothing was passed down by the children, and was at times received from neighbors. The children were often made fun of in school. Sam would never forget the day at school in the eighth grade when Carol and a group of girls walked up to her. Carol had strategically waited for everyone in the hallway to be within hearing distance before she said, "My red dress looked better on me than it does on you. My mother should not have given it to you!"

They learned to fight at an early age, having to defend themselves against taunting, hair yanking, punches, and name calling day after day. Meals were tightly rationed. Stress caused the parents to argue constantly, leaving little time for hugging the children. As each child grew older and left home they were not only scarred by a lack of both nutritional and emotional nourishment but survival of the fittest had been incorporated into each child's personality. Their father hid a shameful feeling of relief from his family. As each child turned eighteen, and was liberated, each exit lightened the load on his wallet. When the last of the children were out of the house the last two before they were even seventeen Ralph was finally able to save a few dollars and Cheryl Ann was free to go out of the home to work and assist with the finances. Even with an empty nest, two incomes and a savings, the couple never pulled their relationship back together. They would continue to live the rest of their lives as dysfunctional as the children they had created.

Sam knew that she was heading for trouble with her rental office for not paying her rent. This was not the first time she'd been so far in the hole with them. There was no need of her going to the manager to ask for a reprieve, because there would not be one forthcoming.

She tried to read the face of the constable standing in her hallway holding what looked to be an official piece of paper. Sam knew it was an eviction notice. She hoped that she could charm him with her flirtatious ways and he'd go away with a telephone number and the piece of paper. She didn't have the money to stop the eviction proceedings and this flirting was a last ditch effort to gain a few more days to come up with the rest of the money before the notice was served to her. As long as it wasn't served she couldn't be accused of being aware of the demand to leave the premises, or to pay up the money owed. Two thousand five hundred dollars was a lot of money to her at the moment. She already had about one thousand six hundred dollars, but the other nine hundred dollars wouldn't be easy.

She could ask her father for assistance, but that would mean admitting to her parents that while living in style of the best fashion models in the top magazines, she hadn't been paying her rent. They wouldn't understand that to look as delicious as she did from day to day meant that she had to be creative when robbing Peter to pay Paul. More often than not Peter and Paul got stiffed. The weekly pay from her job at the Kelvin Accounting Firm was hardly enough to sustain her needs, maybe someone else, but not her.

Yet when she put on her black three inch heeled pumps and felt like she could stop traffic as she walked down the street, the money problems seemed to disappear. At the age of twenty two, she was a shopaholic with damaged credit and more than her fair share of bills in the mail to prove it. She had to find a way to keep her current job, and get another source of income to support her shopping habit, and her bills.

Samantha made the only choice she could, and bought a newspaper to begin the search for a new place to live.

She found an ad for a studio apartment with an affordable rent, and in a nice location. She called the number given and set a time to go see the place.

As Sam approached the building at 105 Shawnee Road, she spotted a woman dressed in a bright lavender colored tent of a dress. She stopped in front of the woman. She wondered if this could be the correct place. How could anyone dressed so tacky be making business choices of any sort?

"Could you tell me where I can find Mae-Belle Smoot? My name is Samantha Kelly; I'm here to see about an apartment." Sam greeted the fashion disaster.

"I'm Mae-Belle. I'm glad you found the place okay."

"It wasn't too hard, but I did have to stop and ask for directions one time," Sam admitted.

"Follow me. The apartment is on the second floor." Mae-Belle said leading Sam into the building.

Mae-Belle pointed to the mailboxes on the wall "Those are the mailboxes for the building. There are tenants in both of these apartments." She pointed to the doors left and right of herself. Sam checked out the condition of the hallway.

"Clean." she thought to herself. They continued up the stairs to the second floor. "There is a tenant in the apartment across the hall from the one that I'm about to show you." Mae-Belle opened the door to the studio. She stepped aside and let Sam enter first. Sam stopped in the middle of the floor. Placing a finger to the bottom of her chin she gave herself a moment of silence to absorb the interior of the apartment.

Mae-Belle broke the silence. "The bathroom is over there." she said pointing to the back corner of the room flight stewardess style arm bent at elbow then straight out finger pointed. Check out the closet space too, again flight stewardess style. I think you'll find it ample."

Sam walked towards the back of the large room and looked into the bathroom, and closet. Then she walked back up front to look in the kitchen. After checking out all of the appliances and the cabinet spaces she turned to Mae-Belle.

"I'll take it, and I'd like to rent it as soon as possible. Am I the only one who inquired or are there others ahead of me?" Sam asked.

"No. You're the first, and you can move in as soon as you'd like. We can go upstairs now to sign the lease if you're ready."

The two women went up to Mae-Belle's apartment and signed the papers needed to make Sam an official tenant. Mae-Belle walked Sam back to the front of the building and they ran into Macy coming up the sidewalk.

"Macy this is your new neighbor Samantha Kelly. She's moving across the hall from you. Samantha this is Macy Jenkins," Mae-Belle introduced the woman.

Macy and Sam locked eyes. Instead of two women, there were two alley cats sizing each other up. Imaginary snarling, purring and sharpening claws. One look at each other and the territorial fight was on. The felines shook hands.

"Just call me Sam, everyone does."

"Nice to meet you Sam, I'm Macy, I'm on the way to dress for work, but I'm sure that we'll be running into each other."

Once she was alone in the hallway, Macy rubbed her hand. It smarted from the squeeze that Sam had given it. Outside Sam allowed her arm to drop to her side, keeping her hand out of view as she stretched her fingers. They ached from the squeeze that Macy had given them. An unheard battle horn had been sounded. Sam flagged down a taxi and went back to her old home to arrange her move.

It took her three telephone calls to get enough strong arms to move all of her possessions in one day. The moving crew helped her arrange the furniture in the new apartment and even flipped a coin to see who would pay for something to eat and drink when the job was done. Sam stood around pointing her well groomed fingers in different directions throughout the apartment. The men knew that she was faithful to no one, yet they still enjoyed being in her company. She had a way of stroking their ego, by playing damsel in distress, and allowing them to show off their masculine abilities to their fullest capacity. One chest tried to out flex the other, and the one lifting three boxes ousted the one that had lifted two. Her petite structure strutted around the apartment like a lioness would grace the jungle. Her blonde hair surrounded her heart shaped face, hanging perfectly down her back like a well brushed mane.

Mae-Belle filled a tall glass with lemonade and took her seat near the window. Soothing breezes blew through her apartment from the water, trees, and shrubbery across the street. She noticed Amber walking down the street. "Probably to work." she guessed. She hadn't seen the girl. But since Amber had not come back upstairs to share anything more of her situation, Mae-Belle did not want to intrude on the girl. She made it clear to everyone that her door was open if they wanted to talk. So she decided to leave things as they were.

Amber left the house heading to work. She dreaded passing the hardware store. Jason had only called once and it was to find out her decision. She informed him that she would have the abortion and of the fee. He wouldn't be able to stop by before then because business was picking up at the store and he was tired. He promised again to bring the money to her the night before, once she informed him of the date. He cut the conversation short stating that he had an emergency to deal with.

Unknowingly Amber found herself standing outside of Jason's store. She wondered if he was there. Maybe she could talk him into agreeing with her that abortion was not the way to solve their problem. Maybe they could go into his back room and he could give her a hug, a kiss, anything to show her that he cared about her. Amber started for the door, and then thought "What if his wife is there? Then we would not be able to speak freely to each other. He would have to act as if he doesn't even know me." A look of jealousy flashed in her golden flecked eyes. A light breeze off the water blew her curly brown hair slightly out of place. For a few seconds the usually angelic face took on the experienced look of a woman scorned, and angry. A thought entered her mind, "If his wife is in there, I'll tell her everything. Why should I care about her divorcing him? He hasn't seemed to care about my feelings. Why should she get to have her beautiful baby and not me? Shouldn't he pay for his play?" Pay for his play, a saying that her aunt used when discussing with Amber the consequences of having pre-marital sex. It took those final few words of thought to bring Amber back to the present. Although the agony of the situation was still surrounding her heart, the devious thought was gone.

Her aunt would not only be saddened by the situation that her niece had found herself in. She would also be disappointed to find out that Amber had gone after the wife. Amber couldn't stomach the thought. She backed away from the door in time for it to be flung open by J.J. and Katie. As the door hit its fullest wideness Amber caught a glimpse of Jason. He also saw her, and quickly turned his head away from her glare. Then the door closed. J.J. and Katie were indulged in a game of tag, and did not notice the woman outside of the store wiping tears from her eyes. Amber sidestepped the child play and continued down the sidewalk to work.

The store was not busy, so Amber spent time organizing shelves, and dusting. She was on her knees in a back aisle straightening, when a bell sounded indicating that someone had entered the store. The bell startled her causing the can in her hand to knock over the cans. She was in no mood for greeting customers so she stayed in the aisle slowly replacing the cans waiting for the person to call out to her, or maybe even go away.

"Hello? Is anyone here?" a woman's voice called out.

Amber replaced the last can, and went to the front of the store. The customer turned toward Amber's footsteps. It was Jason's wife, she stood in front of the counter with a bag of potato chips and four sodas, her swollen belly seemed larger under her horizontally striped maternity smock. Amber's hand went protectively to her own abdomen.

"Hi there." the pregnant woman said cheerfully. "I was wondering if anyone was here. She noticed the look of surprise on Amber's face. "Did I surprise you?"

Amber's mind took in the woman in front of her. She hadn't noticed the sharp facial features on the woman the first time she had seen her in the hardware store. Now she noticed the shoulder length black hair that shined like onyx. Her skin seemed to glow from the effects of sun and pregnancy. The blue of her eyes stood out like ocean water. Her smile was one of a content, self assured woman a woman with a husband, family, and thriving business.

"Oh, I-I'm sorry." Amber said as she walked behind the register. "I didn't mean to keep you waiting."

"Weren't you in the hardware store down the street one day not too long ago? You didn't look too well and I offered you a foot stool to sit down, but then I couldn't find it. I wondered where you ran off to. I found the foot stool, but you left."

"I was fine. Is that all that you'll be getting?"

"I guess so, for now any way. I never know when I'm going to have a craving for something else. Right now its potato chips, later it could be something else. This little bundle runs the show." Debra patted her stomach. "He or she, makes me sleepy one moment, and then wakes me with its kicking the next. This is my third time around and I'm enjoying this one as much as I did the first and second. Do you have any children? I'm Debra Michaels, my husband and I own the hardware store down the street."

"Amber," Amber mumbled in response.

"Any kids?" Debra repeated the rest of the question.

"Huh? Oh, oh, no. I don't have any." Amber answered while reaching for the bag of potato chips to begin ringing up the items. She wanted to get the woman out of the store. She didn't want to hear about Jason's third child kicking in his wife's womb. She needed the woman to leave. Although she had to admit that Debra did not seem to be the bitch that Jason was making her out to be, it was hard for Amber to want to hurt this person by telling her the truth now that she had a face and a name.

"I've got about four weeks to go with this loaf in the oven, so I'll probably be in here a lot chasing down my cravings while I work in the store."

Amber pushed the bag across the counter, and their fingers slightly touched as Debra reached for it.

"Bye for now. I'm sure that my gang is looking for me, wondering where I've gotten off to."

Amber said nothing in return as Debra took the bag and left the store. She ran into the restroom, where she stayed until the nausea, tears, and shaking stopped. Using the telephone in the manager's office she called the clinic and confirmed her appoint for the abortion the following week

Her shift ended, and she tried to walk home quickly to avoid thoughts of entering the hardware store. Once home she napped for an hour, then woke and called Jason.

Chapter 21

Macy found a soda in the refrigerator, crackers in the cabinet, and went up to the roof top. When she stepped out of the doorway she noticed a body stretched out on one of the lounge chairs.

Long, golden blonde hair draped from beneath a straw hat that hid the stranger's face, and an over-sized t-shirt covered most of the body until just above the knees. Perfectly tanned legs stretched to the tips of Flair Red polished toes. Janice sat in a chair in the farthest corner from the door. She was reading a magazine, and sipping a soda.

Macy called to Janice, "Where are my babies?"

"They're down for their naps. I'm grabbing some "mommy time". These baby monitors were one of the greatest inventions yet!" she called back while tapping the hard white plastic gadget.

Macy went over and pulled up an empty seat next to Janice. She sat down and pulled at Janice's magazine cover. "What cha' reading? Something educational I hope."

"Oh yeah, sure, if you want to know the latest number of women impregnated by aliens then I guess this could be called educational."

Both women laughed, causing the stranger under the straw hat to stir. Macy noticed the movement and raised a long, neon orange, with yellow flowers, nail to her lips indicating for herself and Janice to be quiet. Janice made a twisted, comical face causing Macy to giggle again. The stranger lifted an arm and used a well manicured hand to push back the straw hat. A pair of blue eyes peered from beneath.

"You girls care to share the joke?" Sam asked in a languid voice.

"Oh, it's our new neighbor. Macy offered to Janice. "What's your name again?" she asked, being fully aware that the name was etched into her mind.

"Samantha, but please do call me Sam."

"Well Sam, this is Janice from the first floor. Janice this is Sam. She just moved in."

Amber entered the doorway, and both women simultaneously said "Hello."

"So this is where the party is! Where's the music?"

"Does it always get so noisy up here? Sam wasn't concerned with making friends, and allowed her voice to reflect irritation.

Amber looked over at her as if a glass had broken and grabbed her attention. She hadn't noticed Sam when she came through the doorway. She looked at Macy and Janice with a "Who's that?" look.

"Amber, that's our newest neighbor Samantha. I mean Sam. Sam, that's Amber. She lives on the first floor." Macy offered.

"Hi." Amber directed at Sam.

"Hi, to you, too." Sam responded as she pulled the straw hat back over her face, and returned to a relaxed position.

Miz Catfish

The other three women looked at each other, had a moment of silence and then went on with a conversation.

"I'm going to get some hot dog." Janice said.

When Macy and Amber were alone in the corner, Amber said "I need to talk to you later. Will you come down, or should I come up?"

Macy replied "Why don't you come up? You haven't hogged my bed lately."

"That's true; you are due for a little sister visit aren't you?" Amber said in a jolly voice.

Janice returned to her seat "Macy, my mother called. She'll be arriving in two weeks. Maybe you'll get to find out where Mrs. Jenkins is now. You might be able to get some questions answered."

"I'm looking forward to it. I mean meeting your mother. But I'm kind of afraid to ask the questions. What if I find out some things that I can't handle?"

"Well, you old cow! You're not getting any younger, so you better find out anything that you can now!" Janice joked.

Macy gave it back to her, "Who are you calling an old cow? You busted old shoe! I'm only two years younger than you!" All of the women laughed, and Sam wiggled her toes.

The next person through the door was Mae-Belle. "Macy I found someone in the hallway looking for you." She stepped aside and Ortega walked onto the roof. He had a guitar in his right hand. He held the door for Manuel, who followed with a coloring book and crayons. Ortega walked over to Macy and with his left hand, grabbed Macy's hand and gave it a kiss. The women giggled at his attempted Don Juan image.

Mae-Belle hoped that she had not done the wrong thing by bringing the character upstairs. "Anyone for fresh lemonade?" she asked.

Everyone except Sam yelled "Sure." in unison.

Sam lifted her hat to find out what all of the ruckus was about. When she spotted the addition of a male guest, she stretched like a cat after a nap.

"I'll have a glass of that too, please." she purred. Ortega turned his head toward the smooth sound.

"Well! I yam surrounded by beautiful ladees today. Let me play beautiful, sweet music for choo."

No one protested, as the strumming, and then the singing began. The women found themselves swaying to the tunes. Ortega's foot tapped out its own tune as his fingers stroked the chords of his prize possession. He began a traditional Spanish ballad. Sam got up from her chair to do her version of a Spanish mamacita's sway of the hips, demanding to be the center of attention, something that had been hard to do as a child amongst so many siblings.

Ortega began to speed up the tune, and Sam danced faster moving into a spin, with one leg in a ballerina's arch. She turned with her arms outstretched. She turned, and turned, and only Mae-Belle who had just stepped through the doorway with a tray of snacks, and Manuel in a corner coloring, saw Macy stick her foot out.

Sam went down with the grace of a cat sliding on a freshly waxed floor. She did a half split with a glide ending. Ortega dropped his guitar and ran to help her up. The laughs that came from the rest of the audience could be heard at the bus stop down the street. Sam allowed Ortega to help her back to the seat, and pamper her. When the laughter calmed down Mae-Belle tried to take the heat off of Sam.

Mae-Belle handed out snacks. She nudged Macy with the tray as she passed her, and they smirked at each other.

"Are choo okay, lovely ladee?" Ortega asked Sam.

"My leg hurts."

"Would choo like me to escort choo to your home?" he offered.

"Yes, please. That would be nice." She purred.

"Manuel, choo stay here. I mean." he corrected, "Quedate ahi."

He helped her down to her apartment and into the living room. She settled in on the sofa and did not indicate for him to leave until her legs were comfortably elevated on pillows and she had the remote control for the television at her side. She thanked Ortega with a kiss on one cheek and smooth stroke on the other. He more than enjoyed the show of gratitude, and took it as a sign of an invitation of possible things to come, he stroked a hand up her shapely leg to the thigh, at which point her hand stopped his.

"Ah, ah, ah." she chastised. "I can take it from here." she smiled.

"Maybe choo will feel better and one day take care of me, yes?" he grinned.

"We'll see Romeo."

"Do choo feel a lot of hurt? I can help choo with something?" he offered.

"Yeah, I know what you are offering." she laughed.

"No. I can get choo something good for choo pain. It will make choo feel better than making love. And I know choo make love good." He moved his hand to the inside of her thigh.

Sam allowed Ortega's hand to rest on the warm flesh, knowing that it would give her bargaining power in the endeavors that the man was offering. She had an idea that he was alluding to pain killers of some sort, but had to make sure. In the past she had taken pain killers, more to get high than to get rid of an ache. The street value of pills like oxycontin, and Percodan were climbing and it wouldn't hurt to have someone who wanted a piece of you as a provider when you needed a hit.

"Sure, I would like that. But I'll get back in touch with you; right now let me get some rest." She lifted a hand to her forehead, and allowed her head to fall back in theatrical style.

He gave her thigh a soft squeeze and left, returning to the roof top, where he continued to play his guitar for the rest of the crowd.

I'd better get downstairs and cook supper for the kids. I'll see you guys later." Janice said. As she walked past Ortega he said, "Hallo my buddy." Janice snarled at him and kept walking. Macy laughed. She knew how her old friend Jorge Tomas Ortega, the one and only, liked to agitate anyone that he could. He found these games a challenge to break down the opponent's spirit. She decided to go down to her apartment and invited everyone to come; only Amber accepted.

Ortega explained that he had to go home to wait for CeCe so that she could be with Manuel while he went to work.

Macy asked him "What are you doing with little Manuel? Are you running a baby-sitting service nowadays?"

"What?" he didn't understand what she was asking.

"I said, are you babysitting?" she shortened her question.

"No, no. Men don not do those jobs, only ladees. I am married now. Choo took too long, so I find myself another beautiful ladee. She knows how to be a good wife, like the women in Puerto Rico. She doesn't fight all of the time with me." Ortega answered proudly.

"You married who?" Macy asked with doubt.

"I am married to Cecilia, your CeCe."

"Get out of here! You must be joking! How the hell did that happen?"

"Well choo keep kickin' me out of your house, so I met her outside and she fell in love with my handsomeness." he allowed all of his teeth to show beneath the black, bushy tent of a mustache.

"Oh my, someone should have warned that chile!" Macy laughed holding onto her stomach. "Wait until I tell Janice this!"

Miz Catfish

Macy left the roof chuckling to herself about Ortega's news. What was CeCe thinking? Ortega was an absolute nutcase.

After Macy and Amber had been in Macy's apartment for about twenty minutes, the telephone rang. It was Michael.

"Hey babe." he said, happy to hear her voice.

"Hi." Her response was cordial.

"Are you busy?"

"Sort of."

"Should I call you back, or will you call me?" he asked.

"Either, or." she answered plainly.

"Okay, I'll talk to you soon." He quickly gave up, choosing to pick his battles with her.

"Yeah, bye."

She hung up the telephone. Her hand lingered for a few seconds, while her mind wondered about a reason for treating Michael the way she had. He was a decent guy. Maybe he was too normal, too calm, whatever that meant. Honestly she was afraid to trust the innocent attention that Michael gave to her, without asking for anything in return. She was afraid that it would end, because no one that she could vividly remember had showed her such interest, and without it ending. The fact that Michael had been around long enough to have proven himself worthy had not registered in her mind because fear is a strong and controlling emotion, capable of blocking out reason.

Macy knew that she would not call him back as soon he hoped. She was no longer feeling much like entertaining; she wanted to spend some time being quiet. Amber was spending the night, but she didn't have to worry about putting on airs for her friend. As she started preparing to pull out the sofa bed, she felt herself falling into a funk.

She headed over to the fish tank to feed her fish, and sprinkled the multi-colored flakes on top of the water. Macy sat on the floor and crossed her legs. Amber knocked and entered.

"Grab a drink and have a seat. Watching fish is so peaceful for me." Macy shared her thoughts.

Amber took a soda from the refrigerator, and joined Macy on the floor. "Yeah, I enjoy my tank too. I'm glad that I decided to get one."

"So tell me, what's the latest with Mr. Hardware? Oops, I mean Jason."

"His wife came into the store today. She seems to be a nice person. She's definitely very friendly. I almost told her about me and the baby, but I had second thoughts. She was talking to me about her pregnancy. It damn near killed me to listen to her." Amber's eyes filled with tears as she spoke. "She said that she is due in four weeks." Amber absentmindedly drank some of her soda. "I'm still going to get the abortion."

Macy was listening to Amber, but watching two fish chase each other around the tank. She had gone back to the pet shop and bought two more fish. Now the colors in the tank were as colorful as the mural on her wall.

"Macy, are you listening to me?"

Miz Catfish

"Yeah, I'm listening. I just really enjoy watching the fish. Look how graceful they are. Don't you wish you were as confident as they appear to be? They seem to have personalities like people. The pretty fish are all over the tank; the less attractive fish get ignored. I look at them and I wish that I was more like the male guppies, so pretty with color. If I felt that pretty, and confident I'd stride around like that too."

Amber couldn't understand why Macy felt the way she was explaining. From what she could see her friend was beautiful, and seemed to always look well put together without even giving much effort. She didn't know that the woman's thoughts were from the inside.

The catfish glided slowly towards the center of the tank, darted under a plant, and then came back into the center. Its long whiskers searched, feeling its surroundings. It found an area of purple gravel that held a semi-transparent flake of yellow food, and began to eat it.

Macy looked at Amber, who was also watching the fish with a peaceful look on her face. "I feel like we're acting like that catfish. Accepting what falls to the bottom. Why not get the good stuff at the top? If a man like Jason cheats on his wife with another woman, you for instance, that makes his wife the guppy and you the catfish. You're getting the scraps, settling for what he has left to give after giving his wife the cream of the crop. She gets the lovemaking, and you get the sex. She gets the last name, and you get the store phone number. I dance in front of men for money, but they go home to someone else after the club closes. But these are our choices to accept these situations. To settle for what's available, and not wait for what we want, and what we need. We should remember that we deserve the best and demand it."

"How come you didn't tell me that you are a dancer? I was surprised to hear that bit of information," Amber said while continuing to watch the fish.

"Because I don't consider it to be the greatest profession to discuss with just anyone, some people don't agree with what women like me do. I didn't know how you would take it if I told you."

"I poured my heart out to you. Why didn't you feel that you could do the same with me?" Amber asked, finally turning her head from the fish tank to face Macy.

"I've never had close friends like you and Janice before. I'm used to relying on myself to think things through."

"Well I certainly hope that you know better now."

"Yeah, I think I do, but I'm still getting used to the idea."

The catfish went back into a hiding place behind a plant and the two women turned in for a night of slumber side by side.

Amber woke early, she decided to let Macy continue to sleep, and quietly closed the front room door as she left to go home. She showered and made herself some breakfast. A strong knock at the door made her jump; she opened it to find Jason standing on the other side looking innocent and hopeful.

"How are you?" he asked.

"I'm hanging in there."

"May I come in? Or is this not a good time?"

She moved aside to allow him to enter. He removed his jacket. She closed the door, and stood looking at him, he avoided her stare.

"I'm having a slow morning so I thought I'd come visit you. It's been awhile."

"Yes it has been," Amber said quietly.

"Come here."

"Why should I?" Amber asked.

"Because I miss you, and I want to look at you."

"Why would you miss me with such a pretty wife around?" she answered snidely.

"Let's not get into that. I've explained that situation to you already. Now come over here, please."

She crossed the room to Jason and he put his arms around her pulling her to him. She felt at home in his warmth. And just like a woman who is pushing to give birth for the second time pushes with excitement to hold the next child, and forgets the anguish from the first birth, Amber's mind forgot her painful situation as her heart exploded with joy at being back in Jason's arms.

He softly kissed her forehead. Every fiber of her body screamed that this was wrong. That she should make him leave. But how could she when she was melting, melting behind the warmth of his tongue that probed her lips, and the hand that unzipped her shorts.

The strong masculine body lay on top of her, and made love to her softly. Whispers of tomorrow. Just give me today, and tomorrow will be yours. Promises of grandeur. Just give me this moment. Amber gave and Jason took.

When their moment was over, they both lay quietly on pillows on the floor. He got up and began to get dressed,

Miz Catfish

knowing that he'd wash up in the sink in the back room of the store. He did not ask about her condition.

"When I go to my appointment, will you meet me there, or pick me up after?" she inquired.

"I won't be able to make it. I'm running a sale that entire week, and I need to be in the store, as a matter of fact, I'm going to the store now to begin inventory. So I've got to get going. I'll call you tomorrow."

He bent and gave her a kiss on the cheek and left. She continued to lie on the floor. Her hand touched her stomach, as lonely tears began to stream down her cheeks. Amber knew that there would be no telephone call tomorrow. Yet tomorrow would come and she would find herself waiting for the telephone to ring. The light from the window in the kitchen cast a rainbow prism into the fish tank on the counter, and out of the corner of her eye, Amber saw the catfish slink past the glass. With the movement of an ex-cheerleader that she was, she jumped to her feet and with misguided anger; she took hold of the fish tank into her now shaking hands. She walked with a purpose to the bathroom, slipping into the bathrooms door jamb on water that splashed ahead of her onto the floor; she steadied herself, and lifted the toilet seat. The fish scrambled frantically as the hand moved about knocking the decorations out of the rocks that held them in place, and stirred up debris from the bottom of the tank. Within half of a minute all of the fish had been taken from the safety of the tank and thrown into the cold water of the toilet. Amber's hair was tousled from her lovemaking, and now pieces of her bang lay slicked to her brow from the sweat of this latest energetic endeavor. She poured the water from the tank into the water as well, willing in enough logic to be careful that the gravel and decorations not fall in, then flushed the toilet, and slammed the lid shut. Walking back to the kitchen with the now lifeless shape of glass, she mumbled her thoughts, "I can't stand that damn catfish staring at me another minute. Let the damn thing go remind somebody else about their mess of a life."

Chapter 22

Janice sat on the stairs watching the children play. She was waiting for anyone of the other women to come outside, so she could ask about the flowers that were in front of her door that morning.

Macy was out jogging. She had found flowers outside of her door, and so had Sam when she opened her door to take laundry down to the washer in the basement. She had taken them inside and put them in a vase.

Macy returned from her jog and sat to talk with Janice. She mentioned the flowers before Janice could. They were discussing the mystery when Sam came up from the laundry room, and noticed the women. She joined the conversation. No one knew who had left the flowers.

A car pulled up to the curb, and Kenneth got out. He greeted the clan, and Macy did the introductions. Never missing the chance to catch the eye of the opposite sex, Sam began a feline stretch, causing her night shirt to rise, showing most of her tanned, lean legs. She ran her red nails through her hair seductively. The others had not missed the show. Macy looked at Janice and rolled her eyes. Janice smiled.

Kenneth enjoyed the view. He spoke to Sam, "Have you ever thought about showing off that body? You should share that beauty, uh-h, I guess I should ask your name."

Macy spoke up, "I already told you!" she snapped, not hiding her irritation at the scene. "You would have heard me if you weren't so damn busy drooling all over your face and sweating into your ears like a pig!"

Macy's words fell on deaf ears. Sam had picked up on her neighbor's annoyance and was already enjoying it, and Kenneth was seeing dollar signs all over this new found goddess.

"What type of sharing? And the name is Sam."

"Night club dancing. With your body, I think you could get into it and make some people crazy. There'll be some auditioning going on at the club tonight."

She turned to Macy, "Maybe I'll give that some thought." she responded slyly.

Janice snickered to herself. A poem formed in her mind. She could not wait to get in the house and write it in her notebook.

Erica

She was tall, thin and beautiful to my eyes
So I could imagine what kind of magic she held over him
But even though she was a goddess, I never thought
He'd leave me on a whim

I wanted to say all kind if ugly things about her
But in my mind I knew them to be untrue
So instead I kept my opinion lost and this made
My heart feel dark darkest blue

Erica was what he called her

Miz Catfish

And when he said her name I could feel his heart purr
"What is it?" I asked him "that makes her love more special than mine?"
"I'll tell you," he said, "but it will take some time."

The day he walked out with his bags packed
My head fell down very low
He hadn't told me, as of yet
What made him love her so.

Erica was what he called her
With hair so soft if felt like fur
I wondered from time to time
What it was about her that made him so eager
To leave me behind

He came to me one summer eve
And whispered in my ear
That he had never meant to hurt me
And softly wiped my tear

He told me that the secret of Erica
Was not one so easily told
But that her love for him was so strong
That she was the one he'd chose to hold

He said that I should never forget the love he'd felt for me
But that our love was not a love that he felt was meant to be
That I should get on with my life, for someone was waiting there
To hold me tight, every night and cater to my every care

> Erica was what he called her
> As beautiful as a shining star
> And whenever I think of the hurt they caused
> I will forever relive the scar
>
> -Tara Morgan

Macy dug her long sapphire blue claws into Kenneth's arm as she pulled him towards the hallway.

"Ouch! Macy get those knives out of my flesh would you! What's your problem?"

She yanked him. "Just come on!" She didn't speak again until they were inside her apartment. "Why did you invite her to audition?" she asked in a pouty voice. "And I've only told one person here that I dance, now she'll see me there and find out. I don't want her knowing my business."

"She looks like she could be good at it. What's wrong with me bringing in a new money maker? I can't help it if you haven't told your neighbors. Business is business, and I still have to make my money. Don't take it personal. It's all about the business."

"I don't like her. There's something about her. You better keep her away from me!" she warned.

"What's wrong my little turtle dove? Not enough room in this world for two beauty queens?" he teased as he grabbed her around the waist. They fell onto the sofa wrestling playfully, which quickly changed to sex. Afterwards they lay at separate ends of the sofa.

"Looking at this jungle wall doesn't give you a headache?" he asked.

"No it doesn't. All of the colors together like they are make me cheerful."

"Do you want to work tonight?"

"Yeah, I guess I could use the money."

"You're probably sitting on a pretty nice size nest egg. What's the real reason that you want to dance?" He asked the question out of earnest curiosity. He had never been able to figure her out. He hadn't heard of any man at the club getting close to her. Kenneth watched her dance on stage and mingle with the customers without seeming the least bit interested in the variety of propositions that he knew were aimed at all of the women with her type of beautiful face and body. Most of the women in her category that danced eventually got pulled in by the offers and found themselves kept women, or married to a customer after entertaining them for some time. But not Macy, she had a mystery about her that drew the opposite sex, balanced by an evasiveness that kept them at a distance. He had never come to her home and found a boyfriend, or called her on the telephone to find her busy with male company.

She didn't feel like going into the depth of the scars of living in bad foster care homes, and coming away from them with the need to be independent from giving someone the ability to control when she'd eat, or what she'd wear. Only a nest egg as he'd called it could help her accomplish that. She didn't answer his question. Instead she ran her foot from his chest to his private space, allowing her foot to linger there before she continued on to his thigh where she allowed it to rest again. She smiled furtively as he shivered from her touch. Then she changed the subject, "Can you pick me up when I get off work at the store?" she asked.

"Yeah sure. What time?" he knew that she was intentionally avoiding his question and did not try to push for an answer. She had a short temper that he had seen in action. Cornering her would only anger her; it would not get him an answer to his question.

"How about twelve o'clock, that way I'll have time to shower, and change."

"Alright, I'll see you then." He dressed and left. On his way down the hallway he ran into Sam coming up the stairs. "Did you give that audition any thought? It's Sam right?"

"You remembered my name. I feel privileged." Sam flirted.

"How could I forget the name of such a beautiful piece of art?" he returned the favor.

"That's flattering. You have a nice way with words. But I haven't decided if I'm going to come to your club or not. Give me the address just in case I decide to give it a shot. Come on in, you need something to write on." She strutted past him, and he turned back around to follow her. He felt the pull of her animal magnetism. It was as if he were in the jungle scene on Macy's wall. She opened her apartment door and held it open for him to enter, checking him out from head to toe as he did. She liked what she saw. The note pad was near the vase of flowers.

"Pretty flowers, from an admirer I'm sure." Kenneth inquired.

"Actually, they were left at my door. I'm not sure by whom. But they certainly are very pretty."

He wrote the club's address and telephone number on the paper, and then looked up from the paper in time to see her in the middle of a stretch. He enjoyed watching her body, and she enjoyed knowing that she'd timed her movements perfectly. Kenneth moved back into a folded position, and pretended to be checking his writing. He was really hiding a growing bulge in the front of his pants.

His eyes roamed the area around him. The apartment felt very sensual. A large white candle sat on the table beside the flower vase. The mixed smells of cinnamon, apple, and peach blossom told him that a supply of potpourri was placed somewhere near to where he stood. Her furniture was white and looked plush, and soft. He tried to inconspicuously place his hand under the table and push his now swollen member into a more comfortable position. Sam did not miss the movements as he had hoped. She smiled; she had her prey in the area of the trap.

"I'd better get going. I hope to see you tonight." He said as he quickly headed for the door.

"We'll see." Sam replied. She watched him let himself out and smiled at his nervousness, then went to her closet to find something seductive to wear to the club for her audition. Yes, she'd go to the club, this was a chance to make extra money.

Amber knocked at Macy's door. She was barely holding back the tears that were welling up inside. Macy answered the door with two towels for clothing, one around her body and the other around her head.

"Am I bugging you?" Amber asked with a shaky voice.

"No, come on in." Macy stepped away from the door. "I just got out of the shower."

Amber climbed into the black chair and pulled her legs under herself. She hugged a pillow to her chest. Macy was in the closet getting dressed.

"Macy?" Amber called.

"Yeah." Macy shouted back. She could hear the unsteadiness in Amber's voice.

"I never noticed how pretty that butterfly is on the wall near the top of the tree. You know…on the wall."

Macy walked out of the closet. "You didn't come in here to talk about my wall, while you sit balled up in a chair. Do you want something to drink, before you tell me the real reason that you're here?"

Before Amber could respond, Macy was heading her way with two sodas. She passed her one. "Okay, what's wrong?" Macy said in a matter of fact voice.

"Jason came by. He can't take me to the clinic for my appointment tomorrow." she mumbled as she turned the cold soda can between her hands.

"Why can't he? This should be good." Macy snapped.

"He said that the store will be busy, and he won't be able to get away." Amber lifted her head only enough to be understood.

"That's not a good enough reason to let you go through this alone. Is he still going to give you the money? Or has he backed out on that too?"

"No. He's still going to bring me the money on Monday. He said that he misses me. We made love. I miss him too Macy."

"I bet you do honey, but he can't give you anything in return. He's not free Amber. Let him go." Macy said showing sympathy.

"Macy, please don't start on me! I can't handle it right now. Will you come with me? I can't go alone."

"I don't see why you're going at all, but yes I'll go with you. You know I will." Macy said as she went over to the chair and gave her friend a hug.

"Don't mind me," Amber said. "I'm just going to sit here for a while, if that's okay with you."

"No problem." Macy went on about her way, getting ready for work and the packing of her bag for the club.

Kenneth picked Macy up when her shift at work was over. She had a busy night working the crowd and dancing. That night four women tried out for the position of new dancer. The first girl on stage entertained the crowd with her appearance as much as she did with her dance moves. Her deep chocolate skin stood out under the blond hair resting on her head like a bad wig. A pink headband held the hair off her face and matched her press on florescent pink fingernails. Two male customers were lucky enough to get a laugh as they watched her get down on all fours and two of the nails slid across the stage.

The fourth audition almost caused Macy to choke on the drink that she'd been slowly sipping while she sat at the bar. A customer, she's nicknamed "Santa" patted her on the back.

Although some of the auditions were first timers, Sam wasn't, and unless her old friend Clemmy showed up and exposed her no one would ever know this fact. She came on stage dressed in a short camouflage print teddy with matching choker. Her four inch black pumps arched her legs in a way that caused the muscles to appear to be in a flexed state. Her hair was pulled back into a ponytail.

After strutting to the middle of the stage, Sam pulled off her ponytail holder and allowed her mane of straw to flow freely then began a series of movements on the pole that sent the crowd into an uproar. The regular customers took pleasure in the attractive fresh face and body. Kenneth stood back in a dark corner and tried to ignore the feeling of his member rising. Something about Sam made him feel out of control, hungry, and anxious. She collected the money at her feet, and out of the hands of the customers around the stage. As she stepped down from the stage she and Macy locked eyes. Macy snarled at Sam's "cat that ate the canary grin.

The crowd demanded Sam for two more songs before the club closed, and she gladly obliged. She didn't mind showing off what Mother Nature had given her. Sitting in the back seat of a taxi on her way home she counted her riches. She was not disappointed to have to pay the driver fifteen dollars out of her one hundred and seventy dollars earned in one night. It wasn't lost to her that her now rival neighbor Macy was also at the club as a dancer. That made her riches even sweeter because it was one hundred and seventy dollars that she wouldn't get. She'd earn almost twice as much in the following nights to come, as she continued to wild the club as one of its hottest new dancers.

It didn't take long for the gifts and propositions to start coming from big spending customers who wanted to spend off stage time with her. She skirted undesirable suitors, but never turned down gifts, no matter who they came from. The dancing did not bother Sam as it did Macy. Macy was angry at men, sometimes at the world she felt guilty about dancing, showing her body, and being drooled over.

Sam did not have those concerns. She had been hungry, something that she would not allow again if someone desired to give, she was more than willing to take. While continuing her day job, she danced as many hours that Kenneth would schedule her for. Macy stopped trying to control the fact of whether or not Sam danced at the same club, and focused more on reminding Kenneth to make sure that she and Sam's schedules did not coincide. Sam didn't care if Macy danced on the same day as her or not, her concern was to watch her bank account grow. Her closet was becoming crammed with new clothes with price tags still hanging on them. Shopping sprees were carefree again, whether it be indulged alone or with a smitten customer.

Amber spent the night at Macy's on the night before her clinic appointment. Jason had brought the money by as he promised to do, and had also sweet talked her into having sex. He had left her feeling so confused. He was not going on the horrible journey with her. Aside from the money, he didn't even mention the pregnancy. She knew that it was wrong to continue to have anything to do with him now that she knew he was married. She couldn't ignore her feelings for him. When they had sex she ceased to exist as herself and blended into his persona. They moved as one. He said that they'd have plenty of time to have more babies after his divorce and she believed him. After all if he didn't care about her why would he still be making such sensual sex with her? Wasn't that making love? There is a difference between having sex and making love, but Amber had not yet experienced that variation.

Poor Amber could not smell the wolf. She did not mention the sex to Macy. She knew that her friend would scold her. The scolding would not change her mind about Jason, so why even get Macy's mouth going. Amber lay on the sofa bed watching television, and Macy sat in front of the fish tank, while listening to jazz through her stereo headphones. Neither of the two spoke much. Macy turned in first, leaving Amber up alone looking out of the window into the blackness of night. She felt hollow. What if Macy was right about Jason? What if his problems were lies? What if she stopped herself from finishing the next thought. Tomorrow was the day, and at this point she couldn't confuse herself by digging up problems. She cleared her mind and allowed it to blend in with the blackness of the night. Lying back on the bed beside Macy, she fell into a light sleep.

In the morning Amber woke first and continued to lay quietly in the bed, afraid to start the day. Macy was awakened by the alarm clock. She rolled over and looked at Amber.

"Are you awake?" Macy asked.

"Yeah, I'm up." Amber quietly answered.

"Any changes or do we continue on?" Macy asked.

"We continue on." Amber answered without allowing herself time to reconsider her choices.

Both swung their feet over their sides of the bed, and got dressed. They quietly started down the street to the bus stop. Amber began crying as they passed the hardware store. Macy grabbed her around the shoulders and gave her a supportive hug. They took two buses to get to the clinic. Before going into the waiting room they decided to stop for a cup of coffee. Macy noticed that Amber was starting to lag behind; she slowed her pace, allowing the sad face to catch up.

"What's up?" she asked.

"I feel like I shouldn't be having coffee or anything unhealthy for this little baby. Caffeine isn't healthy, is it Macy?"

"Amber, it's up to you."

"I'm sorry; I know I'm babbling on never mind." Amber mumbled.

They entered the coffee shop and made their way to the counter. Macy ordered her coffee light with three sugars, and Amber ordered a cup to tea, both were to go.

They entered the clinic and Amber checked in with the receptionist. She took a magazine off a coffee table and sat down next to Macy. Amber searched the faces of the other women in the room. She felt as if her heart was on her sleeve. Could everyone read across her forehead why she had ended up here? Pre-marital sex, married man, he doesn't want our child. She looked at the others. Some of them were alone; some were with girlfriends like herself. Some were with boyfriends, male friends, or husbands. This made Amber remember that Jason had not been very supportive through this ordeal. She felt envious of the women who sat next to a man, with his arm around her shoulder, or her head on his shoulder. She turned her focus to her magazine. Macy turned to her and nudged her in the side with her elbow.

"Don't you wonder why the others are here?" she whispered.

"I was just thinking, I bet they feel the same curiosity about me." Amber whispered back.

"Any second thoughts?" Macy asked hopefully.

"Please Macy, don't start. I'm trying to stay numb." Amber pleaded.

"Amber Munroe," a voice yelled.

Amber looked at Macy. They took each other's hand. "Come with me, please?" Amber begged. Macy did not need to be coaxed; she would not leave Amber on her own at this point of the journey. Together they walked towards "the voice". A young, plain-clothed woman stood in the doorway of an office. "Amber Munroe?" she asked.

"Yes," Amber responded. Amber and Macy followed the young woman into the office.

"Please come with me." the woman requested. "My name is Mary. I handle the clinic's social service needs. I speak with each client to go over her choices, explain our confidentiality policy, and set up any further services that may be needed. Is this your friend?" she nodded towards Macy.

"Yes, my best friend, Macy." Amber answered proudly.

"So I gather that it's okay to speak in front of her?" Mary asked.

"Yes, it's fine." Amber smiled at Macy. Macy returned a grim smile.

"Well Amber, I see here that you made your appointment yourself after a visit with our doctor. So are you here today to continue with your original plans to terminate your pregnancy?" Mary asked.

"Yes, I am." Amber answered sadly. The word terminate sounded so harsh, so final. But then again this was final wasn't it.

"Have you discussed this with your partner, or does that not apply in your situation?" Mary asked.

"Yes, I've discussed this with him." Amber mumbled. Macy squirmed in her seat.

"Would you like time to gather your thoughts or speak with your friend before we go further?"

Mary asked with concern. She had sat in that room with many young women, looking into their faces, using this time to read emotions, which she had become good at during her years on the job. From Amber's facial expressions, and body language, she read sorrow. Once given time to collect their thoughts, some women backed out of the procedure at this point. She gave the girl time to voice any thoughts. Mary stayed quiet for a minute, faking the action of searching in a desk drawer for a pen. "Well I guess my favorite pen has been swiped again." she smiled as she closed the drawer.

"No, I'm okay. Let's get it over with." Amber said firmly straightening her back into a rigid, upright position.

"Okay then" Mary said. "Here are some forms that need to be filled out in regards to choices of anesthesia." She slid one paper across the desk to Amber and then another. "And this one is for medical history. When you complete these, I'll take your payment, unless you need to go over the fees."

"No, I don't."

The fast pace of the lady's conversation made Amber feel like she was being pushed into a race "Sign these forms, give me money, what are your thoughts, do you understand what I'm saying."

"I'll give you some time to fill out the forms." Mary left the room.

Macy tried to ignore the tears that she saw running down Amber's face as she signed the forms. She bit her lip to keep from saying anything. It killed her to see the girl in such pain, but she knew that she had to hold her tongue.

Mary came back into the room, "Are we ready?"

"Yes." Amber replied weakly.

"Okay, then let's make sure that everything is in order."

She checked over the paperwork for signatures. Then she collected the fee for the service. "This is ready. Okay Amber now I need you to follow me, I'm going to take you into an examination room. Your friend will have to wait for you in the waiting room."

Macy gave Amber a hug, and went out to the waiting room. Amber followed Mary to an examination room, where she left her to wait for a nurse.

A nurse came into the room. She pulled a starched white sheet out of a drawer in a cabinet, and a *johnny* with country blue diamond shapes all over it, from another cabinet drawer, then gave them to Amber.

"Please put this on, and wrap the sheet around your waist. I'll be back in to check your weight, and take your blood pressure." She left Amber alone, giving her time to change. Amber looked around the room, and felt the hair on her arms stand up into goose bumps. It suddenly occurred to her that the room held the imprints of many women before her. Many emotions had filled this room; many *johnnys* had been handed out and then placed in the laundry for the next time. Jars and containers held sticks, swabs, and cotton of various sizes, some wrapped in sterile protective plastic. While struggling with the closures on her bra, Amber backed into the examination table, causing the white paper covering it to crinkle in response. She thought, "There's that crinkle that makes you afraid you're going to tear it, and the nurse will frown at you." Amber worried that the nurse might be outside of the door, and take this noise to mean that she was changed and sitting on the table. She hurried to get her bra off and the *johnny* on; she had already laid her pants across the plastic orange chair in the corner, and stuffed her panties in one of the pockets. As much of her body that the doctor and nurse were about to see, somehow the thought of leaving her panties out in clear view seemed unlady like, and disrespectful.

The nurse returned in her white dress, which added to the sterile appearance of the room. She took Amber's blood pressure, and asked her to step onto a scale in the corner of the room. The woman did not speak to Amber other than to tell her what she required her to do.

Amber felt all alone. She wished Jason was with her, and found herself looking at the door feeling the urge to run out of the room. Maybe this was not the right thing to do; maybe she should take more time to think about her decision. Maybe-e-e. There was movement outside the door, and then the doctor entered the room. He introduced himself, "Hello, my name is Dr. Allen. Are we all set in here?"

"Yes, Dr. Allen. This is Amber Munroe." the nurse said reading the file in her hand, and then handing it to the doctor.

"Ms. Munroe, I see here that you've opted for a local anesthesia. Okay then would you please lie back on the table and put your legs in the stirrups." Dr. Allen read without looking up from the manila folder that he held in his hands.

Amber did as she was instructed. The doctor made small talk about what he was doing, but Amber did not hear him. He may as well have been talking to a dog. She only heard muffled sounds, and saw nothing because her eyes were shut so tight that they hurt. Blackness swam with red splotches, and blue invasions against a white back drop inside her eyelids. Her hands held onto the sides of the table so tightly that her knuckles were on their way to matching the color of the sheet that draped her waist. Amber's back pressed into the table, causing the noisy white paper that lined it to crunch and make crinkle noises. From that point on she barely felt the doctor's touch, or heard the sounds contained in the room.

Four other women sat in various positions in chairs around the recovery room. Amber searched their faces, only one seemed to not be as down trodden as she was. Two nurses went from chair to chair checking blood pressures and offering juice and crackers. She accepted a cup of juice and two crackers as the black cuff squeezed her arm two times. Eventually she was shown back to where Macy waited for her. Macy had the receptionist call them a taxi and they went home. They were as quiet going home as they had been coming. Music from the taxi driver's radio filled the small space. Christina Aguilera belted out her hit "I Am Beautiful". The lyrics bounced against the roof of the car, then were lost under the seat. Neither woman felt beautiful not at the moment. They both felt more like catfish. There was Amber helping Jason clean up his mess and keep it undercover from his wife and there was Macy assisting Amber in the clean-up process. No smiles peered through the windows of the back seat of the vehicle. No one felt like a guppy.

Macy was not sure what to say, and Amber did not want to talk. They were almost in front of the building before Macy broke the silence.

"This is probably a dumb question, but how do you feel?"

"Crampy."

"Any special instructions?" Macy inquired.

"None special enough to speak of."

The taxi pulled up in front of the building. Macy paid the driver, and got out. Standing aside she protectively watched Amber attempt to get out slowly, focusing on twisting her body in the most comfortable manner possible.

"Do you need anything from the store? Ginger ale, crackers, or tea?" Macy asked.

"Yeah, I guess I could use some crackers and tea."

"Okay, you go on inside and I'll go to the store and get some."

"Thanks Macy. You're the best." She gave Macy a hug, and began to cry.

"Don't cry now, you're going to make my cry. Do you want me to go down the street crying like a fool?" Macy teased. "Now go on inside so I can get to the store. Do they know that you're not coming in today? You're not going to try to go to work are you?"

Uh-huh. I told them not to expect me for the rest of the week."

"Well go on, I'll be back."

Macy turned and headed down the street. Amber went towards the building, and into her apartment. Mae-Belle watched from her window.

Macy walked slowly down the street. She could not stop the tears of sadness for her friend that ran down her face. She stopped at the pet shop window. A puppy was leaning on its front paws against the window barking anxiously. It was too bad that she couldn't buy one as a gift for Amber, it might lift her spirits. She went on her way to the store. As she reached the handle of the door, and prepared to pull it, a figure stopped beside her. She turned to see who it was, and it was Jason.

"Have you seen Amber today?" he asked.

"What the hell do you care? You useless bastard! How's the wife and kids!" she snapped at him.

He looked around to see if anyone was coming towards them. He didn't want anyone to hear their conversation. "Hey! Watch it! You don't know."

"Shut up! Before I tell your wife everything, you pig. You're lucky that you pulled this shit on Amber and not me. Because I would have taken you for everything you've got including your balls." Macy hissed in his face, then turned on her heels and continued on to the store.

Big mouth women needed to be put in their place, and Jason wanted to say more to Macy but he couldn't take the risk of causing her to follow up on her threat. He took the thrashing with a stiff upper lip, and went back to his store.

J.J. ran past him chasing the dog. Katie was helping Debra hang safe signs. The sound of the door opening caused Debra to turn.

"Where'd you get off to? I didn't even hear you leave. I turned to speak to you and you were gone."

"I went to the store to get some Honey Barbecue potato chips, but they were out. I guess I'm having your cravings."

She put both hands to her bulging belly, "I think this one is coming about two weeks early. I'm having another contraction."

"How far apart?" Jason asked with honest excitement.

"About fifteen minutes." she smiled nervously.

"What! Why haven't you said anything?" he said going over to give her a hug.

"I wanted to be sure. Don't you remember how many times we ran to the hospital with false labor when I was carrying J.J.?" she laughed.

"Well let's get the show on the road before our latest jewel makes its debut in the paint aisle! J.J. and Katie let's go! I'll drop you two off at grandma's house, and then I'm taking mommy to the hospital to get our new baby." Jason said joyously.

The children jumped up and down. Debra smiled at Jason and the children's excitement. Jason ushered them all out of the door, with the puppy under his arm. Macy was coming back down the sidewalk with a bag full of things for Amber. She saw the stunning pregnant woman holding the car door while the children got in. Then Jason came out of the store. His eyes caught Macy's, and just as quickly he looked away. This was definitely not the time to exchange words with her. He juggled the puppy under his arm as he locked the door, and went around to the driver's side of the car, avoiding any further eye contact with Macy. He passed the puppy into the back seat, to the children.

"Macy please be quiet. God please keep her quiet." he prayed to himself, then closed his door and quickly drove off.

"Jason you're sweating like this is your first time!" Debra laughed swiping at Jason's brow with a napkin from the glove compartment.

Eight hours later Jason cut the umbilical cord of his healthy, screaming son Corey Michaels. After calling family members to report the good news, he left his wife and new baby to do an errand.

"Are you still awake?" he asked Debra as he walked back into her hospital room.

"Yeah. Where have you been, stranger? The baby is in the nursery."

"Don't be so nosy!" he laughed, as he handed her a small package, and a bouquet of roses.

"They're wonderful!" she pushed her nose into the red velvety petals, allowing her nose to both touch and sniff the bouquet of twelve perfect roses. "I'll have to put them in something right away. Please sit them on that counter over there for now." She passed him the flowers, then she opened the gift.

"Oh-h-h sweet-heart! It's beautiful!" Inside the wrapping paper was a navy blue velvet box. The box contained a gold charm bracelet. She lifted it out of the box, and hanging from it was a miniature baseball glove with a gem stone in the color of J.J.'s birthstone. A flower with a gemstone in the color of Katie's birthstone, and a car with a gemstone in the color of baby Cory's birthstone. Debra began to cry, "Jason, I love you!" She pulled him to her and gave him a big hug. They shared a kiss and held each other. Even when the calm came after the excitement of the birth, telephone calls, and gift giving. Amber's terminated pregnancy never entered Jason's mind.

"Macy-y-y!" Amber called.

"What do you want brat!" Macy called back. She was lying on Amber's sofa watching television. She had called a co-worker, and asked him if he could take her place at the store, so that she could stay by Amber's side. She did not mention that she had seen and had words with Jason.

"Could you bring me a cup of tea?" Amber laughed. When Macy bought in the tea Amber hit her friend with a pillow. Macy dramatically fell back on the bed holding her chest. "Ouch!" Amber yelped.

"Oh, I'm sorry." Macy apologized with concern. "What's wrong?" she asked.

"My breasts are tender. The doctor said that it would be about two weeks before my body would realize that I'm not pregnant anymore. That's when my hormones will be back to normal. Macy I feel empty, and I don't know how to handle this feeling. I've been sleeping off and on, has Jason called?"

"No. No, he hasn't."

"If he calls and I'm sleeping, wake me okay?"

"Okay." Macy said half heartily.

"Do you promise?" Amber pleaded, noticing Macy's tone.

"Yeah, yeah!" Macy snapped. She stayed on the bed next to Amber until the girl fell asleep. Macy stayed the night. The telephone did not ring.

Macy woke first the next morning to heavy rain drops hitting the window. Amber continued to sleep. Macy softly slid off the bed. She locked the door behind herself and went to her own apartment. Music played from the direction of Sam's apartment.

Macy showered and dressed, then decided to go to the store to buy Amber a treat, a little something to help with what she had called the empty feeling. When she got to the stairs of the building she noticed Kenneth's car. She was both surprised, and confused. Why was his car in front of her building, but he had not knocked at her door? Maybe he went to the store before coming upstairs. She waited on the stairs thinking that he'd probably come down the sidewalk. After ten minutes she gave up on that idea. The only other reason for him to be at her building would be for him to pick up or drop off Sam. She knew that Sam had been working a full schedule at the club.

She went up to Sam's apartment and had to knock forcefully to be heard over the music. She was about to give up being heard over the tunes when Sam opened the door wearing a bright red kimono style robe. "Hurry back." Kenneth's voice sounded from behind the door. Macy pushed her way past Sam too quickly to be stopped.

Kenneth was lying on his back on Sam's plush white sofa. His muscular arms were tucked behind his head; the rest of his body was naked and sprawled out across the sofa as if he was waiting to have his photo taken. When Macy entered the room he sat up in surprise. The music continued to play as Macy began to bless Kenneth with an unholy tongue. He stood and began to pull on his underwear. Sam had closed the door and stepped across the room to Kenneth's side.

"Why are you getting dressed?" she asked him. "You're not her man are you?!" She said in a smug tone.

Macy answered for him. "He ain't my man, but if he's going to screw anybody, it doesn't have to be someone across the hall from where he screws me!" She took her hands from her hips, and allowed them to hang at her sides.

"Well we're all free agents honey." Sam said in a sassy voice as she sank into the sofa and crossed her legs.

"Kenneth, you better tell her to mind her business!"

"Macy don't start no shit, alright." Kenneth begged. He knew that if he yelled back at Macy that it would only serve to further agitate her. He was now completely dressed, and tried to pull Macy towards the door. She was going willingly until Sam said, "If I knew that you needed permission from another bitch to play I would have asked for a permission slip."

Macy swung free from Kenneth's grasp. "Who are you calling a bitch? You whack ass heifer!"

Before Sam could respond, Macy had taken giant steps back to where she sat. Sam made an effort to stand, but Macy slapped her and caused her to lose her footing. Sam kicked Macy in the stomach sending her back and onto the floor.

Kenneth rushed forward to try to get between the two women. He arrived in time to catch a punch in the groin from Macy that was aimed at Sam, who was diving through the air intending to land on Macy. Kenneth tried to grab for Sam by holding onto her robe. Sam slipped out of the robe, and now completely naked, jumped at Macy. Macy had pulled herself up from the floor and swung at Sam. Kenneth managed to catch his breath and get between the two. "Macy stop, go home will you?" he pleaded. He danced from side to side in an effort to keep the two women from connecting with the blows that each were still attempting to connect, instead he was taking the pummeling.

Miz Catfish

Sam butted in "Yeah, you better, you sorry ass-s-s."

Macy punched her in a naked breast midsentence. The blow winded her and cut off her speech. Macy then turned and slapped Kenneth, "You dog!" She turned to leave the apartment, leaving Sam holding her breast with a growing red bruise and Kenneth who knew not to follow her, as he cupped his now aching private area. They both jumped from surprise when Macy picked up the vase of flowers and smashed it on the hardwood floor. She slammed the door on her way out.

Macy went across the hall to her own apartment to nurse her wounds. Not only the ones on her body, but the ones on her psyche as well. She knew fully well that she and Kenneth had never made any sort of commitments to one another. But they had been sexually involved for the time that she'd known him, and she didn't want to see him with anyone that he was personal with. There was no way that she could stand the thought of sharing anything with that damned Samantha. In other words, Sam had ventured into marked territory. Macy had already peed on that hydrant.

Amber woke expecting to find Macy still beside her. Instead there was no Macy, and no message from her that Jason had called. She called Macy on the telephone.

"Hello!" Macy snatched up the hand set.

"What's wrong with you?" Amber asked innocently.

"Oh, I'm sorry, Amber. I'll explain later. What's up?" Macy used a forced calmer tone.

"Did I get any calls while I was sleeping?"

"No. No phone calls."

"I wonder why Jas-s-s, never mind." Amber mumbled to herself.

"How do you feel?" Macy tried to fill the quietness on the other end.

"I feel alright. The sleep did me a lot of good. Sorry that I wasn't better company."

"Don't be silly! I wasn't there to be company, just to blend into the furniture until you needed me. Do you need anything now?"

"No. I'll be fine. Thanks, anyway. I'll call you later okay."

"Okay."

There was a knock on Macy's door.

"Macy! Macy! Open the door. It's me!" Kenneth yelled. Macy ignored him. She went to the bathroom and freshened her face and hair, then into the closet. Kenneth was still banging. "Macy-y-y! Open this damn door!" he yelled as his fist pounded at Macy's door. "What the hell is your problem?"

When Macy had enough of the pounding, she yelled through the door. "You didn't have to screw someone across the hall from me, you senseless dog! I suppose you were going to come over here next to give me some of her juices. You pig bastard! Get away from my door before I throw hot water on you!" She threw a sandal at the door.

The thump on the other side of the door caused Kenneth to jump. He'd seen Macy go after other dancers and customers with blood on her mind. Kenneth once had to stop her from trying to pick another dancer to death with her high heel shoe, because the girl thought she'd wear the red shoes on her next set. He walked away from the door sulking.

   Amber called Jason. After not hearing from him an hour later, she called him again. She fell asleep waiting for him to respond to her messages requesting that he call her. The morning sun found her balled up on her bed with no messages on her voice mail. She felt crappy, and achy from head to toe. She hadn't eaten anything since yesterday when Macy had given her the tea and crackers. Yet the thought of eating did not appeal to her, she had no appetite. She wanted to hear from Jason. Why hadn't he called to check on her? What was wrong? She had done what he wanted her to. When would his life with his wife change so that he could be with her? His wife was a bitch for using the kids to keep him in the marriage.

   After waiting all day and another night for Jason to call, Amber could not stand not knowing the answers to her questions. She decided to get some answers. After showering and getting dressed, she went down the street to the hardware store.

   Three light blue helium balloons were tied to the door handle. A soft breeze caused the balloons to slightly sway. When she got to the door a different sign hung where the vacation sign had once been. The birth date of baby boy Cory was the same as the date of her abortion.

   No wonder she had not heard from Jason. He was busy with his wife and new baby. He was celebrating the birth of one child, while he left her alone to mourn the decision that he pleaded with her to get. How could he value one child more than another? Amber felt dizzy. She sat down on the curb to get her bearings. Had she been a fool? Cars that were attempting to park swerved around her legs and feet. She sat until she regained her composure enough to stand steadily. She mindlessly walked back to her apartment building. Janice sat on the stairs reading a newspaper. Amber never saw her, nor did she hear her say, "Hello." Janice was not offended, she figured the girl was under stress from the yelling that she had previously heard coming from the apartment.

As for herself, Janice was feeling lonely. It had been a long time since she'd had any male company. It wouldn't be wrong to date would it? Shouldn't she go on with her life? But that meant more than simply choosing to date again. She still had to deal with the fact that she was still married to Shawn legally. *Till death do us part*. Those were the words that they had uttered to one another. There had been no death, physically, to speak of, maybe emotionally, but no, not physically. She had a husband, and she was a wife. The bond that ties one to another is like both a legal and spiritual umbilical cord. Was she ready to cut that cord, even if the other half was connected to someone who threatened her very existence? Could she accept the presence of another man in her life? The warmth of another adult? A man, in her bed? Yes. The sensual touch on her neck, back, or cheek? Yes. The positive side had to be weighed by the negative. What if she chose another abusive man? What if another man raised his hand to slap her, or a fist to punch her, or called her a bitch, or stupid. Would she get out of the relationship immediately? Would she snap and try to kill him? Set him on fire? She couldn't take the risk. The negative side outweighed the positive. She sighed at her decision, and the loneliness settled in beside her on the step.

Miz Catfish

*****

Misty Harrison nervously fidgeted with the corner of the credit card receipt. For three months she'd been intercepting the mail specifically to get the first glance at their credit card bills. Ever since she found a receipt in the pocket of her husband's suit jacket while gathering clothes for the cleaners, she had been on alert for the presence of another woman.

James had not recently presented her with any jewelry, but she saw them listed on a receipt as proof of his purchase. He had been behaving in a withdrawn manner for sometime now. Often coming in long past business meeting hours, and he hadn't even commented on her new hair color or cut. She ran well manicured fingers through her dark auburn tresses. She'd even changed her choices of make up, no longer wearing the dark plum lipstick. The new pink shade of Fluffy Rose made her lips look welcoming. Kissable, so the lady at the cosmetics counter had exclaimed to her.

They'd been married twenty five years. She had seen him through the creation of his company and had walked the floor with him many nights watching him wait for the audits to pass. She had served him ginger ale in an attempt to get the stomach ulcers to calm, and she wouldn't give him up now. The telephone rang "Hello."

"Yeah, is this Mrs. H.?" a gruff voice requested.

"Yes, this is she."

"Yeah, ah. I got your number from a friend."

Miz Catfish

"What friend?" she asked cautiously.

"I don't know." The gruff voice sounded agitated. "Your mechanic?"

"Ok, alright." She soothed. "Are you available?"

"Yeah, I'm available. You sound pretty sexy. What's your deal?"

"Are you serious?! Is that why you think you're calling me?" she huffed.

"Okay, okay, give it to me short and sweet."

"Follow him and stop it. I want my marriage."

"Oh another one of those. Where do you want to meet?"

Misty planned her meeting with the gruff voice on the other end of the line. The owner of the gruff voice did not clean up for the occasion. He appeared with dirty fingernails, a denim jacket with upturned collar and baggy blue jeans with the bottoms stuffed into loosely laced Doc Martin boots. She clinched her pocketbook closer to her stomach under the table as he approached her in the dingy trucker dinette. Misty visibly flinched when he plopped his motorcycle helmet on the red and white checker-board print table top.

In her nervousness she had almost crumbled the 3x5 photo of James she held in her left hand. This was to be one of the only two times she would have to meet face to face with Mr. Gruff voice.

*****

Evening grayness fell upon 105 Shawnee Road, causing Janice to go inside. She felt the need to purge some of her thoughts and decided to write in her notebook.

Someone to Love

I wish I had someone to Love
Someone to call my own
Someone to sit and think about
When I'm feeling all alone

Someone to give me birthday gifts
And flowers for no reason at all
Someone to share my intimacies with
Thru winter, spring, summer, and fall

I wish I had someone to love
A special friend indeed
Someone that I could talk to
During those special times of need

Someone to hold me real, real tight
Someone that I could turn to
Someone I'd love with all my heart
Someone who'd love me too

- Tara Morgan

Amber lay staring at the wall across from her bed. That night the telephone never rang. Macy sat in front of her fish tank sulking. Angry that the men in her life had all seemed to be so piggish. Sex! Everything was based on sex. Sam sat in a hot tub of water, surrounded by large white candles. The water felt good to her aches. The fight with Macy had left a few bruises, the largest one on her ego. It had been twenty four hours and both women were as angry, and competitive in regards to each other as ever before. Mae-Belle hadn't bothered to knock on any doors throughout the day to offer lemonade on the roof top. She had not heard much movement throughout the building. This told her that people were staying in their own space and on their own schedule.

Macy was the first tenant out of her apartment the next morning, and to see the flowers once again outside her door. There were flowers at Sam's door as well. Macy stomped on Sam's flowers, then went back into her own apartment and put her flowers on her kitchen counter. Then she went about her plan of jogging. On her way out of the building she passed flowers at Amber and Janice's doors as well. "Who in the hell is leaving flowers at our doors?" she thought to herself. The coolness of the morning air caused her to put the thought of the flowers on a back burner and to focus on regulating her breathing and her feet hitting the pavement.

Sam opened her door to smashed flower petals and stems on the floor. She pulled off the dark glasses that she had chosen to wear along with a black scarf that was wrapped around her head and neck Hollywood style. So who was the secret admirer? She swept up the mess, put her dark glasses back on and closed her door behind herself. On her way past Amber and Janice's doors she saw their flowers and wondered what harm it would do to take them before they knew they had existed. But if she did take them what would she put them in? Macy the wild woman had broken her vase. She left the flowers alone and went about her way.

Miz Catfish

Janice came out to check her mailbox and picked up the flowers in front of her door. She knocked on Amber's door to make her aware of the ones in front of hers, but got no response. She took hers back into her apartment and left Amber's on the floor.

Amber finally opened her door an hour later to go speak with Macy. She spotted the flowers and began to smile. "Jason." she thought. Jason left me flowers. But why didn't he knock to give them to me? Or call me to say that he was coming over?" she wondered. She called and again got no answer. An hour went by before he called her. She answered the telephone on the first ring.

"Hello!"

"Hi." Jason returned.

"Well! I think you should have more to say to me than a simple, "Hi" she snapped.

"I know, I know. You're at angry me! I deserve it, but I've been really busy. My wife had the baby and there were some complications." he lied.

"I couldn't go far from home. I'm finally getting a chance to return calls and reopen the store. How are you feeling?"

"I'm feeling better now. A lot stronger. It was horrible! I don't ever want to go through that again!"

"You won't have to, don't worry. Are you busy?"

"No. Can you come by?" she asked with hope in her voice.

"Sure, I'll be right there. I need a lunch break. Bye."

They simultaneously hung up their telephones. Amber quickly ran around the house putting things in order, remembering to stop at the fish tank and drop some food in. She forgot about the incident of flushing the fish down the toilet. She had just finished washing her face and brushing her hair when she heard a knock at her door. Her heart fluttered as she ran to it, flung it open, and threw herself into Jason's arms.

He returned the affection. They stumbled through the doorway, not letting go of each other. Jason used his foot to close the door, while continuing to hold onto Amber. Before Amber could get a chance to vent her sadness and disappointment to her lover he was slipping off pieces of clothing from both of their bodies. He had slipped on a condom and pulled her on top of him for sex. It was too soon for her to have intercourse, but she endured it, to be with Jason. There was no conversation between the two of them, until both of their needs had been met.

"Why haven't you called me?" she pouted.

"I've explained that already." he said while kissing her forehead.

"Why are you wearing a condom?" she asked climbing off his lap.

"We can't have any more accidents, Amber. You know my situation."

"Yeah, you're right. Well, aren't you even going to ask me how it was, or how I feel?" she glared at him.

"No, I'm not going to ask how it was, because I don't want to think about that, but I will ask how you are."

"I'm a lot better now." she said snuggling into his side.

He pushed her away enough to see her face. "How many people have you told about this?" he asked.

"Macy is the only one that I confide in. She came with me to the appointment, and she's my best friend. Why do you ask that question?"

"Well, I don't want to be the topic of the neighborhood gossip. It could cause problems for me, you know."

"Don't worry. I won't cause problems for you. God forbid some of this shit should fall into your lap!" she snapped, pushing him as she moved away.

She walked into the bathroom, and turned on the shower. She left the water running as she went back into the living room where she found him putting his clothes in order. He then went into the bathroom and flushed the used condom. She had followed him, and when he turned around to leave she blocked his exit.

"I'd better get back to the store." He hoped to leave without having to make any commitments.

"When will I see you again?" she asked.

"I'm not sure; I told you that there were complications at the birth. I'm needed around the house until my wife can get around on her own again.

"Maybe I should come home with you, so that you can take care of both my and Debra's postpartum needs!" she snapped.

This situation had certainly gotten out of hand. Maybe it was time to bring this tryst to an end. "Hey come on. Don't be that way," he said, lifting a brown curl off Amber's forehead.

"You've got to be patient." He walked over to the counter and picked up his jacket. "I'll call you as soon as I get a chance." He was out the door before she could think of anything to stop him.

She knew that she had been used. He had gotten sex and left her alone again with her emotions.

Suddenly she felt drained. An anger that was long simmering began to grow. She needed to let him know how she felt. She called and left a message for him, but after an hour, he had not called her. She called again, but got a message on a machine. She felt caged like a wild animal. The words that she longed to say to her lover stuck in her throat, while the walls of her living room began to close in around her like those of the emotional cage that held her. If she could not alleviate the emotions that she felt she would have to find a way to keep them tame.

Amber grabbed her keys and wallet, and ran out of the front door. She ran past Janice who was sitting on the stairs. Janice watched her walk down the sidewalk quick paced, and shook her head sadly. She wondered "What in the world had the girl in such a tizzy today?"

Amber couldn't help turning her head towards the hardware store. The sign in the window read "CLOSED". How could it be closed? When Jason left her house, he said that he was going back to the store. The store was supposed to be having a big important sale. "He's playing you for a fool Amber." she thought angrily. "That bastard was not going back to the store; I bet he went home to his perfect little family." her thoughts continued.

She entered the store and went to the wine cooler. She chose a cheap wine, and picked up a six pack of beer. Paying for her choices of indulgence was an embarrassing ordeal. Her co-workers were under the impression that she was at home with an illness. Yet here she was buying alcoholic beverages. With as little conversation as possible, she paid for her purchases at the cash register and quickly left the store feeling more anger and confusion coursing through her body. Janice leaned away from the pathway to be sure not to be in Amber's way as she came scrambling up the stairs.

After sitting on the porch for twenty minutes smelling the flowers that she had found outside her door, Janice had not tired of their aroma. When Ortega made his way to the front of the building, he found her enjoying the flowers so much that only her eyes could be seen above the colorful bouquet. He stopped in front of her.

"How are choo beautiful lady?" he asked Janice.

"I'm okay." Janice replied.

"Choo like the flowers?" he inquired.

"Yeah, they're nice." Her voice gave way to her pleasure.

"Where are choo bebees?"

"What?" she asked with a puzzled look on her face, no longer hidden behind the flowers. From her experiences with talking to Ortega, she knew to get her guard up. He always aggravated her until she cursed at him.

He repeated himself, "I said where are choo bebees, choo kids!"

"They're in the house." Janice answered.

"Why are choo outside enjoying the fresh air and flowers, while choo bebees are in the hot house? Why choo do that? I thought choo look like a smart lady, that is why I bring flowers."

Ortega had broken the floral spell that she'd been under. "You brought me, everyone, flowers?" she asked in surprise.

"Yes, it was me who has been leaving such beautiful flowers. But I will not bring anymore. Maybe I have wasted my time and money, huh?" Ortega said.

"Take your old flowers you pain in the ass! Just because you do nice things, doesn't mean that you can run your mouth all of the time," Janice yelled into his face.

She raised her hand that held the flowers and bought them down on top of Ortega's hat. Multi-colored flower petals scattered the top of his head and shoulders, and the force of the blow caused his hat to fall off of his head. A daisy petal hung carelessly on his eyelash. She threw the stems at his feet and stomped into the building, leaving Ortega standing bewildered and hot under the collar.

Janice went upstairs to see Mae-Belle. After waiting outside long enough to let Janice get out of the hallway, Ortega went upstairs to see Macy.

Macy was making a ham and cheese hoagie to go along with her potato chips and soda when banging began on her door.

"Machie!" Ortega shouted.

"Why in the hell are yo-o?" Macy was yelling as she opened the door. She stopped mid-sentence as she noticed the mess on Ortega's shoulders, and his smashed hat in his hands. "What happened to you!" she asked before she began laughing hysterically. Ortega did not see the humor in having his old world Spaniard ego bruised by a woman. Now one dared to laugh in his face.

"Mujer loca! Ingrata. Necesita un marido que la ensene? Que le pasa a esa mujer? No mas flores, ella esta loca!" he mumbled angrily in Spanish.

"What are you talking about? What happened?" Macy asked through laughter over his angry Spanish words.

"I said that woman down the stairs, she is crazy! She needs a husband to teach her. I brought flowers for everyone here. I try to bring smiles, but instead I get anger." he spoke to Macy, but also to get out his anger. "One of my customers works for a florist; sometimes he gives me the cut flowers from the end of the day. I shared them with all of the women in the building instead of taking them all to my wife."

"Did you say that you brought the flowers to everyone?" Macy asked.

"Si. Yes, I brought the flowers."

"That was nice of you Ortega. So who hit you with theirs?"

"That lady down the stairs I said. Don't choo listen to me, Machie?" he said in an agitated tone. "She is your friend."

"You said something to Janice again didn't you! You should know better by now. Why do you keep talking to her? You're lucky that she didn't do more than that to you. Go into the bathroom and get cleaned up. Maybe you'll want some of my sandwich."

He went off to the bathroom mumbling. She knew that he was mumbling in Spanish so she didn't even try to understand him. She was still laughing about his incident when he returned to the room.

"Do you want some lunch?" she tried to stop laughing.

"What is that choo are having?" he asked.

"A ham and cheese hoagie, some potato chips, and soda, sounds tasty, huh?"

"Choo eat ham? Why? It is not good for choo. What else can we have?" he asked.

"What do you mean *WE*? I'm having what I've already said! If you want something else, go get it!" Macy said in an irritated voice.

"Now choo want to be nasty. I can't be right here today, I guess. I feel tired. May I lay on your chair?"

"No! Go home if you're tired. What do you think this is your second home? Go back to your own house!" Macy snapped. "Isn't CeCe going to start wondering where you are? Maybe she'll hit you with her flowers too!" she teased.

He snatched his hat off of the chair. A few stray pink petals clung to the brim; he plucked them off and threw them on the floor. Macy howled with laughter. Ortega didn't look back as he stormed out of her door.

Janice sat on Mae-Belle's soft green leather chair. Mae-Belle joined her wearing one of her more subtle colored muumuus.

Miz Catfish

"Miss Mae-Belle, my mother is coming to visit me, she's arriving tomorrow. I wondered if you would take me to the airport to pick her up?" Janice asked.

"Sure. I would be happy to do that for you. What time do you need to be there?" Mae-Belle asked.

"Around four o'clock would be fine." Janice said.

"Okay, I'll meet you at the car at three o'clock."

Janice went back to her apartment and woke the children from their nap. She was excited about getting to see her mother again. The children had grown, and emotionally so had she. She was used to sharing everything in her life with her mother, and she missed being houses away from her to continue that special relationship. Yet with all of the joy that she felt about seeing her mother again, she couldn't ignore an underlying feeling of anxiousness. Something was wrong. She could feel it as they talked on the telephone. The woman she thought she knew so well, her mother, was very quiet and nervous when the names of Betty Jenkins and Macy Jenkins were the subject at hand. What was the mystery that she had reopened by calling her grandmother with her questions about the past? She was brought out of the thoughts by Jamie pulling on her shirt tail. Janice found small tasks around the house to keep herself busy until the next morning.

Miz Catfish

Chapter 23

Sam's wheat field of hair flowed behind her from beneath the safety helmet on her head as Lamar drove the black and silver motorcycle up to the curb. She was first to jump off the bike and take her helmet off. Lamar put the support stand down and then he got off the bike as well.

"May I walk you to your door little lady?" he asked.

"Why you sure as shootin' can!" Sam responded with a mock country twang as she handed him her helmet.

He allowed her to walk up the stairway first, enjoying the view from the back. Lamar had watched Sam dance at the club many times. Yet, he had to admit that he was as attracted to her with clothes on as he was when she was taking them off. When she reached her apartment door, she turned to him and saw a smirk on his face.

"Hey, what's that grin on your face for mister?"

"Oh nothing, nothing." he responded slyly.

Once they were inside, and the door was closed, Lamar took his leather biking jacket off and checked out his surroundings. The place looked as he had imagined, soft and feminine. The color white reminded a person to be gentle and careful. Sam handed him a cold can of beer, then he followed her to the sofa where they sat down.

"So when can I get a private show?" he asked.

"You just came from a show. Why do you need another one so soon?" she said with a laugh.

"Because I can't get enough of you, why else! I wanna be selfish and have you to myself. I don't want to hear the clapping of any other hands than my own this time.

"What do I get out of this extra show?"

"You name it babe, it's your call." he said.

"Well it is almost rent time." she said with a pout. "Do you think that you could find your way to helping me out with that situation," she   smiled.

"You've got it." he replied, sliding down further into the sofa's cushions getting comfortable. "Will two dead prez do you good?" he asked.

"Sure, but I don't take checks," she said getting up to put her beer can on the table.

"I'm not talking checks. Don't worry; I never leave the house without a thick roll. I can back my promises up, but I have a reques." he boasted.

"What might that be?" she asked looking at him questioningly from her distance.

"I want the show to be like the ones at the club. I want to see you work your stuff like I know you can. Make me reach my bursting point like you did earlier tonight, only now I'm alone with you and I can go with your vibes."

Sam noticed the small red light blinking on her answering machine, indicating that she had messages. They would have to wait until she made her rent a bill paid in full. She went over to her CD collection and selected one with continuous head beats. Then she went into her closet, used as a dressing room and changed into a red nipple cut out bra with a matching thong. She added a toe ring to her outfit, and a large red manly dress shirt buttoned to the neck.

She re-entered the living room area when the song was on a strong up beat. Lamar was anxious, he was crazy about Sam. He would have given her the rent money just for allowing him into her private space. The dancing was an extra for him. He had a weakness for beautiful women ever since the age of twelve when he began sneaking a peak at his father's nudie magazines.

Sam slowly undid one button at a time as she moved to the beat. Once all of the buttons were undone she allowed the shirt to fall. As the dancing became more seductive, Lamar sipped on his beer, allowing himself to be grooved into a world of flesh. Sam decided to throw her all into the private show. She danced and shimmied her private audience into a frenzy, while Lamar sat on the sofa feeling the excitement building in his body. Sam danced so closed to him that he could smell the sweetness of her body. He reached out to touch her thigh. She backed away just as the tip of his finger made contact with her skin. He felt his toes tense inside his shoes. She approached him again, this time climbing on top of him and thrilling him with a lap dance. He wanted to touch her, but she held his arms above his head. When he could no longer stand the teasing of the mock gyrating motions he attempted to pull his arms away from the grasp of her dainty hands. As she tightened her grasp around his wrists with more strength than he'd assumed she contained, Sam continued the gyrations of the lap dance, until she felt his body go tense. She went for the kill, quickly running her tongue around the outside of his right ear, and then darting it deeply inside its center. Before he could regain his composure from the thrills and chills she was sending throughout his body, he felt his toes release from their position, as well as, a release of warmth in his groin area. He pulled his arms free and grabbed her around the waist pulling her close until a wave of lightheadedness that consumed him passed.

She allowed him the closure, two hundred dollar's worth of closure. She directed him towards the bathroom while she went to the refrigerator to get two fresh beers. He returned to the living room with a sheepish grin on his face. She was sitting on the sofa wearing her shirt, holding the two beers, handing him a beer, she stretched feigning tiredness.

She hinted "I guess I'm going to turn in now."

"I guess that's my cue to leave." he said as he reached into his pocket and pulled out his wallet. He handed her the money as he had promised, plus and extra fifty dollars. He gave her a kiss on the cheek and then left. She was counting the money as his motorcycle roared and then pulled away from the curb side. Sam fell into a deep sleep on her pull-out sofa.

Amber sat in her bedroom holding a glass of vodka left from one of Jason's visits. Each sip of the clear liquid added to a small fire that grew larger in the center of her belly. Along with the flames came numbness throughout her body. She welcomed the feeling, although the feeling of burning was not comfortable. She was not a drinker of hard liquor, and each warm sip went down harshly, and left a bitter taste on her palate that was almost unbearable. She could not deny the peacefulness that it brought to her troubled mind. She had not heard from Jason. She called him and he never called her. Her body was beginning to re-enter a non-pregnant state, but her mind had not. The last disposable diaper commercial had sent her into a crying spell that left her with a headache.

What had she done? When was she going to be able to deal with what was going on in her life without being in so much pain? She fell asleep with her body on her bed, but her arm hung off with a glass of vodka just below her fingertips. She was awakened hours later by knocks at her door.

"Amber. Amber!" Macy knocked for the sixth time.

"I'm coming!" Amber snapped. As she tried to ignore the horrible headache pounding away at the back of her eye sockets. She opened the door not prepared for the effect of the morning sun that caused stabbing pains to course through her temples.

"Whoo! What the hell hit you?" Macy said with surprise as she walked past Amber and into the middle of the living room. "Amber I'm in, you can close the door now."

Amber moved in slow, sluggish motions. "Okay, okay. Just stop shouting will you?"

"You look like you've been through the wringer. Are you okay?"

"Oh Macy I don't know what to do with this mess I'm in." Amber said sadly as she dropped with a thud onto the floor pillow holding her head between her shaky hands.

Macy sat down beside her. She noticed the flowers on Amber's kitchen counter.

"Why do you still have those dead flowers from Ortega on your counter?"

"What did you say?" Amber asked while rubbing her temples.

"I said, why are you keeping those dead flowers," Macy pointed to the flowers, "from Ortega?"

"Ortega? Your friend, CeCe's husband? Ortega?" Amber asked with confusion.

"Yes. Ortega. Ortega is the one who has been bringing everyone flowers. He told me that one of his taxi customers gives them to him. Apparently he got into an argument with Janice who beat him with the flowers he left for her." Macy said the last with a chuckle.

Amber did not smile or laugh at the humor of the story. Nor did she share with Macy the greater sadness that she now felt, because the flowers had not been from Jason as she had thought.

"Hey, ahh, Macy, I have a horrible headache. I'm going to go back to bed." Amber said weakly.

"I'll see you later." she could see that there was a problem with her friend, but did not think it was the right time to push.

Macy left Amber's and went upstairs to see Mae-Belle. She didn't know if she could handle Amber's problems alone. She wasn't sure how to approach Amber's situation with Mae-Belle without feeling like she was revealing her friend's secrets. She began by describing the condition she'd left Amber in before she came upstairs, and that she was almost positive that Amber was hung over from drinking.

"Hi Miss Mae-Belle. Can I talk to you about something?"

"Sure Macy, come on in."

"I'm really worried about Amber. She's in bad shape."

"Yeah I'm worried about her too."

"I think she's into something that's way over her head. I feel bad coming to you like I'm betraying her confidence in me."

"Macy I'm aware of some of Amber's problems so don't feel too bad. You're a real friend that's why you're so worried. But she'll be okay. This type of stuff has been going on since the days of the Bible. We just have to stay supportive of her and she'll pull through. I just hope she stops seeing him."

She was relieved to find out that Amber had already told Mae-Belle about her situation. All Macy had done was to let her in on her recent worries. Mae-Belle suggested that Macy continue to check on her friend, while allowing her to work through her feelings. "She'll let everything out when she's ready. She's been through a lot in these past weeks."

Macy accepted the advice and went back to her own apartment.

Mae-Belle showered and got ready to give Janice a ride to the airport to pick up her mother. Then she stayed in the car with the children while Janice helped her mother with her luggage. Jamie was happy to see her grandmother and clung to her neck until Janice made her let go.

Janice was not sure how to handle the nervousness that her mother displayed. Norma Cowins was normally a very bubbly, friendly, and assertive person. Yet on this day Norma was quiet, and somewhat withdrawn. She allowed Janice to deal with the baggage claim employee and only spoke with Janice and Mae-Belle when they addressed her.

She begged their pardon, and explained that it had been a long flight and she was tired. Norma was relieved to get into her daughter's home so that she could have some time to herself again, as she unpacked her suitcases in Janice's bedroom. She prayed and concentrated on her task ahead.

Mae-Belle's car had pulled back into its usual parking space in front of the building a half-hour after Macy left for work dressed comfortably in cream colored denim jeans and black t-shirt with matching glossy black fingernails. If Macy had been a little slower in her press to get to her job, she might have run into the passengers upon their entrance into the building. Instead she would not meet Norma until the next morning. On Macy's way out of the building she stopped at Amber's door to check on her.

"Amber."

The knocking sounds pushed through the fog surrounding Amber's mind. "I'm coming." she thought in her mind, not realizing that the words were not coming from her mouth. Another round of knocks rang through her mind with more intensity. "Macy I'm coming, stop banging will you!" Amber pleaded as she opened the door and stepped aside.

"Hurry up! I'm on my way to work," Macy said as she entered the doorway. "Why don't you open some windows in here? It's stuffy. Are you going to have your rent money for Mae-Belle? From the looks of you, you haven't gone to work today."

Miz Catfish

"I don't want my windows up, and no I didn't go to work. I don't feel good alright" Amber said in a sassy tone.

"What about your rent?" Macy repeated.

"Rent? What's today's date? Is it that time already?" Amber asked confused.

"Don't worry about the date, just take care of yourself. Have you eaten anything?"

"No, and I'm not hungry."

"You need something, or you're going to get really sick," Macy said walking into Amber's kitchen.

"I called that bastard, and he hasn't even bothered to call me! I can't believe this shit. Macy, what am I going to do?" Amber said half speaking to herself and partially to Macy.

"Amber this is a hard time for you right now, but believe me you'll make it sweetie that I promise you. Here." Macy handed Amber a glass of flat ginger ale from the refrigerator that barely held any food. "I have to get to work. Why don't you take a shower? It'll help you feel better." Macy noticed that Amber's hair was greasy and her clothes rumpled. "I'll check on you when I get off work, okay?" Macy spoke over her shoulder on her way out of the door.

When Macy closed Amber's door, her mind was already settled on what she was about to do. She swung into the hardware store like a December wind. The sound of the door slamming angrily into the door jam caused Jason's head to turn sharply towards the cause. There stood Macy with her hands on her hips.

"Jason, we have a problem!"

"What problem would that be?" Jason asked, coming from behind the counter. A customer stood next to the register looking at Zodiac signs key chains hanging on a pegboard.

"Amber's not bouncing back from her situation that well, she hasn't been to work in a week."

"I don't think that this is the time or place to talk about that problem." Jason said as he turned his head to check on his customer.

"There is no time better than right now. I don't think this conversation can wait." her voice grew louder.

"Sh-h-h! Don't raise your voice; this is a place of business."

"I can and will get louder than this! So you'd better listen to me, and listen good!" Macy said as she shifted from one foot to the other, and keeping her hands on her hips. The one and only customer left the store, almost in a skip avoiding the growing confusion. Jason saw the disgust on the customer's face and turned angrily to Macy.

"You have a hell of a nerve! This shit is between me and Amber, not you!" he yelled.

Macy yelled back, "Yeah, well she's my friend, and I'm not going to let her go down the tubes because of some slick, horny, married pig! So you had better listen up buddy, because Amber is crazy over you, but I don't give two shits about you or your prick!"

"What the hell do you want?" he said.

"It's almost rent time, and her phone bill is probably due too. I suggest that you get yourself a pen so that you can write some checks or fork over the cash. I think you should be able to help her out that much."

"I'll see what I can do." he conceded, but not without feeling trapped.

"Just make it happen, or else!" she smiled wickedly.

"Or else what?" he snarled.

"Or I'll follow you home, and else I'll tell your beautiful wifey everything. Maybe she should look at the telephone numbers on your phone bill more often, you know what I mean?" Macy replied in a teasing tone, arms folded in a sassy manner across her chest.

"I said that I'd see what I could do." he said in an agitated voice, but with less force. He gave in, knowing when he was cornered.

"Well see if you can make your decision today." Macy said as she reached for the door handle. She smiled at Jason, "Amber was right, you are kind of cute." she said as she swung herself out of the door making sure that it slammed shut as loudly as when she'd come in . Jason stood where she'd left him, secretly admiring her spunk, and wondering what the tigress was like in bed.

Jason locked up the store and headed to Amber's apartment. He had been ignoring her calls, and hoping that she wouldn't show up at the store. Macy's threat left him no choice but to go face Amber. He couldn't risk Macy coming back on a day when Debra would be there or seeing her in the CORNER STOP. He checked his wallet to be sure that he had enough cash on him to give Amber what Macy had demanded.

He was not prepared for what he saw when Amber came to the door. The youthful, angelic glow in her skin that had captured his attention was gone; replacing it was a grey hue. Her soft curls were unkempt and matted. She looked tired, and filled with worldliness. When she saw that it was him at the door, she burst into tears and stepped back as if she was seeing a ghost.

"Amber, what's wrong?" Jason asked with genuine concern. To him the events over the past months had been recreational; he had not allowed them to be incorporated into his real life. The abortion had been a strategic move, not personal. He did not even realize that Amber hurt the same way that his wife was feeling the joy. "Why are you backing away?" he asked as he stepped into the apartment and closed the door. Amber still had not spoken a word. She simply looked at him through tired, bloodshot eyes. She made an attempt to lean against the kitchen counter but found her footing unsteady and made an uncertain landing against the counter. Finally he realized that she was hung over.

"My God Amber! What in the hell are you trying to do to yourself?" he asked walking across the floor to where she stood. "Have you eaten?"

Amber's crying became uncontrollable, her sobs loud and erratic. Seeing Jason was too much. Her emotions were as unsteady as her feet. Jason had arrived when her defenses were down. Her anger was lost in the alcoholic haze.

He had caught her off guard. Amber had spent the past few days trying to prepare herself for the fact that Jason was gone for good. Now here he was showing up at her door, rubbing salt into her open wounds. She tried to move away from him, but the concern in his voice and his now out stretched hands pulled her to him like a magnet. She allowed herself to fall.

"Don't cry." he said softly.

"I'm sorry for being so stupid." she apologized between sobs.

"Sorry for what? Don't be silly, I'm sorry that I haven't called you or come by, but I've been so busy. I'm so glad that I decided to come by here today. You look like you could use some help. I'm going to pay your rent and telephone bill for this month so don't worry about that."

He took his hands from her waist to get his wallet out of his back pocket. He put money on the counter, and sat his wallet down as well, and then he returned his attention to Amber.

"Now come on, let's go get you cleaned up." he said as he walked her to the bathroom.

Amber allowed herself to be led. It felt good to be in Jason's arms, and for him to show concern. This was a moment for which she had been wishing. Jason put the toilet lid down and sat her on it, while he turned on the shower, adjusted the water temperature, then helped her out of her clothes and into the water. The wetness felt miraculous against her skin, but not as beautiful as Jason's hands that were moving across her back.

Jason tried to look at Amber's naked body as a mercy mission, but as he wiped the sudsy washcloth back and forth across the small, delicate back he couldn't help but remember how soft, and sweet the skin beneath the cloth was. He was too close to resist.

The warm water both cleared her alcohol induced haze and kept her in a mellow state of sadness. She wondered if her lover washed his wife's back and fixed showers for her too, and his touch became bittersweet. Jason took off his clothing and slipped into the shower behind her. Deep in her own thoughts, she didn't realize that he had joined her in the shower until she felt his wet skin against hers.

He filled his hand with shampoo from a bottle on the window ledge. Quivers ran through his groin and down his legs as he gently rubbed the bubbles through her curls. She bent further into the spray of water to get the soap and shampoo off of her body and felt his wet sweetness enter her. For Jason, the mercy mission was over, nature had won the tug of war. He held her around the waist as he pulled and pushed himself in and out of her welcoming wetness.

She wondered: "How many times had he done this very same thing with his wife?" Tears mingled with the streaming water from the shower head. "This is all so wrong." she thought. "But he feels so good." She turned off the shower, and they left the bathroom together. Jason asked her for clean sheets and helped her change the linen on the bed. He folded back the top sheet, fluffed up the pillows and once they were settled he pulled the clean, fresh smelling fabric up over their still moist skin. Amber felt her eyelids getting heavy as she succumbed to a much needed sleep. Jason checked the clock on the nightstand; he didn't want to go home too late. He allowed her to fall asleep in his arms, and after waiting for her breathing to become heavy and steady, slowly pulled his arm from under her, he dressed and slipped away. He had to get home to another shower before falling in bed next to his wife.

Miz Catfish

Macy did not knock on Amber's door on her way into the building. She hadn't noticed any light through the windows and hoped that her friend was getting some much needed slumber. After getting into her apartment, and putting her pocketbook down, she slipped off her shoes and went to the refrigerator for a drink. With the can of soda in her hand she sat down in front of the fish tank. She opened her soda, took a few sips then sprinkled some fish food into the tank. The guppies and tetra paid no attention to the human watching from outside of their aquatic existence. The catfish poked its head out from behind a plant and then swam over to a corner of the tank. It stayed in the corner, wiggling every now and then for buoyancy. It seemed to stare at Macy, once again drawing the human into a world of association.

Macy stared at the catfish, the cleanup fish. No time for itself to chase the other fish around playfully, or to simply hang out and look beautiful against the tank's decorations. Nope, no time! Something always needed tending to, the ecological balance of the tank depended on her. Amber needed someone to lean on through this trying time, and it was possible that Sam needed one more ass kicking to assure territorial boundaries. And now Janice's mother was coming for a visit, and could possibly give her answers to the secrets of her past. Macy felt the call of the dance tonight, the urge to slide across the stage and hear the roar of clapping and whistles. It was at times like this that the attention from the crowd served to help her feel that she was beautiful, because only beauty demanded the roar of a crowd and calls for more. In these instances it didn't matter whether good or bad attention, it was all attention and she'd take it. She reached for the telephone on the end table.

Macy's fingers tightened around the headset of her telephone as she prepared to poke the numbers that would assist her in accomplishing her goal. Instead of her mind assisting with the completion of the task at hand, it played a nasty trick on her and exchanged the numbers with a flashback to her past.

There was no way for her to know when Mr. Hamin would sneak into the bathroom while she showered. The door made no sound, because dirty ole' man Hamin as the other foster girls called him, had probably oiled the hinges. Macy clearly remembered the first time she pulled the shower curtain back enough to reach for the shampoo and unintentionally glanced up into the mirror locking eyes with twinkling blue eyes placed too closely under unruly thick black eye brows. Forgetting the shampoo she quickly slid the powder pink vinyl back into a closed position and leaned against the wall, in an attempt to pull her naked silhouette away from the curtain that she knew was practically sheer. She tried to ignore the cold moisture on the tile squares caused by remnants of water from the shower head.

Goosebumps rose all over her body. How long had he been standing there? At the age of sixteen Macy was well aware of the reason Mr. Hamin would want to watch her take a shower.

She had to get out of the shower and into some clothes. She shouted to Susan, "Hey, ah Susan, will you bring me some jeans out of my drawer and the sweater off my bed?"

"Sure Macy," Susan returned.

Thank God Susan had been near enough to hear her call out. Macy chanced moving closer to the shower curtain and could see that the door was entirely closed. Mr. Hamin was gone.

She stepped out of the tub and wrapped a towel around herself. There was a knock at the door.

"Macy, it's me Susan. Can I come in?"

"Yeah, come on in," Macy said in shaky voice.

"Here are your things. Hey you look like you've seen a ghost! What's wrong? I brought the under things off your bed too."

"I don't know if I should tell you this, it's about Mr. Hamin."

"Let me guess, he took a peek into the bathroom while you were in here." She put the clothes on the closed toilet seat, and leaned against the sink.

"You say that like it's no big deal." Macy sounded confused.

"It's not so much that It's not a big deal, it's just that he's done it to quite a few of us. I guess he gets off on it. Hey at least he don't rub hisself while he watches, I had a guy do that once."

"It's gross and creepy." Macy hugged her arms around herself." Has anyone told this to the old lady, or their case work-k…"

"Don't bother! There aren't enough foster homes to bounce us around to every time one of us complains about conditions in a place. You're a beautiful girl, get used to it, and use it to your advantage. That's what I do now. Ask him for things; make him pay for the show. Couldn't you use some pocket money, new sneakers, make-up, you get it?" Susan gave Macy a playful punch in the shoulder, winked at her then left.

Macy dressed and brushed the unwashed, unruly, hair on her head into a ponytail. She opened the bathroom door tightly holding onto her possessions, and peeking her head out first to make sure that Mr. Hamin was not lurking in the area. After finding the coast clear, quickly she walked to her room and closed the door, and stayed there listening to the radio until she heard the yell for dinner. Mr. Hamin caught her eye and gave her a sheepish grin, but she caught him staring at her later while he gnawed at his pork chop bone. This time he raised his bushy thick eyebrows in acknowledgement of her attention and smiled around his bone.

"He probably wishes I was that bone. Yuck!" she thought as she quickly turned away. Susan giggled, causing Macy to turn in her direction. The other three girls continued with their own dealings. Macy knew that Susan was tickled by her being uncomfortable with Mr. Hamin's advances.

"Hey Mrs. Hamin! Are you really missing all this action?" Macy thought and wondered what if she spoke her thought out loud? "Would she jeopardize the roof over her head? She preferred living with a family rather than a group home. Once when she was in a group home someone got head lice, and she had to get her hair cut down to a four inch afro in order for the treatments to be effective. Not to mention the fact that in group homes your possessions walked away more often than not you had to fight all of the time with kids that came in from all situations, and who knew what type of mental conditions you were dealing with. She decided to keep her mouth shut this time. At the age of sixteen she only had two years to go before she'd age out and be legally set free from the foster care system into the rest of the world."

Mr. Hamin put his bone down and got up from the table. "Paul are you going to finish your food?" his wife questioned.

"Yeah I'll be back honey."

He returned and directed his attention to his food. Macy scraped remnants of food from her plate and stacked it in the dishwasher, then went back to her bedroom. Immediately she noticed her pillow was not as she'd left it. Her facial features twisted with confusion. Instead it lay in the middle of the bed. Lifting the floral fabric covered goose feathers, she noticed the money immediately. She counted the mixed denominations of bills, and stared at the total of fifty dollars.

Susan entered the room and closed the door. She flopped down on her bed and offered advice, "Put that away and save it for your next trip to the mall. Maybe you'll get a few more pieces in your wardrobe than the rest of us who have to wait for the old lady to decide to use some of the state check to buy us some new underwear much less a new pair of blue jeans. Think of it as allowance slash, payment slash, rainy day fund."

Macy shoved the money under her pillow and slowly spread herself across the bed. The day had ended in an entire haze for her. She lived at the Hamin home for the next year and a half until she turned eighteen, during that time she'd catch Paul Hamin's eyes in the bathroom mirror while she showered at least two times a week. Afterwards, she would find anywhere from thirty to sixty dollars left somewhere on her bed.

Macy came out of her thoughts, "Too bad I can't tell that pig bastard today, what his voyeurism has done for me. I've gone to making more than he could afford for a peek. "She sat with her hand resting on the telephone, finally changing her mind about dancing that night; she decided to hear the voice of someone who saw her for herself and not a sexual object only.

Chapter 24

Sam mixed the store brought mushrooms with the psychedelic drug mushrooms known as 'shrooms that she'd brought from Tiny the petite dancer with the 38 double D breast implants.

Each time the blade of the knife came down to make the beige pieces of work yet smaller the thought of what she was about to do caused a surge of power to run through her body. As the blade loudly hit the wooden chopping block, a thudding pulsation stroked the deepest, wet spot within the golden covered feminine spot between her legs. One hand held the knife midchop while the other gripped the edge of the counter. With her eyes closed to a slither of openings, as felines are known to do in a relaxed state, her thigh and round butt muscles tightened. She shifted her stance to accommodate the oncoming wave of an orgasm.

"Damn girl, get control of yourself." Sam brought her thoughts back to the meal she was preparing for Lamar. She had invited him over for a spaghetti dinner, complete with French bread and wine.

When the forceful knock came at the door, the mushroom mixture was tucked away inconspicuously in an odorous sauce that begged to be sopped up by pieces of absorbent bread. The lights in the apartment were low, the table was set and the candles lit.

Sam answered the door dressed in a yellow midrift t-shirt, and "lay on the bed to squeeze into me" blue jeans that closed just above the pubic area revealing the strings of a neon yellow g-string that hugged her waist. Her dainty bare feet with red painted toe nails sank into the plush carpet as she stepped aside allowing her guest to enter.

"Well good evening handsome." She smiled.

"Good evening to you too. Damn girl!" Lamar stopped in the middle of the floor watching Sam as she closed and locked the door. "What's for dinner? You or the spaghetti sauce I smell?"

"How about both? I'm flexible with the menu tonight." She stepped to him, and wrapped her arm around his waist.

Lamar could feel emotions stirring with in his stomach and groin. The excitement in his groin area was understandable, but what was causing the tightening in his stomach? He had felt this feeling many times before, but usually when he was nervous or in a dangerous situation, like the time he had to fight at Kelsey's Bar and had to knife a guy. He knew that Sam was no innocent newby, she'd been around the block as the saying went, but that fact didn't make him afraid to spend time with her. Ever since she'd become a new dancer at the club, he'd had an uncontrollable urge to stroke her skin, and have her stroke his in return.

"Would you like to hear some music?" Sam asked.

"What ever you want."

"Are you this easy to please all of the time?" she released him from her hold and moved to the stereo to put on a jazz CD. "Let's move over here to the counter while the food is nice and hot. I made this meal with a special touch. I hope you don't mind." She smiled.

They moved together to the counter and while Lamar sat, Sam prepared two plates, and placed them in their positions. She cut two pieces of bread, then poured their wine, placed them in their positions then sat opposite her guest.

"Let's dig in."

Lamar twisted his fork in the spaghetti and enjoyed a mouth full of flavor. He ate four mouths full of food to her two and drank two glasses of wine to her one. Sam reached her bread across to Lamar.

"Have a bite."

"Any time a beautiful woman offers to feed me I wouldn't dare say "No". he smiled and took a bite.

"If you've had enough let's move over to the sofa."

After swallowing another mouthful, Lamar agreed to the move. Sam had already begun to feel the effects of the 'shrooms. The walls around her appeared to be breathing, they attempted to extend and touch her as she walked to the living room. Lamar followed close behind and noticed her slight weave and dodge motion.

"Hey what are you doing?" he laughed.

"I put a special spice in the food and I think it's starting to fuck with me."

"Put a spice huh? I thought I was imagining the twirling feeling in my head. I wasn't going to say anything. What special spice did you feed me?"

"I had a friend do a little cow tipping for me." She fell backwards onto the sofa. "Phew! I didn't think I'd make it."

333

Lamar sat on the floor at her feet. "Make it where?" his breathing was labored.

"To the sofa. Sh-h-h, stop talking, they're breathing." She put a manicured finger to her lips.

Lamar began an uncontrollable laugh that continued until his chest felt constricted. He took his shirt off in an attempt to make room for his lungs to expand. He laid his head on Sam's lap trying to concentrate on regaining control of his breathing. Sam covered her eyes with her hands, thinking she'd wait out the pulsating movement of the wall beside the sofa. The white paint had moved close enough for her to see the stroke marks from the paint brush, and then pulled away like it was being sucked in. When she pulled her hands away she realized that Lamar had removed his shirt.

"Where's your shirt?"

"Over there." He pointed to the shirt lying in a heap at the door.

"Why did you take it off?"

"I couldn't breath! How much of that stuff did you put in there?"

"Not that much. Why? You can't hang or something?" she challenged.

"I said no such thing."

"I got a joint, want some?"

"Damn you tryin' to kill me in here?" he laughed.

"Don't worry; if I do I'll bring you back."

"Yeah, so you say. I'll smoke with you if you'll take those jeans off and let me enjoy the rest of the sunshine hidden under them." He traced her navel with his finger.

"It's a deal."

She disappeared on shaky legs into the closet. Returning with the joint, cigarette lighter, and no longer wearing blue jeans. She joined him on the floor, still feeling the giddiness from the 'shrooms. Lamar had removed his shoes and blue jeans. Sam straddled him, put the skinny white stick between her lips, lit it, and pulled in until she had a mouth full of pungent smoke. She inhaled deep and exhaled into Lamar's face, kissing him long and hard with the lost bit of her smoke being exchanged between the two of them. She passed him the joint and suddenly noticed what appeared to be a slight movement in his chest hairs.

"Stay still, there's something on you." she began to part the hair on his chest.

Lamar blew out smoke. "Like what?" he pulled on the joint, which was now smaller. He quickly released the smoke when he felt a sharp pain on his chest. "What are you doing?!"

"I'm looking for it!" Sam moved her fingers through the hairs on Lamar's chest as is she were a mother chimp looking for mites on her baby. Her beautiful facial features serious as she concentrated on her task.

Lamar pushed her hands away. "Ouch! Here take this!" he passed her the remnants of the joint which at this point was dangerously close to burning the fingers of it's possessor. A euphoric feeling filled his body. Leaning his head back onto the sofa, he allowed his body to go limp. He teetered on the edge of feeling like he was in the room and being on a soft cloud with nothing but fluffy cotton beneath him and cool air surrounding him. Only in parts of the moment did he feel Sam tugging his boxers past his hips and down his legs. The removal of the thin fabric from his private area released the sweet smell of freshly showered male sexuality into the room. It mingled with the scent of the joint and the affects of the 'shrooms, causing Sam's senses to heighten to a peak.

A sudden flood of pleasure in Lamar's thighs and groin area caused him to look downwards. Sam had taken him into her mouth and was stroking him in and out of her beautiful pouty lips. He pulled her back into her previous straddle position on his lap. Leaving the yellow string on but pulling it aside, he motioned for her to lift her body slightly. He then reached under her, positioned himself, and allowed her to slide her body down into place. The place where he met her. She felt hypersensitive pleasure everywhere that he touched her. The hands that held her tight butt cheeks felt like a girdle, his tongue probing her mouth tasted like the sweetest flavor of a cherry lollipop being twirled in her mouth, and oh as he entered her where they met, she felt as if she had been impaled by something the width of his hand. She pulled her body upwards in a stroke once, twice and on the sixth let go with an explosion soon to be accompanied by Lamar's. They fell sideways onto the plush white carpet which had served as clouds in his delusional state. Both exhausted and dripping with sweat, they fell asleep with Sam waking first.

She continued to lie still until she was sure that she felt in control of her senses. Noticing that Lamar was still sleeping, she carefully pulled her leg from beneath him and her arm from beneath his neck. Sam didn't mind participating in a

Miz Catfish

little drug activity every now and then; especially when she had a plan of action based around it, and today was one of those days. She picked up Lamar's pants and removed the wallet from the back pocket. Letting the pants fall back to the floor, she opened the stiff leather and pulled out the green dollar bills. Four hundred twenty three dollars, not bad. Sam didn't know what Lamar did for a living and she didn't ask. If the "Don't ask, don't tell" policy had worked for the government, it was certainly good enough for her. She put one hundred seventy three dollars back, and kept two hundred and fifty. Then she thought about the cost of the 'shrooms and the joint, and took twenty dollars more. Sam closed the wallet and put it back. She could have asked him for money and he would have given it to her, but she didn't want to allow him to choose the amount, or give up the feeling of being naughty and in control. She allowed him ten more minutes of sleep, and then began to nudge him with her foot.

"Hey, wake up sleepy head."

"Hum-m-m?"

"Get up. I've got and appointment to get to." She lied. She had no more use for him now. The party was over, she had entertained and been paid for her services.

He sat up and reached for his boxers pulling them on in his seated position. "You know something Sam, you're like the river, and no one ever knows which way you're flowing beneath the surface. That beautiful face always gets ya."

Sam handed him his pants. He stood and pulled them on. She gave no response to his comment, instead she handed him his shirt, all the while watching him with a peaceful, angelic look on her face. Once Lamar was completely dressed, he pulled out his wallet.

"I like that little yellow number that you're wearing, but how about you surprise me the next time with something green. That's my favorite color." He opened the leather and counted the dollar bills quickly realizing that he was short by quite a bit. He looked into her face which still looked peaceful as she lay on her sofa, stretched out in all of her glory.

He didn't say anything; he figured he could only blame himself. Who could miss the mischievous glare in the girl's eyes? She was high maintenance and probably used to helping herself stay that way. He would have to remember to never leave his money where she could help herself to it unless he wanted her to, if there was to be a next time. She was lucky he was still tipsy from their night of fun. He had to get completely back to a clear head to see how he really felt about her serving him 'shrooms. He'd never done them before and hadn't been interested in trying. What if he'd had some bad trip? No, he'd definitely have to look at this situation with a clear head. He had to consider how he felt about this night of events. Any other female of lesser beauty and charisma, would have put herself in a dangerous position and come to harm right there on the spot, to top the night off she'd stolen money from his wallet.

He hid his thoughts. "Well I must admit that was a whopper of a meal. Koodles to the chef!" he laughed.

"Oh, that was just a little something, something." She smirked.

He bent over her and kissed her on the forehead. "Give me a call later."

"Sure thing cutie." She replied. She knew she wouldn't.

*****

Amber stretched her leg towards the middle of her bed, expecting to feel Jason's leg. Instead she felt emptiness, and opened her eyes to a vacant opposite side of the bed. When had Jason slipped away? Why had he come as if he were bringing comfort and hope only to crush her again? Amber got up from the bed, reached for her robe slipping it on as she walked towards the living room. He was definitely gone, but his wallet was on the counter. She looked at the folded brown leather laying still like a turtle in it's shell, it, too, waited to have its hole poked to see what would come out. She rubbed her hand across the smoothness of the wallet trying to hold back the urge to search its contents. Finally giving in to the temptation, she unfolded the leather to reveal a wallet size photo of the children from the hardware store introduced to her as Katie and J.J., enclosed in a plastic pocket. They were sitting on the Easter Bunny's lap. She flipped the photo and stared into the strawberry patched face of a new baby. A name was typed across the bottom in gold. Apparently Cory Phillip Michaels had been eight pounds one ounce at birth. The small, ruddy cheeked face, with a round bald head, looked peaceful and innocent.

Would he ever find out that he would have had a sibling months younger than himself? Maybe she'd tell him when he got older. Maybe she'd tell the other children about their missing sibling as well. When Amber regained focus on the object in her hand, she was looking into the twinkling, welcoming eyes of Debra. An unseen fist punched Amber's empty belly with a one-two motion, not allowing her to catch breaths in between. No doubt about it Debra was as beautiful on paper as she was in person. Was she smart? Did the woman in the photo make love to him longer than she did? Did he stroke his wife's shiny black hair the same way he stroked her curls?

Amber pulled the yellowing, hard plastic driver's license from its snug slot opposite the photos. Jason wore a school boy smile that hid the fact that he was eight years her senior. With all of the misery Amber felt she could not deny her attraction to the handsome face behind the plastic. Nine Woodlawn Drive. Jason's address wouldn't have stood out brighter if it had been in orange letters. Amber wondered what the house at nine Woodlawn Drive looked like on the inside. Did Jason mow the green grass of the lawn, or did he pay a neighbor's kid to do it? Did he push his cute little girl on a swing in the back yard? Did white smoke curl out of a chimney when snow covered the ground?

Jealousy and curiosity nudged her to find a piece of paper to write down the address, Jason's birth date, and his social security number, then she flipped back to baby Cory's photo and wrote down his birth date. She counted the money in the fold. He had eighty-two dollars. She took out the eighty dollars, put them in the pocket of her robe, and left the two dollars behind. What was coming over her? Here she was snooping, stealing, drinking herself into a stupor and crying over a married man. She was losing herself in this new life away from her aunt and uncle.

The telephone rang, startling Amber. She picked up the receiver with shaky hands, "Hello."

Miz Catfish

"Amber, did I leave my wallet there?" Jason rushed.

"Yeah your wallet is here, but why can't you at least say, "Hello" or

"Good morning?" Amber snapped.

"I will if you give me a chance. Good morning. I'll be there to get the wallet in about fifteen minutes." He hung up before she could say anything else.

Amber was dressed in t-shirt and jeans when Jason's knocks rang through the apartment. Jason rushed in through the opening that Amber created. "I have to get back to the store. Where is it?"

Amber closed the door, but continued to stand beside it with her arms folded in a defiant manner. "It's on the counter." she said in a flat tone. He picked up the wallet from the counter and opened it, hoping that Amber did not notice the nervousness in his movements as he quickly checked through each compartment. The photos were in place, but the money looked thin. He didn't want to count it in front of her and risk offending her. His driver's license was upside down, he hardly had cause to pull it out of its slot, so he was sure it was always left in place right side up. He pulled it out and replaced it to a right side up position.

"Amber, did you look through my wallet?"

"Why? Is there something in there that you wouldn't want me to see?"

"Did you look through it or not?" he turned to face her. Amber, don't try anything dumb." He said in a warning tone, taking a step toward her.

"Don't threaten me Jason." Amber warned through a mischievous grin,

"I don't hear you complaining that anything is missing. So what's your problem?"

"I don't have time for this; I have to get to the store." he said reaching for the door knob "Oh yeah, and tell your bitch of a girlfriend, Macy, to mind her own business!" he pulled the door open and slammed it behind himself. Amber ran to the window, lifted it, and said, "Cute family! Is Woodlawn Drive close by?" she warned.

He didn't look back, the words caused the hair on his neck to stand on end. "Damn this shit is out of control!" Jason thought. "Now what the hell am I going to do? She knows my address; of course she looked through my wallet!" His thoughts pushed him down the street at an even faster pace as panic quickened his footsteps. He reached the store, unlocked the door and closed it behind himself with a forceful shove. He had to do some damage control with Amber.

Amber threw the money from Jason's wallet to the floor, then stepped on it and pushed it across the floor. The dingy, worn green and white paper scattered in multi directions and lay useless where they landed. They would serve their purpose when she gave them to Mae-Belle for her rent, but at the moment they were a reminder of Jason's visit. She was angrier and more confused now that she'd seen him again this morning, than she'd been waking up to an empty bed. He'd retrieved the wallet and left like a scolded dog, not like a person who had slept with her hours ago. "Why had he come yesterday, just to have sex with her? Why help with her bills?

Why was he gone without as much as a kiss on the cheek? Was he ever coming back, did she want him too?"

She put on sandals and started out for answers, she wouldn't be dismissed so easily. Amber didn't understand that being a mistress means to be dismissed quite often without explanation. Hell, would it be the truth even if there was an explanation? Jason was surprised and nervous to see her walk in. What if Debra decided to stop in for a visit with the children?

"Amber, what are you doing here?" he said not hiding his irritation, then thinking better of his tone remembering that he needed to keep her calm and away from his home, he said in a more soothing manner, "You were in quite a state when I got to the house yesterday. I thought you'd sleep for days." he said in one breath, hoping to not sound as uncomfortable and irritated as he felt.

"Why did you leave without waking me?" she asked ignoring what she considered babble.

"I had to open the store." he said in a matter of fact tone.

"Are you coming back tonight?" she asked as she moved closer to him.

"I'm not sure," he replied, leaning back from her gaze and trying to avoid touching her body, "and you shouldn't have gone through my wallet Amber, that was wrong."

"Why haven't you called me?" she asked jumping around with her thoughts.

"Amber don't star-r," he did not get to finish his sentence.

"Please hold me Jason." she pleaded, now standing toe to toe with him, and her arms around his waist.

"Amber, this isn't the place for that." he said firmly trying to push her away.

She didn't let go easily. While trying to kiss his neck she caused him to lose his footing. They stumbled backwards into the counter.

"Amber, stop! This is crazy!" he yelled forcing her to release her grip around his waist. "Have you been drinking again?"

She stepped back as if he had pricked her with a pin. "No, I haven't been drinking! You didn't care about that when you were humping me last night, you bastard!" she slapped his face.

"Amber don't do that again. You'd better leave!" he resisted the urge to rub the smarting area of his cheek.

"Why? The little lady coming here today? Maybe you don't want her to see us here alone? But then again, why should you care if she sees us together or not, you're going to divorce her remember? Remember?" she yelled hysterically.

"Amber! Good-Bye! I won't discuss my home life with you. I've got a lot of work to do. I'll call you later."

"Yeah, well I won't hold my breath," she kicked him in the shin and walked out of the store.

She went to the convenience store, bought more beer and wine and went back to her apartment. The bottle of wine and cans of beer clinked and clanged in the large brown paper bag. As soon as she got into the apartment she locked the door and opened the bottle of wine. She knew that Jason would not call but still she found herself waiting for the telephone to ring.

Norma dried the breakfast and lunch dishes, as Janice dressed the children. After they were dressed and released by their mother, they ran back to sit in front of the television. Johnny had come to enjoy the cartoons as much as his sister and with his bottle nipple clinched between his teeth, he ended up in front of the television before her. Norma heard the commotion and smiled at the growth and contentment that she saw in her grandchildren.

"Ma, do you want to meet Macy now? I can go upstairs, or call her down. Even better than that we can all go upstairs to the roof. It looks nice outside," Janice called to her mother.

Norma took a deep breath and called back, "Yes, you can go ahead and call her; but I think that we'd better stay inside, so we don't have any disruptions."

Janice was anxious to put the two women together. Finally there would be some answers to the mysteries that her grandmother and mother held from her over the telephone lines.

She almost tripped over one of Johnny's toys as she quickly made her way to the telephone.

"Hi Macy, it's me Aish…" She caught herself before completing the name that she'd been hearing since her mother's arrival. "Um-m, it's me Janice. My mother is here, why don't you come on down. We can ask her all the questions about Mrs. Jenkins." She ended excitedly.

"Okay, I'll be right down," Macy replied. They hung up their telephones, and each took a moment to deal with the emotions surrounding the call.

Janice had almost called herself by her real name of Aisha. She was reminded of her old life as that person. Her mother's arrival had opened a small black box full of Aisha Brown's life, joys, and the pains that Janice constantly tried to keep separate from life as it currently was. Before her mother came she quietly lived the life of a single parent with two children. No one asked questions. No one in the state of Massachusetts knew that she was afraid of being found by her abusive husband. They only saw her tough exterior. Her black eyes and bruises had healed many moons ago leaving behind scars hidden from the human eye in a forbidden place in her mind.

She had become used to the privacy of the unknown. Her mother was a part of the old life. Looking at her forced Janice's mind to allow the intrusion of old demons. As she enjoyed her mother's home cooking, she couldn't help but think about the leftovers from some of these same types of meals that were once in her and Shawn's refrigerator.

Macy apprehensively started down the stairway to Janice's apartment. Maybe she shouldn't bother sleeping dogs. She had made it through life this far without knowing any information about her biological parents, maybe she should go back to her own apartment and go on with life's mysteries intact. Her thoughts ended when she realized that she was in front of Janice's door.

Absentmindedly, she knocked. An anxious and smiling Janice opened the door.

"Hey girl, get on in here!" Janice shouted with excitement.

Miz Catfish

Macy stepped into the apartment and closed the door behind her. Jamie ran across the room and threw her arms around Macy's waist, Macy returned the embrace. Johnny paid her entrance no attention as he watched an animated cat and mouse run across the television screen.

"Come here Ma, Macy is here!" Janice yelled out to her mother like a happy child.

Norma took a deep breath and stepped from the kitchen into the living room. She still had to turn to her left to see the young woman standing near the front door. She didn't know what to expect. Maybe it wasn't her, how would she know? Certainly she wouldn't recognize the girl at first sight. After all, the Macy that she remembered had been a mere child the last time she'd seen her. She did not know how to expect the adult Macy to look. There was one thing that would make identifying her Macy certain, a pear shaped dark brown birthmark at the nape of her neck, which seemed fitting because pear had been her favorite snack throughout the stressful pregnancy.

When she turned to face the women, the first thing that she noticed was the uncanny resemblance between her granddaughter Teri, and the woman whose waist the child clung to. Janice shooed the little girl away.

"Teri go over there with your brother, the grownups need to talk," she commanded. Jamie reluctantly released Macy and pouted the entire distance from where she'd stood to where Johnny sat.

"Ma, this is Macy Jenkins. Macy, this is my mother Norma Cowins," Janice said.

"Hi how are you?" Macy said offering her hand for a proper handshake greeting.

"I'm fine. It's nice to meet you." Norma responded, receiving the outstretched hand.

The skin of the hand was smooth, and warm. Norma felt weak. It had been so many years since she'd felt that hand. Was this really happening? Both of the young women stood proudly poised. Although they were night and day in their physical characteristics, they were a stunning pair to lay eyes upon. Little Jamie pulled the two together genetically having sprang from Aisha's loins, but looking exactly like Macy. Norma could stand no longer.

"Well, come on girls, let's sit over here." she said walking over to sit on the sofa before she fell down from the shock of things.

Macy and Janice followed behind her. Janice spoke first, "Teri looks a lot like Macy, doesn't she?" Janice asked her mother.

"Yes, she does." Norma replied.

"She reminds me of myself when I lived with Miss Jenkins in Pittsburgh. I called her Mama. Miss Norma do you remember Betty Jenkins?" Macy joined the conversation.

"Yes, I remember Miss Betty. We were neighbors in Pittsburgh." Norma responded.

"I think I remember playing with Macy at Miss Betty's house. Do you remember me playing with Macy? Do you remember her?" Janice asked.

Miz Catfish

"Yeah, I think I remember playing with Janice too, but I don't remember the name Janice." Macy said.

"That's because my real name is Aisha. I had to change it because I'm hiding from a crazy husband. That's how I ended up in Boston. The kid's real names are Teri, and Shawn Junior. My husband's name is Shawn Brown. I had to leave my whole world behind for safety sake. I couldn't tell you because that would be risking my safety. It's a small world, and you never know who knows who." Janice explained, happy to be able to share her burden with a friend.

"Oh." Macy said, "I was wondering why you just called Jamie "Teri when you told her to go sit down".

Norma took a deep breath and took control of the conversation. "You two are right, you did play together. I always wondered if this day would come, and now that it has I'm almost speechless. I'm afraid that I'll wake from a dream and find that this didn't happen. You're both beautiful young women. Macy do you have any children?"

"No, I don't."

"Ma, how come you never called us back to answer these questions that we're asking now. You and grandma were acting so strange. What's the big deal?" Janice asked.

"I'll explain that, give me a chance. Aisha I met your father in high school. We became sweethearts. When I got pregnant with you, we got married. The marriage didn't last long; he was not responsible enough to take care of a family. We got a divorce and he went on his way. I went back home to my mother's house, and that's how we came to live near Betty Jenkins. She had bought the house next to your grandmother's.

She cared for foster children. There were always children playing, and running in her yard. She had more than enough love for them all. She'd bring each one over to our house as she got them, to introduce them to me and my mother. When you, Aisha, got old enough to play outside, we allowed you to play with the children.

I got a job at a grocery store to afford to buy your clothes and necessities. Your father was nowhere to be found. A man by the name of Liam McDougal was the owner of the store. I didn't have a way home when the weather was bad, or if I was weary from a busy day so he began giving me rides. We'd wait until everyone was gone before we went to the car. Our friendship had to be kept quiet because he was white, and people in our town were not comfortable or happy about black and white relationships. Your grandmother knew that I was accepting the rides from Liam. It was of no concern to her, but she warned me of the bigotry we'd experience from the community if I was seen getting in, or out of his car.

"After one month of spending time with Liam during the rides home, he expressed a desire to sleep with me. I told him, "no," and explained to him that I was still trying to get over the disappointment of my relationship with my ex-husband Vernon." She turned to Macy, "Aisha's father.

I didn't have a problem with his color, I just wasn't ready. He said that he understood, but two weeks later, he asked me again. I told him, "no," and explained to him I wouldn't take any more rides home from him. I didn't think it would be fair to him to continue. Maybe I would have, if I wasn't still trying to deal with my past, but I just wasn't ready. At work the following day, as I was preparing to leave, Liam walked up to me and pulled me into an embrace. I asked him to stop, and tried to push him away. As if it were yesterday, I can still see the pain of rejection on his face, his eyes grew big and round like saucers, and they welled up with tears.

"He started tugging at my clothes, while constantly repeating over and over again how much he wanted, and needed to be close to me. I continued to struggle, but I could not stop his hands from making their way up under my skirt and ripping down my underwear. I threatened to scream for help, and he reminded me that it was late and no one would hear me. He also said that he would deny everything I said, and because I was black he'd be believed before me. I cried and pulled at his dark brown hair."

Norma stopped, and audibly took in a gulp of air, as if struggling to keep her breathing regular. She looked from Janice to Macy's face looking for signs of judgment or rejection. She saw none, only the expectation of the forth coming information registered, and she knew that she owed Macy everything that she could remember of how the girl came to be, and why she'd been given up for adoption.

The television released bonking noises as Tom hit Jerry over the head with a frying pan, causing the shape of the small mouse to imprint into the stainless steel. Jamie warned Johnny to back away from the television in a big sister's authoritive tone. The children continued on in their enjoyment of innocence, oblivious to the life changing conversation being had feet away.

Macy sat back into the cushions of the chair for support. She wasn't sure if she was absorbing what this stranger was offering. Norma looked at Macy, waiting for her to look her way. Macy felt Norma's glare and looked up to find the woman staring at her. There was no denying the similar features that exposed the shared blood line, the strongest differences being caused in the child due to what she now knew to be bi-racial paternity. Macy looked away; feeling uncomfortable with the direction Norma's story seemed to be going.

Norma wondered how the girls in front of her, women of the world, but forever her girls, were going to look at her after she'd finished her story. Would they be ashamed of her for giving away her own child? Would Aisha stop speaking to her? She couldn't imagine her life without Aisha and the children. But the past had caught up to her and she had to deal with the consequences.

She started again, "anyway, like I was saying, I pulled at his hair and beat at his chest, I tried kicking and biting but nothing stopped him. Liam was a handsome man; he stood about six feet, with broad shoulders like a football player. I couldn't stop him, and when everything was over I lay on the floor with my clothes all twisted around my body, my skirt above my waist, and my torn underwear around one ankle. He stood up, straightened his clothes and apologized. He offered his hand to help me up from the floor, but I pulled away confused by his actions. He left the room, I got up and with my hands as shaky as they were, tried to make myself look as decent as I could. I left the store, walking home as quickly as I could, constantly looking over my shoulder, afraid that he would follow me in his car. I struggled with whether or not to tell my mother what had happened. I was afraid that she'd accuse me of bringing the situation on myself by accepting the friendship from the beginning, and I couldn't prepare myself to speak out loud what had been done to me.

"I entered the house, and went straight to the bathroom. I showered over and over again, until you Aisha began to continuously knock at the door with your little hands, wanting me to play with you. I avoided my mother hoping to keep her from noticing my nervousness as my hands continued to shake. Every time a car passed the house, I worried that Liam was coming to stop me from telling what he'd done. It wasn't realistic that he'd come to my home, but that was my fear.

"I never returned to the store again, and stayed as close to home as possible, afraid to run into Liam. When my period didn't come the following month, I knew that I had a decision to make. I hadn't been with anyone else sexually since Vernon, and that had been too long ago to even be considered. The fact was that I was carrying Liam's baby. I kept my secret to myself, trying to decide what to do. I knew women, who had chosen to have an abortion. I could have gotten information from them on how and where to get one, but I didn't feel that was the choice for me. When I played with the little girl I already had, I couldn't imagine not bringing the next tiny life into the world.

I'd hid the pregnancy from my mother for two months before I got up the courage to tell her. She held me, and cried. She didn't want to see me and the baby scorned by the hateful, ignorant people in town. Liam and I never spoke again. I saw his sister when I was around seven months along. She said she'd mention to Liam that she'd seen me. She congratulated me on the new baby and said that she missed seeing me at the store. Not long after that day I saw Liam's car drive past the house. I was in the yard and our eyes met as he slowly drove by. His eyes dropped to my stomach then he drove on. I don't know if he came again after that day, I know in my heart that he knew it was his baby.

The baby growing inside of me was part of what was a nightmare for me, but I wanted to keep it. My mother convinced me that it would be best to give the baby up. She promised that it would be adopted by a family somewhere else where it would be accepted as a bi-racial child, and no one would question me on who the father was.

"I longed for labor to begin so that I could be in a non-pregnant state again, but on the other hand, I dreaded labor because it meant that I'd no longer be able to protect my child from the cruelties of the world, and once it was out of my belly, I'd have to part with it.

"By the time I went into labor I had worked myself into frenzy. I couldn't bear to part with the child. So your grandmother came up with a way to help ease the pain of the adoption procedure."

Norma stopped to gain her composure, and swipe at the tears that had been running down her cheeks.

"Ma, what's wrong?" Janice handed her mother a tissue.

Macy was feeling an odd anxiousness throughout her body. What was this woman getting at? White man, pregnancy, and adoption. Her mind began to whirl as if she was entering an out of body experience. What was this woman saying? Could it be?

Norma took a deep breath and continued. "When my baby was born they allowed me to hold her one time before they turned her over to the adoption agency. I cried so long on that day that I made myself sick. I couldn't eat and even vomited the tea and crackers that the nurse brought me. I'll never forget how the weather on that day reflected my mood. It was rainy and solemn, and the rain drops seemed to pop against the hospital room windows. Even when I stopped crying it felt like I still was, because of the rain water running down the windows. My mother left you, Aisha, with Betty Jenkins while she tended to me. I wondered if anyone but me would want my beautiful baby girl. She carried the tell tale signs of being bi-racial. Her hair was curly and light brown. Her skin was soft and fuzzy like a peach. She turned bright red as she cried, while I counted her fingers and toes. When she stopped crying and the redness faded away, her skin was golden tinged. I knew that she wouldn't get any darker. Her beautiful light brown eyes drew me into her heart and her into mine.

When the nurse took her my mother held me and whispered into my ear

"Don't worry baby, you'll see her again. I talked to the adoption people. The baby is going to Betty Jenkins's home."

"When I was released from the hospital Miss Betty had the baby at my house. I walked into a dream. There was my first born Aisha Renee, and my new secret Macy Jennifer. I told Miss Betty the names that I had chosen and she gave them to the adoption agency to put on the birth certificate." Norma stopped talking and allowed her words to sink in for her two daughters who were now looking at her as if she had just told them that she was really a man.

"Are you saying that Macy is your daughter, the baby you gave up for adoption? Is that what you said?" Janice asked in a bewildered tone.

"Yes." Norma managed through fresh tears.

She looked at Macy who was sitting quietly with her own tears streaming down her face. The stranger looking at her had just said that she had named her Macy Jennifer. That was her name, but maybe she wasn't the Macy that Norma was remembering.

"Maybe I'm not the same person that you are thinking of?" Macy voiced her thoughts out loud.

"My baby had a pear shaped birthmark at the nape of her neck.

Without responding verbally, Macy turned her body sideways on the sofa and flipped her hair up to show the birthmark.

Norma gasped "Good Lord! You've brought my baby back to me!" she managed through joyous sobs. Her hands went up in praise.

Macy turned back around and allowed herself to fall into Norma's arms. Norma held her child. She pulled away from Macy and took her face between her hands.

"Your skin is still soft like a peach." she said between sobs. "I knew that you wouldn't get much darker than what you were at birth, and those eyes are still piercing. You have your father's eyes. "

"Ma, are you saying that Macy is my little sister?" Janice asked, still bewildered by what was happening in front of her.

"Yes, this is your little sister," Norma gave a shaky laugh, "My second baby. I've been miserable through the years wondering if you were alright. I was afraid that you were with people who weren't taking care of you after you left Miss

Betty's house. As long as you were next door to me, I could watch you grow up, and participate in your upbringing. I used to keep you with me as often as I could. But in those days the social workers used to check out the foster homes frequently, and without notice of when they were going to show up. So we had to be careful. If they came too often and you weren't there they would have thought that Miss Betty was not really caring for her foster children herself, and removed them all. Aisha, you used to take care of Macy when you two got big enough to be outside together. You'd drag her around like a mother hen. It was a blessing from God to me, that I was able to keep Macy with me a lot, and you two got a chance to bond. When Miss Betty got up in age and took ill, the foster children were removed from her home. I thought I'd lose my mind with sorrow; a piece of my heart had been ripped out. I wanted to tell the social services people that I wanted you to come back with me. But my mother, family, and friends drilled into my head that I'd be causing problems for you and Aisha. People would point fingers at you like a circus animal and Aisha would hurt to see your pain, and also be hurt by the things she'd hear people say to her about her sister and mother. In my heart I knew that my decision was wrong, I should not have let a bunch of ignorant people dictate to me if I should keep my child or not. I was a coward not to stand up for myself and my child. You did not ask to come into this cruel world. I should have protected you. I never stopped thinking about you. I hoped that one day you will be able to forgive me, and allow me into your life in some way. I'm so happy that you have found your sister, and have a relationship."

Macy and Janice looked at each other hesitantly. "We're sisters!" Janice said in quiet amazement. The three women sat quietly. The cartoon that the children were watching took on the largest presence in the room.

"Ma why didn't you tell me before? You've gone all of these years with this secret? It must have been tough for you." Janice said sympathetically, not being able to imagine having a child in the world away from her own care.

Macy stood up. "Why didn't you try to find me?" she asked, turning away from the woman's glare.

"It was not that simple in those days. Adoption was complicated and records were available only to social workers. The children, including you, were taken so quickly that I didn't even have time to think about what my choices were. An ugly white van showed up, all of you children were put into it and it drove away. Miss Betty never recovered from her illness and passed away."

"Did my father ever acknowledge me?" Macy asked sadly, cutting off Norma's words.

"Not publicly, no."

"Do you think he's still in Pittsburgh?"

"He was a few years ago. My mother, your grandmother, has run into him a few times around town. She doesn't speak to him. To her he's the devil because of the way he handled the entire situation."

As much as Macy tried, she could no longer hold back her tears. Janice and Norma moved closer to embrace her.

"We're sisters!" Janice said to Macy. "No wonder you and my Teri look so much alike. You're her auntie. Janice gave Macy's chin a gentle shake,

"I always wanted a sister."

"Macy, I beg your forgiveness. I thought that I was doing the right thing at the time. It didn't take long for me to realize that I was wrong. I'm so sorry. Can you forgive me?" Norma asked Macy.

Macy gave Norma a hug, and they cried together.

"I need some time to absorb this." Macy pulled away from Norma to reach for a tissue.

"I can understand that. I won't pressure you, but know that I love you dearly. My Macy Jennifer, my baby." Norma tried to hold back any further show of tears in an effort to allow Macy to deal with her own sounds and thoughts.

"I really need some time." Macy said as she got up to leave. "I've got to go now." She quickly walked past Janice avoiding eye contact with either of the women.

Macy left her newly found family behind as she went back to her own apartment. She wasn't sure how to handle all of the information that she'd just received. She slumped into one of her chairs and folded her legs under herself. Staring at the jungle scene on the wall until she imagined herself entering the deep green brush pushing aside the tall palm leaves. The spider monkey hung from a tree making primitive sounds of laughter. A bird flew overhead dropping a bright red feather at her feet. The white butterfly painted to sit peacefully on the rock beside the pond, took flight at the sound of her foot pushing a small rock across the ground. The rock landed bringing Macy into herself in the room and she exited the scene. After thirty minutes she knew that she had to distract her mind. She picked up the telephone and called Kenneth. He was surprised to hear from her. She told him that she wanted to dance, but not the same hours as Sam. She also promised not to hit him in the groin again. After hanging up the telephone, she got her bag packed, sprinkled fish food into the fish tank, and then called a taxi to get to the club. While she waited for the taxi she called Michael. He was always supportive of her when things got tough. The telephone on his end rang six times before he answered. Macy almost hung up. He answered the telephone, and his smooth voice flowed into the telephone wires and filled her heart with comfort.

"Hello."

"Hi babe. It's me." she hoped she didn't sound emotional.

"This is a nice surprise. What made you decide to call me? I mean, not that I don't appreciate whatever the reason, but you never call me twice in a month."

"I got some good, but crazy news today. I don't have time to tell you now. Can you come by my house tomorrow?"

"Yeah, what time?"

"How about nine o'clock tomorrow morning?" she asked.

"Okay, I'll see you then."

The taxi blew its horn. She danced until her existence outside of the club became a blur. She could be who ever she wanted when on the stage. No one in the club knew the mixture of emotions going on in her heart and her mind.

The mystery of her identity was gone, but in its place came questions of how to deal with the new mother and family that she'd stumbled upon. As well as an anger and pain at knowing that her father had not claimed her. She was used to being a loner. Was she supposed to call this Norma woman *mother*? Would her relationship change with Janice now that she knew that her neighbor was actually Aisha, her older sister? After being in uncaring foster homes for most of her life she was unsure of how to feel emotionally attached to another human being. Michael had taken her as close to those emotions as she had come in years. And although she had become attached to Amber and Janice she had not considered them more than neighbors.

There was a positive emotion standing out amongst the turmoil. At least she had found out that she was not alone in the world. There had actually been someone out there thinking about her. Concerned for her well-being, and loving her. Would her sleeping heart waken and allow her to embrace the answered prayer that used to dominate her mind when she was younger?

A customer yelled "Swing that ass baby!" and brought Macy out of her private space. Her thoughts returned to the dimness of the club setting and she realized that it was Sam that stood beside Santa at the bar. Her hand was touching his arm and she threw her head back in a feminine chuckle.

"Damn how long has that bitch been there?" she wondered.

The well dressed man sitting at the bar was actually James Harrison according to the photo in his pocket. He had followed the person he called "Mr.H" from his office to this club on the outskirts of town.

The cute little blonde number that had been standing beside him had been touching his hand and arm in a flirtatious way long enough for Mr. Gruff voice to come to believe that she knew Mr. H. well and was more than likely the interloper in the Harrison marriage. He'd seen exactly what he had come for and had his own sweet thang at a motel waiting to give him some business, so there was nothing more for him to do there tonight but to make his mental notes finish his beer and take his leave. He stuck a dollar bill in a passing by thong on the way out the door.

Macy finished her set and quickly left the stage. Someone yanked her thong and shoved a dollar bill between her skin and the elastic fabric, causing the paper of the bill to scratch her hip. "Damn don't be so rough!" she yelled in the direction of the aggressor. The floor was sticky with spilt liquor and beer as she made her way to the bar.

"Sam aren't you needed by one of your Johns?"

"Well I guess somebody is in a cranky mood." Sam snickered.

"Is there a problem ladies?" John asked.

"No, it's just that Sam seems to like my choice of friends." Macy threw Sam a snare.

"Is that your mean face? Oh I'm shaking." Sam teased.

"Wait a minute, it seems like there is something going on here that I'm not aware of." James asked more than stated.

"Nope, nothing worth mentioning, except I'm kind of parched." Macy hinted.

"Oh forgive me." James slapped the counter top two times, "Bartender."

The next set began. Sam drained the last of golden liquid from her glass and turned to leave. "See ya later James." She cooed.

"I don't suggest you do that unless you want a repeat of what happened at home." Macy warned.

"What happened at home?" James questioned. "You two know each other that well?"

"If you want to call it that." Sam called over her shoulder as she walked away.

James turned back to Macy. "Why the pout on that pretty little face?"

"That bitch you were just talking to is not on my best gal pal list. You should really be more careful who you hang out with."

"I wasn't actually hanging out with her. She came over and asked me to buy her a drink. I admit she's easy on the eye, but I'm not a newby my little flower in the rough." He touched his finger to the tip of her nose. "I think I can hold my own. And I didn't get where I am by allowing just anyone into my wallet."

"Well I'm just sayin' be careful."

"Do I see a sign of the green eyed monster?" he chuckled.

"Hell no! I just don't like her ass." She swirled the straw in her drink.

"Okay." He gave her hand a squeeze. "I'll keep that in mind."

"How come you never tried for more than seeing me here?" she asked.

"I'm a little too busy and long past being sucked in by just the sight of ass and plump breast. I just enjoy the conversation, eye candy and giving pretty gifts. I've always enjoyed giving gifts.

She didn't ask why he wasn't giving the gifts to his wife. He didn't bother to hide the thick, gold; diamond encrusted wedding band on his left hand ring finger. The customers' home lives were not her concern unless they wished to share on their own. But she had gotten used to the special feeling that he came only to spend time with her.

*****

Amber's mind was in as much turmoil as Macy's but she lacked the ability to see through the fog. Jason had not called or come back to visit since her visit to the hardware store. She had attempted to call him at the store before it closed, but Debra answered. Amber could hear the baby crying in the background, and she hung up immediately without using one of her phony names to ask for Jason, or leave a message.

Six beer cans sat on the floor beside Amber's bed; she held another one in her hand. Maybe if she got some air her head wouldn't feel so heavy and stuffy. She took her beer can and went out to the front stairs. It was too late for Janice to be in her usual spot on the stairs, and Amber was glad because she didn't want to talk to anyone.

The air outside felt cool against her skin compared to the stuffiness in her bedroom. The water across the street rippled in the darkness of night. The peaceful sounds had an effect on her like a silent whistle to a dog. With some difficulty, she raised herself from the stairs leaving the now empty beer can sitting on the top step.

She crossed the street and stopped at the tall brush separating her from the water that called to her. Any thoughts that may have entered her mind were lost in an alcoholic haze. She found a gap in the brush and stepped through. Once on the other side, staring only into darkness the first thought she was able to control was of Jason as all of her thoughts of late seemed to be. It would be nice to be standing here with Jason. The sound of the waves would make our love making so beautiful. Then she remembered her anger at Jason. The thoughts changed, "Maybe he had already been in this spot making love to his wife. Maybe their baby had been conceived near this water after they closed the store."

She neared to the water's edge. The bushes behind her crinkled as the wind ran its fingers through the leaves. She walked even closer to the water's edge, close enough to feel the water licking her toes that were clad in open-toed house slippers.

Her mind replayed the telephone call to the hardware store. As if still on the telephone, she heard Debra's voice and the baby in the background. Did Jason go to console little Cory while his wife answered the telephone? How dare he! She couldn't console her baby when it cried. He didn't care about her, their, baby crying. She touched her hands lightly to her belly.

The abortion had been a mistake. She had gone against her own judgment for the sake of a love that apparently would never be hers. Why had she done such a thing? The trance of an orgasm lasted too long to make important decisions. Her decision had been made at that joyous, passionate point. Now she couldn't stand herself, she wanted to get out of the stupid person's body. Two more steps took her farther into the water. It was cold, and she shivered as a wave came to shore pushing wetness farther up her pant legs. She clinched her fists and teeth to brace herself for another dose of iciness as another strong wave came to shore.

Mae-Belle took her hair scarf off and allowed her tufts of dark hair to fall to her shoulders. She placed the scarf on the coffee table and picked up her hair brush, then went over to the seat in front of her window. As a car came down the dimly lit street with its head lights on high beam, she noticed a figure standing at the water, then along with the glare of the head lights, the figure was gone. A chill went through her causing her to drop her hair brush onto her lap. Who would be at the water this time of night? It was every bit of twelve thirty. The only reason she was up herself was because she'd taken a long nap earlier and now couldn't get back to sleep.

She put on her slippers and left her apartment headed for the other side of the street to check on the figure in the head lights.

Amber had not noticed the car's lights with all of their brightness until they were upon her. She attempted to duck the beam of light before she was seen. A wave came to shore while she stooped, and almost knocked her down into the water. When the light passed she stepped farther into the water bringing its level up to her waist. The alcohol continued to numb her mind as the cold water numbed her body. She wanted to punish her ignorance, and the choices that she could not reverse.

Mae-Belle raced through the hallways, and out of the building, making her way to where she thought she had seen the figure. She went through the brush and there stood Amber up to her waist in the water.

"Amber!" she yelled. "Amber! What are you doing?" Amber turned around and looked at Mae-Belle as if she were staring at a ghost. Mae-Belle was unnerved by the blank, hollow stare in the girl's eyes.

"Amber, what's wrong? Come out of that water before you get sick!" Mae-Belle yelled out.

"Leave me alone!" Amber yelled back. "I want to die. I've made a mess of things. Just let me be!"

Mae-Belle took a few steps closer to the water. "Amber, please honey. It's not worth dying for, whatever the problems are. Everyone in the building loves you; we'll all help you through this. Please Amber, come back.

"I can't do this. It hurts. Mae-belle it hurts," Amber cried.

Mae-Belle walked to the water's edge and held out her arms. "Amber, come on baby, come on," she said repeatedly. Amber turned towards Mae-Belle and began to slowly walk out of the water to the outstretched arms. When she reached Mae-Belle's hands she reached out her own and allowed Mae-Belle to guide her out of the waves.

"Girl! What in God's name were you doing out there! If you felt that bad why didn't you come to me or Macy? You're not alone, you know that don't you?" Mae-Belle said as she guided the now shivering, crying, girl back to the building. Slowly they walked up the stairs to Mae-Belle's apartment. She left her on the sofa while she went back downstairs to

Amber's apartment to get some clean and dry clothes. When she got back upstairs Amber was in a fetal position crying uncontrollably. She coaxed her out of the wet clothes and into the dry ones. Then she put her back on the sofa with a blanket and pillow.

"Do you want to talk?" Mae-Belle asked.

"What is there to say? I'm a mess! You told me that he was married, and I still allowed him to wreck my life. I'm so stupid." Amber said through tears, and sharp, snort, heaving breaths.

"What did he say about the pregnancy?" Mae-Belle asked.

"He gave me the money to get an ab-b." Amber loss control to the tears. Mae-Belle went over to her and rubbed her back. "Amber, you've got to take back control of your life. All that you can do now is ask your God to forgive you, and give you peace with your decision, because you can't change, or undo the past. Chalk it up to experience sounds simple for this occasion, but it's really all that you can do sometimes in this life. You're young honey, you'll cry more times than this. Get strong from this, and never let another person make life changing decisions for you. If it doesn't feel right in your heart don't do it".

"But Mae-Belle, he said that he loved me. He promised me a future in return for our unborn child's life. It's my fault that I fell for the lies instead of protecting my child. How can I live with that? How? He never intended to leave his wife did he?" Amber pleaded.

"Probably not sweetie, no one wins when it comes to dealing with a married man. Even if he had left his wife you would have to worry about him doing you the same way that he did his wife. There would be no trust. I had a girlfriend that went through this same situation of a relation with a married man. She survived it, and so can you. You can't have a relationship without trust." Mae-Belle advised.

"How could the love feel so real to me, and mean totally nothing to him?" Amber questioned.

"That is an ageless question. I don't think any one will ever be able to answer why people do the things that they do. One cannot read another person's mind." Mae-Belle answered softly as she stroked Amber's temple.

Amber fell to sleep at Mae-Belle's touch. She allowed the older woman's touch of kindness and wisdom to guide her to temporary tranquility.

As Aisha slipped into her bed she couldn't find sleep, and wondered if Macy and Norma could. The day had been too exciting with both joy and sweet sorrow. She found quiet time to put pen to paper. She tried to imagine some of her mother's prayers and feelings of hopelessness as described during the visit with Macy. The words formed by the gentle strokes of her black pen enveloped the thoughts and silent fears of Norma who had just found a lost child.

Heaven

Swirling, swirling swirling downward
This world so dark and I am a coward
So many things that I want to say
About the ways of the world today
But the words just refuse to come out right
They're tucked away, way down deep and tight
I wish that I had the courage to do
What needs to be done to save me and save you?
I look around and all is so grim
The light all around me is becoming so dim
Downward, downward, downward I go
Until the hole envelopes me so
The darkness so harsh, so black, and so cold
Could it be that I'm getting old
And all of the demons of life's futures and pasts
Are starting to haunt me fast, fast, fast
The world of the worlds that I wished it to be
Is swirling right past and I cannot see
What it should have become and not what it is
Thank God that the Lord claims this world to be his
Something to look forward to and all is not lost
Look up to the sky, pray, whatever the cost
Ask for forgiveness with all of my heart
Knowing someday, of this earth, I will part
Get down on my knees, and I pray, and I PRAY!
Hoping to someday see beyond the stars and the clouds
To see angels and angels in crowds and in crowds
The swirling will stop and the demons will flee
And of this darkness and coldness I will finally be free

Miz Catfish

-Tara Morgan

Amber woke at eight thirty the following morning to find Mae-Belle moving around in the kitchen making breakfast. The smell of fresh coffee actually smelled inviting.

"Good morning," Amber said sheepishly with embarrassment.

"Good morning," Mae-Belle returned.

"I guess I really lost it last night huh?"

"Uh-huh, you could call it that." Mae-Belle said as she crossed the room with a tray holding coffee and toast.

"That smells good, but I don't think that I could stomach any of it right now." Amber said apologetically.

"You need something in your stomach sweetie. Just sip at the coffee, and nibble on the toast. Before you know it you'll notice a difference."

"Okay, I'll try. Thank you Mae-Belle, you're a Godsend."

"Godsend or not, don't you ever let yourself get to that point again!"

Mae-Belle quipped at Amber as she playfully slapped her against the side of the head "No man is ever worth you taking your life!"

"It all just hurts so bad." Amber said sadly.

"This too shall pass sweetie. Believe me. If you let it, it will pass."

Miz Catfish

*****

Misty ran in the door to get the ringing telephone almost twisting her ankle and dropping her bags of groceries in the process.

"H-h-hello?" she was winded.

"Yeah, Mrs. H?" came the gruff voice

"Yes."

"I've seen your husband, ah, Mr. H"

"Was I correct? Who is she? How old is she? Is she pretty? The bitch!" she hadn't taken a breath between questions.

"Whoa, whoa, give me a chance will ya? She's a stripper; she's beautiful, blonde, and about twenty two, twenty three years old."

"A stripper? A stripper?! What is he doing with a dirty piece of trash like that? Does he go to the, that place where ever she works?"

"Yep"

"I'm sure it must have been really tough on you to follow him into that place multiple times. You men-n."

"Hey, hey, lady! I'm not the one who's the big, rich, mucky-muck hanging out in the dives after hours behind my wife's back. Don't go blowing your money bought self righteous smoke up my ass alright. What you're doing right now ain't gonna be all that worthy of a metal of honor at no swanky country club you know what I mean. So stay focused will ya'. Just tell me what do you wanna do now?"

"Alright. Have you seen him with her more than once?"

"Yep." He lied.

"I want-t-t." Mitsy felt the pressure of tears welling in her chest. "Give me a minute to digest this news and then…" the tears had reached the bottom of her eye lids and threatened to spill, her breathing was becoming labored, and damn it how could this be happening. Why wasn't she enough for her own husband?

"I'm sorry I have to go." He barely heard her say as she hung up.

Macy had been up since six o'clock and had already gone out for her morning jog. On her way out of the building she had thought about knocking on Amber's door to ask if she wanted to join. Then she decided to let the troubled girl sleep. Once back from the jog she began a shower. It was nine thirty when she heard the telephone ring, wrapped in a large towel she answered.

"Hello." she answered

"Good morning, Macy," Michael said.

"I thought you were going to come by."

"Just checking first. You change like the wind, girl. Is the offer still good?" he asked.

"The offer is still good and I'm waiting. Tic–toc tic-toc," she laughed.

He arrived one hour later, and as soon as she opened the door he pulled her into a hug. She allowed him to hold her.

They moved over to the sofa with their conversation and Macy explained as best as she could her shocking news and mixed emotions.

Michael listened and let her vent. That was all that Macy needed. She completed her story with a large sigh and suddenly realized that during moments of confusion and crisis in her life, if anyone, Michael seemed to give her more comfort than any other she'd allowed into her personal space. Yet, for years she had kept him at arms length until she needed him. Suddenly she couldn't make sense of why. She was so emotionally unguarded from the discovery of her mother that she was able to recognize the goodness of his presence that had been with her for a long time unappreciated.

Her arms squeezed his waist tighter, as she snuggled close against his chest. He felt good. Why fight it any longer? What she was feeling at that moment felt better than dancing. It was better than the thought of a one night stand, or quickies with Kenneth. Michael was a good man. Wasn't that what women dreamed of finding? Yet when the real thing comes along, women tend to over look them? Why did the bad boys stand out brighter? Maybe it was time she thought about keeping the good guy. A guy, a sister, niece, nephew, Amber, and maybe others to come, finally a complete picture.

"Michael, I love you." she allowed herself to say.

"You don't know how good that sounds. I've been waiting for this day. I love you too." he replied, giving her a squeeze.

She opened up and let nature take its course. Sure she felt shaky like a colt freshly born, but she also felt full.

Norma had completed two days of holding her breath while she waited for Macy to come back to Janice's apartment with a reaction to the news dropped in her lap.

Finally the knock came at the door, and Macy walked in and gave her a huge, affectionate hug. She embraced her, and Macy embraced the truth, and the love that she had always longed for.

One revelation had been revealed, now Norma had to reveal another. She had a newspaper from home in her suitcase. She had taken it out and laid it on Janice's bed where she would see it. Janice came into her bedroom from putting the children down to naps in their bedroom. She picked up the newspaper and skimmed the happenings back home in Pittsburgh. On page one was a small article concerning a man's body found in an alley. The body had been there for a number of days. There was no wallet or items of value found at the scene, and no suspects as yet.

What a shame she thought "The poor soul and his family whoever they may be." She read further, the poor soul as she'd called "it" had been identified as Shawn Brown. According to the article the deceased was believed to be a known drug addict. The report read that a brutal beating had caused the death and may have been due to a drug transaction of some sort gone sour. Maybe he owed money, or had stolen from the wrong dealer. Whichever, it had cost him his life and an investigation was under way. Janice the hidden was at that moment uncloaked as Aisha the wife, the abused mother of two, daughter to Norma, sister to Macy. The paper fell to the floor, as Aisha's fingers lost their grip and all went black.

Norma had been quietly entertaining Macy waiting for her daughter's reaction. Aisha was good at internalizing her emotions, but she didn't expect the girl to be able to contain a reaction to the news printed in black and white on the paper she'd so cowardly dropped on the bed. She heard a thud and ran to Aisha's room, where she found her slumped over. She yelled to Macy, who unbeknownst to her had followed her out of concern, to get a damp face cloth. She wiped her face with it until Aisha came to.

"Are you going to be okay?" Norma asked, "I'm sooo sorry."

"Oh my God! Ma, why didn't you tell me? Oh my God!" Aisha repeated.

"I didn't know how to baby, I didn't want to give you such horrible news. You've been through so much already."

"Ma, I didn't mean for anything to happen to him. He's the father of my children. I used to love him." she cried softly. "I wouldn't wish death on anyone, not even him."

"I know that baby, I know." Norma said as she cradled her sobbing daughter, and Macy stroked her back.

Norma carried her last bag to the front door. "Aisha take good care of my babies, you hear!" she said as she gave big hugs to each of her grandchildren. Mae-Belle came downstairs and knocked at the door.

"Is everybody ready to go?" Mae-Belle asked.

"Yes, we are." Norma replied.

Norma picked up the two larger bags as Aisha took the carry-on bag, and Macy grabbed Johnny's hand. Teri ran ahead of everyone out of the building to the car. Mae-Belle drove them to the airport in enough time for hugs and chatty good byes, and Norma to get in line to board her plane. But not before hearing the words that she had waited twenty eight years to hear.

"I forgive you. I guess you did what you thought was best. I haven't experienced motherhood, and I don't think that I should judge you on doing something that I can't even imagine ever having to do."

Norma's heart was free from its own maternal prison. Her children were together finally as sisters.

Miz Catfish

*****

Macy hadn't discussed with Norma which of them would make the next move to continue their new relationship.

She didn't want to risk reaching out to the woman who had been used to having one daughter and now may not want a stranger in her life after all this time. Would she, Macy, be an intruder? No one since Betty Jenkins had been her family and loved her, or cared about her. Why would a stranger who did not know her from another person on the street? She felt it was too risky to believe in this type of fairytale.

She'd have to do some thinking on how this situation would move along. After all this required trust and that was something Macy didn't have a lot of. She did what she always did in times of stress and confusion, she called Kenneth.

Macy worked the pole tonight mostly in a standing position, while attempting to prevent lines of frustration from showing on her face. She was irritated by the continuance of the song being played by the DJ. She could see the bar over the crowd and even after her warnings to Santa and Sam to stay away from each other; she could see Sam leaning in close to him. Her blonde mane was pulled into a ponytail from her previous set on the stage earlier in the night. Santa's shoulders moved up and down slightly in a chuckle from the words that passed between them.

The bartender stopped in front of Sam and James. "Hey Sam." He placed a shot glass full of clear liquid on the bar and gave it a slight push, causing it to slide and come to a stop in front of Sam.

"That guy down there" He nodded his head to the right, "sent this to you. He said to tell you "Thank you for the meal." He turned to leave, and then turned back. "Oh yeah, he said something else, something about he still owes you for such a good time." He hunched his shoulders and walked away. He made it a point not to get in the girls' business.

Sam leaned forward and peered in the direction of the bartender's nod. There sat Lamar, he wore a scowl on his otherwise handsome face. As soon as her eyes locked with his he raised his hand to his forehead using his fingers to salute her in military style. His scowl remained as he dropped his hand to the position of picking up the drink that sat in front of him.

James had noticed a slight change in Sam's expression and turned his head in the direction of her stare. "Hey that guy doesn't look too happy. Do you know him?"

Sam cleared her throat and turned her attention back to the shot glass resting in front of her. She lifted the glass to her mouth and sucked in the clear liquid then swallowed in one gulp, the only way to enjoy a shot of Patron Tequila Silver.

She returned the glass to the counter and smiled. "He's just a friend. I owe him a phone call is all. I guess he's a little clingy." Sam joked in her response to James but the truth of the matter was the look on Lamar's face had given her a chill. She had not called him after their last date together when she had fed him the 'shrooms and stolen money from his wallet. He had every reason to be angry with her, but she wasn't going to worry about it tonight. In all honesty, she probably wouldn't worry about it tomorrow either.

"It's been nice talking with you again. Maybe you'll see your way to taking me out for a nice dinner one night." She winked at him as she turned and left the bar.

The song droned on as Macy took a stroll around the pole. When she returned to her previous position Sam was gone, but Santa was still in his seat.

"Lucky for her" Macy thought "cuz if she had still been there when my set was over I'd snatch that ponytail off her head."

He sat in the darkest corner of the club watching an ivory complexioned beauty complete a full split while squeezing her own breast nipples between her long red fingernails. She fell back onto her ass cheeks to get into a position of sitting and continued to play with her now very perky nipples. A voice yelled out "Yeah babe! I wanna be breast fed please!" and the crowd gave up a roar of laughter. Mr. Gruff voice laughed too, then returned his attention to the blonde at the bar giggling and smiling too broadly at Mr. H. sitting beside her. He stood and headed for the exit, tonight just might be the night.

"Good night Kenny." Sam patted Kenneth on his behind and shifted her duffle bag to the opposite shoulder.

"I don't even need to turn around to see who's speaking to me when ever I hear the name Kenny. You're the only one who calls me that or could get away with it."

"That's cuz I'm special. Goodnight see ya later." Sam stepped out into the darkness and cool breeze of the alley.

She never heard or saw the figure step from behind the steel, royal blue dumpster. Mercifully the hot piercing entry smaller than the size of a dime entered her brain in the targeted area that prevented suffering on machinery. Her body slumped to the ground, her beautiful corn silk mane of hair now stained and becoming matted with deep velvet red fluid and brain matter. No more breath forced its way through her lungs, and when found she would be referred to as "the body". Dehumanized to housing, a shell for the spirit. A selfish, manipulative, conceited spirit. Yet someone's daughter, sister, beautiful specimen on the stage.

The dark shadow quickly stepped over "the body" and left the alley quickly making the steps required to blend in with the few pedestrians waiting at the cross walk for the light to turn red, and the dark orange hand image to turn bright and into the image of a person.

The motorcycle headed for the on ramp of the expressway merging it's owner, operator into the sea of lights at break neck speed.

Sheila was next to leave the club through the back door and almost tripped over Sam's duffel bag causing her to look down. Her scream pierced the darkness.

Miz Catfish

Chapter 25

Macy removed herself softly from the sofa bed to answer the ringing telephone. She answered it on the second ring so that it would not wake Michael sleeping soundly beside her.

"Hello." she whispered quietly into the telephone

"Hey wild thang!" Kenneth responded.

"I can't talk now." she whispered.

"I just wanted to know if you could dance tonight. A dancer quit on me."

"No, I can't dance tonight. I won't be dancing anymore Kenneth. So don't call me." she softly hung up and crawled back into bed next to Michael.

"Who was that?" he asked.

"No one." she said slightly startled. "No one you need to concern yourself about. Sh-h-h, go back to sleep." She kissed him on the cheek and lay still until his breathing assured her he'd fell back into peaceful slumber.

Kenneth's words hadn't allowed Macy peace. His words had immediately struck a spot in her mind and lingered in her thoughts. "A dancer quit on me." Was what he'd said. Huh! That was his reason for needing another girl on? Who had he called to come in when he was down a girl the night after Sam was killed? Yes the business was all about the skin and the money, but had it been that easy for the club to just call someone else to replace her too?

Sure there had been no love lost between her and Sam, but she wouldn't wish death on anyone. Sam's death had also forced her to realize how vulnerable dancers were on a daily basis, and how quickly life could change. She had gained a family and just as quickly Sam's family had lost a member. Funny how death of one person makes others take inventory of their own existence.

*****

Two days passed before Amber felt good enough to leave her apartment. After her episode with the alcohol and water she was physically, as well as emotionally wiped out. Today was the first day that she could control the tears of emotion that seemed to want to flow excessively. She had called her job and asked to be put back into the schedule as soon as possible. Mae-Belle had made her promise that she'd get back on her feet. She kept her promise. She had been put back on the schedule for her old hours. The warm air of the afternoon actually felt good to her entire body. As she got closer to the windows of the hardware store she got nervous and tempted to turn back for the shelter of her home. But then she remembered her promise to Mae-Belle, and she continued along her way. When she walked in front of the windows of Jason's store, she tried to look straight ahead, but lost the battle. Jason looked up from his task in time for him and Amber to lock eyes. He smiled sheepishly and she stuck up her middle finger and kept walking. She felt light on her feet the rest of the walk to work. After she'd been there for an hour Macy came in for bread and milk.

"Where have you been stranger?" Macy asked, "I haven't seen you in years."

"Ha, ha. You're the one who's been missing. I needed you."

"I'm sorry I wasn't around. There has been a lot going on. Did Mae-Belle tell you about Sam?"

"Yeah, crazy huh? I hope they catch the person. Man it's crazy to think one of your own neighbors would be murdered. That's too close to home." Amber shook her head.

"What time do you get off work? I need to bring you up to speed. You won't believe what I've got to tell you." Macy spoke as she bagged her own groceries.

"Well I need to bring you up to speed too." Amber replied, "I'll be off at four o'clock."

"Okay, I'll see you then. Bye." Macy called over her shoulder.

Jason came into the store. He walked to the cold cooler for a soda, then brought it back to the counter and put it down with a thud.

"Why did you stick your middle finger up at me?" he asked innocently.

"Because I felt that you deserved it."

"Why haven't you called me? he asked

"Gee, do you think that maybe you could answer that one yourself?" she said in an agitated tone.

He smiled a boyish grin. "Can I come by to see you tonight? I miss you."

"You miss me? How could you have time to miss me, when you're so busy with your little family?"

"It's not as perfect as you think Amber." He allowed the lie to roll from his tongue, "I miss you." He took her hand and led her out from behind the back of the counter. Every thought pattern in her brain screamed, "Don't let him touch you, don't!" Her body did not listen. She allowed him to pull her close, to smell her scent, and to kiss her neck. It took that moment only for her wall of anger to come down, and along with it went the most recent memories of the painful ordeal with the water. All that she could feel was the warmth and strength of her lover's arms. "If he holds me like this in public here in the store, he must not be afraid of his wife seeing us." she rationalized. Ignoring the warning screams again late that night when her lover held her again, this time between the crisp sheets on her bed. When he got out of the bed, washed up and went home to his wife she felt the old familiar sorrow return. Mixed with the sorrow was the excited energy of knowing that he'd be back again. She didn't know she was making a pact with Satan to dismiss the here and now to receive the latter. Because her soul would be in one of the greatest battles of her life, the battle of knowing right from wrong and being pulled to choose wrong.

*****

Misty's hands shook with such force she could hardly hold the morning's paper. The small black print read about the mystery of a dancer's body found in an alley behind a strip club. The story reported that the girl had been shot to death.

The article served as the confirmation that her request had been fulfilled. Misty searched herself for a twinge of remorse for wishing another human beings life force to end. But she found none, not a twinge or a twinkle. James was hers and she'd keep him at any cost to anyone.

They met at the truck stop off the main highway. Misty allowed just enough of her head to show above the dash board as a sign of proof that indeed there was a live person in her vehicle. For this meeting she begged off from the idea of going inside and again sitting at the sticky checker board topped tables. This parking lot was as far as she wished to go. A hairy knuckle bumped twice against the window. Misty scooted upwards peering once again into the face of Mr. Gruff voice.

She pushed the window control button to the left, causing the window to glide down slowly and only enough to accomplish what she had heard referred to on television as "the drop". With a shaky hand, as if preparing to pet a rabid dog, Misty lifted a white business length envelope containing ten thousand dollars behind its sealed flap to the window. The flap was smeared with the slightest trace of Fluffy Rose lipstick left when she had old school method licked the glue to cause its stickiness to activate. She had only to allow the corner of the envelope to poke from behind the glass.

Mr. Gruff voice took hold of it and snatched it from her fingers. It had barely cleared the glass before Misty began to push the window control button to the right, sending the glass upwards, thereby closing off her availability to the unsavory person standing on the other side. As the window slide smoothly to a stop in its groove, she felt the sudden urge to pee. A common side effect to fear.

"Shit!" she thought "I'm looking at a real life killer."

She didn't know what to do next. Did she say "Thank you" through the glass? Call me later? What does one say to their hired hit man when the job was done?

Mr. Gruff voice took the pressure of the wonderment from her mind by turning and walking away from the car. He walked quickly back to his motorcycle, placed his black helmet on his head and revved away. She really had to pee.

James guided his black Mercedes away from the curb and headed north towards the center of the downtown business district. His cell phone rang distracting his attention from the fact that the traffic light facing him had gone from yellow to red. His Mercedes floated with the grace of a sail boat caught in wind through the red light and into the intersection. Much too late James looked up to see a black motorcycle helmet preparing to smash against his windshield, and again he was too late to notice the traffic light pole in direct line with the nose of his car.

The Harley Davidson then lodged under his grille and dragged it's rider with it. The mangled mess of black steel, silver metal, flesh, and denim came to a stop against the traffic pole signaling the air bag in the steering wheel to deploy and express it's sole purpose to cushion it's occupant from harm. Instead its forceful arrival smashed into James chest, breaking his ribs, which in turn, punctured his lungs.

The first firemen to arrive on the scene took turns yelling into the glassless window to James, challenging and encouraging him to "hang on". They promised they'd have him out of the tangled wreck in a few more minutes. Though the few more minutes James did not have. He loss consciousness to a white light being focused into his right eye, and took his last breath of life before the white light of the ambulance attendant's small examine tool moved to his left.

Another team of firemen attended to the body pinned under the vehicle. A dusty black Doc Martin boot lay in the middle of the street. The black scraped helmet lay closer to the bootless foot of the owner. The lifeless man was dislodged and placed on the waiting stretcher. His denim jacket released a white envelope from an inside pocket. A passing policeman picked up the envelope. It was addressed to no one. He flipped it over and over in an attempt to find some distinguishing sign of ownership, but could find nothing but a trace of pink.

Miz Catfish

Chapter 26

The Labor Day weekend rolled around bringing with it the end of summer, and the wearing of white shoes.

Mae-Belle hated to feel the angry breeze that pushed through her windows. It meant the end of lemonade on the roof top. She decided to get all of the tenants together for one last gathering of the summer. She wrote up invitation notes for everyone in the building inviting them to the roof top for homemade lemonade and a cook out: "Hot dogs, hamburgers, spareribs and potato salad! Let's take the summer out with a bang, come one, come all!" she wrote on each, and then went about preparing to slip them under everyone's door.

When she reached the second floor she realized that she'd actually made the number of invitations including the poor deceased girl. It was hard to remember that someone had snuffed out the light of a person so young, beautiful and full of life. Samantha had been mischievous but surely that did not warrant the loss of her life. She stood with her hand landing softly on what had been the door to Sam's apartment. Quietly she whispered "Please bless her Lord," then moved on down the hallway about her task.

Macy got ready for the cookout upstairs. Michael was going to meet her on the roof top. She washed the dishes left in the sink and took a quick glance around the room, making sure that everything was in its proper place. The fish tank caught her eye. She hadn't fed the fish. As she shook the colored flakes across the top of the water, she noticed something that made her laugh. The catfish came darting up to the roof top of the water again to grab food. She was sure now of what she'd seen. "Go catfish! Go!" she thought to herself smiling. No more bottom feeding. She stooped to look into the tank. The catfish did a fancy twist to the bottom of the tank. Then Macy was totally thrown. The catfish swam up to the glass and appeared to wink at her. Macy shook her head in disbelief and laughed.

"What the hell was that?" she said out loud. Then there was a knock at her door. Before she turned away from the tank, the catfish returned to its shelter behind the plant.

"Come in." she yelled, standing up from her squatting position.

"I went upstairs looking for you. What's your hold up lady?" Michael said smiling.

"Oh nothing, I'm coming, I'm coming," Macy took one last glance at the tank.

Leaving for the roof top with Michael she reached for a strawberry cheesecake on the kitchen counter on their way out the door, her contribution to the cookout. She did most of the talking as they went through the hallway. Michael allowed this, enjoying the fact that Macy seemed content. The woman was usually so moody, that whenever she was in a joyous mood he would gladly play the role of the silent partner. As they neared the top of the third floor stairs the presence of Ortega was confirmed by the sounds of his guitar chords bouncing off the tiled hallway walls.

Michael held the door for Macy. There sat Ortega in a grey steel folding chair with his guitar in his lap. He strummed a long drawn out Spanish tune, and allowed his right foot to thump, thump, thump loudly against the tar and gravel surface of the roof. "Floppee Ladeee" he crooned directly at Aisha.

Macy began greetings to her neighbors. CeCe sat to Ortega's left. She was reading a novel in Spanish, and she looked up from the book to see who had come through the doorway.

"Hi, CeCe."

"Hello." CeCe said with a smile before returning her eyes to her novel. She had nothing in particular against Macy, but she wasn't sure of the reason for Ortega's frequent visits to her apartment before coming to his own home. She realized that the two had been friends before she met him, but she wasn't comfortable with the American culture of married men visiting female friends in their homes. In her culture a woman who allowed such company would be called less than friendly names. Manuel, Teri and Shawn played with building blocks and small cars. Macy walked over to her new family members who now went by their given names of Aisha, Teri and Shawn and gave Aisha a hug. "Aisha, this is Michael, my fiancé. Michael, this is my big sister Aisha."

"Your fiancé?" Aisha said with a raise of her eyebrows.

"Yes, my dear" Macy smiled.

"Well! You haven't completely brought me up to speed on everything going on in your life have you missy?" Aisha said in a mock stern voice.

"Well now Michael, what are your intentions towards my sister?"

Ortega stopped playing his guitar and joined the conversation. "Be careful my friend, that ladee there." he pointed to Aisha, "is very tough. She is like a bull by the horns. She is to Machie's life a donkey with his ear to the ground. Nothing can get past her."

"Ortega! You better shut up before I play your guitar for you!" Aisha snapped across the roof top.

Macy laughed and turned to Michael, "I hope this doesn't scare you off."

"Dealing with you and your mood swings is a lot tougher than all that I'm hearing now." he said with a smile."And I haven't run away yet."

Macy continued on with her salutations. "Over there is my buddy Amber." Amber waved with a free hand, while the other nursed a frosty glass of lemonade. "Don't sleep on my side of the bed please!" she joked. She was yet to tell Macy that she had missed her period. But then again, she hadn't told Jason yet either.

"I see that you've got quite a bunch here. No wonder you never needed any company," Michael laughed as he picked an empty chair and sat down.

Mae-Belle was at one of the corner grills flipping burgers when Macy spoke to her. Standing with her was a leggy red-head in a conservative, white linen dress.

"Hi Macy, and Michael, that cheesecake looks heavenly! Please put it over on the table. Well, Ro-o. Oh my, where are my manners? You haven't been introduced to your new neighbors. "Everyone let me introduce you all to our newest tenant, Rowan O'Connor. Rowan turned to greet her new neighbors with piercing emerald green eyes. She nervously shifted from one foot to another. All adult eyes shifted uncontrollably to the size eleven feet housed in black leather flats. Rowan cleared her throat, causing all eyes to shift to the size of the porcelain complexioned Adam's apple that moved up and down. "Just a tad too big." Aisha thought, while unconsciously bringing a hand to her own throat.

"Hello everyone." Rowan greeted softly.

"Girl, you better practice a heavier voice if you want to hold down a spot in this building full of women." Aisha yelled across to her.

Everyone laughed. Mae-Belle suddenly shouted "Who would like the first burger, and whoever put these pigs feet on the grill? I think they're ready."

Questions for Discussion

1. Did you identify with any of the characters?

2. Mae-Belle knew Jason's background. Do you think she should have told Amber as soon as she realized what Jason was doing?

3. Did reading about the emotions Macy experienced while dancing cause you any specific thoughts about women that strip or nude dance?

4. Macy shared some of her experiences in foster care. How did you feel about her experiences and the appearance of the foster care system through her eyes?

5. When do you think Amber became responsible for her part in the affair with Jason?

6. Is it possible for someone to encourage you to do something against your will as Jason did when he encouraged Amber to get an abortion?

7. Did it take Aisha/Janice too long to leave Shawn, or should she have stayed with him until he got clean of the drugs and saved their marriage?

8. Can abusive relationships be repaired?

9. Do you understand the extent of the decision CeCe made to get a better life for her son?

10. Would you marry for necessity like CeCe did?

11. Could you have a friend like Sam?

12. How did you feel when you first found out Sam had been killed?

13. Did Misty overreact to the relationship between James and Macy? Would you consider their friendship cheating?

14. How many of the book situations could you relate to Biblical Scripture or stories?

Miz Catfish

About Portia Gray Goffigan

Portia Gray-Goffigan is a native of Virginia Beach, Virginia. She is a divorced mother of four, a grandmother of one, and enjoys a relationship with her blended family. Portia currently resides in Attleboro, Massachusetts. This is her second published book.

Miz Catfish

Miz Catfish II is coming!!!

- Get to know the newest member of 105 Shawnee Road: Rowan O'Conner. Why is her Adam's apple so big?

- Will you support Amber through her second pregnancy, and how will Jason react to the news? Will Amber continue to see Jason?

- Will Macy be able to enjoy her newly found family and accept Michael's affection without suspicion of their intentions? She said she's done dancing but is she?

- Can Aisha love again, without becoming further part of statistics by getting into another abusive relationship? Will she trust another man at all?

- Will CeCe come to have heart felt love for Ortega?

- Who will move into the empty apartment on the third floor? And what excitement or drama will they bring to the building?

- Get to know more about the colorful, muu muu wearing Mae-Belle Smoot.

Made in the USA
Middletown, DE
11 March 2019